THE STORIES OF MARY LAVIN

Volume II

By the same author

Novels

THE HOUSE IN CLEWE STREET

MARY O'GRADY

Short Stories

TALES FROM BECTIVE BRIDGE

THE LONG AGO

THE BECKER WIVES

THE LIKELY STORY

A SINGLE LADY

THE PATRIOT SON

THE GREAT WAVE

THE STORIES OF MARY LAVIN (Volume 1)

HAPPINESS

A MEMORY

THE STORIES OF

Mary Lavin

VOLUME II

CONSTABLE

LONDON

This selection first published 1974 by
Constable and Company Ltd
10 Orange Street, London WC2H 7EG
Copyright © 1974 Mary Lavin

ISBN 0 09 459720 0

Set in Monotype Garamond
Printed in Great Britain by
The Anchor Press Ltd,
and bound by Wm Brendon & Son Ltd,
both of Tiptree, Essex

For my daughter

CAROLINE WALSH

Contents

The Green Grave
and the Black Grave

It was a body all right. It was hard to see in the dark, and the scale-back sea was heaving up between them and the place where they saw the thing floating. But it was a body all right.

"I knew it was a shout I heard," said the taller of the two men in the black boat that was out fishing for mackerel. He was Tadg Mor and he was the father of the less tall man, that was blacker in the hair than him and broader in the chest than him, but was called Tadg Og because he was son to him. Mor means "big" and Og means "son". But Mor can be taken to mean greater and Og can be taken to mean lesser than the greater.

"I knew it was a shout I heard," said Tadg Mor.

"I knew it was a boat I saw and I dragging in the second net," said Tadg Og.

"I said the sound I heard was a kittiwake, crying in the dark."

"And I said the boat I saw was a black wave blown up on the wind."

"It was a shout all right."

"It was a boat all right."

"It was a body all right."

"But where is the black boat?" Tadg Og asked.

"It must be that the black boat capsized," said Tadg Mor, "and went down into the green sea."

"Whose boat was it, would you venture for to say?" Tadg Og asked, pulling stroke for stroke at the sea.

"I'd venture for to say it was the boat of Eamon Buidhe," said Tadg Mor, pulling with his oar against the sharp up-pointing waves of the scaly, scurvy sea. The tall men rowed hard toward the clumsy thing that tossed on the tips of the deft green waves.

"Eamon Buidhe Murnane!" said Tadg Mor, lifting clear his silver-dropping oar.

I

"Eamon Buidhe Murnane!" said Tadg Og, lifting his clear, dripless, yellow oar.

It was a hard drag, dragging him over the arching sides of the boat. His clothes logged him down to the water and the jutting waves jostled him against the boat. His yellow hair slipped from their fingers like floss, and the loose fibres of his island-spun clothes broke free from their grip. But they got him up over the edge of the boat, at the end of a black hour that was only lit by the whiteness of the breaking wave. They laid him down on the bottom boards of the boat on top of their haul of glittering mackerel, and they spread the nets over him. But the scales of the fish glittered up through the net and so, too, the eyes of Eamon Buidhe glittered up at them. And the live glitter of the dead eyes put a strain on Tadg Mor and he turned the body over on its face among the fish; and when they had looked a time at the black corpse with yellow hair, set in the silver and opal casket of fishes, they turned the oar blades out again into the scurvy seas, and pulled toward the land.

"How did you know it was Eamon Buidhe Murnane, and we forty pointed waves away from him at the time of your naming his name?" Tadg Og asked Tadg Mor.

"Whenever it is a thing that a man is pulled under by the sea," said Tadg Mor, "think around in your mind until you think out which man of all the men it might be that would be the man most missed, and that man, that you think out in your mind, will be the man cast up on the shingle."

"This is a man that will be missed mightily," said Tadg Og.

"He is a man that will be mightily bemoaned," said Tadg Mor.

"He is a man that will never be replaced."

"He is a man that will be prayed for bitterly and mightily."

"Many a night, forgetful, his wife will set out food for him," said Tadg Og.

"The Brightest and the Bravest!" said Tadg Mor. "Those are the words that will be read over him – the Brightest and the Bravest."

The boat rose up on the points of the waves and cleft down again between the points, and the oars of Tadg Mor and the oars of Tadg Og split the points of many waves.

"How is it the green sea always greeds after the Brightest and the Bravest?" Tadg Og asked Tadg Mor.

"And for the only sons?" Tadg Mor said.

"And the widows' sons?"

"And the men with one-year wives? The one-year wife that's getting this corpse" – Tadg Mor pointed down with his eyes – "will have a black sorrow this night."

"And every night after this night," said Tadg Og, because he was a young man and knew about such things.

"It's a great thing that he was not dragged down to the green grave, and that is a thing will lighten the nights of the one-year wife," said Tadg Mor.

"It isn't many are saved out of the green grave," said Tadg Og.

"Mairtin Mor wasn't got," said Tadg Mor.

"And Muiris Fada wasn't got."

"Lorcan Og wasn't got."

"Ruairi Dubh wasn't got."

"It was three weeks and the best part of a night before the Frenchman with the leather coat was got, and five boats out looking for him."

"It was seven weeks before Maolshaughlin O'Dalaigh was got, and his eye sockets emptied by the gulls and the gannies."

"And by the waves. The waves are great people to lick out your eyeballs!" said Tadg Mor.

"It was a good thing, this man to be got," said Tadg Og, "and his eyes bright in his head."

"Like he was looking up at the sky!"

"Like he was thinking to smile next thing he'd do."

"He was a great man to smile, this man," said Tadg Mor. "He was ever and always smiling."

"He was a great man to laugh too," said Tadg Og. "He was ever and always laughing."

"Times he was laughing and times he was not laughing," said Tadg Mor.

"Times all men stop from laughing," said Tadg Og.

"Times I saw this man and he not laughing. Times I saw him and he putting out in the black boat looking back at the inland woman where she'd be standing on the shore and her hair weaving the wind, and there wouldn't be any laugh on his face those times."

"An island man should take an island wife," said Tadg Og.

"An inland woman should take an inland man."

"The inland woman that took this man had a dreadful dread on her of the sea and of the boats that put out in it."

"Times I saw this woman from the inlands standing on the shore from his putting out with the dry black boat to his coming back with the shivering silver-belly boat."

"He got it hard to go from her every night."

"He got it harder than iron to go from her if there was a streak of storm gold in the sky at time of putting out."

"An island man should not be held down to a woman from the silent inlands."

"It was love-talk and love-looks that held down this man," said Tadg Mor.

"The island women give love-words and love-talk too," said Tadg Og.

"But not the love-words and the love-looks of this woman," said Tadg Mor. "Times I saw her wetting her feet in the sea and wetting her fingers in it and you'd see she was a kind of lovering the waves so they'd bring him back to her. Times he told me himself she had a dreadful dread of the green grave. 'There dies as many men in the inlands as in the islands,' I said. 'Tell her that,' I said. 'I told her that,' said he. 'But they get the black grave burial,' she said. 'They get the black grave burial in clay that's blessed by the priest and they get the speeding of the green sods thrown down on them by their kinsmen.' 'Tell her there's no worms in the green grave,' I said to him. 'I did,' said he. 'What did she say to that?' said I. She said, 'The bone waits for the bone,' said he. 'What does she mean by that?' said I. 'She gave another saying as her meaning to that saying,' said he. She said, 'There's no sorrow in death when two go down together into the one grave. Clay binds close as love,' she said, 'but the green grave binds nothing. The green grave scatters.' 'The green grave is for sons,' she said, 'and for brothers,' she said, 'but the black grave is for lovers,' she said, 'and for husbands. The faithful clay under the jealous sods.' "

"She must be a great woman to make sayings," said Tadg Og.

"She made great sayings for that man every hour of the day," said Tadg Mor, "and she stitching the nets for him on the steps of the pier while he'd be salting fish or blading oars."

"She'll be glad us to have saved him from the salt green grave. It's a great wonder but he was dragged down before he was got."

"She is the kind of woman that always has great wonders happening round her," said Tadg Mor. "If she is a woman from the inlands itself, she has a great power in herself. She has a great power over the sea.

Times – and she on the cliff shore and her hair weaving the wind, I'd point my eyes through the wind across at where Eamon Buidhe would be in the boat back of me, and there wouldn't be as much as one tongue of spite rising out of the waves around his boat, and my black boat would be splattered over with white sea-spittle."

"I heard tell of women like that. She took the fury out of the sea and burned it out to white salt in her own heart."

The talk about the inland woman who fought the seas in her heart was slow talk and heavy talk, and slow and heavy talk was fit talk as the scurvy waves crawled over one another, scale by scale, and brought the bitter boat back to the shore.

Sometimes a spiteful tongue of foam forked up in the dark by the side of the boat and reached for the netted corpse on the boards. When this happened Tadg Og picked up the loose end of the raggy net and lashed out with it at the sea.

"Get down, you scaly-belly serpent," he said, "and let the corpse dry out in his dead-clothes."

"Take heed to your words, Tadg Og," Tadg Mor would say. "We have the point to round yet. Take heed to your words!"

"Here's a man took heed to his words and that didn't save him," said Tadg Og. "Here was a man was always singing back song for song to the singing sea, and look at him now lying there."

They looked at him lying on his face under the brown web of the nets in his silver and opal casket. And as they looked another venomous tongue of the sea licked up the side of the boat and strained in towards the body. Tadg Og beat at it with the raggy net.

"Keep your strength for the loud knocking you'll have to give on the wooden door," said Tadg Mor. And Tadg Og understood that he was the one would walk up the shingle and bring the death news to the one-year wife, who was so strange among the island women with her hair weaving the wind at evening and her white feet wetted in the sea by day.

"Is it not a thing that she'll be, likely, out on the shore?" he asked, in a bright hope, pointing his eyes to where the white edge of the shore-wash shone by its own light in the dark.

"Is there a storm tonight?" said Tadg Mor. "Is there a great wind tonight? Is there a rain spate? Are there any other signs from the sea?"

"No," said Tadg Og, "there are none of those things that you mention."

"I will tell you the reason you asked that question," said Tadg Mor. "You asked that question because that question is the answer that you'd like to get to that question."

"It's a hard thing to bring news to a one-year wife and she one that has a dreadful dread on her of the sea," said Tadg Og.

"It's good news you're bringing to the one-year wife when you bring news that her man is got safe, to go down like any inlander into a black grave blessed by a priest and tramped down by the feet of his kinsmen on the sod."

"It's a queer thing him to be caught by the sea on a fine night with no wind blowing," said Tadg Og.

"On a fine night the women lie down to sleep, and if a woman has a power over the sea, with her white feet in the water and her black hair fighting the wind and a bright fire in her heart, the sea can only wait until that woman's spirit is out of her body – likely back home in the inlands – and then the sea-serpent gives a slow turnover on his scales, one that you wouldn't heed to yourself, maybe, and you standing up with no hold on the oars; and before there's time for more than the first shout out of you the boat is logging down to the depths of the water. And all the time the woman that would have saved you, with her willing and wishing for you, is in the deep bed of a dark sleep, having no knowledge of the thing that has happened until she hears the loud-handed knocking of the neighbour on the door outside."

Tadg Og knocked with his knuckles on the sideboards of the boat.

"Louder than that," Tadg Mor said.

Tadg Og knocked another, louder knock on the boat's side.

"Have you no more knowledge than that of how to knock at a door in the fastness of the night and the people inside the house buried in sleep and the corpse down on the shore getting covered with sand and the fish scales drying into him so tight that the finger-nails of the washing women will be broken and split peeling them off him? Have you no more knowledge than that of how to knock with your knuckle-bones?" Tadg Mor gave a loud knocking with his own hand on the wet seat of the boat. "That is the knock of a man that you might say knows how to knock at a door, day-time or night-time," he said, and then he knocked again, louder, if it could be that any knock could be louder than the first knock.

Tadg Og listened and then he spoke, not looking at Tadg Mor, but looking at the oar he was rolling in the water. "Two people knocking would make a loud knocking entirely," he said.

"One has to stay with the dead," said Tadg Mor.

Tadg Og drew a long stroke on the oar and he drew a long breath out of his lungs, and he took a long look at the nearing shore.

"What will I say when she comes to my knocking?"

"When she comes to the knocking, step back a bit from the door, so's she'll see the wet shining on you and smell the salt water off you, and say in a loud voice that the sea is queer and rough this night."

"She'll be down with her to the shore if that's what I say."

"Say then," said Tadg Mor, pulling in the oar to slow the boat a bit, "say there's news come in that a boat went down beyond the point."

"If I say that, she'll be down with her faster than ever to the shore without waiting to hear more, and her hair flying and her white feet freezing on the shingle."

"If that is so," said Tadg Mor, "then you'll have to stand back bold from the door and call out loudly in the night, 'The Brightest and the Bravest!' "

"What will she say to that?"

"She'll say, 'God bless them!' "

"And what will I say to that?"

"You'll say, 'God rest them!' "

"And what will she say to that?"

"She'll say, 'Is it in the black grave or the green grave?' "

"And what will I say to that?"

"You say, 'God rest Eamon Buidhe, that will be put down in the black grave in the holy ground, blessed by the priest and sodded by the people.' "

"And what will she say to that?"

"She'll say, likely, 'Bring him in to me, Tadg Og!' "

"And what will I say to that?"

"Whatever you say after that, let it be loud and raising echoes under the rafters, so she won't hear the sound of the corpse being dragged up on the shingle. And when he's lifted up on to the scoured table, let whatever you say be loud then too, so's she won't be listening for the sound of the water drabbling down off his clothes on the floor!"

There was only the noise of the oars after that for a time, till a shoaly sound stole in between the oar strokes. It was the shoaly sound of the pebbles dragged back from the shore by the tide.

A few strokes more and they beached, and stepped out among the sprawling waves and dragged the boat after them till it cleft its depth in the damp shingle.

"See that you give a loud knocking, Tadg Og," said Tadg Mor, and Tadg Og set his head against the darkness and his feet were heard grinding down the shifting shingle as he made for the house of the one-year wife. The house was set in a thrifty sea-field, and his steps did not sound down to the shore once he got to the dune-grass of the thrifty sea-field. But in another little while there was a sound of a fist knocking upon wood, stroke after stroke. A strong hand coming down on hard wood. Tadg Mor, waiting with the body in the boat, recalled to himself all the times he went knocking on the island doors bringing news to the women of the death of their men. But island wives were the daughters of island widows. They knew the sea gave food, but it gave death. Life or death, it was all one in the end. The sea never lost its scabs. The sea was there before the coming of man. Island women had that knowledge. But what knowledge of the sea and its place in the world since the beginning of time had a woman from the inlands? No knowledge at all. An inland woman had not knowledge to bear her up when the loud knocking came on her door in the night. Tadg Mor listened to the loud, hard knocking of his son Tadg Og on the door of the one-year wife of Eamon Buidhe that was lying in his casket of fishes on the floor of the boat, cleft fast in the shingle sand. The night was cold. And even though it was dark the fish scales glittered in the whiteness made by the breaking of the waves on the black shore. The sound of the sea was as sad if sadder than the sight of the yellow-haired corpse, but still Tadg Mor was gladder to be down on the shore than up in the dune-grass knocking at the one-night widow's door.

The knocking sound of Tadg Og's knuckles on the wooden door was a human sound and it sounded good in the ears of Tadg Mor for a time; but, like all sounds that go on too long, it sounded soon to be as inhuman as the washing of the waves tiding in on the shingle. Tadg Mor put up his rounded palms to his mouth and shouted out to Tadg Og to come back to the boat. Tadg Og came back running over the shore, and the air was grained with sounds of sliding shingle.

"There's no one in the house where you were knocking," said Tadg Mor.

"I knocked louder on the door than you knocked on the seat boards," said Tadg Og.

"I heard how you knocked," said Tadg Mor. "You knocked well. But let you knock better when you go to the house of her neighbour to find out where the one-night widow is from her own house this night."

"If I got no answer at one door is it likely I'll get answer at another door?" said Tadg Og. "It was you yourself I heard say one time that the man that knows how a thing is to be done is the man should do that thing when that thing is to be done."

"How is a man ever to get knowledge of how to do a thing if that man doesn't do that thing when that thing is to be done?" said Tadg Mor.

Tadg Og got into the boat again and they sat there in the dark. After four or maybe five waves had broken by their side, Tadg Og lifted the net and felt the clothes of Eamon Buidhe.

"The clothes are drying into him," he said.

"If I was to go up with you to the house of Seana Bhride, who would there be to watch the dead?" said Tadg Mor, and then Tadg Og knew that Tadg Mor was going with him and he had no need to put great heed on the answer he gave to him.

"Let the sea watch him," he said, and after a wave went back with its fistful of little complaining pebbles he put a leg out over the side of the boat.

"We must take him out of the boat first," said Tadg Mor. "Take hold of him there by the feet," he said as he rolled back the net, putting it over the oar with each roll so it would not ravel and knot.

They lifted Eamon Buidhe out of the boat and the mackerel slipped about their feet into the place where he had left his shape. They dragged him up a boat-length from the sprawling waves, and they faced his feet to the shore, but when they saw that that left his head lower than his feet, because the shingle shelved deeply at that point, they faced him about again toward the waves that were clashing their sharp, pointy scales together and sending up spires of white spray in the air. The dead man glittered with the silver and verdigris scales of the mackerel that were over his clothing, every part.

Tadg Mor went up the sliding shingle in front of Tadg Og, and Tadg Og put his feet in the shelves that were made in the shingle by Tadg Mor because the length of the step they took was the same length.

The sea sounded in their ears as they went through the shingle, but by the time the first coarse dune-grass scratched at their clothing the only sound each could hear was the sound of the other's breathing.

The first cottage that rose up blacker than the night in their path was the cottage where Tadg Og made the empty knocking. Tadg Mor stopped in front of the door as if he might be thinking of trying his own hand at knocking, but he thought better of it and went on after Tadg Og to the house that was next to that house, and that was the house of Seana Bhride, a woman that would know anything that eye or ear could know about those that lived within three islands of her. Tadg Mor hit the door of Seana Bhride's house with a knock of his knuckles, and although it was a less loud knock than the echo of the knock that came down to the shore when Tadg Og struck the first knock on the door of the wife of Eamon Buidhe, there was a foot to the floor before he could raise his knuckle off the wood for another knock.

A candle lit up, a shadow fell across the windowpane and a face whitened the door gap.

"You came to the wrong house this night," said Seana Bhride. "The sea took all the men was ever in this house twelve years ago and two months and seventeen days."

"It may be that we have no corpse for this house, but we came to the right house for all that," said Tadg Mor. "We came to this house for knowledge of the house across two sea-fields from this house, where we got no answer to our knocking with our knuckles."

"And I knocked with a stone up out of the ground, as well," said Tadg Og coming closer.

The woman with the candle-flame blowing drew back into the dark.

"Is it for the inland woman, the one-year wife, you're bringing the corpse you have below in the boat this night?" she said.

"It is, God help us," said Tadg Mor.

"It is, God help us," said Tadg Og.

"The Brightest and the Bravest," said Tadg Mor.

"Is it a thing that you got no answer to your knocking," said the old woman, bending out again with the blowing candle-flame.

"No answer," said Tadg Og, "and sturdy knocking."

"Knocking to be heard above the sound of the sea," said Tadg Mor.

"They sleep deep, the people from the inland?" said Tadg Og, asking a question.

"The people of the inland sleep deep in the cottage in the middle of the fields," said Seana Bhride, "but when they're rooted up and set down by the sea their spirit never passes out of hearing of the step on the shingle. It's a queer thing entirely that you got no answer to your knocking."

"We got no answer to our knocking," said Tadg Mor and Tadg Og, bringing their words together like two oars striking the same wave, one on this side of a boat and one on that.

"When the inland woman puts her face down on the feather pillow," said Seana Bhride, "that pillow is like the seashells children put against their ears; that pillow has in it the sad crying voices of the sea."

"Is it that you think she is from home this night?" said Tadg Mor.

"It must be a thing that she is," said the old woman.

"Is it back to her people in the inlands she'd be gone?" said Tadg Og, who had more than the curiosity of the one night in him.

"Step into the kitchen," said the old woman, "while I ask Brid Og if she saw the wife of Eamon Buidhe go from her house this night."

While she went into the room that was back from the kitchen, Tadg Og put a foot inside the kitchen door but Tadg Mor stayed looking down to the shore.

"If it is a thing the inland woman is from home this night, where will we put Eamon Buidhe, that we have below on the shore, with his face and no sheet on it, and his eyes with the lids not down on them, and the fish scales sticking to him faster than they stuck to the mackerels when they swam beyond the nets, blue and silver and green?"

Tadg Og stepped a bit further into the kitchen of Seana Bhride. "Listen to Brid Og," he said softly.

"Brid Og," said the old woman, "is it a thing that the inland woman from two fields over, went from her house this night?"

"Yes. It is a thing that she went," said Brid Og.

Tadg Og spoke to Tadg Mor. "Brid Og's talk is soft in the day, but her talk is soft as the sea in summer when she talks in the night in the dark."

"Listen to what she says," said Tadg Mor, coming in a step after Tadg Og.

"Is it that she went to her people in the inlands?" Seana Bhride asked.

"The wife of Eamon Buide never stirred a foot to her people in the inlands since the first day she came to the islands, in her blue dress with the beads," said the voice of Brid Og.

"Where did she go then," said the old woman, "if it is a thing that she didn't go to her people in the inlands?"

"Where else but where she said she'd go?" said the voice of Brid Og. "Out in the boat with her one-year husband?" There was sound of rusty springs creaking in the room where Brid Og slept, back behind the kitchen, and then her voice was clearer and stronger like as if she was sitting up in the bed looking out at the black sea and the white points rising in it, lit by the light of their own brightness. "She said the sea would never drag Eamon Buidhe down to the green grave and leave her to lie lonely in the black grave on the shore, in the black clay that held tight, under the weighty sods. She said a man and a woman should lie in the one grave. She said a night never passed without her heart being burnt out to a cold white salt. She said that this night, and every night after, she'd go out with Eamon in the black boat over the scabby back of the sea. She said if he got the green grave, she'd get the green grave too, and her arms would be stronger than the weeds of the sea, to bind them together for ever. She said the island women never fought the sea. She said the sea needed taming and besting. She said there was a curse on the black clay for women that lay alone in it while their men washed to and fro in the caves of the sea. She said the black clay was all right for inland women. She said the black clay was all right for sisters and mothers. She said the black clay was all right for girls that died at seven years. But the green grave was the grave for wives, she said, and she went out in the black boat this night and she's going out every night after!" said Brid Og.

"Tell Brid Og there will be no night after!" said Tadg Mor.

"Time enough to tell her. Let her sleep till day," said Tadg Og, and he strained his eyes past the flutter-flame candle as the old woman came out from Brid Og's room.

"You heard what she said?"

"It's a bad thing he has got," said the old woman.

"That's a thing was never said on this island before this night," said Tadg Mor.

"There was a fire on every point of the cliff shore to light home the men who were dragging for Mairtin Mor."

"And he never was got," said Tadg Mor.

"There was a shroud spun for Ruairi Dubh between the time of the putting-out of the boats to look for him and their coming back with the empty news in the green daylight," said the old woman.

"Ruairi Dubh was never got."

"Mairtin Mor was never got."

"Lorcan Og was never got."

"Muiris Fada was never got."

"My four sons were never got," said the old woman.

"The father of Brid Og was never got," said Tadg Og, and he was looking at the shut door of the room where Brid Og was lying in the dark, the candle shadows running their hands over the door. "The father of Brid Og was never got," he said again, forgetting he had said the same words before. "Of all the men that had yellow coffins standing up on their ends by the gable, and all the men that had brown shrouds hanging up on the wall with the iron nail eating through the yarn, it had to be the one man that should never have been got that was got." Tadg Og, opened the top-half of the door and let in the deeper sound of the tide.

"That is the way," said Tadg Mor.

"That is ever and always the way," said the old woman.

"The sea is stronger than any man," said Tadg Mor.

"The sea is stronger than any woman."

"The sea is stronger than women from the inland fields," said Tadg Mor, going to the door.

"The sea is stronger than talk of love," said Tadg Og, going out after him into the dark. It was so dark, he could not see where the window of Brid Og's room was, but he was looking where it might be while he buttoned over his jacket.

Tadg Mor and Tadg Og went back to the shore, keeping their feet well on the shelving shingle, as they went toward the sprawling waves. The waves were up to the sea-break in the graywacke wall.

The boat was floating free. It was gone from the cleft in the shingle. And the body of Eamon Buidhe, that had glittered with fish scales opal silver and verdigris, was gone too from the shore. It was gone from the black land that was scored criss-cross with grave-cuts by spade and shovel. It was gone and would never be got. The men spoke together.

"Mairtin Mor wasn't got."

"Muiris Fada wasn't got."

"Lorcan Og wasn't got."

"Ruairi Dubh wasn't got."

"The four sons of Seana Bhride were never got."

"The father of Brid Og wasn't got."

The men of the island were caught down on the bed of the sea by the tight weeds of the sea. They were held by the tendrils of the sea anemone, by the green sea-grasses and the green sea-reeds, and the winding stems of the green sea-daffodil. But Eamon Buidhe Murnane would be held fast in the white arms of his one-year wife, who came from the inlands where women have no knowledge of the sea but only a knowledge of love.

Sarah

Sarah had a bit of a bad name. That was the worst her neighbours would say of her, although there was a certain fortuity about her choice of fathers for the three strapping sons she'd borne – all three outside wedlock.

Sarah was a great worker, strong and tireless, and a lot of women in the village got her in to scrub for them. Nobody was ever known to be unkind to her. And not one of her children was born in the County Home. It was the most upright matron in the village who slapped life into every one of them.

"She's unfortunate, that's all," this matron used to say. "How could she know any better – living with two rough brothers? And don't forget she had no father herself!"

If Sarah had been one to lie in bed on a Sunday and miss Mass, her neighbours might have felt differently about her, there being greater understanding in their hearts for sins against God than for sins against his Holy Church. But Sarah found it easy to keep the Commandments of the church. She never missed Mass. She observed abstinence on all days abstinence was required. She frequently did the Stations of the Cross as well. And on Lady Day when an annual pilgrimage took place to a holy well in the neighbouring village Sarah was an example to all – with her shoes off walking over the sharp flinty stones, doing penance like a nun. If on that occasion some outsider showed disapproval of her, Sarah's neighbours were quicker than Sarah herself to take offence. All the same, charity was tempered with prudence, and women with grown sons, and women not long married, took care not to hire her.

So when Oliver Kedrigan's wife, a newcomer to the locality, spoke of getting Sarah in to keep house for her while she was going up to Dublin for a few days, two of the older women in the district felt it their duty to step across to Kedrigan's and offer a word of advice.

"I know she has a bit of a bad name," Kathleen conceded, "but she's a great worker. I hear it's said she can bake bread that's nearly as good as my own."

15

"That may be!" said one of the women, "but if I was you, I'd think twice before I'd leave her to mind your house while you're away!"

"Who else is there I can get?" Kathleen said stubbornly.

"Why do you want anyone? You'll only be gone for three days, isn't that all?

"Three days is a long time to leave a house in the care of a man."

"I'd rather let the roof fall in on him than draw Sarah Murray about my place!" said the woman. "She has a queer way of looking at a man. I wouldn't like to have her give my man one of those looks." Kathleen got their meaning at last.

"I can trust Oliver," she said coldly.

"It's not right to trust any man too far," the women said, shaking their heads.

"Oliver isn't that sort," Kathleen said, and her pale papery face smiled back contempt for the other women.

Stung by that smile, the women stood up and prepared to take their leave.

"I suppose you know your own business," said the first one who had raised the subject, "but I wouldn't trust the greatest saint ever walked with Sarah Murray."

"I'd trust Oliver with any woman in the world," Kathleen said.

"Well he's your man, not ours," said the two women, speaking together as they went out the door. Kathleen looked after them resentfully. She may not have been too happy herself about hiring Sarah but as she closed the door on the women she made up her mind for once and for all to do so, goaded on by pride in her legitimate power over her man. She'd let everyone see she could trust him.

As the two women went down the road they talked for a while about the Kedrigans but gradually they began to talk about other things, until they came to the lane leading up to the cottage where Sarah Murray lived with her brothers and the houseful of children. Looking up at the cottage their thoughts went back to the Kedrigans again and they came to a stand. "What ever took possession of Oliver Kedrigan to marry that bleached out bloodless thing?" one of them said.

"I don't know," said the other one. "But I wonder why she's going up to Dublin?"

"Why do you think!" said the first woman, contemptuous of her companion's ignorance. "Not that she looks to me like a woman would ever have a child, no matter how many doctors she might go to – in Dublin or elsewhere."

Sarah went over to Mrs. Kedrigan's the morning Mrs. Kedrigan was going away and she made her a nice cup of tea. Then she carried the suitcase down to the road and helped Kathleen on to the bus because it was a busy time for Oliver. He had forty lambing ewes and there was a predatory vixen in a nearby wood that was causing him alarm. He had had to go out at the break of day to put up a new fence.

But the bus was barely out of sight, when Oliver's cart rattled back into the yard. He'd forgotten to take the wire-cutters with him. He drew up outside the kitchen door and called to Sarah to hand him out the clippers, so he wouldn't have to get down off the cart. But when he looked down at her, he gave a laugh. "Did you rub sheep-raddle into your cheeks?" he asked, and he laughed again – a loud happy laugh that could give no offence. And Sarah took none. But her cheeks went redder, and she angrily swiped a bare arm across her face as if to stem the flux of the healthy blood in her face. Oliver laughed for the third time. "Stand back or you'll frighten the horse and he'll bolt," he said, as he jerked the reins and the cart rattled off out of the yard again.

Sarah stared after him, keeping her eyes on him until the cart was like a toy cart in the distance, with a toy horse under it, and Oliver himself a toy farmer made out of painted wood.

When Kathleen came home the following Friday her house was cleaner than it had ever been. The boards were scrubbed white as rope, the windows glinted and there was bread cooling on the sill. Kathleen paid Sarah and Sarah went home. Her brothers were glad to have her back to clean the house and make the beds and bake. She gave them her money. The children were glad to see her too because while she was away their uncles made them work all day footing turf and running after sheep like collie dogs.

Sarah worked hard as she had always done, for a few months. Then one night as she was handing round potato-cakes to her brothers and the children who were sitting around the kitchen table with their knives and forks at the ready in their hands, the elder brother Pat gave a sharp look at her. He poked Joseph, the younger brother, in the ribs with the handle of his knife. "For God's sake," he said, "will you look at her!"

Sarah ignored Pat's remark, except for a toss of her head. She sat down and ate her own supper greedily, swilling it down with several cups of boiling tea. When she'd finished she got up and went out into the wagon-blue night. Her brothers stared after her. "Holy God," Pat said, "something will have to be done about her this time."

"Ah what's the use of talking like that?" Joseph said, twitching his shoulders uneasily. "If the country is full of blackguards, what can we do about it?"

Pat put down his knife and fork and thumped the table with his closed fist.

'I thought the talking-to she got from the priest the last time would knock sense into her. The priest said a Home was the only place for the like of her. I told him we'd have no part in putting her away – God Almighty what would we do without her? There must be a woman in the house! – but we can't stand for much more of this."

Joseph was still pondering over the plight they'd be in without her. "Her brats need her too," he said, "leastways until they can be sent out to service themselves." He looked up. "That won't be long now though; they're shaping into fine strong boys."

But Pat stood up. "All the same something will have to be done. When the priest hears about this he'll be at me again. And this time I'll have to give him a better answer than the other times."

Joseph shrugged his shoulders. "Ah tell him you can get no rights of her. And isn't it the truth?" He gave an easy-going chuckle. "Tell him to tackle the job himself!"

Pat gave a sort of a laugh too but it was less easy. "Do you remember what he said the last time? He said if she didn't tell the name of the father, he'd make the new born infant open its mouth and name him."

"How well he didn't do it! Talk is easy!" Joseph said.

"He didn't do it," said Pat, "because Sarah took care not to let him catch sight of the child till the whole thing was put to the back of his mind by something else – the Confirmation – or the rewiring of the chapel."

"Well, can't she do the same with this one?" Joseph said. He stood up. "There's one good thing about the whole business, and that is that Mrs. Kedrigan didn't notice anything wrong with her, or she'd never have given her an hour's work!"

Pat twitched with annoyance. "How could Mrs. Kedrigan notice anything? Isn't it six months at least since she was working in Kedrigan's?"

"It is I suppose," Joseph said.

The two brothers moved about the kitchen for a few minutes in silence. The day with its solidarity of work and eating was over and they were about to go their separate ways when Joseph spoke.

"Pat?"

"What?"

"Oh nothing," said Joseph. "Nothing at all."

"Ah quit your hinting! What are you trying to say? Speak out man."

"I was only wondering," said Joseph. "Have you any idea at all who could be the father of this one?"

"Holy God," Pat cried in fury. "Why would you think I'd know the father of this one any more than the others? But if you think I'm going to stay here all evening gossiping like a woman, you're making a big mistake. I'm going out. I'm going over to the quarry field to see that heifer is all right that was sick this morning."

"Ah the heifer'll be all right," Joseph said. But feeling his older brother's eyes were on him he shrugged his shoulders. "You can give me a shout if she's in a bad way and you want me." Then when he'd let Pat get as far as the door he spoke again. "I won't say anything to her, I suppose, when she comes in?" he asked.

Pat swung around. "And what would you say, I'd like to know? Won't it be all beyond saying anyway in a few weeks when everyone in the countryside will see for themselves what's going on?"

"That's right," said Joseph.

Sarah went out every night, as she had always done, when dusk began to crouch over the fields. And her brothers kept silent tongues in their heads about the child she was carrying. She worked even better than before and she sang at her work. She carried the child deep in her body and she boldly faced an abashed congregation at Mass on Sundays, walking down the centre aisle and taking her usual place under the fourth station of the cross.

Meantime Mrs. Kedrigan too was expecting her long-delayed child, but she didn't go to Mass: the priest came to her. She was looking bad. By day she crept from chair to chair around the kitchen, and only went out at night for a bit of a walk up and down their own lane.

She was self-conscious about her condition and her nerves were frayed. Oliver used to have to sit up half the night with her and hold her moist hands in his until she fell asleep, but all the same she woke often and was frightened and peevish and, in bursts of hysteria, she called him a cruel brute. One evening she was taking a drop of tea by the fire. Oliver had gone down to the Post Office to see if there was a letter from the Maternity Hospital in Dublin, where she had engaged a bed for the following month. When he came back Oliver had a letter in his hand. Before he gave it to her, he told her what was in it. It was an anonymous letter and it named him as the father of the child Sarah Murray was going to bring into the world in a few weeks. He told Kathleen it was an unjust accusation.

"For God's sake, say something, Katty," he said. "You don't believe the bloody letter, do you?" Kathleen didn't answer. "You don't believe it, sure you don't." He went over to the window and laid his burning face against the cold pane of glass. "What will I do, Katty?"

"You'll do nothing," Kathleen said, speaking for the first time. "Nothing. Aren't you innocent? Take no notice of that letter."

She stooped and with a wide and grotesque swoop she plucked up the letter. Then she got to her feet and put the letter under a plate on the dresser and began to get the tea ready with slow, tedious journeyings back and forth across the silent kitchen. Oliver stood looking out at the fields until the tea was ready and once or twice he looked at his wife with curiosity. At last he turned away from the window and went over to the dresser. "I'll tear up the letter," he said.

"You'll do nothing of the kind," Kathleen said, and with a lurch she reached the dresser before him. "Here's where that letter belongs."

There was a sound of crackling and a paper-ball went into the heart of the flames. Oliver watched it burn, and although he thought it odd that he didn't see the writing on it, he still believed that it was Sarah's letter that coiled into a black spiral in the grate.

The next evening Sarah was sitting by the fire as Kathleen Kedrigan had been sitting by hers. She too was drinking a cup of tea, and she didn't look up when her brothers came into the kitchen. No one spoke, but after a minute or two Sarah went to get up to prepare the supper. Her brother Pat pushed her down again on the chair. The cup shattered against the range and the tea slopped over the floor.

"Is this letter yours? Did you write it?" he shouted at her, holding out a letter addressed to Oliver Kedrigan – a letter that had gone through the post, and been delivered and opened. "Do you hear me talking to you? Did you write this letter?"

"What business is it of yours?" Sarah said sullenly, and again she tried to get to her feet.

"Sit down, I tell you," Pat shouted, and he pressed her back. "Answer my question. Did you write this letter?"

Sarah stared dully at the letter in her brother's hand. The firelight flickered in her yellow eyes. "Give it to me," she snarled, and she snatched it from him. "What business is it of yours, you thief?"

"Did you hear that, Pat? She called you a thief!" the younger brother shouted.

"Shut up, you," Pat said. He turned back to his sister. "Answer me. Is it true what it says in this letter?"

"How do I know what it says! And what if it is true? It's no business of yours"

"I'll show you whose business it is!" Pat said. For a minute he stood as if not knowing what to do. Then he ran into the room off the kitchen where Sarah slept with the three children. He came out with an armful of clothes, a red dress, a coat, and a few bits of underwear. Sarah watched him. There was no one holding her down now but she didn't attempt to rise. Again her brother stood for a moment in the middle of the floor irresolute. Then he heard the outer door rattle in a gust of wind, and he ran towards it and dragging it open he threw out the armful of clothing, and ran back into the room. This time he came out with a jumper and a red cap, an alarm clock and a few other odds and ends. He threw them out the door, too.

"Do you know it's raining, Pat?" the younger brother asked cautiously.

"What do I care if it's raining?" Pat said. He went into the other room a third time. He was a while in there rummaging and when he came out he had a picture-frame, a prayer book, a pair of high-heeled shoes, a box of powder and a little green velvet box stuck all over with pearly shells.

Sarah sprang to her feet. "My green box. Oh! Give me my box!" She tried to snatch it from him.

But Joseph suddenly put out a foot and tripped her.

When Sarah got to her feet Pat was standing at the door throwing her things out one by one, but he kept the green box till last and when he threw it out he fired it with all his strength as far as it would go as if trying to reach the dunghill at the other end of the yard. At first Sarah made as if to run out to get the things back. Then she stopped and started to pull on her coat, but her brother caught her by the hair, at the same time pulling the coat off her. Then, by the hair he dragged her across the kitchen and pushed her out into the rain, where she slipped and fell again on the wet slab stone of the doorway. Quickly then he shut out the sight from his eyes by banging the door closed.

"That ought to teach her," he said. "Carrying on with a married man! No one is going to say I put up with that kind of thing. I didn't mind the other times when it was probably old Molloy or his like that would have been prepared to pay for his mistakes if the need arose, but I wasn't going to stand for a thing like this."

"You're sure it was Kedrigan?"

"Ah! didn't you see the letter yourself! Wasn't it Sarah's writing? And didn't Mrs. Kedrigan herself give it to me this morning?"

"Sarah denied it, Pat," Joseph said. His spurt of courage had given out and his hands were shaking as he went to the window and pulled back a corner of the bleached and neatly-sewn square of a flour bag that served as a curtain.

'She did! And so did he, I suppose? Well, she can deny it somewhere else now."

"Where do you suppose she'll go?"

"She can go where she bloody well likes. And shut your mouth, you. Keep away from that window! Can't you sit down? Sit down, I tell you."

All this took place at nine o'clock on a Tuesday night. The next morning at seven o'clock, Oliver Kedrigan went to a fair in a neighbouring town where he bought a new ram. He had had his breakfast in the town and he wanted to get on with his work, but he went to the door of the kitchen to see his wife was all right and called in to her from the yard. "Katty! Hand me the tin of raddle. It's on top of the dresser."

Kathleen Kedrigan came to the door and she had the tin of raddle in her hand.

"You won't be troubled with any more letters," she said.

Oliver laughed self-consciously. "That's a good thing, anyhow," he said. "Hurry, give me the raddle."

His wife held the tin in her hand, but she didn't move. She leaned against the jamb of the door. "I see you didn't hear the news?"

"What news?"

"Sarah Murray got what was coming to her last night. Her brothers turned her out of the house, and threw out all her things after her."

Oliver's face darkened.

"That was a cruel class of thing for brothers to do. Where did she go?"

"She went where she and her likes belong; into a ditch on the side of the road!"

Oliver said nothing. His wife watched him closely and she clenched her hands. "You can spare your sympathy. She won't need it."

Oliver looked up.

"Where did she go?"

"Nowhere," Kathleen said slowly.

Oliver tried to think clearly. It had been a bad night, wet and windy. "She wasn't out all night in the rain?" he asked, a fierce light coming into his eyes.

"She was," Kathleen said, and she stared at him. "At least that's where they found her in the morning, dead as a rat. And the child dead beside her!"

Her pale eyes held his, and he stared uncomprehendingly into them. Then he looked down at her hand that held the tin of red sheep-raddle.

"Give me the raddle!" he said, but before she had time to hand it to him he yelled at her again. "Give me the raddle. Give it to me. What are you waiting for? Give me the God-damn' stuff."

At Sallygap

The bus climbed up the hilly roads on its way through the Dublin Mountains to the town of Enniskerry. On either side the hedges were so high that the passengers had nothing more interesting to look at than each other. But after a short time the road became steeper and then the fields that had been hidden were bared to view, slanting smoothly downward to the edge of the distant city.

Dublin was all exposed. The passengers could see every inch of it. They could certainly see every steeple and tower, although as these spires and steeples rose up out of the blue pools of distance they looked little more than dark thistles rising up defiant in a pale pasture.

The sea that half-circled this indistinct city seemed as grey and motionless as the air. Suddenly, however, it was seen that the five o'clock mail boat, looking no bigger than a child's toy boat, was pushing aside the plastery waves and curving around the pier at Dunlaoghaire on its way to the shores of England.

"There she goes!" Manny Ryan said to the young man in a grey flannel suit who shared the bus seat with him. "The fastest little boat for her size in the whole of the British Isles."

"What time does it take her to do the crossing?" the young man asked.

"Two hours and five minutes," said Manny, and he took out a watch and stared at it. "It's three thirty-nine now. She's out about four minutes, I'd say. That leaves her right to the dot. She'll dock at Holyhead at exactly five forty."

"She's dipping a bit," said the young man. "I suppose she's taking back a big load after the Horse Show."

"That's right. I saw by the paper this morning she took two thousand people across yesterday evening."

"You take a great interest in things, I see."

"I do. That's quite right for you! I take a great interest indeed, but I have my reasons. I have my reasons."

Manny put his elbow up against the ledge of the window and turned on his side in the tight space of the seat so that he was almost facing his companion, who, having no window ledge to lean upon, was forced to remain with his profile to Manny while they were talking.

"You wouldn't think, would you," said Manny, "just by looking at me, that I had my choice to sail out of Dublin on that little boat one day, and I turned it down? You wouldn't think that now, would you?"

"I don't know," said the young man uncomfortably. "Many a man goes over to Holyhead, for one class of thing or another." But it was clear by his voice that he found it hard to picture Manny, with his shiny black suit and his bowler hat in any other city than the one they had lately left. So strong was his impression that Manny was – as he'd put it – a Dubliner-coming-and-going, that he hastened to hide this impression by asking what business Manny had in Holyhead, if that wasn't an impertinence? He forgot apparently that Manny had never actually gone there, but Manny forgot that too in his haste to correct the young man on another score altogether.

"Is it Holyhead?" he asked in disgust. "Who goes there but jobbers and journeymen?"

"London?" asked the young man, raising his eyebrows.

"Policemen and servant girls," Manny said impatiently.

"Was it to the Continent, sir?" said the young man, and the "sir" whistled through the wax in Manny's ears like the sweetest note of a harp, plucked by a clever finger.

"To the Continent is right," he said. "I was heading for Paris – 'gay Paree,' as they call it over there – and I often wish to God I hadn't turned my back on the idea."

"Is it a thing you didn't go, sir?"

"Well, now, as to that question," said Manny, "I won't say yes and I won't say no, but I'll tell you this much: I had my chance of going. That's something, isn't it? That's more than most can say! Isn't it?"

"It is indeed. But if it's a thing that you didn't go, sir, might I make so bold as to ask the reason?"

"I'll tell you," said Manny, "but first of all I'll have to tell you why I was going in the first place." Taking out a sepia-coloured photograph from an old wallet, he passed it to the young man who looked at it, holding it close to his face because it was faded in places and in other places the glaze was cracked. But he made out quite clearly all the same a group of young men sitting stiffly on cane-back chairs, their legs rigid in pinstripe trousers, their hair plastered down with oil, and their

B

hands folded self-consciously over the awkward contours of trombones, fiddles and brass cornets. In the centre of the group, turned up on its rim, was a big yellow drum wearing a banner across its face with the words MARY STREET BAND printed on it in large block letters. "That was us," said Manny, "the Mary Street Band. We used to play for all the dances in the city, and as well, we played for the half-hour interval at the Mary Street Theatre." He leaned over. "That was me," he said, pointing to a young man with a fiddle on his knee, a young man who resembled him as a son might resemble a father.

"I'd recognise you all right," said the stranger, looking up at Manny's face and down again at the photograph. Both faces had the same nervous thinness, the same pointed jaw, and the same cleft of weakness in the chin. Only the eyes were different. The eyes in the photograph were light in colour, either from bad lighting on the part of the photographer or from youthful shallowness in the sitter. The eyes of the older Manny were dark. They had a depth that might have come from sadness, but whatever it came from, it was out of keeping with the cockiness of his striped, city suiting and his bowler hat. "There was a party of us – the few lads you see there at the back, and the one to the left of the drum – and we were planning on getting out, going across to Paris and trying the dance halls over there – palais, they call them. We'd stuck together for three years, but these few lads I'm after pointing out to you got sick of playing to the Dublin jackeens. I got sick of them, too. They were always sucking oranges, and spitting out the pips on the floor, and catcalling up at the artistes. We heard tell it was different altogether across the water. Tell me this, were you ever in Paris, young fellow? 'Gay Paree' I should be saying."

"No, I can't say that I was," said the young man.

"Man alive!" said Manny. "Sure that's the place for a young fellow like you. Clear out and go. That's my advice to you. Take it or leave it: it's my advice to you, although I don't know from Adam who you are or what you are. That's what I'd say to you if you were my own son. Cut and run for it." Manny gave a deep sigh that went down the neck of the lady in front and made her shiver and draw her collar closer. "Paris!" he said again, and again he sighed. "Paris, lit up all night as bright as the sun, with strings of lights pulling out of each other from one side of the street to the other, and fountains and bandstands every other yard along the way. The people go up and down linked, and singing, at all hours of the day or night, and the publicans – they have some other name on them over there, of course – are coming to the door every minute with aprons round their middle, like women, and sweeping the pavement outside the door and finishing off maybe by swilling a bucket of wine over it to wash it down."

"You seem to have a pretty good idea of it for a man who was never there!"

"I have a lot of postcards," said Manny, "and myself and the lads were never done talking about it before ever we decided on going at all. In the end we just packed up one night and said, off with us! There had been a bit of a row that night at the theatre, and somehow or other an old dead cat got flung up on the stage. Did you ever hear the like of that for ignorance? 'Holy God,' we said, 'that's too much to take from any audience.' "

"All I can say is, it's no wonder you packed your bags!" said the young man.

"Is it now?" said Manny. "That's what I tell myself. My bag was all packed and strapped, and what was more, before very long it was up the gangplank and on the deck of that little boat you see pulling out there!"

They looked out the window of the bus, down over the falling fields of the mountainside, to the sea and the vanishing boat.

"Is that right?" said the young man.

"That's right. Me and my bag were on the deck and there was Annie below on the quay, with the tears in her eyes. That was the first time I gave a thought to her at all. Annie is my wife. At least she is now. She wasn't then. I gave one look at her standing there in the rain – it was raining at the time – with her handkerchief rolled up in her hand ready to wave as soon as the boat got going. The porters were pushing past her with their truckloads of trunks and hitting up against her. Did you ever notice how rough those fellows are? Well, with the rain and the porters and one thing and another, I got to pitying her, standing there. I got to thinking, do you know, of all the things we'd done together. Nothing bad, you know. Nothing to be ashamed of, if you understand, but still I didn't like to think of her standing there, watching me going off, maybe for good, and she thinking over the things I'd said to her at one time or another. You know yourself, I suppose, the kind of thing a man's apt to say to a girl, off and on?"

"I do," said the young man.

"You do? Well, in that case you'll understand how I felt seeing her standing there. I felt so bad I tried to go back down the gangplank

for a few last words with her before the boat pulled out, but there were
people coming up against me all the time and I was having to stand
aside every other step I took and crush in against the rails to let them
pass. And some of them were cranky devils, telling me to get the hell
out of the way, to come if I was coming, and go if I was going, and –
for God Almighty's sake – to take my bloody bag out of the way. It
was jabbing them in the legs without my noticing it, and as sure as I
pulled it to one side it jabbed into someone on the other side. There was
terrible confusion. You'd think, wouldn't you, that the officials would
be able to put a stop to it? But I declare to God they were worse
than the people that were travelling. There was one of them clicking
tickets at the bottom of the gangway, and all he did was let a shout at
me to say I was obstructing the passage. Obstructing!"

" 'Come on up, Manny,' shouted the lads from up above on the
deck.

" 'Goodbye, Manny,' Annie said in a little bit of a voice you'd hardly
hear above the banging of cases and the screaming of the seagulls."

"You didn't go down?"

"Down I went."

"And the boys?"

"They were staring like as if they were transfixed. They couldn't
believe their eyes. They kept calling down to me from the deck above,
but the wind was going the other way and we couldn't hear one word
they were saying. Then the whistles began to blow, and the sailors
began spitting on their hands and pulling at the ropes to let the plank
up into the boat. The train was getting ready to go back to Westland
Row: it was going to pull out any minute.

" 'I knew you'd come to your senses,' Annie said. 'Have you got
your bag?' I held it up. 'Your fiddle?' she said. By God, if I hadn't left
the fiddle above on the deck! Would you believe that? I started
shouting up at the lads, and Timmy Coyne – that's the little fellow
with the moustache sitting next me in the photo – Timmy put his
hands up to his mouth like he was playing a bugle – it was the piano
he played in the band, by the way – and he shouts out 'Wha-a-a-at?'
like that, drawing it out so's we could hear it.

" 'The fiddle!' I shouted. But 'fiddle' isn't a word you can stretch
out, you know. No matter how slow you say it, it's said and done in a
minute. 'Fiddle.' Try it for yourself. 'Fiddle.' It's a funny sort of
word, isn't it, when you say it over a few times like that? It sort of

loses its meaning. Anyway, Timmy didn't hear me. 'Ca-a-a-n't – hea-er-ear!' says he. A couple of people round about me began to shout up too. 'Fiddle.' 'Fiddle,' they shouted. The boat was pushing off from the pier. Suddenly one real game fellow that was after putting a fine young girl on the boat, and after kissing her too in front of everyone, ups and pulls off his hat, and crooking it under his arm, like it was a fiddle, he starts pulling his right hand back and forth across it for all the world as if it was a bow and he was playing a real fiddle. Timmy takes one look at him and down he ducks and starts rooting around on the deck. The next minute he ups and rests the fiddle case on the rails.

" 'Catch!' he shouts, and over comes the fiddle across the space of water that was blinding white by this time with the foam from the moving boat.

" 'It's into the water!' someone shouts.

" 'Not on your life!' shouts your man on the wharf, and he leaps into the air to catch it. But you know how slippy them wooden boards on the wharf are – with that green slimy stuff on them? You do? Well, to make a long story short, your man's foot slips, and down comes the fiddle on one of the iron stumps they tie the boat to, and fiddle and case, and even the little bow, were smashed to smithereens under my eyes. You should have heard the crowd laughing. I always say it's easy enough to raise a laugh when you're not doing it for money!"

"What did Annie say?"

" 'It's the hand of God,' she said."

"What did you say?"

"Sure, what could I say? There was no use making the poor fellow feel bad, so I had to let on to make a joke of it. I went over and gave a kick with my foot to the bits of wood, and put them floating out on the water, along with a bucketful of potato-peels and cabbage-stalks that were just after being flung out of a porthole." Manny looked down at the grey feather of smoke on the horizon that was all that now remained of the mail boat. "Whenever I see that little boat," he said, "I get to thinking of the sea and the way it was that day, with the swill lapping up and down on it and the bits of the fiddle looking like bits of an old box. Walking back to the train, we could see the bits of it floating along on the water under us, through the big cracks in the boards. I never can understand why it is they leave such big spaces between those boards anyway. And just as we were going out the gate to the platform, what did I see, down through the splits, but a bit of the bow. And here's a curious thing for you! You could tell what it was the minute you looked at it, broken and all as it was. 'Oh look!' you'd say if you happened to be passing along the pier, going for a walk and not knowing anything about me or the boys. 'Look!' you'd say to whoever was with you. 'Isn't that the bow of a fiddle?' "

"Did you ever hear from the boys again?" the young man asked.

Manny shook his head. "If they wrote we never got the letter," he said. "I heard they broke up after a bit. After Annie and me got married we opened a shop in South King Street and we went to live over the shop. You know South King Street? Our shop is down past the Gaiety. The shop took up pretty near all our time on account of us knowing nothing about business. We never got a minute to ourselves. Nor now either. Look at today! I've been out since early morning trying to find someone that would deliver eggs to the door. That's what I'm doing now, going up to Sallygap to see a man I was told about by one of the dealers in Moore Street. The dealer gets his eggs from this man twice a week, and I didn't see why he couldn't bring us in a couple of dozen at the same time. If he does, we'll put up a card on the window saying, 'Fresh Eggs Daily.' The Dublin people go mad for a fresh egg. Did you ever notice that?"

The conductor came down the aisle and leaned in to Manny.

"We're coming near to Sallygap now," said the conductor.

"Is that right?" said Manny. "Give a touch to the bell so, and get the driver to stop. Anywhere here will do nicely." He turned to the young man confidentially. "I have to look for the place, you see."

"I hope you find it all right, sir."

"I hope so. Well, good day to you now. Don't forget the advice I gave you." Manny pointed with his thumb in the direction of the sea. Then he got off the bus and for the first time in years found himself on a country road alone.

The farmhouse Manny was looking for was easy enough to find. And the farmer obligingly promised to send him down the eggs twice a week, and three times if the orders got bigger. He wanted to know if Manny ever tried selling chickens or geese? Manny said his wife took care of the orders. The farmer asked if he would mention the matter to his wife. Manny agreed to do so. They said goodbye and Manny went back to the road.

By that time Manny wanted a drink. He wasn't a drinking man, but he wanted a glass of beer just to take the thirst off him. He remembered that they had passed a public house a while before he got off the bus. He started walking back toward it.

As he walked along he thought of the boys again. It was the boat had put him in mind of them. And the young fellow that had been sitting beside him was just about the age he was himself in those days. A nice young fellow! Manny wondered who he was, and he wondered, just as idly, at what time he himself would get a bus going back to Dublin.

But it was nice, mind you, walking along the road. He didn't care if the bus was a bit slow in coming. It was not as if it was raining or cold. It was a nice evening. He'd often heard tell of young lads from Dublin coming up here on their bicycles of a fine evening, and leaving the bicycles inside a fence while they went walking in the heather. Just walking, mind you; just walking. He used to think it was a bit daft. Now that he was up here himself, he could see how a quiet sort of chap might like that class of thing. Manny looked at the hedges that were tangled with wild vetches, and he looked at an old apple tree crocheted over with grey lichen. He looked at the gleaming grass in the wet ditch, and at the flowers and flowering reeds that grew there. They all have names, I suppose, he thought. Could you beat that!

Walking along, he soon came to a cottage with dirty brown thatch from which streaks of rain had run down the walls, leaving yellow stripes on the lime. As he got near, a woman came to the door with a black pot and swilled out a slop of green water into the road, leaving a stench of cabbage in the air when she went in. It was a queer time to be cooking her cabbage, Manny thought, and then he chuckled. "For God's sake," he said out loud, "will you look at the old duck?"

A duck had flapped over from the other side of the road to see if the cabbage water made a pool big enough to swim in. "Will you just look at him?" Manny said to himself, the road being empty. He was giving himself very superfluous advice though because he was staring at the duck as hard as he could. But as he stood there a geranium pot was taken down from inside one of the small windows of the cottage, and a face came close to the glass. They don't like you stopping and staring, I suppose, he thought, and he moved along.

His thoughts for some time were on the smallness and darkness of the cottage. He wondered how people put up with living in a little poke like that, and his own room behind the shop in South King Street seemed better to him than it had for a long time. After all, he and Annie had a range. They had gaslight. And they had the use of the lavatory on the upper landing. He was pleased to think of the many advantages he had over those people who had been peeping out at him. He used to think sometimes that South King Street was a dungeon in which he was imprisoned for life, while other men went here and went there, and did this and did that, and some of them even went off to Paris. But at that moment he felt it was a fine thing after all to have a place of your own to keep things in, a place where you could lie down if you were sick or worn out. And it was within a stone's throw of the Pillar.

He didn't get out enough – that was the trouble. If he got out and about more he'd have the right attitude to the house, and maybe to the shop, too. No wonder he was sick of it, never leaving it except like this, to do a message. He should take an odd day off. Man! What was he talking about? He ought to take a week. He ought to run over to Paris and look up the boys. Then, as if aghast at the magnitude of his revolt, he gave himself an alternative. He should go over to Liverpool, anyway, for one of the weekend race meetings. With a bit of luck he might make his expenses, and that would shut Annie's mouth.

The public house came into view just then, and very opportunely, because Manny walked in with the confidence of one who is contemplating a sojourn in distant lands.

He ordered his drink. There were two or three locals leaning against the counter, and a large man, obviously a commercial traveller, stood cleaning his spectacles and asking questions about the locality. The locals were looking sheepishly at their empty glasses that were draped with scum. The traveller gave orders for the glasses to be filled up again. He looked down the counter at Manny as if he would like to include him in the order, but there was a repelling air of independence about Manny, due perhaps to his bowler hat, which sat self-consciously upon the bar counter.

Manny listened to the talk at the other end of the bar. Once or twice the locals mistook the traveller's meaning, but Manny felt a warmth in his heart towards them. Their dull-wittedness gave him a feeling of security. He felt a great dislike for the talkative traveller. He hoped that they would not be on the same bus going back to the city.

Just then the sound of a motor stole into the stillness outside. The bus was coming. Manny drank up, and put out his hand for his hat. Out of the corner of his eye he saw the traveller buttoning his overcoat. He heard his jocose farewells to the locals, who were already leaning back with greater ease against the counter.

Manny went towards the door. The traveller also went towards the door. In the doorway they met.

"I see you are taking this bus too?" said the traveller.

Manny had, of course, intended going back on that bus. He had no idea when there would be another one. But he took a great dislike to the idea of journeying back with the large, talkative man.

"I'm waiting for the next bus," he said impulsively.

"Sorry!" said the traveller. "I should have been glad of your company. Good evening."

"Good evening," said Manny, and he stood back from the dust of the bus as it started up again.

When the dust had blown into the hedges, Manny stepped into the middle of the road and doggedly faced the way the bus had gone. He would probably be walking for a long time before another bus caught up with him, but he did not care. A rare recklessness possessed him, and when shortly after night came down this feeling of recklessness strengthened. He walked along, looking from side to side, and in his heart the night's potent beauty was beginning to have effect. But he felt confused. The dark hills and the pale sky and the city pricking out its shape upon the sea with starry lights filled him with strangely mingled feelings of sadness and joy. And when the sky flowered into a thousand stars of forget-me-not blue he was strangled by the need to know what had come over him, and having no other way to stem the tide of desolating joy within him, he started to run the way he used to run on the roads as a young lad. And as he ran he laughed out loud to think that he, Manny Ryan, was running along a country road in the dark, not knowing but he'd run into a hedge or a ditch.

Yesterday, if anyone had come to him and suggested that he'd do such a thing, he would have split his sides laughing. And tomorrow, if he were to try and persuade Annie to take a walk out in the country, she'd look at him as if he was daft. The Dublin people couldn't tell you the difference between a bush and a tree. Manny stood to recover his breath. And he thought of his wife with her yellow elbows coming through the black unravelled sleeve of her cardigan, as she leaned across the counter in the dismal shop, giving off old shaffoge with any shawley who came the way and had an hour, or maybe two hours, to spare. He thought of the bars filled with his cronies talking about the state of the country for all they were fit, men that never saw more of it than you'd see from the top of a tram. He thought of the skitting young fellows and girls outside Whitefriar Street after late Mass on a Sunday, and he thought of the old men standing at the pub ends of the streets, ringing themselves round with spits. He thought of the old women leaning against the jambs of their doorways, with white crockery milk jugs hanging out of their hands, forgotten in the squalor of their gossip. He thought of the children sitting among the trodden and rancid cabbage butts on the edge of the pavements, repeating the gossip they had heard when they crouched, unheeded, under some public-house counter. He thought of the young and the old, the men and the women, and the pale, frightened children, who were shuffling along the kneelers in churches all over the city, waiting their turn to snuffle out their sins in the dark wooden confessionals. And it seemed as if the cool green light of day scarcely ever reached those people, and the only breezes that blew into their lives came from under their draughty doors thickened with the warm odour of boiling potatoes. The loathing he'd felt for the city, years before, when he first came to Dublin, stole over him again as it had done on that night long ago in the little theatre in Mary Street. Dublin jackeens! he thought.

"Dublin jackeens!" he said then out loud, the gibe coming forth from a dim corner in his mind where the memory of a buttercup field, and a cobbled yard pricked with grass, gave him the right to feel different from them. Once more he longed to get away from Dublin. But this time there was a difference. He wanted to get away from Dublin – yes – but not from Ireland. He didn't want to go away from Ireland, he thought with anguish. Not away from her yellow fields. Not away from her emerald ditches. He wanted only to get away from the stuffy Dublin streets and the people that walked them. Even to get away occasionally for an hour like this would satisfy him.

Wasn't it well, after all, he hadn't gone to Paris? Things always turned out for the best in the end. If he had gone away he might never have come up here to Sallygap, and then he would never have found out that peace was not a matter of one city or another, but a matter of hedges and fields and waddling ducks and a handful of stars. Cities were all alike. Paris was no better or no worse than Dublin when you looked into the matter closely. Paris was a wicked place too, by all accounts, even if people did have a good time there at night, with the lights and the bandstands. Who ever heard of the boys from the Mary Street Band since they went? Where were they? God alone knew! They were playing, maybe, in some cellar done up with striped table-cloths and posters on the walls, like he'd seen in the pictures, with smoke cutting their guts, and women with big thighs and dresses torn open to the waist sitting on their knees and cracking the strings of their sinews with the weight.

A sweat broke out on Manny, and he had to stand still on the road to let the wind cool his burning face. He was damn glad he had stayed at home. What was the need in anybody going across seas when all a man had to do, if he got sick of himself, was to take a bus and come up to a place like this? As long as a fellow could come up to a place like this, what was the need of going farther?

I'll come up here again, he thought, upon my word I will. At last he had found his real escape from the sordidness of the life he led, and perhaps in time the seed of sensitiveness that had lain sterile in his heart through his bleak and unnatural spring and summer might have had a rare and wonderful autumn flowering. There are gentle souls who take nothing from their coarse rearing, and less from their chance schooling, but who yet retain a natural sensitivity, and some-times it flowers, as Manny's did, in the hills.

"I'll come back again," he said out loud. "I'll come back again all right." He turned and took a last look at the hills before he went round a bend in the road, where the houses and shops of Rathfarnham would hide them from view.

With the first shops and the first beginnings of the city and its dazzling tramlines, its noises, and its shoving crowds, Manny felt a tiredness he had not felt in all the miles of rough road he had walked. His feet burned, and his back was weighed down with a knapsack of weariness. So at Terenure he took a tram and sat on the edge of the only seat that was vacant, his light weight joggling with every motion, and the elbow and hipbone of a fat woman on the inside of the seat nudging him with the insistence of inadvertency. Smells of gas and oil sickened him. Broken lights strained his eyes. But most of all a dread of returning home came over him as he remembered that Annie had told him to hurry back. The sharp notes of her voice echoed sudden and loud in his ears, and it seemed impossible that he had for-gotten what she said. He felt like a little boy who had blotted his copy, a little boy who had lost the change, a little boy creeping in under fear of the whip.

The fear of Annie's tongue hung over Manny all the way through the suburbs. When he reached home and saw the closed shutters of the shop, his hand was so stiff and cold that when he put it into the letter-box he could hardly find the string by which the latch of the door could be pulled back from outside. His hand clattered the letter-box for a time before he found it. Then he pulled the string and the door opened. He went in and felt for the knob of the kitchen door, not seeing that the door was wide open because the room was dark and the fire only a powdering of hot grey ash. Then a red spark fell into the ashpit and he realised the door was open after all and that Annie was sitting by the range. Next minute his eyes became used to the dark, and, the customary position of things supplementing his eye where it failed, enabled him to reach the fire and sit down opposite her. He said nothing but sat watching her and wondering when she would speak.

Annie did not speak. The truth was that she had been so excited by his unusual absence that she was unfit for any emotion at his eventual return.

Marriage had been an act of unselfishness on Manny's part. He married Annie because he thought that was what would make her happy, and he was content to give up his own freedom for that object. She, however, had not thought of marriage as anything but a means of breaking the monotony. And she had soon found it a greater monotony than the one she had fled from, and, unlike the other, it was no ante-room of hope leading to something better. Manny accepted her so complacently from the first day that she was bored in a week with his unchanging kindness. At first she exhibited an artificial irritation at trifles in the hope of stirring up a little excitement, but Manny was kinder and more gentle on those occasions than he was before, and gradually her irritability and petulance became more daring until these sins could scarcely be classed as venial. Finally, what had been slyly deliberate became involuntary, and the sour expression on her face hardened into a mask. She sought in the throbbing pulse and rippling flux of anger the excitement she had unconsciously hoped to find in her marriage bed. But her angers, too, were sterile, breeding no response in Manny. He was the same always. It seemed, however, that she could never believe this, and she tried from time to time to break the strength of his weakness, and she fought against his kindness as if it were her enemy, as, in an obscure way, it was. What Annie really wanted was the flaming face, the racing pulse, the temper that raised red weals on the skin, the heat of bodies crushed together in rage. And this need of her nature had never been satisfied except vicariously, leaning over the shop counter listening to the whispered stories of other women; stories of obscene blows given in drunken lusts, stories of cunning and cupidity and flashes of anger and hate that rent the darkness of the tenement hallways in the vicinity, when she and Manny had been in bed for hours.

"Ah, woman dear," these other women would say to her, "sure you know nothing at all about life." And then, as if she was to be pitied, they'd roll up their sleeves indulgently and show her scalds and scabs. "Take a look at that!" they'd say.

And sometimes, standing at the hall door in the dark at night after the shop was shut, she might hear a scream in a room across the street, or round the corner, followed maybe by children's voices sounding as if they were frightened out of their wits. Or perhaps a neighbour might come down the street loudly sobbing, linked on either side by her children, sobbing louder and telling her in high childish voices not to mind; not to mind. Not to mind what? Annie wondered. Which of the inciting words and gestures she had heard the neighbours tell about had provoked this woman? She used to draw back a bit into the doorway while they were passing, her thin shoulder-blades pressed against the wall so they wouldn't see her spying on them and she might then catch a glimpse of Manny sitting in the kitchen with his stocking-feet upon the cooling range, while he read the paper. Her eyes would flicker with hatred and resentment, and she would have an impulse to be revenged on him by going in and poking the range, to send clouds of ashes over him till he'd have to get up and go to bed.

This evening, when he did not come back on time, she set her mind to planning some taunt for him when he'd come into the shop. If there were customers there, so much the better. One time she wouldn't have risked a row before the customers, but she'd found it helped trade more than it hindered it, particularly when Manny never answered back or made trouble. But as the evening wore out and there was still no sign of him, she began to think better of him. She began to think that maybe in his weak way he was defying her at last. Maybe he was getting his temper up with drink? He wasn't a drinking man, but there was always a first time for everything.

A wild elation welled up inside her, waiting for a torrential release in shouting and screaming. Perhaps she had battered in his patience at last? At last he was going to try to get even with her. Well! She was ready. She went into the kitchen, leaving the door into the shop half-open while she knotted her hair as tight as she could, the pricking pain on her neck giving her a foretaste of the fight she would have, and her eyes glittered. She let the customers go without giving them their usual bit of chitchat. She put the shutters up before the time. Where was he? It was getting very late now for a timid man like Manny. And he had had no dinner. She lifted the saucer that was covering his plate on the range. She ought to let him get a bite of food into him before she started the row. But where was he?

She was on her way out to the door to look up the street when she saw the silhouette of the poorhouse hearse passing the door. Supposing he was gone for good? The little skunk! It would be just like him to go over the river wall, like a rat in the dark, and never be heard of again. She would be cheated in this like everything else. Then the blackness lifted a little in her heart and she began to consider other possibilities. Maybe he'd skipped off to better himself somewhere and given her a miss? Again anger throbbed in her breast, but it eased when she remembered that he wouldn't have any money. Thanks be to the Almighty – and to her own good sense – she hadn't given him any money for the eggs. She wondered if he'd got them. Had he gone for them at all?

One after another, then, pictures of horror came into her mind. She saw a sodden corpse, white and hideously swollen, being carried in across the shop, dripping water from muddy clothes upon the thirsty floorboards. She saw herself at the wake, moaning and rocking from side to side, with everyone pitying her.

He wasn't a bad sort really, always wanting to take her to the Gaiety when the opera was on. He wasn't to blame for being so weak. His hands always went dead when he was cold. His face got a terrible blue colour in frosty weather. She thought about the peculiar habit he had of sleeping with his feet outside the bedclothes. And she began to feel uneasy about the past as well as about the future. She walked up and down the dark room, letting herself be mauled now by remorse.

Once in a while she went into the street and looked up and down. She did that in an effort to anticipate the terror that she felt was coming nearer every minute, rounding each corner more rapidly than the one before. But the evening winds were cooling the air and breathing their clear sweet peace even into the city streets. The lights were lighted, but their rays were not yet drawn out from them because the day had still some brightness of its own. They kept their gold carefully folded inside their glass globes, against the hour when their light would be needed, and it seemed as if they had no other function than to decorate the streets with gilt stars. The trams too were lit up, and they sailed like gilded galleons down the evanescent evening blue. The noises of trucks and drays sounded singly in the stillness as if to say that they were going off as fast as they could, and that soon the city would be given over to cars and taxis travelling to gaudy cinemas and theatres pearled with light.

The evening was so fair and so serene, so green and gilt, it threatened to rob her of all her dreads and to soothe her fears. It was better to sit by the whitening fire and imagine that the city outside was dark and vicious as she had often felt it to be, crossing it late on winter nights; a place of evil shadows, with police standing silently in the alleyways, and its shops shut down and barricaded with boards like coffin lids, and all the private houses fortified with battered ashcans lined up along the path, and, dreariest of all, the dark Green with its padlocked gates and its tree-high railings, through which you heard the agonies of a thousand cats wailing in the shrubberies.

She did not know which of her black forebodings she felt to be the more likely, but the ones that brought terror without robbing her entirely of the object of her terror were the ones that most appealed to her. And so she more or less expected a living Manny to be brought home to her, but one in whom some latent mutinous instinct had at last set up a twanging of chords that would echo throughout the rest of their lives and put reality into their relationship. She waited for his coming with more eagerness than when he was coming to court her.

But the instant she heard his footfall she knew he was the same old Manny. He was all right. And he was sober. Her fears faded out in widening ripples, leaving stillness and stagnation in her heart once more. When he put his head inside the door she knew by his apologetic cough that whatever it was had kept him out late it was no high-riding revolt, just a pale and weedy shoot from the anaemia of his character. It was certainly not a bursting into leaf of unsuspected manliness.

She sat by the fire without moving.

At last Manny was driven to break the silence himself.

"Did you keep my dinner, Annie?" he asked timidly, going over to the range, stooping his head as he went to avoid a slap of the wet sheets and towels that hung across the kitchen on a piece of string. He opened the door of the oven and bending down looked in. There was nothing there, and he shut the door quietly and stole a look at Annie. She was sitting scratching her head with a hairpin she had pulled out of the tight knot of hair on her neck. When she had finished scratching she stood up.

"Get out of my way," she ordered tonelessly, and, taking down a damp cloth off the line over his head, she took a hot plate from the top of the stove and went over to a pile of rubbish in the corner of the room. Pulling out a piece of brown paper she put it under the plate before she set it on the table. "Light the gas," she ordered.

The nauseous smell of gas roamed around the room in streamers that soon ran together into one thick odour, and the glare of the gaslight took away the only dignity the room had – its darkness. Manny sat down to the meal set before him on the brown paper. It was a plate of meat flanked on two sides by tallow-yellow potatoes and a mound of soggy cabbage that still held the shape of the fork with which it had been patted. Meat, potato and cabbage were all stuck fast to the plate. And around the rim of the plate, the gravy was crusted into a brown paper doily.

"It looks good," Manny said appeasingly, "and it smells good."

"It smelled better four hours ago," Annie said, cleaning a knife with her fingers and putting it down beside the plate.

Manny wondered if this reference to keeping the dinner hot was intended as an opening for him to say where he had been, and what had kept him, but when he looked at her he decided on saying nothing.

He ate his dinner in silence, and tried as best he could to keep the food in his mouth from making noises, but the sounds of chewing seemed so loud in his own ears that after a few mouthfuls he began to swallow down the coarse lumps of beef unchewed. Soon the silence became so terrible he could eat no more. He pushed aside his plate and sat staring at the ring of grease it had left on the absorbent brown paper. He was reminded waywardly of the brown paper he had used the night before his wedding to get a grease stain off the sleeve of his best suit. In those days he used to read in bed and he'd get his clothes covered with candle grease, because he used to hump them under the candlestick to raise it higher beside the bed. That was a long time ago, but the past had been coming into his mind all day. He used to hear his mother say that you re-lived all your life in your mind before you died, but he hated those ignorant old superstitions. They'd drive you mad. Yet the silence in the kitchen was enough to make a man mad.

He turned around in the chair and deliberately drew down the lash of her rage. "I went up to Sallygap to get the eggs, but I missed the bus and walked home."

"From Sallygap?"

He had expected a tirade. He looked at her. She was picking her teeth with a bit of brown paper she'd leaned over and torn off the paper under the plate.

"Gets in your teeth, doesn't it?" he said, in a fainthearted hope that there was not going to be any row.

"Are you finished?" she asked.

He looked at his plate. "Finished," he said. "All except my tea. I'll wet the tea myself if you like."

"The tea is in the pot," she said, and as he poured the spluttering water into the cold teapot she got up and went over to the dresser and took down a cup and saucer. She put them on the table.

The cup had not been washed since it had last been used. There was a sediment of moist sugar in the bottom of it, and the outside was streaked with yellow tea stains.

"This cup is a bit dirty," he said, moving over to the sink.

"It's your own dirt, then," she said to him. "It was you who had it last."

He stood irresolute, and then he said he'd like a clean cup.

"There's a quarter pound of sugar in the bottom of that cup," Annie said, and then she snapped a question at him suddenly, with some apparent relevancy in her own mind. "What did you do with the return ticket?"

He rooted in his pockets and took out the half-ticket. She snapped it up and looked at it closely, and then she stuck it down in a jug that was hanging by its handle on the nail of the dresser.

"Is he going to send the eggs?"

"Every Monday and Friday."

"Give me that cup." She went over to the sink where she ran the cold tap on it. She clattered it back on the saucer, wet. Cold drops splashed on to his hot hands from her wet hands. She stood looking down at him. "It's a queer thing when a man disgusts to himself!" she said.

Her eyes were greener than ever. They used to remind him of the sea at Howth, where they used to go walking when they were courting. They were the same colour still, but now they reminded him suddenly of the green water under the wharf at Dunlaoghaire. And as the sticky sea that day had been flecked with splinters of his broken fiddle, Annie's eyes above him now were flecked with malevolence.

Ever since their first quarrel, he'd been afraid of her sharp tongue. But it had been the fear of a timid soul. Now, looking up into her eyes, his immature and childish fear fell from him, and instead of it there came into his heart a terrible adult fear; a fear that came from his instincts, from his blood. He thought of all the talk he had heard at different times in public houses, talk of morgues and murders, and he remembered what he had said to himself up at Sallygap about the people of Dublin: that they were ignorant, with clogged pools in their blood that clotted easily to unjust hate. They hugged their hate. He thought of Paris, with its flashing lights and its flashing hates, its quick flashing knives; but the dangers in Paris seemed vivid and vital compared with the dead anger in the sullen eyes that were watching him. Desperately he thought of the hills, but the thought of them gave him no refuge. The happy hills were fading from his mind already. He would never seek a sanctuary among them again.

For there was no sanctuary from hatred such as he saw in Annie's eyes, unless it came from behind some night, from a raised hatchet brought down with a crack on his skull, or from a queer taste in the mouth followed by a twisting in the guts. She had him imprisoned for ever in her hatred. His little fiddle had crashed on the pier the day he gave up all his dreams for her, and it had floated in splintered sticks on the dirty water. He thought of it for a moment, and then he thought of nothing at all for a while, but just sat watching her as she went about the room.

Then he remembered that she had said something to him when she clattered down the wet cup on the saucer in front of him a little while before. He tried to think what it was she had said. He couldn't remember.

But he did remember, distinctly, thinking at the time, that whatever it was, it was true.

The Nun's Mother

Well, it was all over now anyway. Mrs. Latimer closed her eyes and laid her head back against the horsehair cushions of the taxi. It was all over, and she was certainly grateful for that much. As they drove down the avenue from the convent she kept her eyes closed. And she would keep them closed she decided – at least until they reached the gate-lodge, when the taxi would jolt over the spud-stone – up with a little bump – down with a little bump – and Luke and herself would joggle together no matter how tightly they clung to the crusty hand-straps. Their feet would lift a little from the rubber flooring like corks on a wave-wash, and then plop into place again. Her hair would probably catch on a ravelled thread of the wiry horsehair upholstery, and the cat hairs on her neck would pinch – only for a second of course. But since they'd got grey those cat hairs looked too untidy for words unless they were pinned into the rest of her hair, which was hardly grey at all. Mrs. Latimer sighed. Her hair had certainly got greyer all over in the last month. Even so it still wasn't so very grey. Most people thought she was younger than she was. And she could see for herself that she was much younger-looking than Luke. Here Mrs. Latimer stealthily opened her eyes – mere slits – and looked at her husband. Poor Luke! This last month had told on him. He was worn out. It had taken more out of her all the same. She closed her eyes and sighed again, remembering that until quite recently her hair had been as brown as when she was a girl. But what could one expect after all? One couldn't stay young forever, alas. And this summer had been so frightful. The final week, of course, being almost unendurable.

Ah, they had reached the gate. Up with a little bump. Down with a little bump. Then out over the spud-stone and into the main road. And as they joggled together, Luke – as she knew he would – steadied himself by placing a hand on her knee, and when they wheeled into the tarred road he left it there. To show his sympathy! But she stubbornly kept her eyes closed. If she'd opened them he might have felt obliged to express concern for her – to say something to the effect that things

43

must be worse for her than for him – as a Mother he'd mean.

It was then Mrs. Latimer realized why she didn't want to open her eyes. She was afraid Luke might see that her eyes were empty – empty, that was to say, of all appropriate expression. For she felt, at that moment, absolutely nothing. Nothing but relief that all was over.

She certainly was not suffering. Not anything like him. Poor Luke! He was not only hurt but perplexed. Men had such an irrational horror of the cloister. Their views on the religious life were positively medieval. Luke himself until quite recently always spoke of convents as nunneries! Such a word!

Really and truly he could hardly have been more upset if Angela had got into trouble – yes, yes – even that kind of trouble! If anything like that had happened, Luke would have been shocked, grieved, worried, but deep down he would have been able to understand that such things could happen even to a well-brought-up girl like Angela. He would have had a hard time swallowing that such a thing could happen to his own daughter, but if it had happened, he'd have had to swallow it. What his daughter had, in fact, done, however, was something absolutely incomprehensible to him. His nature rebelled against it. He'd found it unnatural, abnormal – abhorrent.

She herself – as a woman – didn't feel quite the same. Women had a curious streak of chastity in them no matter how long they were married or how ardently they had loved. And so, when a woman heard that a young girl was entering a convent – most women at any rate – felt a strange triumph in their hearts for a time – and, as they moved around the house that day they felt a temporary hostility to their husbands and to the things of his household. For no reason at all they'd flick a dishcloth irritably in the air and send a mist of fine rain through the hot kitchen, their minds invaded by visions of green girls (who might have been themselves) going garlanded with lilies (or white flowers of some kind) down cloisters ivied over by centuries. And these young girls would be going away gladly, without once looking backward to where, behind them on summer lawns, and sunny river banks, others, with lovers, lay dallying.

Yes, Mrs. Latimer was satisfied that that was undoubtedly how most women felt on such occasions. How else could one account for the success of novels and films like *The White Sister* (it had just been re-issued and would soon be showing in their local cinema)? But that was not how she felt. And why induce feelings? Hadn't she always tried to be sincere? Sometimes, of course, she failed, but she had always tried. And now that it was over and done with, if she were asked to tell – truthfully – how the loss of her daughter Angela affected her she would have to say that – now at this moment anyway – it only meant no more fun going shopping in town (sober purchases from now on), no more visits to the small women's department (matrons and outsize now for ever), no more need to be constantly on the lookout for bargains in linen at the January sales (even when things were going for for a song). No reason in short to remain young.

Now, no longer could she dream of going gaily down the years (blithely negotiating the narrow causeway of age) with a prancing two-in-hand. It would be single gallop from now on, and one that would get faster and faster with the years. Faster and faster she would go from now on, speeded all along the way by the voices of other women, calling after her. "Well for you, Mrs. Latimer: well for you with a daughter a nun to pray for you."

A nun to pray for her? Her daughter Angela! Such a notion! It was utterly absurd.

She had faith, of course. She believed in prayer – to a certain extent – prayers of praise and prayers of contrition – but not prayers of petition: Dear God, please help me to find my brooch – Dear God, don't let it rain today when I've no umbrella – that kind of thing. That wasn't real prayer. That she despised. And prayers for her soul's salvation, from her daughter Angela – well, that too she would quite frankly discount. To think of depending on the prayers of Angela. Angela! Who was in pigtails till the beginning of the summer? Angela, who up to her last day at home always sat so immodestly with her bare thighs showing? Oh it was hard, even now, to believe she was really going to be a nun – a nun!

There now! That was the truth. That was what she felt about the whole business – disbelief. Not grief. And certainly not the joy which was what some people seemed to think she ought to feel! As for pride that the Lord should have chosen the fruit of her womb! Well, to be perfectly honest she did not believe He had chosen Angela. Angela had taken it into her head and gone.

But why? Why? That was what Mrs. Latimer hadn't been able to discover. The girl had made her choice alone, without once consulting them, and calmly announced her decision without caring – it would seem – how badly they felt. And here was poor Luke – Mrs. Latimer did not need to glance at him, she knew how he'd look – here he was sitting beside her in the cab, like a dummy.

And here she was herself – she was just about to describe herself to herself as turned into stone when she realized how much worse it was than that – here she was turned into A Nun's Mother!

It was quite a title. A Nun's Mother. She could imagine how people would fasten on it. "May I introduce Mrs. Latimer, who has a daughter a nun. Have you met Mrs. Latimer? Mrs. Latimer has a daughter in the convent."

Mrs. Latimer. Mrs. Latimer. Her Christian name would probably be dropped – fall out of use – become forgotten. Even Luke might, in time, feel Meg too frivolous a name to call her except perhaps when they were alone. Once already today – talking to the Reverend Mother – he had – to her astonishment – called her Margaret. She would become a sort of exhibit. Would she perhaps be obliged to assume an attitude? Expected to dress differently? More discreetly? To give up smoking? In public anyway! To put up holy pictures even in her *downstairs* rooms? And what else? Oh yes – to punctuate her conversation with pious little tags like *God willing, Thanks be to God* and *God between us and all harm*. So many women sprinkled their conversation with these ejaculations, like holy water. Holy water? That was another thing. She shuddered. Friends and neighbours would now be for ever bringing her home presents of little labelled bottles of Lourdes water, which would lie about in drawers, accumulating. Oh dear! What else would the mother of a nun be expected to do? Ah yes! Donate settees to the convent parlour. Settees and upright pianos!

It was really unfair to think how little notoriety was attached to being the father of a nun. Luke did not realize it yet, but when he'd go up to the convent to visit Angela he would be treated quite normally. Angela wouldn't blush if his tie was too bright, or be embarrassed if unthinkingly he raised his voice a little too loud in the convent parlour, or blew his nose too noisily – like a trumpet, as he sometimes did.

Oh yes, it was all very well for Luke. When he'd get used to it, Luke would quite enjoy going up to Mount Saint Joseph. He would look forward to his walks around the convent grounds step by step with his stately daughter, her high virgin bust firmly tightened into pleated, black gaberdine and her profile enhanced by her coif and wimple. He'd soon be going up there every chance he got – as often as Reverend

Mother permitted. He'd gradually give up other things he used to enjoy like going to the Club or the occasional game of golf. Even the cinema. Good Lord! A simply frightful thought occurred to Mrs. Latimer. He might want to give up their annual trips abroad! Oh but she must not, she knew, she must not, let resentment mount against him. Poor Luke! It was devoutly to be hoped that he would in time become resigned, but he might not achieve resignation for a long time – might not indeed ever become resigned – at all. For who could tell? Not her! He had always been so inarticulate – compared with her – and certainly in the past few months one would have thought at times that the cat had taken his tongue!

When he'd first been told of Angela's intention – not by Angela herself of course (the girl had always had a knack of avoiding unpleasant tasks, and pushing them over on others) – he said only one word: Angela? Like that! As if they had several daughters and she, their mother, had mixed up their names. They were in their own bedroom at the time and Luke had sunk down on the bed, stunned. She had, of course, seen that he was stunned, and later most likely he had said something else, but if so it was nothing she could remember. Nothing important. Nothing remarkable. Usually, of course, his lack of loquacity didn't bother her. She was used to it. But that day it infuriated her.

And now again – sitting beside him in the taxi – she was suddenly furious with him again when he moved on the seat and his elbow jostled her again because she guessed – she *knew* – he was turning around to try and catch a last glimpse of the convent. How could anyone be so stupid! Even with her eyes shut she knew it was out of sight by now. And as if anyone in their right mind would want to look at it anyway, the hateful place – that ugly, bare building. And to think that Angela – oh she couldn't bear to think of that! Just then, anyway, Luke faced forward again and patted her knee with the hand that still rested on it. Poor dear. He was so considerate of her always. He probably thought it was out of consideration for *him* that she was silent! Yes! His hand was pressing her again, tenderly, as if to thank her. Thank you, my dear, it seemed to say, thank you for giving me this respite. When we get home we can talk.

Talk? As if she didn't know what that meant! Talk about other things! About this and about that – maybe even about practicalities necessitated by Angela's departure. But not about Angela herself. Not about their loss. Nothing of that kind. But perhaps, for that, she ought to be thankful? What would be the use of a post-mortem? Shutting the stable door after the filly had bolted!

Indeed it would be too frustrating if Luke where to ask in retrospect the same clumsy questions with which he had tormented her all summer – never mentioning a name, of course. Are you sure she knows what she's doing, Meg?

If he asked that once he must have asked it a hundred times. At first she used to shake her head, being – if he only knew – twice as confused as him. But as the summer went on and the event they dreaded drew near, she lost patience with him.

"Who are you talking about?" she asked once coldly, because, curiously enough, the more helpless and pathetic he began to look the more he annoyed her. She began to take out her own disappointment on him – to torment him like he was tormenting her – to give as good as she got – because the long and short of it was that he had let her down. Why had he not seen that she had mismanaged her end of the thing? Why hadn't he taken up where she had failed? Why hadn't he himself gone to Angela and (with a masterfulness he had shown himself to be capable enough of when she was a child) asked her outright, what they both wanted so desperately to know, why she – their lovely, lovely Angela – was going away and leaving them for ever? And ever!

Instead of that he kept pestering her, as if she had some inside information.

"Does she know what she is giving up, Meg?"

Did *he* realize how often he asked that – and at the oddest times too – coming out of the lavatory for instance – although she could follow his line of thought there, could see how any man would have felt – but what another man would have come straight out with – forthrightly.

"I suppose she does," she'd heard herself reply wearily one evening towards the end. By then she'd been too tired to care, because by then Angela had become a regular slave-driver, whipping her on, and running her off her feet with the preparations for the Big Day. "I suppose she does," she'd said. And after that, each time he asked the same silly question she gave him the same silly answer. But why, oh why had she not run to him and thrown herself into his arms, and drummed her fists on his chest – as she had often done successfully in other situations? Why had she not confessed openly that she didn't know either – any more than him – that she was afraid to ask – and that if one of them didn't do something quick it would be too late?

How odd that she, who was usually so free with her tongue, should have been afraid to ask her own daughter one simple question. And if, as was proved, she did find it impossible to be frank, why hadn't she done what she had done on innumerable other occasions – asked a series of small, trivial but subtle questions whose answers she could have put together later like a jigsaw.

Oh well – why blame herself now? If she had asked a direct question Angela would almost certainly have given her a rebuff. And if she had employed the other – and let's face it – the meaner method, the girl would have seen through it, and despised her even more than she seemed to do already. Yes – Angela really did despise her at times. She knew that. She didn't flinch from the thought. Daughters were sweet. But no one could pretend they were easy to rear! Later, when they married it was probably different, but Angela – Oh dear, Mrs. Latimer felt the tears welling into her eyes and she did not dare dab at them with her handkerchief in case Luke would notice.

If only they had had a son! Then this situation would never have arisen. Then, things would have been taken out of her hands anyway. If a boy of theirs had taken some crazy notion – like Angela – and announced that he was going to become a priest, Luke would undoubtedly have handled him wisely. He would have taken him aside and had a down-to-earth talk with him.

Men were straightforward with each other. There would have been no nonsense. Look here, my boy, Luke would have said, tell me frankly, son, have you considered this? And the *this* would have been love and the bodies of men and women. Luke would have spoken in the most matter-of-fact manner – perhaps even with a slightly humorous note – but the outcome would have been satisfactory. Things would have been settled at once. The boy would either have stood his ground and gone ahead with his plans or else agreed to give himself a little time to think over his father's words – even, perhaps, wait a few years until he was older and had had some experience of the world. Either way, Luke and herself would have felt absolved from responsibility for his decision.

But could they feel absolved from Angela's decision? Was their daughter sufficiently experienced to have made the choice she had made – taken the drastic step she had taken? That step might not, nowadays, be considered absolutely irrevocable like it would at one time have been but that only seemed to make matters worse. If in a year or so the girl were to come out again she would probably go through life with feelings of guilt – or a sense of failure. Would one *want* her to change her mind now? Would one want, oneself, to go through the whole ghastly process in reverse? Oh God, no! Hadn't they had enough, all of them? Mrs. Latimer's heart froze at the thought of re-opening the whole painful business.

But why oh why was it so hard for women to be honest and above board with each other? They didn't behave like that with men! With men – well, with some men anyway – women – well, some women – such as herself for instance – could be startlingly frank. But with each other it seemed it was virtually impossible. Or so she had found it. Even at school! All that awful lumpy shuffling that used to go on under their clothes when they were dressing or undressing in the dorm. As if they were trussed up in sacks! An elbow protruding here, and a knee there under their slip or their nightgown! No simplicity. No grace. And not only when they were at school but later when they were supposed to be mature, in the fitting-rooms of shops and at the dress-maker. To say nothing of their wedding night.

But here Mrs. Latimer nearly laughed out loud, remembering Luke's face on the first night of her own honeymoon when she was endeavouring to wiggle her arms, one by one out of the sleeves of her dress in order to take off her bra under the sort of the tent she'd made of her dress! Luke was so funny about it. "Who do you think you are, Meg? Houdini?" he said. How they laughed. He himself stepping out of his trousers as carelessly as if he was in the presence of his tailor. To tell the truth she'd been slightly shocked the whole time on their honeymoon by the insouciance with which he'd walked around their room sometimes with absolutely nothing on. But when she saw how appalled he was one day that a chambermaid, thinking the room was empty, opened the door she'd realized for the first time the difference between false and true modesty. She'd realized how at one she and Luke had become. And that was the end of her nonsensical girlish prudery.

Mrs. Latimer smiled to herself. Then her smile faded, because since they'd got older she had found herself returning unconsciously to her former ways. But now it was for another reason. There was an excuse for delicacy when the body got – well, got old. But all the same, when one thought about it, it was odd that even in youth it should be the woman who felt exposed, whereas, in fact, the female form was so much more secretively and subtly moulded than the male.

Oh dear – if only it was the other way around in real life! Then there would be none of the awful falsity – that clutching at a towel or a sheet if the door-knob rattled, and the silly shrieks of warning – *Just a second. Don't come in for a minute please.* All that rubbish. Above all there would be none of that deadly silence between mother and daughter, a silence based on embarrassment, and not, as between a mother and son, upon mystery and respect.

She had always been conscious of a curious embarrassment – it would not be going too far to call it revulsion – between herself and Angela. Well no – not always, but certainly since the girl reached adolescence. And in their last few months together Angela herself seemed wary of intimacy. Whenever they were alone the child had adopted an almost defiant attitude – as much as to say, *Speak now if you dare, about me and my private affairs.* It was an attitude that effectively sealed her mother's lips anyway.

But Luke knew nothing about this. Nothing! She could have strangled him at times, particularly when they'd got into bed, and she'd put out the light. That was always when he piped up with his tiresome questions. She had to admit he had changed his tune slightly during the girl's last week at home. "Do you think you ought to have another word with her, dear?" he'd asked, one night, adding that he thought it might be advisable. Advisable! In the dark he could not see her face but she hadn't dreamt he'd miss the irony in her voice when she'd replied in the affirmative, saying she had had a nice long chat with the child. A nice long chat! Only a fool would have missed the irony of that! But Luke evidently – God help him – was only too eager for reassurance. He had taken her words at face value – gobbled them up indeed and with a sigh of relief hunched up the blankets, turned over, and settled down to sleep.

She knew she had more or less burned her boat that night. She knew she could never confess to having been sarcastic – not about a matter so serious and of such concern to them both. Come to think of it, after that night she didn't get a second chance anyway. Luke gave up his foolish questioning of her and, apparently relying totally on her ability to handle the situation, he developed instead another, a new and even more irritating habit, the habit of throwing Angela and herself together on every possible occasion. "Wouldn't you two like to run along?" he'd say, coming home, perhaps, from Mass. "I'd like to stop and get the papers." Sometimes he said this without remembering that they had got the papers on the way to Mass and he had them, at that moment, under his arm. Maddening! Or else he'd come into a room and finding they were talking (about nothing) he'd scuttle out with an apology as if he was an intruder. It was a wonder she hadn't run after him and hit him over the head with something – with anything.

Poor Luke! It wasn't fair to blame him for taking her at her word: for trusting her. She had only herself to blame for that. And also for the way he began to act towards their daughter – treating the girl as deferentially as if she was too saintly to be treated any more like a mere daughter! Because, for him – as a man – the only important difference between the world and the cloister was the difference of the flesh and the flesh denied. Poverty and obedience didn't matter a rap to him. "Poverty," he'd always scoffed. "Haven't the nuns more money than anyone? Isn't it the nuns who have bought up all the big properties in the country? And not content with that, they have to build on huge extensions and annexes and God knows what – until you'd need a scooter to go from one end to the other! Poverty, did you say? You must be joking?"

He had not seen Angela, as she, her mother, had seen her on her last day at home distributing her little treasures among her friends. Her velvet toque that was so becoming she had given to that really plain little girl next door, whom it certainly would not suit. And the photos of film stars that had been pasted all over the wall of her room she had given to the maid! (She must remember to warn that creature to peel them off carefully or else the plaster would come off with them.) But oh dear, oh dear – for a girl like Angela, who was like a little jackdaw the way she stored up junk – letters, theatre programmes, postcards – even luggage labels – a vow of poverty would surely be a kind of little death in life? Mrs. Latimer sighed. That, of course, she reminded herself, was what it was supposed to be!

And the vow of obedience? For that, too, Luke had no time. "Obedience? You'd have to be a lot more obedient in an office," he said. "And no roses in heaven for it either!"

But chastity? Ah, that was another thing altogether. About that Luke had nothing to say – not a word. Chastity floored him. To think that a daughter of his – the child of his own delight – should choose to live a celibate life – that was utterly beyond his capacity to understand. It was inevitable that he would end by persuading himself she was a being apart – unlike other mortals made of perishable clay. Poor Luke! She'd caught him looking oddly at herself sometimes, for all the world as if he were longing to ask if she could have done it? If anything would have induced her to give it all up? But, of course, he never had the gumption to ask. If he had, they might have got down to brass tacks and confronted Angela together. To do it alone was too much to expect of one parent. Girls of Angela's age – as she knew from bitter experience – were past masters in covering up what they thought and felt – specially about boys and that kind of thing. If she had taken Angela aside and managed to stammer out a few words on that most difficult of all subjects, it was probable that Luke and herself might still be sitting here in this taxi having left her behind there in that awful convent. Because the likelihood was that Angelia wouldn't have paid the slightest heed to them.

Well, it was all over now. For better or for worse. But oh dear, what an unfortunate phrase that was! Mrs. Latimer bit her lip. Yet could one deny that for most people, marriage was more often worse than better? More of a cross than a crown? She herself had not found it so. Far from it – poor dear Luke – but a number of her married friends had told her things, confidentially, of course. (Not that she'd needed to be told, they were things she had guessed.) And thinking of some of those confidences now, she could almost feel relieved that Angela was going to be spared the risk of that kind of thing!

It was only when she thought about herself and Luke that Mrs. Latimer felt bad – swamped with pity – not just for themselves but for poor little Angela as well.

Angela was going to miss it all. Mrs. Latimer tightened her clutch on the hand-strap. Her mind rambled back over the past – and indeed the not-so distant past – and she thought about the bliss – oh the bliss of – but better not to think about such things, especially of the nights when they were first married and young and inexperienced and when – No. No. She must stamp out those thoughts. She must suppress those blissful memories. Bliss was a silly word anyway, yet how else could one describe – oh dear – she must control her thoughts. She must! Otherwise she would not be able to comfort Luke who – although he'd never, never speak about it – would be thinking exactly the same as her, especially tonight when they'd go upstairs to their room and see Angela's empty room (she must try and remember to go up first and shut the door). Mrs. Latimer glanced covertly at him again then. She ought to begin this minute to take a new attitude towards the whole business, and try to put the best possible complexion on Angela's action, even if it meant going along with the view of others that God had called their child to Higher Things. If she was to make Luke feel this was so, she would have to try to feel something of that sort herself – would have to begin by suppressing her thoughts with regard to – how should she say it – with regard to the pleasures of the body.

At her age anyway should she not have begun to feel a certain – well, not shame – but a certain feeling of unsuitability perhaps about . . .? Mrs. Latimer did in fact flush slightly as she recalled a night not long before, but this time she deliberately let her mind dwell on it because it really might be helpful in their new situation if she felt a little, well, say, more reserve about certain matters. Yes, reserve was the right word. Shame was too strong. Reserve. But when she tried to think more clearly about that night – and she was doing so very very deliberately – she found her thoughts were dim and vague. There had been the langour of sleep as well as the langour of love.

Wait a minute. Surely she ought to be able to feel some compunction on Luke's behalf – some shame for him? He had looked so abandoned – his head thrown back, his mouth half-open, and a large vein like a worm in his forehead throbbing. She stole another quick look at him, where he sat bolt upright on the slippery horsehair seat, in his pinstripe suit and his bowler hat with his umbrella between his knees, his hand tightly grasping it by the crook. Surely she ought to feel compunction that she had – and so many, many times – reduced this natty man to the indignity of blindly feeling fingers, faltering breath and, finally, to prostration? But the answer was no. No. No. No. Instead she was flooded with pride in her own power, and her breast rose carrying aloft the cameo brooch he had only recently given her. The end was nowhere in sight either, she thought, with even more grievous pride. None of her friends – or so she suspected – had lived with love as long and intimately as her.

Then she let out her breath, and the cameo brooch fell into the hollows again. To think that her only daughter – her only child – would have her hair shorn, and her body wrapped up in black sacking – oh it was very hard to take!

How had those nuns succeeded in talking the girl into taking such a step? But need one ask? She herself had only to think of their try-ons with her when she was Angela's age! The Church had the trump card when it came to talking about love. The fulfilling of the law. Greater love hath no man! All that bosh. Even if she had tried to compete with those nuns, what chance would her stumbling words have had against quotations two thousand years old, no matter how they were garbled and distorted.

Supposing just for a moment that she had managed to corner Angela and had blurted out her question. What do you know, Angela, about human love? Physical love? The love of a man for a woman? Supposing – just supposing – she'd got that out! And supposing – just supposing – Angela had taken it from her – what then? Supposing the girl had admitted she knew nothing? And asked to be told? Good God! What would she have said then? Not that love was noble. Not that it was kind. Generous? No. Gentle? No. Dignified? (That was laughable!) In short, love was nothing that could be described in a way that would have an appeal for an idealistic young girl whose head was full of poetry. Why even the poets themselves hadn't been able to describe it. *There had fallen a splendid tear from the passion tree at the gate.* Lines like that might convey something to one when one was a bit older and understood the underlying suggestions – but at Angela's age it only added to the idealism – the unreality. Yet, Luke thought it could be done with a word. *Did you have a word with her?* Fool! She changed her position to shake off his hand, but not obviously – not hurtfully – or so she hoped. Then she returned to her thoughts. Even if love could be described with a word – or twenty words for that matter – would it have been right to interfere with what, after all, one was supposed to consider a Divine call? The fact that she herself never had much faith in the idea of a voice from Above speaking directly to one soul in a million (one in a million million if one wanted to be more exact) her disbelief did not necessarily mean that the thing was altogether impossible. It was all a great mystery. Life itself, she meant. Hadn't she heard of cases where interference with a so-called vocation had been disastrous? Only recently she had heard about a girl who was determined to be a nun, and whose parents tried to prevent her. And what happened? One night the poor girl climbed out a skylight on to the roof in her night-dress with a crucifix in her hands. They managed to coax her down but she had to be sent to a mental home. And never came out again either. That was certainly worse than going into a convent, no matter what way you looked at it.

If she and Luke had attempted to baulk Angela in this, they might have regretted it bitterly in time to come. How could they have assumed such a heavy responsibility?

But here Mrs. Latimer detected a trace of insincerity in herself. Hadn't they long ago accepted responsibility for Angela – when they brought her into the world? Indeed she herself had accepted it eighteen years ago when the child was conceived. As soon as she'd become aware she was pregnant she'd felt the weight of that responsibility. And immediately after the birth, when Luke had gone out of the room and the nurse had fixed her up and drawn the curtains, leaving her to rest, her joy as she lay in the darkened room had been tempered by a vague feeling of apprehension for the fate of the child she had just borne. To this day she could remember the strange thought that came into her mind, it was almost a vision. Lying there and looking down the years ahead, she had seen herself as a portal from which not only her child had come out, but the child of her child, and then that child's child and so on – until a great multitude of people spread out over the world – a horde of human beings – who all, all had issued forth from her. She thought of them – *saw* them – like people coming out of a cinema, singly at first, then forming into pairs, and then when they reached the street merging into threes and fours until they were soon spreading out over the whole city, the whole world in an ever-widening wedge. And – this was the awful part – all those people – those strangers – had her features and they were all looking back at her over their shoulders with looks of reproach – looks of accusation. Only for you we would never have been born, they seemed to say. Because in her physically depleted state it had seemed that one and all the lives of these unborn people would be dark, tragic – even evil. Better far, it would seem for them, never to have been brought into this wicked world.

Later, of course, when she was rested and felt stronger and when the flowers and telegrams began to arrive – above all when they'd brought back the baby and put it into her arms (ah – the anguish now to think that infant was Angela) – then of course she felt differently. Yet here, now, in the taxi at this moment, she shuddered. Why had she herself not gone away one summer day like Angela, her face washed clean with honest soap and water, her body shrouded in black, with flat-heeled shoes on her feet?

For Angela would never sit like this in a taxi, an old woman – well, say an ageing woman – shrinking from the thought of something long done and utterly irrevocable. With Angela life would come to an end, like a flower fallen into a stream and carried under the water before its seed had time to ripen and bear fruit.

But here Mrs. Latimer sat up straight as she woke to a new significance in her daughter's rejection of the world. By taking this vow of chastity Angela was freeing her, too, from the future – and from her fear of it, whether foolish or not. A great sigh escaped her. The seed of her seed would be for ever barren. And viewed in this light suddenly the attitude of other women – at which she had so lately sneered – seemed different, seemed more acceptable to her. For the first time in the dismal days, weeks, months that had passed she began to see that God might indeed have conferred a great grace upon her. And upon Luke. Perhaps in His infinite wisdom He had looked mercifully on them and instead of impoverishing them He had bestowed His bounty upon them. All at once Mrs. Latimer felt more carefree than she had felt for years. And into her heart – like when she was young – there flew a bluebird of happiness – to make its nest there again and – of this she felt sure – to dwell there now for ever. And like she had always done she wanted to share her happiness with Luke – to open her eyes and let her happiness fly forth into his in a flutter of smiles.

But just as she was about to turn towards him, Mrs. Latimer hesitated. Could it be possible that she, who had always prided herself on knowing exactly what she felt, even deep down (although she had never gone along with all that probing into the subconscious that had become a mania with some of her friends), could it be that, all the same, deep down somewhere inside her, that old fear of responsibility had continued to lurk? Dear God – had it perhaps shown in her face? What about the day Angela had given her the list she'd got from the novice-mistress – the list of things she had to get? Angela's manner that day had been so antagonistic. She'd held out the piece of paper. "Here is the list of what I've got to get," she'd said almost brutally. That list had made everything so final, and in any case within a week the job of finding all those ridiculous, those crazy, items, had both of them flattened out and quite incapable then of talking about anything. They didn't get time – not once – for a cup of tea or coffee – much less to slip into a cinema, as was their normal pattern after a day's shopping in town.

Such peculiar things as were on that list! They didn't know where to look for them. At the end of the day her own feet ached and Angela was so unbelievably irritable that once or twice she'd felt like giving her a good slap as if she was still a child. Laced corsets, for instance. Where would one go for laced corsets? They tried about twenty shops before

C

they got them finally in some sort of medical suppliers – remedial garments, no doubt. The sales-girl looked commiseratingly at Angela – thinking at first she must be saddled with an invalid mother. Then when she realized they were for Angela herself she must have guessed her purpose in wanting them and stared at her as if she was off her head.

The next item on the list was white stockings. White? The sales-girl was astonished and asked to look at the list for herself in disbelief. Angela, poor child, was in a continual state of embarrassment. There were some articles – articles of underwear in particular – that seemed really immodest, and made one think of fat women at the seashore undressing under a bathing sheet before going in for a dip – silly women who would only paddle, or flop up and down on the edge of the waves without letting their tops get wet. One of the sales-girls had such a smirk on her face as she said she had no notion where one would find such outlandish things – she had managed to convey there was something outlandish about them, Angela and herself as well as the garments. They left the shop so flustered – Angela was actually blushing – that when they got out into the common light of day she herself exploded. "Bad enough to be a fool! But to be recognized for one is another thing," she said. At that moment she didn't care if she alienated Angela for good. She'd soon be gone from her anyway.

In the end they had to get a dressmaker to make some of the under-clothes. There was no use slogging to any more shops. Those things had gone out with the dodo. But even then a sadistic streak (why not admit it) made her go on persecuting the child. "You'll have to tell the dressmaker why you want those things," she'd say. "Unless you want her to think you're stark, staring mad!"

That was so unkind. But every second word out of her mouth was unkind in those last weeks. Sharp, unkind, bitter. She couldn't help it though, every hour brought new annoyances. The old dressmaker became a pest. She showered Angela with medals and scapulars and gave her mortuary cards of her father and her mother, beseeching her to keep them in her prayer book and pray for them! No doubt daily!

Then there was the dreadful day when the old dressmaker came to deliver some flannel shifts, while a boy from down the street was visiting – David Something-or-Other – a nice boy. He had taken Angela skating the previous winter – but really and truly it was hard to avoid the suspicion that he called from curiosity, having got wind of Angela's intentions. He was a gossip – young as he was. To think it was in his hearing the crazy old fool of a woman had told that truly shocking story about the bandages on the statue – the bandages that started to bleed when – oh but why repeat it? Why not blot it out of one's mind? That kind of thing was part of the appalling superstition that she herself had always despised until – but Mrs. Latimer put a stop to such thoughts. It was so easy to become totally confused – to be back in Square One. She wearily tried to press her head deeper into the unyielding cushions of the taxi. It was painful how Angela had reddened that day – oh what a horrible, horrible old woman! She had almost reduced the child to tears, because Angela probably guessed – and who wouldn't? – that that nasty boy would not be above repeating the story. He was quite capable, indeed, of saying that it was Angela who had told the story. Well, he could hardly go that far! Not if he knew Angela – Angela who had always leaned more to scepticism than to superstition; and who right up to the week before she went away had scoffed at so many things that other people (even Luke and herself) had at times felt obliged at least to pretend to accept.

The girl must, surely, have had a real vocation to have withstood the arrival – almost every day during that last week – of the most awful conglomeration of tasteless presents (to say nothing of the tactless wording of the gift cards attached). Holy pictures, holy water fonts, prayer books, hymn books (as if the Order couldn't supply the latter), rosary beads, crucifixes, and – who could believe it? – a quartz angel so hideous that when they were unpacking it Pook the Pekingese took one look at it and moved fastidiously away. There was no end to the rubbish that was piling up on the hall table – Angela made no effort to take the things up to her room – and as one watched her untie the parcels, it was impossible – quite impossible – to suppress the thought that it ought to have been wedding presents she was receiving: finger bowls and decanters, cushions, towels, silver salvers and so on.

Did Angela never think this herself as she unwrapped those wads and wads of tissue paper? Knowing what would be inside, did she never at times have any regrets – even superficial regrets? You certainly could not tell by the expression on her face.

What in the world had come over her? It was sheer nonsense to say she didn't know what she was doing. At least with regard to poverty and obedience she must have realized what she was sacrificing – if not perhaps altogether in the bodily sense. To come back to the latter – goodness knows hadn't she seen (one would have thought so) enough films? And hadn't she played postman's knock at those innumerable parties to which they seemed to be for ever escorting her – as well as the parties in her own home which they had been at pains to give for her every year (never never counting the cost)?

Say what you liked, there were countless ways in which girls got accustomed to life and learned what it was all about. Mrs. Latimer frowned. How had she herself found out? She couldn't remember exactly, but she had a vague memory of her cousin Charlie saying something (surely not *doing* anything?) one afternoon when she was going into the pantry with a tray of glasses in her hand.

She'd got a fright. And afterwards she'd started to weep. "Cry baby!" he hissed. "I suppose you'll run and tell your Ma on me." But she didn't tell her mother – or for that matter, anyone. She'd gone upstairs to her room and sat for ages thinking about him in the half-light. And indeed that Christmas she'd set up stitches to knit him – Cousin Charlie – a pullover – she could remember well it was canary yellow. But Charlie went to Canada at the end of the festive season, and a short time later she had met and become engaged to Luke. Mrs. Latimer smiled when she remembered how she'd hunted up the rest of that canary wool and finished the pullover for him – Luke.

Good old Charlie! To this day she felt grateful to him for – well, for some sort of awakening if you liked. Up to that she had been a bit of a prude, or so her sisters always maintained. They used to tease her unmercifully and they used to tell one particularly obnoxious story about a day when Pappa brought them out to the fields to see a young heifer and she had asked – Oh it was too stupid for words, what she'd said. To this day it embarrassed and annoyed her to be reminded of it. She found it hard to believe she'd said such a thing. Her sisters had surely made it up. To plague her. If it was true of course she must have been the most innocent creature that ever lived. But good old Charlie. On the whole, he had apparently done more harm than good with his kisses. (Was that why he was despatched to Canada?) But not in her case.

Had nobody ever kissed Angela? Perhaps no one ever dared. She was very cool and inaccessible looking. Like a water lily.

Should they have given more parties for her than they did? (That was hardly possible.) Should they have let her go away – as she'd wanted more than once – on holidays with her friends and without any adults along? (Several parents of their acquaintance had been bitterly sorry for giving their girls that kind of liberty.) Mrs. Latimer sighed. The taxi was travelling fairly fast. Soon they would be home. She'd have to stop heaping blame on herself. After all, in the final analysis what nice girl, brought up in a decent home, and going to a convent school had any real experience of boys? Yet their ignorance did not seem to hamper them – didn't, as it were, put a stop to their gallop!

Quite suddenly Mrs. Latimer decided finally and firmly there *must* be something in the notion of a Divine Call. How else on earth could one account for a pretty girl like Angela – some people thought her quite beautiful – deciding to shut herself up in a convent? And so suddenly! It was the suddenness of the decision that had been the real shock. They might have been better prepared to accept it if she had ever shown the slightest signs of unselfishness – or if she'd been delicate, or plain. Even if she'd been aggressive about the rights of women (pretty girls seldom were, of course). But no. Nothing of the sort. No wonder Luke and herself were dumbfounded. Naturally, they had not begun to think of her as marriageable, but it would never have occurred to them that, when the proper time did come, she'd have any trouble in finding a husband – a girl so fitted – you might say, so decked out – to attract men. She was beautifully balanced. Mentally as well as physically. And she was generally reasonable – for a girl. And this was as true of her when she was a child as it was right up to this summer.

Never had a child been more normal. From the time she was four or five, there was never need to tell her to take the hair out of her eyes, to wash her hands, or pull her socks up, or that kind of thing. She kept herself as neat and tidy as a cat – as if from a natural instinct to please. And when she did occasionally have to be scolded it was for something unimportant like looking around her in church, or fidgeting during the sermon. One Sunday they'd been furious with her when they saw her (across the aisle from them when they couldn't do anything about it) frizzing her hair with her fingers. Yet looking back – although Luke was scandalized – she herself was really only angry because of the way it would make her hair fuzzy and hard to comb. As a matter of fact, Luke's mother, who was on a visit with them at the time, had taken Angela's part and said it was a natural trait in a small girl – that prinking and preening – even in church. Prinking. Preening. They were indeed endearing traits.

What had come over her? What had interfered with that simple happy vanity? It was not as if she'd ever been pious or really religious. She never remembered to take her prayer book to Mass, or even her Rosary beads. And if her father lent her his beads she put them down on the pew in front of her and went on yawning and looking around her, just as restless and anxious as anyone else for the Mass to end. And when it did end she'd be the first to stand up, trying to get out before the congregation blocked the aisles. Indeed, she wasn't above pushing – surreptitiously – you'd think she was in a football stadium.

This summer, after she'd thrown her bombshell at them, and after they'd been up to the convent and seen the Mistress of Novices and all was arranged, she was, if anything, less devout than ever. One Sunday when Luke asked if she'd take her grandmother (Luke's mother was staying with them *again*) to late Mass, in case the old woman got dizzy in the crowded church, she lost her temper. "It's not fair. I've been to Mass already!" she said, and she actually stamped her foot. As if to ask her to go to two Masses in one day would be an unpardonable imposition. Well! Mrs. Latimer almost stamped her own foot on the floor of the taxi. Well! How many Masses would she have to sit through now, in the convent? High Mass at that – with all that endless chanting.

Ah but they were nearly home. Luke had laid his hand on her knee again. She opened her eyes.

"Luke?" Suddenly she didn't care if he guessed the truth – if he knew she hadn't spoken to the child. She didn't care what he thought about it because she couldn't stand not having some answer herself to the very question which he had nearly driven her mad by asking. His guess would be as good as hers. "Luke?" she repeated, because he hadn't seemed to hear her.

"Just a minute, dear," he said, then. He had turned around and was looking out again through the back window of the cab. (What now?)

"Did you see that man, Margaret – standing under a lamp-post back there?" he asked, and he turned back to her because they were travelling fairly fast on this quiet residential road and the man was obviously out of sight now.

"No, I didn't," she said flatly. It was hard to accept that his mind had not been on Angela at all.

"Well I saw him," he said strangely. "And what's more I have seen him before – on and off since Easter. Up to no good, I'd say. Probably gone in the head. I think I'll give the police a ring and have them keep

an eye out for him. He might give somebody a nasty fright." Sensing
that she didn't quite get his meaning he must have felt the need to be
slightly more explicit. "Not properly dressed, you know. Probably no
real harm in him. Not a pretty sight though!" But the taxi had drawn
up outside the house and he had to get out to settle with the taxi-driver
in the light from the headlamp.

Mrs. Latimer remained seated inside until Luke was ready to give
her his arm. Her mind had ceased spinning round, throwing out
thoughts at random like sparks, but a great weariness had come over
her. It was hard being a mother. Hard from start to finish. Hard to be
vigilant night and day, and at the end not to know whether you had
failed or not. As Luke put his hand under her elbow and she stepped
down on to the pavement already dark with the coming of night – a bit
prematurely dark perhaps on account of the trees at the top of the road
which were considered to give the area a secluded aspect – she suddenly
remembered the maniac that Luke said he had seen under the lamp-post.
The madman's face, although she had not seen it, was vividly present
in her imagination. And in her imagination he was not standing under a
lamp-post, but on a river-bank, bending down and reaching out beyond
reeds and rushes with fat sweaty fingers – to grasp at something floating
on the surface of the water – a water lily! A water lily, white and shim-
mering and stiff as wax – but which, when his foetid breath fouled it,
shrank and went limp. Whether he reached it or not, whether he
touched it or not, she couldn't tell, because just then the nightmare was
interrupted by the sound of her own hall door being flung open by the
servant girl, who ran out to meet her and taking her arm – Luke's
hand supported her on the other side – hurried her into the house.

"I heard the taxi, ma'am," the girl said, "and I put on the kettle. I'll
make you a nice cup of tea in a minute." And when they went into the
drawing-room Mrs. Latimer saw that her slippers as well as Luke's were
warming on the fender. "Sit down, Mrs. Latimer, ma'am," said the
young servant girl in a voice that was wonderfully kind. It was hard
to believe she was only with them a few months. Her attitude had the
inimitable blend of familiarity and respect of a servant who had been
in the family for years. Like an old friend, indeed.

Mrs. Latimer sank gratefully into a chair, but her heart sank too.
Everyone would be kind to her from now on, and everyone would
treat her with respect, for she had proven herself; she was the mother
of a nun.

Brother Boniface

Brother Boniface sat in the sun. The sun shone full on the monastery wall, and brightened the gold coins of its ancient lichen. Its light fell through the leaves of an elm tree and littered the grass with yellow petals. It splattered the green and white palings that shut off the kitchen garden from the blazing flower-beds on the lawn and it fell full on the rough stone seat where Brother Boniface sat smiling.

There was no one to be seen out under the hot midday sun but Brother Boniface and the monastery cats. There were five cats. There was a big marmalade tom with green eyes, stretching his long paws up the bark of an elm. There was an old white cat sitting solemn in the grass, with her eyes shut tight against the piercing rays of the sun. There were two fat cats abask on the stone seat, one each side of Brother Boniface. And there would have been great peace in that sunny place had it not been for the fifth cat. The fifth cat was young and slender and she ran among the grasses. Her fur was grey with markings of gold, and her eyes were amber. She could not stay still for a second. She ran at the falling leaves. She ran at the splatters of sunlight and tried to pin them against the palings with her paw. Brother Boniface watched her for a little while, but with the other cats all around him closing their eyes every other minute – blinking, narrowing, then closing them – his own eyelids soon grew heavy and he, too, took a little nap.

Brother Boniface was sleeping soundly, with his chin on his chest, when a cinnamon-coloured butterfly, with black and brown spots on its wings, flew unsteadily over the flower-bed. At once the young cat sprang after it, leaping lightly through the flowers, but all the same the stem of a flower snapped and broke under her weight. The fat cats opened their eyes. The old white cat sat up. Brother Boniface jerked his head up and looked from right to left. When he saw the broken stem of the flower he rose to his feet as quick as he could, clapping his hands together and shuffling the gravel with his sandalled feet he called out to the cat.

64

"Pussy! Pussy! Pussy! Come out of that at once." He waved his arms in distress. "Pussy! Pussy! Pussy! Come out of that at once!"

The young cat started up with a pretty fright. She laid her ears back against her sleek head and arched her back fantastically. She looked at Brother Boniface and forgot the cinnamon butterfly, which fluttered away, but after a minute her body slackened and she leaped out of the flower-bed again and ran away, capricious, giddy and full of grace.

Brother Boniface watched the young cat as she ran away into the shade of the trees where she began to scramble from shadow to shadow whenever a breeze lightly moved the branches overhead. In his brown worsted habit he himself was almost too hot to move. The heavy folds seemed to tug at him with an insufferable weight. When he was a young monk he used to think that the folds of his sleeves and the scoop of his cowl gave him an added speed as he strode along the corridors, the way the sails of a ship speed it on before the wind. But at eighty the weight of the wool wearied him, although, in places, it was worn so thin it was little more than a network of thread. Still he got to his feet and shuffled over to the flower-bed to examine the broken flower. There was more than one broken! Two? Three! In dismay Brother Boniface picked up three flower heads that had been severed from their stems, and laid them sadly on the grass. Three flowers less before the high altar on the feast of Corpus Christi. The old monk sighed. He was looking forward to the great feast day, when there would be hundreds of candles blazing before the Host and hundreds of flowers as well. He would have to keep a more constant eye on that young cat. He went back to the stone seat, moving slowly over pebbles that had been rounded and smoothed by the soles of thousands of sandalled feet, and raked every day, winter and summer, by Brother Gardener.

Brother Gardener had joined the order exactly ten years after Brother Boniface, and so Brother Boniface always looked upon him as a very young man, although Brother Gardener himself was then fifty years in the garb of God. The day Brother Gardener came up the driveway to the monastery with a red carpet-bag in his hand, Brother Boniface was clipping the ivy on the chapel wall and the air was scented with its sap. The young man had asked to see the Father Abbot, and Brother Boniface got down from the ladder and went around with him to the door of the Abbot's office. While they stood waiting for the Father Abbot to come out, they began to talk.

"Ivy should not be cut at this time of year," said the young man, who had been a gardener out in the world before he got the notion of entering a monastery. Brother Boniface was just going to ask his reason for this statement when the Father Abbot – Abbot Anselm, God be good to his soul – opened the door, and, hearing the last sentence, joined in the conversation as if he had known the young man all his life.

"Will it grow again?" he asked.

"You can't kill ivy," said the young man. "But it looks better if it's clipped before the new growth starts."

"I'm glad to know that," said the Abbot. "Still, we can't leave it the way it is!" He looked at the barren grey patch on the wall where Brother Boniface in his youthful vigour had perhaps been a bit too drastic with his shears, and then he looked at the rest of the wall where the ivy was so thick it gave shelter to hundreds of bees – and even a few birds – who, darting out, made the young leaves flutter as if they too had wings. He turned back to the young man and, glancing at his red carpet-bag, he looked him straight in the eye before he spoke again. "Leave your bag in the hall, young man," he said, "and finish clipping that ivy. But see that you cut it at the right time next year," he paused, "and the year after and every year," he said. He took the shears out of Brother Boniface's hand. "You can help Brother Sacristan to clean the brasses," he said. That was the kind of man he was, Father Abbot, God be good to his soul. He liked a job to be done right. Brother Boniface was very fond of him.

The young monk was given the name of Juniper, but it wasn't long till he was known as Brother Gardener, in the same way that Brother Boas was called Brother Sacristan, and Brother Lambert was called Brother Vintner. But Brother Boniface was always called by his own name because he never did anything well enough to be left at it for long. He was always being changed from one task to another. He cleaned the brasses and snuffed the candles. He sharpened knives and he fed chickens. He peeled apples and he turned the churn. He waxed the oak pews in the chapel and he chopped logs for the kitchen fire. And every October he went out with a basket and picked elderberries. Later he took the scum off the wine vats. He had a thousand tasks to do, and he loved doing them all. He helped with everything, and one day Father Abbot said he should have been called Brother Jack, because he was Jack-of-all-trades.

But when the Father Abbot felt his end had come, it was for Brother Boniface he sent, and although all his monks clustered round him, he wouldn't let anyone minister to him but Boniface. It was Brother Boniface who wet his lips. It was he who wiped the sweat from his brow and held the crucifix up for him to kiss. It was he who kept the candle firm in the Abbot's hand when the old man's soul was finally loosed to God. And when that soul had fled its clay, the hands of the corpse and the hands of Brother Boniface were bound together by a rope of twisted wax that had knotted its way down the candle, drop by drop, to their clasped hands.

Every year when the ivy was cut, and its green sap freed upon the air, Brother Boniface prayed for the old Abbot, and as he prayed thoughts of the past came back to him. His memories were not many but they were vivid. Memories stay greener where memories are few. There had never been much time, of course, for remembering anything at all. The years had gone by so swiftly one after another; it seemed they had been but as the flight of the swallows that darted out at dawn from under the eaves of the chapel, almost faster than the eye could follow.

The earliest thing Brother Boniface could remember was standing between his father's knees in the big wagonette, painted black and yellow, with slippery leather cushions, as it rolled along a dark road in the middle of the night under rustling poplar trees. He had never been out so late. His mother hadn't wanted him brought. She thought it would be bad for him to stay up so late, but his father insisted, saying he could sleep in the brake coming home.

The journey home in the brake had been the real enchantment for Barney. It was the part of the picnic he remembered best. The rest of the day was a broken memory of sun and trestle-tables and people laughing and swaying from side to side on benches. He remembered a tall man pouring out lemonade from a bottle that foamed at the mouth. And he remembered a lady with a green feather in her hat who kept telling him to run away and play like a normal child. But he remembered every single moment of the drive home, along the darkening roads, up hill and down, with everyone singing. The voices volleyed back from the hills they passed between, and the horses' hooves, when they hit the road, rang like bells. He remembered looking down over the sides of the brake at the road that was travelling too, but travelling backwards, and he remembered his mother pulling him by the sleeve.

"Look up, Barney Boy," she said. "It will make you sick to lean down over the sides like that." So he looked up, and when he did, another wonder of the world appeared. As his head jerked up he saw a shower of brilliant sparks riding down through the skies – riding straight towards him it seemed – and he screamed with fear and excitement, and everyone in the party was startled.

"Oh, look! Look, Father," he shouted, as the gilt stars rode downwards.

"Where? What?" said his father, looking up in fright. "What do you see?"

"Look," shouted Barney, and he pointed at the stars.

"Is it the stars you mean?" his father said, and he gave a laugh and winked at the lady with the green feather in her hat.

"Is that what you call them?" Barney said, his voice full of awe. "Why are they up in the sky?"

"They're always there," his father said. "You often saw them before." His father laughed again but a bit uneasily.

"Were they there last night?" Barney asked.

"I suppose they were."

"Why didn't I see them?"

"You were in bed."

"Were they there last Sunday night?"

"They were. Now that's enough about them!" said his father, who had got quite testy. But Barney was persistent.

"When will I see them again?" he asked.

"If I have my way it will be many a day!" his father said, and he nudged the lady with the feather and she began to laugh and soon everyone was laughing as the brake went rolling along under the rustling trees, and Barney himself, who was staring upwards, felt his head begin to reel.

After that every night Barney used to beg to be let stay up until the stars came out. But long before that he was in bed, and although he tried hard to stay awake he always fell asleep before they rode forth. And so, in time, he forgot about them. And when he went to school he learned, among other things, that it was silly to get excited about common things like stars and even rainbows. They were natural phenomena, the teacher said, and he spent two days teaching Barney how to spell the word phenomena, because Barney was backward at his books.

All during his school days, Barney was slow. It took him all his time to avoid being made the butt of the master's jokes. And except for one poor lad that was simple in the head he would have been at the foot of his class. Of course, if he had had more time to do his homework and look over his lessons in the evenings he might have made better progress, but his father did not believe any real work could be done sitting down, and so Barney was more often helping in the shop than reading his books. His father kept him on the move. At nine o'clock he had to open the shop, although no one ever came into it until after ten. But between the time of taking down the lice-eaten shutters and the appearance of the first customers there were a hundred and one jobs to be done. He had to sprinkle the floor with tea leaves to keep down the dust before he swept the floor, and after he'd swept the dirt out into the gutter, he had to sweep the pavement in front of the shop as well.

One morning when he was sweeping the pavement his father came out and saw he had sprinkled tea leaves on it the way he sprinkled them on the shop floor and his father gave him a clout on the ear. "Waste not, want not," his father said, and after that Barney had to be more attentive.

Sometimes there were large packing-cases to be splintered open with a chisel, and cups and saucers and statues and lamp globes taken out and counted, one by one, and the tissue paper that was stuck to them peeled off with his fingernails. Then the articles had to be arranged on the shelves, and after that the sawdust had to be gathered up, and bits of shavings picked out by hand from the cracks in the boards, and carried in to the kitchen fire without any of it let fall. There was something to be done every minute, and on a Fair Day there was so much to be done Barney had to stay home from school.

On the night before the Fair Day he was up until ten or eleven o'clock rolling empty beer barrels into the street and nailing boards across them to make barriers to protect the plate-glass windows of the shop-front from the horns of the big heavy cattle. All the same he still had to hop out of bed at four on the morning of the Fair, and go out in the street and stand with an ash plant in his hand, ready to beat off any beasts that made bold enough to butt at the barrels.

One morning when Barney stood in the dawn with his stick in his hand, a great red heifer gave a puck to one of the barrels and before Barney got time to raise his stick she had butted against it with such force the nails in the boards were lifted out and a board rose up and crashed through the glass.

That was the worst day in Barney's life. He stood on the cold pavement while his father warmed his ears with curses and the drovers all came over to gape at the hole in the window. The cattle themselves were terrified and butted one another backwards and forwards and some of them slipped and fell on the wet dung that covered the street. When a beast fell the drovers yelled at it and kicked its rump and hurled curses at it so loud that in the end Barney couldn't hear the half of his father's curses.

But later that morning when he was thinking about it, the thing that seemed worst of all to him was the way his father kept flinging questions at him to which he had no answer. Why weren't you looking at what you were doing? Why didn't you see the beast? Where were your eyes?

And he was frightened because he couldn't remember looking at anything else but the big red-chalked barrels, and the dusty boards, and the great steaming nostrils of the cattle. He was looking at them all the time, and if he looked away it could only have been for a second when in the grey dawn a wisp of scarlet cloud floated out between the chimney of the barrack and the spire of the church. But later in the morning when he was thinking things over it seemed to him that there might be something odd about him, and that ordinary successful people – people who were respected in the town, like his own father – would never be foolish enough to stand and stare at a cloud.

But if Barney was beginning to notice a difference between himself and the other young fellows of his age in the town, his father, too, was beginning to notice it. One night, late, when his father was coming back from the railway station where he had been lading crates of china, he came upon Barney, leaning against the yard gate staring up into the sky. His father looked up too, but there was nothing in the sky only the everyday stars and the common, ordinary moon. The father flew into a rage. "Are you soft in the head, I wonder?" he said as he pushed past Barney and went into the house, and Barney could hear him, telling his mother on him. "That son of yours is abroad in the yard," his father said, "leaning up against the gate-piers, with his hands in his pockets, staring up into the sky like a half-wit. Can he never find anything to do without being driven to do it?"

"Leave him alone," his mother said. "You drive him too much as it is. You're always yelling at him, and sending him here and sending him there. He never gets a moment to rest his poor feet."

"It's not his feet he's resting out there in the yard, gaping up at the sky," his father said. Then Barney heard his step on the stairs, and he knew he was gone to bed leaving his mother alone in the kitchen. He was going to slip in then, when, happening to look around, he saw that every window of every house in the town was shuttered and curtained. And he shivered, partly because of the cold night air, partly because of the fear that he felt in his heart in case he was different from other men. He dreaded going into the lighted kitchen where his warm-hearted mother sat waiting for him, because he even felt different from her. All the same he opened the door and went in.

"Are you cold, son? Sit over here by the fire," his mother said, kindly, pulling a chair across the tiles with a clatter. "What were you doing out there in the dark by yourself?" she asked.

"Nothing," Barney said, and he felt her gentle glance upon him although he was staring into the flames.

"People will think you're daft if you stand about like that gawking up at the sky," she said, but he felt she was asking for an explanation rather than giving him advice. He knew that the simplest explanation would have made her his champion, but the need that drove him out into silent places, away from the company of his fellows, was a need too vague to be expressed even in thought, much less in words. He remained silent.

His mother felt rebuffed. "It must be true for your father," she said. "You must be soft in the head. I don't know what kind of a person you are at all. But I know one thing! The devil makes work for idle hands! That's an old saying and it's a true one." She picked up a candle and went out into the hall with her lips pursed together in annoyance. But half-way up the stairs she stopped and leaned down over the banisters and watched him as he sat without a word by the fire. Barney knew she was watching him, and his own perplexity deepened. He wanted to please his parents, but every day that passed made him feel more certain that their way of life was small and mean and he felt sure that there must be another way – one that would leave some time for taking in the glory of the earth and the heavens above it.

The week that his father found him in the yard gazing into vacancy, Barney was given more work to do than ever. Even in the evenings, when other boys went off to the ball-alley to play handball, or went off with their girls for a walk around the old town ramparts, Barney was often sent out on his bicycle into the country to deliver some parcel that could easily have been left for delivery next day. His father and mother were determined to prevent him from idling. They were determined to keep him on the go. But although for a long time there may seem to be something vague and indecisive about a man's destiny, after a certain point has been reached it often becomes clear, not only that there was a continuity in the events of his life but that the very events, which seemed to impede, had in fact accelerated his progress. So, cycling along the country roads on messages intended to stop him from dreaming, Barney's eyes were being opened more and more to the beauties of nature and he began to wonder more and more how it was that all the men he knew spent their leisure hours as drearily as their working hours, and only exchanged the stuffiness of the storehouse for the stuffiness of the card-room or the pool-room.

At first when he cycled out into the country Barney was little better than a city man, seeing only the blatant beauty paraded in the hedgerows, the wild rose, the hawthorn and the rambling honeysuckle. But after a time he learned to probe for subtler pleasures. Then he used to get off his bike and leave it on the side of the road and climb over the fences to penetrate into the green deeps of the fields where small flowers, harmless to him, gave up their secret fragrance only when he knelt and parted the grasses and found them where they hid close to the earth. And it was in a field one evening, with the curious cattle standing idle around him, that he resolved at last to evade the way of life that his father and mother had destined for him.

At first Barney's vow was pale and simple and merely freed him from the dread of spending his life behind the counter of a shop. But as time went on he realized that he must choose some other way of earning his bread. He set himself at once then to choose a way that would allow him some time to stand about and stare. But it was not an easy thing to find. For the first time in his life he was seen to take an interest in his fellow townsmen. He was seen to walk around the town, in such apparent search for something that people came out into the streets after he'd gone back home and furtively shuffled a foot in the gutter in the hope of some anonymous gain. But Barney was only looking for an idea. He stood at the great dark doorway of the smithy and watched the golden sparks threading up the flue. He stood at the door of the livery stable and watched the stable boy groom big horses with trembling withers, strange dappled roans, strawberry and grey, and bays and chestnuts dappled with their own sweat. He watched at the doors of shops bigger than his father's, and the only difference he could see between them and his own was that the big shops were noisier and had more spits on the floor.

Then one evening when he was out in the country on a message for the shop, just as the last of the last light was ebbing from the sky, he saw a man sowing seeds in a few final furrows of his field. The picture the man made against the darkening sky was startling and it made Barney think for a moment that he himself had found the right life at last. But when he went nearer he saw that although the man made a picture of great grandeur standing out against the horizon with his raised arm flinging the unseen seed, the man himself was unaware of his grandeur, and never lifted his eyes higher than the hand that groped in the sack for the seed, to toss it on the ground. Realizing this, Barney stepped down from the bank where he had been standing almost in a trance, and went sadly home.

And as he cycled home that night his sadness deepened, for it seemed to him that whether you cobbled or whether you hammered, whether you weighed up rice on a scales or led a young colt round and round in a ring, or whether you stood at evening in a field opening or closing your hand to let fall a shower of seeds, you had to keep your eyes upon what you were doing, and soon you forgot that there was a sky overhead and earth underfoot, and that flowers blew and even that birds sang.

So at last he settled down to follow the life his father had planned for him. He let his mother buy him a yellow dust-coat to keep his trousers clean when he would be weighing out whiting or weedkiller. And everyone said that he was shaping out much better than had been expected. The canvas coat kept the dust from his trousers, but there was dust getting into his soul, and soon he would have been weighing the whiting and the weedkiller in the bag in order to make up weight and using newspaper to wrap up his customers' purchases in order to spare bags. And in no time at all he would be taking down the shutters from the shop windows five minutes before nine, instead of nine, in the hope of making an extra penny. But before he had quite relinquished the last shreds of his dream, a message came down to the shop one day from the Abbot of a monastery that was a few miles outside the town. The Abbot wanted to know if the monastery could be supplied with a gallon of colza oil three times a week, and if it could be delivered?

"There's no need for you to go with it, Barney. I'll send one of the shop boys," his father said, because his father was anxious not to impose too much on him just when he was beginning to show some interest in moneymaking.

"I think I should go myself," Barney said. "I might arrange to supply them with candles as well as colza."

"Good man," his father said proudly and he took the dust-coat out of Barney's hands. "I'll hang that up for you, my boy," he said. "And take your tea before you go. It's a long push on a bicycle out to that monastery, and, if I remember, there's a rise in the road most of the way."

There was many a rise in the road, and Barney was so tired by the time he reached the monastery gate he left his bicycle at the gate-lodge and walked up the avenue. The night was coming down between dark yews and cypresses, and there was a scent of flowers in the air. But Barney's mind was occupied with thoughts of what he would say to the monk who would open the door.

It was an old monk who came to the door, and he seemed to be deaf. He took the can of colza oil from Barney and looked past him at the open door. "Shut that door," he said, and then he told Barney to wait for the can, while he himself doddered off down a corridor. Barney was left alone in the bare hallway where the yellow floorboards were so slippy with wax he was afraid to move a foot. All of a sudden Barney felt very young. He looked around him, and through the high, arched windows he saw the sharp-pointed stars, because the windows had no curtains. And suddenly it seemed to him that of all the silly things in the world the silliest was to hang a curtain across a window and blot out the glory of the sky and its welter of stars.

When the old monk came back with the empty can, and handed it to him, Barney took it silently and went out into the dark. There was no sound but the closing of the monastery door, and he thought of all the foolish words another man would have wasted upon the simple transaction. The monk was a wise old man, he thought, and he was thinking about him as he walked down the driveway.

Half-way down the avenue there was a great elm tree, and Barney had nearly passed it when, by the light of the moon, he saw that underneath the tree a young monk was standing. There was such a strange stillness in the standing figure that Barney stopped and stared. The young monk's face was turned upwards to the stars, and his hands were lifted in adoration of the Creator. Barney raised his head. And it was all he could do to keep himself from falling to his knees and joining his own hands in adoration too.

All that night and all next day Barney thought about the young monk whose face was lifted to the stars, and at the end of the second night he knew that his own eyes had been blinded for ever to the gross glare of coins. But the only difference his father and mother saw in him was that his yellow dust-coat was getting short in the sleeves.

So, one night soon afterwards his father was wakened in the early hours by what he thought was a rat down below in the shop and he went down in his nightshirt, with a spluttering candle stuck in a bottleneck, to see what was afoot. He got a shock. All the counters were piled with carefully weighed-out bags of tea, sugar, whiting, grass-seed, tacks, lime and a lot of other commodities. There was enough of everything weighed out to last all winter, and when he asked Barney why he had weighed out so much he was almost relieved at the answer he got, because when he first saw the laden counters he thought his son's tardily developed interest in business had driven him completely out of his mind.

Next evening Barney took an old fibre suitcase belonging to his mother, put a few of his things in it, and tied it to the back of the bicycle.

"I'll send one of the boys up to bring back the bicycle," his father said.

"He can take back the case too," Barney said. "I won't need it after today."

His mother wiped her eyes on the corner of his dust-coat which she held in her hand.

"Are you sure you'll be contented, Barney, inside those high walls?" she said.

"Remember," his father said, "there's only seven acres, all told, timber and pasture, inside those walls. It's a small place to spend the whole of your days."

But Barney was thinking of the uncurtained windows up at the monastery and the great expanse of sky over it, and it seemed that the monastery was as wide and spacious as the whole world. And there, men had time to meditate and dwell on all the beauty the Lord had laid out before their eyes.

That evening, in fact, after he'd been shown to his cell, Barney found that the monastery was so big it was like a city and it took five or ten

minutes to go from one end of it to the other. You'd need a scooter
for the job. Three lengths of one corridor were equal to half a mile.
He was shown over the whole place by a young and active lay brother,
and when they came back to the place from which they had started out,
the arches of Barney's instep were aching and he could hardly believe
that it was only nine o'clock, and time to go to bed. Nine o'clock
seemed a ridiculous hour to retire to his pallet, but Barney was so
tired he was glad to lie down. He meant to get up later and look
out the narrow window of his cell at the garden below, but he fell
asleep.

In the middle of the night Barney was wakened by a loud knock
on the door of the cell and he sprang to the floor in fright because
through a great windy crack in the door he had seen a flickering tongue
of flame. Flinging open the door he was about to rush out, when a
dash of holy water, cold as ice, cooled his face. The flame was only the
flame of a candle in the lay brother's hand.

Dominus vobiscum.

Young Brother Boniface hastily donned his habit and joined the
thronging feet that were descending a great flight of stone steps to the
chapel. Once there, the knocking of wooden rosary beads, the sliding
of sandals, the swishing of the monks' habits, the praying, the singing,
but above all the blaze of candles on the altar, made him forget it was
night and gave an impression of broad and busy day-time.

When the real day-time came at last and the birds began to chirp
and fly out from under the eaves, Brother Boniface was set the task
that always fell to the last member to join the order, and that was
peeling potatoes. It took a lot of potatoes to feed seventy-two monks,
specially when they didn't eat meat. But it didn't take long to eat them.
Brother Boniface was used to eating quickly and he would have been
finished as soon as anyone, only he was so interested in the gospel
story that the Brother Lector was reading during the meal that he had
to hurry at the end and leave his meal half finished in order not to be
left behind.

After the meal there was community prayer. Then there was private
prayer. And after that there would have been recreation, but on that
day some important person was coming to visit the monastery, and
the Father Abbot wanted all the community present in the hall to
receive her. The visitor, however, didn't arrive at the time arranged.
She was so late coming that the monks had only seventeen minutes for

supper; and it was a great rush clearing away the meal and laying the table for breakfast, before the great bell rang out to announce the hour of evening prayer. Next day an old monk died, an old monk who had clung to life longer than anyone could have imagined possible, and still at the end his soul lingered among the souls of the living while even the candle-flames around his pallet strove to part from the wick and fly heavenward. Boniface had never seen anyone dying before and death made a great impression on him. At dawn, when at last he went to his cell he stood for a while at his slit of window and said innumerable *pater* and *ave* for the dead man, but his thoughts were centred on the deathbed scene he had just witnessed, and then his mind flew forwards to thoughts of his own last end. Afterwards, when he tried to remember whether the stars had gone in or not, and whether the moon had waned or not, he could not remember.

Next day Brother Boniface had to help dig a grave for the dead monk and the ground, under its rich covering of grass, was remarkably hard and strong and had to be attacked with a pick-axe. This took most of the day because the work had to be interrupted for prayers and meals and also for all the daily chores that would have had to be done by the living even if it were the Father Abbot himself who had died.

After that week there was a very wet week, and in wet weather there were always a great many things to be done in the monastery. Corridors were waxed, brasses shined and benches and pews were up-ended and examined to see that they were free from wood-lice. But on the evening of the seventh day when the rain ceased at last Brother Boniface went out into the grounds for a few minutes. Through the leafy branches of the trees he saw that the sky was pricked with stars and he walked a little way down the avenue towards the elm tree under which he had seen the young monk standing in adoration the first night he himself had come up to the monastery on a message. He was there again! As Brother Boniface had not made this monk's acquaintance, he stepped into the grass and was about to go across to him, when he saw that the young monk's eyes were closed and that his lips were moving. He was saying his office, and not looking at the stars at all. And Brother Boniface remembered that he himself had not yet said his office. So raising his eyes to heaven he began to say it there and then where he stood, in the damp evening grasses, under the starry heavens. But he soon found that he could not pray with his eyes open. The stars distracted him. He had to close his eyes, and when he came to the end of his office and opened his eyes again the sky was overcast.

That first year went flashing by so fast that at the end of it Boniface did not feel he was a week in the monastery. And in spring and summer when his father and mother came up to see him, if he was working in the fields he was often so busy working he did not see them and when his father called out to him by name – "Barney! Barney!" – the other monks had to pluck him by the sleeve, because Brother Boniface had almost forgotten that he had once answered to the name of Barney. Time went flashing past fast as the wind, and life was blown with it as the wind blew the leaves from the trees. And Brother Boniface had stepped into his sandals some twenty thousand mornings before he realized one fine morning that he was eighty years old.

On the morning Brother Boniface was eighty he was coming out of the bakehouse with a trough of dough that he had kneaded for Brother Breadmaker, when he met the monastery doctor in the middle of the courtyard.

"Good morning, Brother Boniface. You get sprightlier every day," the young doctor said, but he looked closely at him and watched after him when he went on his way. Then the doctor turned and went back to the Abbot's room.

"I met Boniface in the yard," he said to the young monk who was Abbot at that time and who was a personal friend of the doctor's. "I didn't like the way the veins on his forehead were swollen," he said. "He was carrying a heavy tray of dough. He does too much for a man of his age."

"But he loves work," the young Abbot said.

"That is the kind of person who needs rest most. He must be made to take life easier."

"I will see that he is released from some of his duties," the Abbot said.

"That's not enough," the doctor said. "He must be freed from all duties. He must sit out there in the sun, and remain as quiet as possible."

"Poor Boniface," the young Abbot sighed, as he and the doctor stood at the window in the Abbot's office and looked out at Brother Boniface, who had left the dough in the bake-house and was now going across the grass with a saucer of milk, followed by five cats. As he went along, some of the cats ran in front of him with their tails up stiff as sticks, and others circled around him and lifted themselves up on their hind legs to caress him with the backs of their necks.

"You can't call that hard work?" the Abbot said.

"Any work that never ceases is hard work," the doctor said.

"I suppose you're right," said the Abbot. "Very well, I'll send him out tomorrow morning to sit in the sun and I won't let him inside the door till night-time, except for meals and of course for prayers."

Brother Boniface took to the sun like the monastery cats. He sat on a stone seat, and he had nothing to do but follow the ballet of the butterflies, or gaze—like the cats—who sometimes slit open their lazy eyes to gaze into the grass at a glossy black insect, perhaps as it ran up a green blade and bent it down.

And as he sat there Brother Boniface thanked the Lord that he had been led through the hustle and bustle of life to the peace and quiet of age. And he wondered what he had done to merit such happy contentment and rest. He tried to remember what it was that had first turned his thoughts to the cloister. He remembered the shop where he used to scatter tea leaves to keep down the dust. He remembered he wore a shop-coat that got too short in the sleeves. He remembered going out into the country on his bicycle to do errands for his father. And he remembered once when he was a small boy he had gone on a picnic with his father and mother in a black and yellow brake, under rustling poplar trees, while singing voices volleyed in the hills and stars showered down through the sky. And when he remembered that starry sky he slapped his hand on his knee and he gave a laugh, at which all the cats sprang up and arched their backs. But seeing they had nothing to fear, they relaxed, except for the young cat, who walked away in disdain.

Brother Boniface continued to chuckle. He realized that he had entered the monastery in order to have more time to meditate upon the glories of the earth, but his life had circled round, from matins to lauds, from daylight to starlight, with greater speed than it could possibly have sped by in the world. It had gone by so fast that he could hardly tell the colour of the leaves on the trees, and whether the stars were blue or green. But he was filled with joy to think that now, at the end of his days, having diligently earned his leisure, he would at last be able to spend long hours in appreciation of God's handiwork. Just then, however, there was the sound of another stem snapping and Brother Boniface had to get himself on his feet again. The young grey cat was chasing another butterfly, and once more she had jumped into the flower-bed. When she saw Boniface stand up she sprang out, but a yellow dahlia lay broken on the grass. Brother Boniface clapped his hands and toddled over to the flower-bed, but at that moment there was a light step on the gravel and the agile young Abbot came down the path, his flowing sleeves and his ample cowl, that belled out in the breeze as he walked, giving him an impressive air, although he was the youngest Abbot that had ever been anointed.

"Good morning, Brother Boniface," he said, and quicker than Boniface he stooped and lifted up the broken dahlia. "What will we do with those cats?" he said, shaking his head. "The feast of Corpus Christi is only a few days away and we need every flower for the decoration of the altars. I wish we could dispense with the cats, but there are unfortunately too many mice for that – did you hear them behind the wainscoting in the chapel this morning?" As he spoke he was bending to examine the stem of another dahlia that looked a bit lopsided. "What will we do?" he said, and then he snapped his fingers. "I have an idea," he said, and he strode across to the casement of the refectory, and brushing aside the strands of ivy he tapped on the window. "Brother Almoner!" he called out, in his clear young voice. "Hand me out a paper bag."

Old Brother Almoner could be heard shuffling around inside, and pulling out drawers and opening cupboards. At last he came to the window and handed out a tinfoil tea-bag, open at the mouth. The Abbot came striding back across the grass, and when he reached the gravel path where Boniface sat on the stone seat he bent and gathered up a handful of pebbles from the square of gravel under the seat and he threw them into the tinfoil tea-bag. Then nimbly bending down again he got another handful, and another. When the bag was filled to the top with pebbles, he set it down on the seat beside Brother Boniface. "Here is a small job for you, Boniface," he said. "You can do it without standing up – without moving an inch. Every time you see a cat going near the flowers, all you have to do is take up a little pebble and throw it at him and frighten him away. In spite of the cats we'll have a magnificent blaze of flowers yet for Corpus Christi."

Brother Boniface took up the bag.

"I'll keep it in my lap," he said.

"I'm delighted to have you out here, Boniface," the Abbot said. "Now I need not worry about the flowers. I know I can depend on you." Smiling, he went back to his own work.

Brother Boniface sat on in the sun. When the Abbot's footsteps died away, there was no sound in Boniface's ears but the ringing of the bells of silence. Beside him once a brilliant red insect crawled up a blade of grass, and Boniface watched the blade slowly bend until the insect was almost back on the ground. The little creature put out a feeler and caught on to another blade that was shorter and stabbed into the air more stiffly but when it started to crawl upward, this blade too began to bend. Boniface shook his head. Where were those little creatures heading, that they took such dangerous and devious paths?

But just then he heard another stem snap. The young cat was in among the dahlias once more. Stems were breaking to all sides and petals were scattering to the ground because this time there were two butterflies and the young cat sprang at each of them in turn.

"Pussy! Pussy! Pussy!" Brother Boniface shouted. "Pussy! Pussy! Pussy! Come out of that at once!" He stamped his foot and he groped for a pebble in his tinfoil bag. "Pussy! Pussy! Pussy! Come out of that at once!"

And years and years afterwards, when Brother Boniface was long laid to rest in the close and secretive clay, the young monks who entered the monastery were told about his industry. They were told he was never, never idle for a moment. They strove to follow his example. And when they themselves were old they in their turn told younger men about him. And the part of the story that the old monks liked best to tell, and the young monks liked best to hear, was about the last days in the life of Boniface, when he was so old he couldn't even hear the bells of silence. Because then he was busiest of all. Day in and day out his voice could be heard, as he guarded the flowers for the feast days of the Mother Church, throwing pebbles at the cats and calling out to them.

"Pussy! Pussy! Pussy! Come out of that at once!"

Say Could That Lad Be I?

This is my father's story. It isn't mine at all. I wrote it down one night so soon after hearing him tell it, I remembered every word. My father is not a man to bother writing a thing down, unless a message to pin on the stable door for the herd, or the boy that feeds the dogs. He's not exactly a talking man either, unless about horses. Most of his yarning goes on in his head while he's walking the Meath fields, or leaning over the gate of a paddock. When I think of him, I think of him as I so often saw him, walking green fields dusty with buttercups, stopping only to stare at his prize cattle, cropping the rich grass, or to scotch a thistle with a blade he had fitted to the butt of his walking-stick. His eye was always quick to see the weeds that seemed to spring up over-night, and which, if left uncut, self-sowed themselves and multiplied seven times seven. In Meath a man must restrain the land, or it would strangle him. But in Roscommon, where he was born, the fields were thin and the grass wiry and sparse. There, poverty had the dignity of a lost cause well fought. When my father talked of his bare-footed boyhood in blue Roscommon, it seemed very far away to me, as if he was a different person from the boy he talked about.

I think he must have found it hard himself sometimes to believe that he was once that boy – as hard as the boy would have found it to believe that he would one day be this quiet man who would not leap over a wall if there was a gate or a stile, and who, if he went out in the evening-time, would go out only, as the poet says, to stand and stare.

But if I found it hard to imagine the lad he remembered was him, this story is his all the same, and not mine. It is his, even in the way one word goes before another.

"Did I ever tell you about a dog I had?" he asked me one day, "a dog by the name of White Prince? He was the wonderfullest dog in the world. He was a cross between a wire-haired terrier and a blood-hound, and he was pure white, with the hair bristling on him like a hedgehog when he smelled a fight. A dog was no good to a fellow in those days if

82

it wasn't a fighting dog. That was all we kept dogs for: to set them on one another. Every fellow in the village had a dog. And the fellow that had a dog to beat all the other dogs was a fellow that was looked up to the length and breadth of Roscommon. I used to have great dogs. But White Prince was about the best I ever had. I was very proud of him and I took him with me everywhere. On Saturdays I was sent over to my grandmother's to do the shopping for her in her own village that was a lot bigger than our village. My grandmother lived seven miles away, but by going over the fields as I did that was nothing – not in those days. And naturally that Saturday I brought White Prince along with me. We set off, the two of us, the dog and me – I was whistling, and kicking at sods of dry grass that were thrown up by the hooves of an old mare that was always breaking loose and clattering over anyone and everyone's few acres. The dog was running along in front of me barking for joy. I was glad I had him along with me for company, although I knew my grandmother hated the sight of him. Yes – well I knew it.

"We got to my grandmother's house about two o'clock in the afternoon. It was drawing in towards winter and the evenings were getting short, so although it was only two o'clock the night was beginning to show in the sky already. My grandmother was sitting on the side of her old settle bed, and she said she was sitting there for two hours waiting for me. 'Take care would you think of bringing that blaggard of a dog into the village with you,' she said, knowing he'd fight every dog in the village and that he wouldn't come home till he did. Nor me either. 'And take care would you think of leaving him here,' she added as an afterthought.

"I didn't know what to do. I thought things over for maybe a minute, and I decided that perhaps it was just as well not to bring my brave fighter into a village that was still strange to him. I called him into the house and waited till my grandmother turned to the dresser to take down her knitting. Then I went out quickly, stopping the dog from coming after me by blocking the door with the butt of my boot. When I was outside and the door shut I drew down the hasp. There used to be a hasp on the outside of the doors of most houses in those parts then and when it was caught down no one who was inside could get out. It seems queer, now that I come to think of it, but then it seemed the most natural thing in the world. When I put down the hasp my grandmother and the dog were locked inside, and my mind was at rest on one score anyway. My grandmother was a kind woman at heart, and even if that was not the case, she was feeble. and I knew she wouldn't be fit to lift a hand to the dog. There was only one thing she would do to him if she could, and that was the one thing I made sure she couldn't do: let him out and stray him on me.

"I went down the pebbly lane, jingling the coins in my trouser pocket, and feeling a very big fellow, when all was said and done. But I was only half-way down the lane, when I heard a shattering noise behind me, and I looked around in time to see my fighting dog come leaping into the air through a gaping hole he'd made for himself in my grandmother's window. He glittered all over with sparkles of broken glass, and behind him on the sill a pot of red geraniums was reeling around like a drunk. I didn't wait to see if the pot fell, but went running down the lane, with White Prince after me, and now he was barking and yelping and snapping at my heels with his pride and his joy and his devilment. The more the dog ran the more excited he got. But the more I ran the more frightened I got. It was only when I came in sight of the village I stopped running and sat down on a stile, and took out the silver shilling my grandmother had given me and the six heavy coppers. Fast and all as I had run I hadn't lost the money. I looked at it for a long time and I felt a bit better. I felt some of the importance creeping back into me that I'd felt when I set out from the door after putting down the hasp. I started to plan in my mind the way I'd ask for my messages in the shops, but when I tried to remember what I was to buy I couldn't for the life of me remember. And I was afraid to go back and ask my grandmother to tell me them again.

"I'd get her tea and sugar anyway, I decided, and a loaf of bread, and if there was any money left, I'd get her a piece of bacon. She'd be so mad about the broken window she wouldn't open the parcel till after I'd be gone home. But I was sorry I reminded myself of the broken window, because the thought of it gave me a queer feeling. I looked around at the dog, thinking to give him a kick by way of thanks for all the trouble he'd got me into, but he was sitting in the middle of the road looking up at me, with his head cocked to one side and one ear up and the other ear down and I hadn't the heart to touch him. I couldn't think to do anything more than give him a whistle to get up and come along with me. And after that the two of us made for the main street of the village, trotting along together as great pals as ever we were.

"It was half-dark by this time and the lamps were being lit in the shop windows. In every shop I could see shop-boys kneeling into the window spaces to trim the wicks of the lamps and in some shops they'd already touched a match to the wick and were putting down the globes over the flame. The lamps in the shop windows were hanging-lamps, and after they were lit they swung back and forth for a few minutes, sending big unnatural shadows of the shop-boys out over the footpath, in a way that would make you scared to look at them. I looked into the shops instead, where the lamps were fastened to the walls and their yellow light was steady. The crinkly tin reflectors behind them reminded me of our kitchen at home.

"I went into the biggest shop in the street. They sold drapery on one side, but on the other side they sold tea and sugar and bread, and bulls'-eyes in jars – a thing I never saw anywhere else but there. The window on that side was filled with plates of raisins and plates of flour, and plates of rice and plates of prunes. The window on the drapery side was filled with ladies' bonnets and caps, and yards of lace and coloured tape and strings of bootlaces in black and brown. I liked doing messages in this shop. We hadn't any as big as it in our own village. I liked looking into the glass cases, and I liked looking at the big lamps as long as they were still and not sending their shadows flying about. Most of all I liked looking at the big ball of twine inside a tin canister with a hole in it, and listening to the whirl and spin of the twine every time a shop-boy gave it a tug and drew out enough to tie up a parcel. I liked the noise of the money, too, rattling about in a drawer under the counter, when the drawer was pulled out to give someone change.

"I was so happy that evening looking around me and taking notice of everything, I didn't heed what my brave fighter was doing. The last I'd seen of him he was only smelling around, doing no harm to anyone, and, as long as no other dog came into the shop, I felt it was safe enough to let him smell around as much as he liked. But, as I was leaning on the counter watching the boy totting up the price of my messages, I felt something brush past my leg, and I looked down in time to see the white stump of the dog's tail disappearing under the counter. There was a space between two of the counters, so the shop-boys could get in and out if they wanted, but there was a board across the opening, and they had to lift up that board going in or going out. The board was to keep out people that had no business behind the counter, but you'd never know there was a passage underneath, if you didn't happen to look close. White Prince wasn't the sort to miss much though, I can tell you, and he didn't miss that passage between the counters. He went inside, and I held my breath.

"He was very quiet for a while. Then all of a sudden one of the boys bent down to pick up a penny he'd let drop, and he must have seen the white stump of a tail wagging away in the darkness under the shelves, because he let a yell out of him, and started ordering the poor dog out, stamping his feet at him and waving a sweeping brush that he'd grabbed up in a fit of rage. I don't know what the poor dog was doing, but whatever it was the shop-boy must have thought it was something he shouldn't be doing. And to make matters worse the shop-boy that was yelling at him to get out was standing up against the counter and blocking the way out all the time he was yelling. So I suppose the poor dog got confused. I suppose he was sure and certain the fellow would kill him with the big sweeping brush if he didn't get out quick somehow. You never know what an animal is thinking, but they have very clever ideas. When White Prince saw there was no regular way out I suppose he started planning on getting out some irregular way. I suppose he said to himself if a trick was worth doing once it was worth doing twice! Anyway, however, it was with the dog in his own mind, the next thing I saw was my flashing fighter rising up in the air and leaping into the window, knocking the bonnets to right and left and slapping up against the glass with a crash. Then there was a sound of splintering that was ten times worse than the one I'd heard in the lane back at my grandmother's, and down came a ten-times heavier shower of splinters as White Prince went flying into the street with his four paws stiff out under him and streamers of lace and ribbon and tapes trailing after him into the street outside. I was struck cold with fright. I couldn't lift up a foot from the floor, much less get out of the shop. I thought as true as God I'd be put in prison for life. The shop was in an uproar, everyone running out and shouting and holding up their hands and whistling for the dog to come back, with one breath, and with another calling God to witness what they'd do to him if he did! Then everyone ran out into the street, shading their eyes with their hands and peering into the blackness to see which way the dog had gone, although it was easy to see the way he went, with the stream of muddy tapes and bonnet-strings he'd left behind him. Ribbons and tapes stretched half-way up the street, and maybe further, only it wasn't bright enough to see far. Then the shop-boys started after him. The shop-keeper himself was fit to be tied. He divided his time between shaking his fist into the dark and running over to the window and pushing bonnets back through the hole in the glass.

"There was a terrible lot of talk, I needn't tell you. Everyone was asking everyone else how much the cost of new glass would be. And the women were asking whether the things that got muddy would be sold off cheap. I was alone in the shop but I could hear the talk outside in the street because the hole in the window made it easy to hear. I'd have run off like the dog, if I had got my change, but I'd have thought it as bad to go back to my grandmother without that as I'd think it to go to prison with the dog. So I stood waiting in the shop, and cursed White Prince and planned what I'd do to him when I got him. But when I thought of the big bullies of shop-boys that were chasing after him at that minute, I got very sorry for him. And at the thought that if they caught him I might never see him again, I made up my mind that if only they'd come back and give me my change I'd go looking for him myself and I swore that if I found him I wouldn't hurt a hair on his head.

"I was standing in the shop for a long while, because the shop-keeper had got a hammer and a fistful of nails and he was nailing boards over the broken window. Then when he came in at last he took up a piece of paper and a pen and he started to draw up a notice. But he found the pen-work hard going and catching sight of me he said I looked as if I was at school long enough to be able to write. 'Write down BUSINESS AS USUAL,' he said. I am glad to say just then one of the shop-boys, that had gone after the dog, came back, and took the pen out of my hand and wrote it himself, although he was panting fit to burst his ribs. If only I'd had my change that would have been the time for me to make off, when the fellow was winded, but I hadn't got it. I was glad to see though that he hadn't forgotten about the change. 'I'll have it for you in a tick,' he said, and sure enough he gave it to me. When I counted the change and saw it was right I started for the door. But before I got to it, the shop-keeper called me back. 'Which road are you taking out of the town, young lad?' he said. I went stiff with fright. I thought they'd found out the dog was my dog. But no! 'Whichever way you're going,' he said, 'let you keep an eye out for that tinker of a dog. I'll give you sixpence if you come back with him!'

" 'All right, sir,' I said, and I was just going to go out of the door when he came after me again and insisted on escorting me into the street. 'The cur was all white, but for an odd spot of black here and there on him I think,' he said.

" 'He was pure white, sir,' I said politely. 'There was no black on him at all.'

" 'Is that so?' said the man. 'You've a good pair of eyes.' He looked around at the crowd. 'That information is worth something I suppose,' he said, thinking maybe to encourage others to turn informer. 'That information is worth at least a bag of sweets, I think.' he said, and he went back inside the shop and I had to wait while he took down the jar of bulls'-eyes and shook them into a big paper bag with a mitred mouth on it. He filled the bag so full it wouldn't close over in the end. He had to swing it round and round, till it had two little paper ears sticking up on it. But the ears made me think of the way the dog cocked his ear when we stopped on our way into the village, and I wished I hadn't brought him with me at all. I took hold of the bag of sweets though, and I pelted off down the road towards my grandmother's, and I can tell you it was no snail's pace I went, at least until I was out of the village and was back in the decent dark of the country road. I slowed down then because according as the road between me and the shop was growing longer the thought of the broken window of the shop was getting fainter, although according as the same road got shorter between me and my grandmother the thought of her broken window was getting stronger. But I was glad the dog had gone off with himself because it would have ruined everything if he'd come running up to me wagging his tail before I got out of the village. If he did there wouldn't be one in it that wouldn't know he was my dog, and there wouldn't be one that wouldn't be after me as well as him. I'd have had no chance at all against so many, and some of them maybe with bicycles. I hope he went home, I said to myself. I hope he didn't get himself lost.

"I didn't need to worry. When I came out into the real open country, what did I hear in the dark ahead of me but a growl and after that I heard a sort of scuffling on the gravelly road, and then more growling – and snarling too. I wasn't long telling that the loudest snarl of all the snarls was the snarl of White Prince. Then I caught sight of him – shining bright against the black hedge. He was up on a rise of the bank, and there was a half-circle of dogs around him and he was snarling at them and baring his teeth. Not one of the other dogs would dare go an inch nearer to him, but not one of them would draw back an inch from him either. Then White Prince must have heard my footsteps, because he took courage, and giving a fiercer snarl than any that went before, he put his teeth into something that was lying on the grass beside him, and made off down the road, with all the other dogs after him barking fit to wake the dead. That was the way I put it to myself that night. But I remember thinking, too, that as far as I was concerned they could wake every corpse that ever was planted – as long as they didn't draw down the living on us. I looked back nervously in the direction of the village. There was nothing to be seen of it only a light here and a light there winking through the trees. So I ran after the dogs. I caught up with them in a bit. White Prince had stopped again on top of another bank and left down his precious load, whatever it was. But the half-circle of mangy curs was around him again in no time, this time, and the poor dog gave me a look as much as to say, 'What are you standing there for? Beat off these devils of dogs, will you, and come and look at what I have here!' I felt myself it was high time to put a stop to things as they were, and I took up a stick and began to beat off them dogs. It was no easy job, but I drove them off one by one until in the end there was only one lanky yellow cur left. But he was as hard to shake off as twenty dogs. Forty times he slunk off and forty times he slunk back, till at last I threw the stick at him and gave him a good crack on the skull. At that he let out a yell at the scudding clouds and off with him to wherever he came from.

" 'Come on now, you!' I said to White Prince, and I was about to set off again for my grandmother's house. I forgot he had been carrying something. But after a while I began to think it strange that he wasn't frisking along in front of me, and when I looked around there was the poor dog, staggering under the weight of whatever it was that he had hanging out of his jaws.

" 'What have you got, you blaggard?' I said, and he dropped it down at my feet. What do you think it was? A leg of mutton! White Prince stared up at me. His little bright eyes were glinting, and his tail was wagging like a bush in the wind.

"I was ready to kill him there and then on the road for the robber and thief he was, when all of a sudden I remembered how mad my grandmother would be waiting for me, and I remembered, too, that she might still be hasped into the house, which would make her ten times madder. I got an idea.

" 'Good dog!' I said, patting him on the head, and taking the parcel

D

from him. 'Come on!' I shouted, leaping over the hedge and into the fields with the groceries under one arm and the leg of mutton under the other.

"May God forgive me, I washed that leg of mutton in a stream of clear spring water, and before my grandmother had time to know I was back at all I had the leg of mutton planted down on the kitchen table. Then I ran out again to where my white fighter was waiting for me, and half a hundred stars as well, that had slipped out without my noticing them. We went back home, the two of us over the fields again, and the dog ran along in front of me, barking and wagging his tail again, as if nothing at all had happened. And if that dog was as happy as me, he had no conscience either."

Sunday Brings Sunday

"Prayer is an efficacious thing," said the curate with the white face, and, as he glanced up at the wet windows of the cold out-parish church, the light caught on the glass of his spectacles and gave a startling impression that his eye sockets were vacant, or filled only with a pale watery fluid. "Prayer, as I have said before, is an efficacious thing. It is a good thing for all of us to go down on our knees and humble ourselves by prayer."

He paused and the congregation shuffled their feet in the silence made by the pause. The curate had now looked down again from the windows and fixed his eye on the knob of the door at the end of the small cement chapel. "It is the duty of all of us to pray." He swung the white tassel of his stole around in a slow arc. "We should all of us try to cultivate the habit of prayer. Every man and woman should be aware of the power of prayer.

"Fathers and mothers should give an example to their children in this matter. Heads of houses should not be ashamed to be seen by those under them kneeling down at the appointed times and saying a few devout prayers. They should not be ashamed to be seen on their knees by their children, or by their friends, or by those in their charge, servants and employees and the like. When the Angelus rings they should make the sign of the cross openly and not be ashamed, and, when convenient, they should go down on their knees.

"It is a common thing, especially in towns and cities, but sometimes indeed in country places like this as well, for people to be ashamed to be seen kneeling down. A thing like that is a great mistake. I hope no one here listening to me today would be in danger of making that great mistake." He looked away from the knob of the outer door and fixed his eyes on the knob of the door that led up to the organ loft.

"Prayer is an efficacious means of obtaining favours for ourselves and those belonging to us. But we should not pray for favours only. We should pray at all times and without waiting to be in trouble.

"The man or woman who never takes the time to kneel down and say a prayer when he is in good health, with everything going well, cannot expect God to fly to his assistance the minute that man, or that woman, as the case may be, throws himself down in time of need to implore God's help.

"Yet how often we find that man, or that woman, when he or she is in trouble of one kind or another, as, for instance, the sickness of a valuable beast or some such animal, or the sickness of a child or of some person dear to them, how often we find that man, or that woman, complaining that God will not come to his or her assistance.

"How often that man or that woman expects God to be ready and waiting to cure that child or that beast, as the case may be, just because that person has thrown himself down in time of need to ask for help, forgetting that when he was in good health, with everything going the way he wanted, he never took time out of the long day and night to offer up one prayer for any purpose whatsoever." The curate looked up again, and again his eye sockets filled with reflections of the white and vacant sky.

"There are a great many people in this parish and what I am saying here today does not apply to them, although few of us are perfect, and that is not what I wish to convey either, you understand – God is grateful to those people – mostly old people and pious women – and let us hope they never slip out of their pious practices.

"It is to the people who have slipped out of this pious practice that I wish to speak here today, and speak very seriously. So if there are any such people here, mostly growing young people and men, who used at one time never to pass the church without raising their hats and saying a prayer for themselves, or for those belonging to them, or for the dead of the parish, but who, through vanity or shame or some other worldly temptation, have fallen away from this habit, all I can say to them is that they ought to repair this state of affairs before it is too late and they are deprived, perhaps for ever, of the chance to do so.

"It is to those people I would like to say a few words this morning. But I will not keep you long because it is a very wet morning and many of you, I know, have come a long distance to this church this morning." The rain struck the window-pane once more as if to corroborate the curate's words.

"Just a few words then, to those who may have slipped out of the habit of saying their morning and evening prayers or the habit of saying the Angelus or offering up a few words to God at any of the other times that Holy Mother Church ordains to be a suitable time for prayer.

"I will ask those people if it is a thing that they think they will be on this earth for ever? Because if that is what those people think, they are, as we all know, greatly mistaken. And when these people are on their deathbeds, as we all of us will one day be, great and small, rich and poor, the highest and the lowest, they will say then, when it is too late, 'if only I had not abandoned the habit of prayer!' They will be sorry in that hour that they went their own way, wilful and not caring whether they were acting in accordance with the right ideas or not. Then they will be regretful. Then they will be remorseful. Ah, it is then they will lament that they did not continue in the practice laid down by the Church as the most efficacious means of ensuring that we do not stray from the state of sanctifying grace. On that day those people will present a very sorry sight indeed to the eyes of the be-holders who will stand back, helpless, and have to watch him or her, as the case may be, turning over and over in the pains of death and calling out with a pitiful voice and bewailing that he, or she, had not given up the pious habits they had been taught to believe in when they were innocent children going to school. It is a very pitiful scene that I paint for you, and one which I hope none of you will ever have the sorrow of witnessing. But I ask you to turn these things over in your mind, and if there are any of you who have dropped, unconsciously it may be, into the habit of getting into bed at night, on a cold night perhaps, or after a hard day's work, without first kneeling down for a few minutes to thank God for having safely passed through another day, then let that person be resolved from this day forward not to let such a thing occur again.

"I ask you to turn over in your minds whether it is better to get down on your knees for three minutes or to spend an eternity in the dark pit of damnation, lit only by the flames of hell; those flames that never quench. It is a terrible thought, but one which it is helpful to keep constantly before us."

The curate had been knotting and unknotting the cord that tied his stole, but now, by giving it a sharp tug and tying it into a tight knot he gave the congregation a hint that the sermon was near its end.

"That will be all that I will say on this matter for this morning, but remember that prayer is an efficacious thing and that it is the duty of all those who have young people under their care, whether of either sex, to see that those young people are given a good example in this matter. Next Sunday I will say a few words about the different kinds of prayer and the different times that it is meet for us to pray."

The curate swung back to the altar. The Mass continued. The tassels on his stole soon were still.

Outside the rain could be heard falling on the corrugated roof of the shed where the priest kept his car on wet days or days of dangerous frost. At intervals now and then the wind pushed against the thin panes of cheap green glass as if it would crash its way through, drenching the congregation with a shower of broken glass. Inside, the altar boys answered the responses in shrill voices that sounded bleak and undeveloped, and the grey colour of their badly laundered surplices gave them a dreary appearance as they huddled together chattering the Latin verses without comprehension of their meaning. The candle flames gesticulated uneasily. A smell of rubber came up between the pews from the raincoats of the schoolchildren. And from the woollen shawls of the women and the felt caps of the men there came that strange cold stench that rises off a hairy sheepdog coming in to a fire with wet fur.

The Mass ended. Before the priest left the sanctuary he knelt on one knee at the foot of the altar and called out loudly:

"A prayer for the eternal salvation of all deceased members of this parish, and this congregation:

"O God Who . . ."

The congregation repeated after him:

"O God Who . . ."

"Through the infinite merits . . ."

"Through the infinite merits . . ."

"Of Thine only . . ."

"Of Thine only . . ."

"Beloved Son . . ."

"Beloved Son . . ."

When the prayer had dragged a weary centipedal way from beginning to end, the priest and the servers rose and went towards a small door to the left of the altar. Before they reached it, this door, which led into the vestry, was opened from inside by a woman in black with a few sticks of kindling wood in her hand. She was not so much seen as known to be there by the rest of the congregation, and as they filed out of the cold church, above the heavy trudging of their feet on the wooden boards and over flagstones that marked the graves of former priests of the parish, from the vestry there could be heard the thin, finely drawn, but insistent sounds of hot fat spitting on a pan.

Once outside, the congregation went quickly towards the gate. The altar boys were flinging wide the wooden doors of the shed where the priest's car was kept and kicking away a brick from the back wheel to let the car slip out of the shed in readiness for the curate when he had finished his breakfast. A few men were stooping down with bright red faces to pump the tyres of their bicycles. And some people were already across the road, banging on the door of the local shop to get their week's provisions. Horses and ponies were being led out from the stables behind the shop and the idle shafts of traps and carts were being lifted from the wayside grass. A few motorcars were being turned in the gateway of the chapel with the help of becks and nods from a group of young fellows standing under the wall they would have sat up on had it been fine.

The people moved like actors in a play, actors who have rehearsed their lines and gestures so often that they could go through them in their sleep, but had long ago lost all understanding of the play's significance. And, huddled in a corner of the chapel yard, under a dripping tree, like an old woman from a Greek chorus, whose part, even in the fresh beginnings of the play, was to create an antique sense of wariness and sorrow, there was a half-crazed hag who kept crying out in a cracked, wailing voice:

"Sunday brings Sunday! Let you listen to an old woman. Sunday brings Sunday, as ever is and as ever was!"

Mona raised up her bicycle from the wet grass by the chapel wall and a shower of drops fell back into the grass from the shining spokes and gleaming handlebars. She wheeled the bicycle over the yard and leaned it against the ivy on the front wall of the chapel while she clapped her red hands together to warm them. The blood soon tingled back into her fingers and she blew her breath on them to ease the tingle. Then she went over to a piece of slate that had been lifted off the roof a good while back by a big wind, and she stamped her feet on it a few times till her feet tingled too. It was a lovely feeling, the ready blood coursing back into her numb limbs.

By now the last stragglers were streaming out of the chapel yard and coming through the narrow gate. On to the road. And after them the old mad hag went strealing, with her dress slopping down, torn, into the wet and mud.

"Sunday brings Sunday!" she kept saying. "Sunday brings Sunday. It's wet today. It will be fine tomorrow. It's winter now. It will be summer on another day. Sunday brings Sunday."

Mad Mary seldom went into the chapel. During Mass she stayed around the yard picking up bits of fallen twigs. Sometimes she spent the time tearing up handfuls of grass and cleaning the wheels of the priest's car. Occasionally she went inside the door and then she could be heard, over the chilly voices of the servers, and even over the curate's reading of the framed prayers in front of the tabernacle, as she talked to herself. Over and over, then she could be heard saying her private litany. What it meant no one troubled to ask, because everyone put some meaning or other into the words for himself and left it at that.

"Sunday brings Sunday! Sunday brings Sunday!"

It was like one of those sayings that sound true no matter what is meant.

When Mona got the feeling back properly into her fingers she got up on her bike and started to go out of the yard. She was one of the last to leave. There was a slope down the centre path and the rains had made it steeper by washing runnels in the gravel. Mona was going out the gate freewheeling, when, just as she got to the granite piers and was turning into the road, one of the young men who were standing under the chapel wall put out his foot in front of the bicycle and she had to swerve abruptly. The bicycle skidded and she crashed into a big laburnum bush that showered down its raindrops on her and drenched her face and hands with icy drops. But she held tight to the handlebars and steered the bicycle back to the centre of the road again.

She went off down the road then, with cheeks red from shame, but red also from health, and from the gentle thrashing of the rain. And as she went she could hear the young fellows laughing behind her and she wished, she wished like anything, that she was sixteen.

When she got to be sixteen they wouldn't take liberties like that with her. They wouldn't as much as turn around then when she rode out of the chapel yard. They'd keep facing to the wall, and scuffling the ground, and shoving each other, and wrestling. And if one of them got caught stealing a look at her legs when she'd be getting up on the bike, he'd have to say "How' you ?" real respectful, and give her a beck of his cap.

It would be a great thing to be sixteen and getting looks from the fellows under their caps. The minute a girl went into service the fellows all quit treating her like a child and began looking to go walking out with her.

Mona wondered which of all the young fellows that hadn't any steady girls would be the first to say "How' you" to her, and look to go walking out with her. Sometimes when she was in the kitchen at home, doing her sums on winter nights, or starching her pinafore for school, she'd hear voices outside on the dark road, voices that rang clearer if the night was frosty. You'd know by the ring of the voices that the people they belonged to were having a great time. Other nights, walking along the road by herself, on a message perhaps, or just walking, she'd hear giggling inside a gate and she'd have to step out faster and not let on she'd heard anything. Fellows and girls couldn't stick having kids around, spying on them. That was what she'd been told anyway. But in a few months now she'd be leaving school, and then the fellows outside the chapel would give over their codding, and treat her proper. They'd say "How' you?" They'd beck their caps. They'd act respectful.

It didn't seem that there could be anything in the world as wonderful as hearing a fellow saying "How' you?" and having him beck his cap. Next to the cackly voice of the chapel-yard hag saying "Sunday brings Sunday" she kept hearing in her ears all the way home "How' you? How' you?" Soon there wasn't one fellow in the whole village that Mona hadn't imagined stepping out a piece from the others and saying the first "How' you" to her. And when her mind ran out of fellows she knew she began making up fellows she had never seen anywhere, and they were forwarder far than the real fellows. The people streaming out of the chapel would all be gaping at her, and the chapel-yard hag would be strealing after them and saying that Sunday brings Sunday.

Mona loved hearing the old hag giving out her crazy talk. She loved hearing her shouting out that Sunday brought Sunday, because that was what Mona wanted most of all. She wanted the Sundays to come on faster and faster. She wanted the time to pass. The days of the week were all more or less the same. They weren't easy to mark off from one another. There were the same things to be done on every one of them. But Sunday was different. Some Sundays were sunny. Some were rainy. There was a frost some Sundays and other Sundays the leaves were lashed about with the wind. If she was put to it, Mona could tell you what it was like on every single Sunday, back as far as you'd like to go. But who could remember what it was like on a Monday or a Wednesday? Mona couldn't tell you what it was like last Friday, let alone last Wednesday or last Monday!

On Sundays you could feel the year was travelling. You could know there was a big stir on the year when you sat listening to the sermons of the curate because the curate kept close to the season of the year in the words he gave out to the people during Mass. Mona loved sitting up for the sermon and listening to every word. She kept thinking how far they had got since the Sunday before, and she kept thinking how far more they'd have got by the next Sunday.

In November there were sermons about the souls of the dead. Mona, listening to the curate's words about the dead, could almost see them writhing out from under their gravestones in the churchyard and circling up through the skies, past the green glass windows of the chapel; like slow curls of smoke from a fire that wasn't drawing well.

In December there were sermons about Ember days and fasting and the bright star over Bethlehem. In January there was Lent coming toward them, and then in no time it was the month of May and the curate was telling them about the beneficial practice of keeping a May altar in the home, and putting wildflowers in front of it if you didn't have any better. Devotions like that were what kept the faith alive, he said, and many a poor exile was saved on his death-bed by thinking of the simple faith of the people at home with their May altars always decorated to the best of their ability.

That was the sermon Mona liked best. That was one she remembered word for word from the last time it was given out. Didn't she herself always have the best altar in the village and the other scholars from the school came in to see it when they were passing home? Last week the curate heard about it from the teacher, and he made Mona stand up and he gave her a picture to put in her prayer book. That day Mona took a short cut home across the field where Kineelys kept the bull, so she'd get home quicker to tell her mother. Her mother was very proud, and the next Sunday, coming out from Mass, her mother and Mrs. Kineely had a long talk about it.

"The priest had a touch of a cold on him this morning, I thought," said Mrs. Kineely.

"He's a lovely man, isn't he?" said Mona's mother.

"I hear he gave your Mona a holy picture for her prayer book when he was over in the schoolhouse?"

"He did," said Mona's mother. "He's a nice man."

"He takes a great interest in everything," said Mrs. Kineely. "But he's not strong. I'm afraid he's delicate, the poor man. But no wonder."

"No wonder indeed," said her mother. "It's a hard life they have, up out of their beds till one o'clock in the day without as much as a cup of tea inside their lips."

"Yes, and when they do get their bit of breakfast, think of them having to be victimized by eating it in that poke-hole of a sacristy with Nonny Kane's dirty cooking?"

"I don't like to think of it, and that's the truth."

"I don't understand why they have the like of Nonny Kane cooking for the priest in the first place. I wouldn't eat bit or bite in that one's house if I was to be without crust or crumb for forty days and forty nights. And that's the truth for you."

"I can believe it. It's a wonder to me he has her at all, but I suppose he couldn't very well pass over her and she living next door to the chapel."

"She's all right in her own way, I suppose, but I'll tell you what it is, I wouldn't trust her to lay out the best penny she had for a piece of bacon. Would you?"

"I wouldn't. I wouldn't trust her an inch. Isn't it terrible? I declare to God if I was cooking for the priest I'd be up the best part of the night skinning the bacon and rinsing out the kettle."

"I know you would. There's no need to tell anyone that. All Nonny Kane does is slap the food up to him any old way. I didn't care much for the smell of the rashers she was frying for him this morning, did you?"

"Now that you mention it, I did not. Maybe I'm over particular, but I thought to myself that they didn't smell the way I'd like them to smell."

"You're not over particular in the least. And when it comes to cooking for the priest it would be a hard thing to be over particular, no matter how particular you were. If they don't deserve the best, I'd like to know who does?"

"The poor man! I declare to God, I often felt like asking him to step across the road to my place and have a cup of tea out of a teapot that wouldn't be rinsed out twice but ten times or twenty times."

"I often heard my Mona say just that very thing," said Mona's mother.

"Your Mona is very fond of him. She's a good girl, that one is."

"You should see the altar she has up!" Mona's mother said.

"That's because of what the priest said about altars the last Sunday but one, I suppose?"

"Why else? Why else?" said her mother. "That girl drinks in every word the priest utters. She's a good girl, even if I am her mother and say it myself. Do you know what it is, Mrs. Kineely? I believe in my heart that if the priest told that girl of mine to cut off her right hand she'd do it without thinking another thought."

"You don't need to tell me. I'd know that by the way she sits looking up at him every Sunday."

"She is a good biddable child. There's no saying against it."

"She'll be getting a good job one of these days. Isn't she near the age to be leaving off school?"

"This coming summer," said Mona's mother, and then she looked around her and drawing her coat tighter across her chest, she leaned a little nearer to Mrs. Kineely. "I wouldn't want to say too much, you understand, Mrs. Kineely," she whispered, "but we have reason to hope that there's a position ready and waiting for her the minute she leaves off school, and not too far from where we're standing this minute either, if you understand me?"

Mrs. Kineely nodded her head.

"If that's the case," she said, "she's only getting what she deserves, a nice good biddable little girl like she is!"

"I hope you understand, Mrs. Kineely," said Mona's mother anxiously, "about my not being able to mention any names. The whole thing hasn't gone any further than the exchanging of winks, if you know what I mean?"

"I know what you mean, of course. What's the use of letting too much of your business get out and about? I respect you for keeping your affairs to yourself, not that I don't understand perfectly well the party you're making reference to, and I'm glad to think the little girl is doing so well for herself. That party will give her the right training."

"That's what I say," said Mona's mother. "But isn't it a wonder they're taking her at all and she not trained in any way?"

"It's no wonder at all. Aren't they getting a fine strong little girl, and willing and clean? And wasn't the last girl this party took in a fully trained girl and yet I hear she was always upsetting his instruments and all the world knows there's a strict law in that house – and always was as long as I can remember – against anyone going next nor near the surgery, let alone touching his instruments."

"Mona is the very girl they want so, if that's the case, because a better girl to do what she's told I never met, if I do say it and I her own mother. That girl never did a pennyworth of harm to a living soul unless it was for want of knowing there was any harm in what she was doing."

"You may be sure too this certain party we were mentioning a while back is well informed on that score. She's a lucky girl, Mona! They'll give her a training up at that house will stand to her all the days of her life. Would you mind telling me how it came about?"

"I'll be glad to tell you, Mrs. Kineely. You're a good friend to Mona, and I'm sure she'd be glad for you to know! She was coming out the yard of the school a week or so back and there was this party's car coming down the road . . ."

The story Mona's mother told Mrs. Kineely was accurate in every word, but her knowledge of the story was mainly due to her own industry in putting the right questions to Mona, who was inclined to put no heed at all on the incident at the time it occurred and who even forgot to tell her mother about it at all for several days.

"Why didn't you tell me this before?" said her mother.

"I forgot."

"I don't see how you could forget a thing like that," her mother said, looking at her sharply. "You're quick enough to run in off the road with every little tittle-tattle that's said to you by people of no importance."

"Ah sure I put no pass on it," Mona said.

"You put no pass on it? What do you put pass on, so, if you didn't put pass on this? Let me tell you, miss, it's about time you put pass on the proper things. What did they say to you? Tell me that!"

"They said nothing, Mother."

"Is it a fool I have for a daughter? They didn't drive up in their motorcar just to look at you, did they?"

"They asked me my name."

"I hope you gave your full name?"

"I said 'Mona'!"

"What did they say?"

"They said 'Mona what?' "

"And what did you say?"

"I said 'Mona Clane.' "

"You should have said your confirmation name: Mona Bernadette Clane. But never mind. What did they say then?"

"They asked me what class I was in."

"What did you say?"

"I said I was in the sixth class."

"How do they know what that means? You should have said you were in the last class in the school. But what harm! He's an educated man; I suppose he'll have an idea what you meant. What else did they say?"

"They asked how my father was."

"And what did you say?"

"I said he was all right."

"What business had you to say the like of that? What kind of a girl are you? Wasn't it you yourself put the plaster on his back last week?"

"But the plaster was only because he was stiff after shearing the sheep."

"No matter what it was for, you had no business to say he was well and he going around with his back nearly burnt off him with a plaster. And let me tell you another thing, a man isn't well if he has to have a plaster put on him after shearing the few sheep we have out there in the pen. What else did they say?"

"They didn't say any more."

"Did *she* say anything?"

"She asked who washed the pinafore I had on me."

"I hope you said you did it yourself?"

"But it was you, Mother!"

Her mother jerked her shoulders with impatience. "Ah well!" she said then resignedly. "I suppose it can't be helped now. Never mind. What else did she say?"

"She asked me why my hair was cut short. Why did she ask me a thing like that?"

"She was afraid of ringworm. What did you say?"

"I said nothing."

"Why didn't you say it took up too much time combing and brushing it?"

"*He* said that!"

"Who?"

"The doctor."

"I thought you said they didn't say anything else?"

"They didn't ask any more questions, but when I said nothing about why my hair was cut short he took a look at me and he laughed. 'It takes up too much time, I suppose, brushing and combing it,' he said. 'It's pretty hair, healthy and thick.' "

"What did she say to that?"

"She said she hoped I washed it often."

"What did you say to that?"

"I said nothing."

"What did she say then?"

"She didn't say anything else to me."

"Did she say anything to him that you could catch?"

"She said, 'That's all, I think' to him, and he said 'Goodbye.' "

"Did she say goodbye?"

"She sort of smiled."

"How did he say goodbye?"

"He said 'Goodbye, Mona. You're a good girl. Stand back now from the splatters.' "

"Did he say anything else?"

"He said to tell my father he'd look in on him some day during the coming month."

"He said that?"

"Yes, Mother."

"What kind of a girl are you? Why didn't you tell me that in the first place and not be putting me to all these rounds?"

Mona's mother ran over to the half-door leading out into the yard and she called out to Mona's father who was rolling a cartwheel across the cobbles.

"Come in, will you," she said, "when you know I want you. What kind of a man are you?"

Mona's father rested the wheel up against the house.

"That wheel is warped," he said. "I'll have to tighten the spokes. Say what you have to say and let me get on with my business."

"What I have to say is more your business than what you're doing," his wife said. "I want to let you know you may be expecting the doctor to drop in on you one of these days to talk about getting Mona into service with his wife."

"How do you know?" Mona's father asked.

"He didn't say anything about that, Mother," Mona cried.

"Will you let me talk, both of you!" said the mother, and she turned to the father. "Don't hold out for too much money," she said, "because she's not trained, but don't let her go too easy either, because she's a good girl and very biddable." She turned to Mona. "Run up the street, Mona, like a good girl and repeat all you're after saying to me to your Aunt Brigid. But tell her not to let on to a soul, and tell her not to mention names on any account. Tell her the whole thing hasn't gone beyond a wink in the dark yet. But tell her we're in hopes. And then come back as quick as you can and tell me everything she says to you. Don't make any reply if anyone stops you in the street and starts asking you questions. Say you don't know to everything anyone asks you. Run off now, like a good girl."

Mona ran up the street, and as she ran by the chapel she went inside for a minute and knelt on the floor near the holy water font. She said a prayer for the souls of those poor sinners that the curate said were to be found walking the streets of the cities of the world with not one to say a prayer for them. Mona thought that sermon was the saddest sermon she'd ever heard, and she never let a day pass without praying for the poor sinners who were walking around the world with their sins heavy on them. The curate had spoken so sadly about them, looking up at the green glass windows and telling how Holy Mother Church made a special point of emphasizing the need on the part of the faithful to pray for all those who, through weakness or ignorance, had the misfortune to give up the protection of the sacraments.

Mona did not know what those cities of sin were like, but she felt that whatever they were like it was a good thing not to be in them. It was a good thing to be walking along lanes and cart roads between the safe mearings of hedge and ditch. On those roads and in those lanes no greater harm could come to you than a prick from a bramble. Even the ditches were shallow.

The ditches were shallow and there were yellow flowers growing in them, and the hedges were bloomy with rose, when the doctor's car drew up to the house and it was arranged that Mona would go into service as soon as she left off school. But school didn't break up till the middle of July and there was a long month to go.

Every evening all through that June, Mona heard the voices of the fellows and girls who were working at the haymaking by moonlight and they seemed to be having great larks together. Late in the night, too, when she was in bed, she could hear their voices still, out beyond the haggard, out beyond the paddock, down on the road leading to the mill pond. And the voices were as insistent as the scent of the hay coming in through the small square window. She could neither see the hay whose fragrance was so sweet, nor guess at the identity of those whose laughing voices made her lean up sleepily on her elbow to listen.

Outside in the hay-scented moonlight the wind was weaving the grey ghosts of the future; but weaving the ghosts of the glad hours only. In her big bed, that filled the room so the door didn't open the whole way, and the chest of drawers had to be put sideways, Mona lay impatiently whittling away at the hickory stick of her childhood. She had no heed for the hours ahead that she must have known vaguely would be filled with the noises of dirty wash sousing and grey slop spilling, coal hods clattering and the noiseless run of wet wood splinters into the soft wet palms of her hands.

But Sunday brings Sunday, and so the time came along at last for Mona to scrub her cheeks and get up on her bicycle and go away to service with the doctor's wife. She scrubbed her cheeks till they shone as bright as a polished apple, and she put her suitcase over the handlebars of the bicycle and went off down the road. It was two miles by the main road and only a mile and a bit by the cross-country road, but it was all ruts and it took longer going that way. She had to sleep in. But she had Wednesdays free, and Sunday evenings free as well. It was much better than most jobs. All this her mother kept telling her as she was getting up on the bicycle. But she wasn't half listening. What did she care as long as she was through with school, and out on her own?

Mona went home the first Wednesday. And the Sunday after that, on her way into the chapel, she got a chance to whisper to her mother that she'd be home that evening too if the weather kept up.

The weather kept up, but Mona didn't get home. Just as she was going out of the chapel-yard after Mass the doctor and his wife stopped to talk to her father. She stood waiting for them, back a bit from the car because she didn't want to get in till she was told. The fellows were sitting on the wall. They were shoving and codding with themselves. But Jimmy Carney was standing a bit off from the others, and Mona just happened to look at him. Jimmy's face got red. He drove his hands into his pockets and then he pulled them out again, and then he got redder still, and she saw he didn't have any cap on. But just as she was thinking that, he gave a beck to the yellow forelock that was hanging down over his eye. She could just barely hear him saying "How' you" in a slumpy sort of way, but she knew by the sort of smile he gave after saying it, that she was making no mistake. The next thing he'd be looking to go out walking with her! She knew! She knew! It was just like she thought it would be!

And sure enough, that afternoon, there he was, waiting in the laurels when she came freewheeling down the doctor's driveway. And he had a new cap on, one with a stiff peak on it and the button shut like a city fellow's cap.

They left her bicycle in the laurels.

It was sort of awkward at first walking linked, but she got used to it after a bit.

"I mustn't forget to get the bicycle going back," she said.

"It's all right," said Jimmy, "the laurels are thick."

There wasn't much to say. But soon the moon came out and then the silence wasn't so bad because anything they said seemed to stay echoing in the air for a long while after they stopped saying it. And other sounds from over the fields, the sound of a dog yelping and of cans being got ready for milking, and once, the sound of a train, all served to fill in the silences just as good as talk. But no one could say they were laughing or having great times. She could hardly expect that, perhaps, the first night. But Mona kept thinking of the laughing she used to hear on the roads at haymaking times when she was lying in her bed. It might be better another night, she thought.

But it was the same the next time, and the next. She and Jimmy never had much to laugh about, not when they were alone anyhow. If they caught up with other fellows and girls walking in the grey shadows of the trees that the moon threw down across the roads, the others began nudging and laughing and then Jimmy began nudging her and she began laughing and they had pretty good times then. It was getting late in the year and the smell of the honeysuckle was heavier than the smell of the hay in June had been when she used to sit up in bed and hug her knees and wish like anything that she was sixteen and out in service. There had been something delicate about the scent of the hay, but the scent of the honeysuckle was sickly and strong. Mona knew before the honeysuckle faded that the laughing she used to hear was the laughing of threes and fours, and that when a fellow and girl were walking along alone, or sitting on a gate, they didn't feel much like laughing. There wasn't much to laugh at. And they didn't have much to talk about if it came to that. Once you stopped talking it was hard to get started again. It was all very heavy, the talk and the air, and even when the scent of the honeysuckle was gone there was a strong heavy smell from the leaves that were beginning to turn yellow, and in the ditches the fallen leaves sent up a stifling odour that you'd kind of have to like, all the same. So Mona thought anyway. You wouldn't know what Jimmy was thinking, unless he told you. And he didn't tell things much.

Would it be nicer, and kind of fresher, when spring came, or, better still, when the summer came? There'd be good times at the haymaking. That was one thing anyway. She was sorry she'd missed it this year. She had only missed it by so little. She could remember the way the fresh hay scent came in through the window, and with it the sounds of the voices in the valley. She remembered the way the window sash spread out its pale shadow on the floor, a shadow twice as big as the window itself. She remembered it all the time she was walking with Jimmy that late summertime and she remembered it more than ever when the evenings began to get chilly and they started going into Ruane's hayrick out of the cold. The first thing she thought of every time they plumped down on the hay and put the smell of it waving up through the air was the nights long ago when she was longing for this; having a fellow treating her proper and the other fellows having to give over their tittering at her as if she was of no account.

But in Ruane's the dark shadow of the hanger fell across the hayrick and the close hay had a stronger smell than the hay had when it lay drying out in the fields. They didn't have anything to laugh at there. There was only their two selves. They didn't have much to say, either, and Jimmy's voice wasn't clear or gay like the voices she used to hear long ago. Jimmy's voice was thick like as if he had a cold. And he didn't have a cold. His voice was always thick when they were in Ruane's hayrick, lying down on the hay and pressing out its odours with their weight.

No matter how bright the moon shone out, no matter how deeply the tree shadows stained the pale blue road in the moonlight, no matter how brilliantly red Mona scrubbed her glossy cheeks, the evenings were not what she had expected, and it was always stuffy and odorous in the hayrick back of Ruane's, and Jimmy's voice always got thick, and his hands got sweaty and clumsy the minute they began tricking or pushing each other about, the minute, that is to say, they began to have any fun at all.

When the real winter set in, Mona was sorry in one way, but in another way she was glad. It was all one, though, anyway, whether she was sorry or not, because her mistress wouldn't let her out after dark.

"I wouldn't be responsible!" the doctor's wife said to her husband. "I hope she won't mind, she's such a child! I'll have a talk with her. She's so innocent."

"Is she giving satisfaction?" the doctor asked.

"She's excellent," said his wife, "for her age and her lack of training. She's willing and able. She's a good little girl."

"She never went near the surgery, that's one thing," said the doctor. "I could tell in a second."

"Even if you couldn't tell, I could reassure you. She is so obedient. She does everything I say and just the right way. It's such a relief. I hope she won't be discouraged about not getting out during the coming months. There will be a stretch in the light after January. I hope she won't mind. But I couldn't be responsible."

"She won't mind," said the doctor confidently, "if you have a little talk with her."

Mona didn't mind. It was put so nicely. The mistress came right down and sat on the edge of the table.

"I couldn't be responsible for you, Mona," she said. "I'd feel as responsible as if you were my own child. You're very young. You're very inexperienced. You have no idea of the dangers. That's why I'm speaking to you so frankly. I couldn't be responsible for you these dark nights coming back along the road. Think of the by-roads! Think of the tinkers! The dark laurels! The avenue! Everything! Write to your mother or tell her next time you're over. She'll understand, I'm sure. And you'll find plenty to do here. There's a gramophone in the attic. You can take it down, and I think there's a pack of cards in the drawer of that table." She pulled out the drawer, and while she rooted among the cutlery she said that the winter wouldn't last very long. "A few short months and it's over," she said. "And there's knitting. I forgot there was knitting. You knit, don't you?"

So Mona only saw Jimmy on Sundays going into Mass and coming out. He was always sitting on the wall with the other fellows, but if ever he got a chance while the doctor was heating up the engine he'd edge over along the wall till he got near enough to say "How' you". If he didn't get a chance for that, he always got a chance to wink. It was a great break in the week, anyway, because the six of spades and the three of diamonds were missing out of the pack of cards, and the only records she found for the old gramophone were some songs in a foreign language. Sunday made a great break. And the year was travelling.

"Sunday brings Sunday." No matter how much of a racket the doctor's car made and no matter how loud the doctor was talking, Mona could always hear the old chapel-hag. It was a great comfort to her, just like it always was. It made her think the summer was coming in long leaps, from one Sunday to another, travelling tirelessly. Soon it would be warmer and the evenings would be bright again. She and Jimmy would be out in the grey moonlight at haymaking.

Or maybe she'd be out with a different fellow; one that would be twice as nice as Jimmy! Poor Jimmy wasn't bad. He was all right in himself, but she'd like a fellow more well up. She'd like if some other fellow came and said "How' you" to her some Sunday when Jimmy was codding with the other fellows on the wall, and if the new fellow came up the drive of the doctor's ahead of Jimmy she'd dodge in by the laurels and give Jimmy the slip and go off with the other fellow.

Jimmy was slow. He was all right, but he was slow. He was the first fellow that ever said "How' you" to her and he told her the last time she saw him that he wanted her to stick with him no matter what happened. But he wasn't well up. He wouldn't know how to act if anything queer happened. His voice thickened up and his hands sweated.

And the night the dreadful thing did happen, in the hayrick back of Ruane's, he got up and ran out of the haggard and when he came back he had his hands in his pockets like he was trying to let on he knew everything, and that it was all right. But the minute he saw her sitting on the hay he flung himself down on his face and started to cry. It was awful. When she shook him and asked him if it was any harm what they did, he said how did he know. And he said how could it be any harm when lots of fellows did it. But he went on lying on his face all the same and she had to shake him with both hands.

"And what about girls? Is it any harm for them?"

"I don't know about girls," he said. "I never went with any till you."

"But how could the fellows do it without girls?" she asked, but his head was smothered up in the hay so she had to say it louder.

"Quit yelling, will you? Do you want to be heard in the house?"

"They often heard us before!"

"That was different!" he said.

"How was it different?"

"I don't know."

That was true for him. He didn't know anything. She didn't know herself, but you'd expect a fellow would know. It was his fault. If it was any harm it was his fault. Poor Jimmy. She was kind of sorry for him. Even if it was his fault he didn't have to be so scared about it. As long as you didn't mean to do any harm it was all right. Wasn't it?

The sweat came out on him when she asked him that. It came out in white drops on his white face. She thought of the great white faces of her father's sheep when they were penned up waiting their turn for the shearing. The eyes of the sheep used to be dark and full of dread in their white faces and that was the way Jimmy looked in the dark hayrick, as if something dreadful was going to happen and he didn't know rightly what it was. He was no good in any kind of trouble. He was twice as scared as she was.

"You're leaving your cap after you, Jimmy," she had to say. She had to put it into his hands. His hands were cold as ice. A minute before that they had been as hot as hot.

If only in the summery time that was leaping in long leaps from Sunday to Sunday she could meet a fellow with nice hands, a fellow so full of life he'd be always laughing and wanting to go dancing two towns away, she'd never give another thought to Jimmy. Then when there'd be no darkness anywhere on the roads but the darkness from the great tree shadows, they'd walk along linked and laughing. Even when winter came again and they had to shelter in Ruane's hayrick – or maybe they'd go to another hayrick, one that would be bigger; one that would be nicer and brighter – she wouldn't have any need to be scared as long as the fellow knew a bit more than Jimmy. Jimmy was slow. Jimmy was stupid.

As Sunday brought Sunday Mona longed more and more for the summer, and the more Sundays that passed the more she longed for some other fellow besides Jimmy to give her a beck of his cap and link her off down the road before everyone, and leave Jimmy gawking.

The thought of Jimmy was a hot thick thought, and even in the chapel where everything was cold – the stone floor and the cheap green glass – the thought of Jimmy was hot and clammy. Even when the curate, with the light glinting off his glasses, started reading the list of the confraternity guilds that were to go to confession the next Saturday, even when a vicious wind scourged the window-panes with a scatter of rain, when Mona thought about Jimmy, she felt sort of sick.

One Sunday her hands got so cold her fingers swelled up and when she tried to see herself in the brass pole that held up a green silk banner on the end of the pew, she could see that her cheeks were white and she wished they'd redden up and be like they used to be when she was at school. If only she could have a cup of hot tea, right then, she might feel better. Her cheeks would flush up a bit, for a while anyway.

She'd give anything for a cup of hot tea. She wondered what would happen if she got so cold that she had to stand up and go out of the chapel to stamp her feet on the broken slate in the yard? Would everyone stare? Would her mother give out about it the next time she went home? And going back in the car would the doctor be asking what was the matter?

There was nothing the matter, only that she couldn't warm up. She couldn't warm up no matter what she did. For about a week now, or maybe two, maybe three, she hadn't taken any stock of how long it was, the cold kept her awake half the night, and in the morning the cold floor and the cold wind coming in between the sashes of the window made her head reel and she felt queer all over, ever until she got a cup of strong hot tea down her throat.

If only she could have a cup of tea now. She looked up at the cold white marble of the altar and a shiver went through her, under her shoulder blades. Her shoulders ached. She wanted to sit up, but it wasn't the time to sit up yet.

When the time to sit up came around at last, and the curate turned about to give the sermon, Mona felt better. But when he looked up at the windows and the white rain-sodden light glittered on his glasses, for the first time in her life she didn't heed what he said, and the long sermon with its familiar Latin words fell heavily on the air with the falling force of dead things.

It was hard to sit up straight. It was easier to listen when she slumped down and shut her eyes.

"It is an efficacious thing," the curate said, "to kneel down on your knees for a few minutes out of the twenty-four hours that go to make up a day and say a few prayers in order not to let it be said that you passed the day in the pursuit of your own interests regardless of the higher things that should occupy the minds of all those Christians who are worthy to be called by the name.

"I know that the people of this parish are, for the most part, good-living people who say their prayers regularly, but there are a great many sinners in other parts of the world, not so much in our own country, I am thankful to be able to say, but in other pagan places, who have abandoned the habit of prayer. It is easy for us to see how great a mistake this is for such people because it is by prayer that we avoid sin.

"It is a very pious practice for those who have themselves received the grace necessary for living a good holy life, occasionally to say a prayer for those who have not of themselves had the wisdom necessary to pray for the grace to avoid temptation. As I have said, it is by prayer that we obtain the grace to avoid sin."

Mona looked up. She'd heard the last sentence. She sat up straighter. Her back didn't ache so bad. She wasn't shivering so bad. It is by prayer that we avoid sin. Well! She said her prayers every night. She never missed a night. She never went by the chapel without going in to say a prayer. She wore a medal all the time; she wore it in bed even. And every time she heard the medal knocking off the sink or the coal bucket she said an ejaculation.

She looked up at the curate. He knew everything, she supposed. He knew everything that was right and everything that was wrong. He had to know everything on account of hearing confessions. She never said anything to him in confession about Jimmy and what happened. It wasn't any harm. You couldn't do any harm if you didn't mean to do harm. Or could you? And how could she tell him, anyway? What way would she say it?

If he'd only say something from the altar about what was wrong and what was right. If only he'd say something about kissing and that kind of thing. But he didn't. How would he say it anyway? It would sound queer. Still, if he only just gave people a hint. All he said was that company-keeping wasn't right. But anyone could see that was only talk. Didn't everyone keep company? Wasn't her own father always talking about the time he and her mother were company-keeping? Weren't the old people always laughing till their sides split whenever there was a sermon on company-keeping? "Where would he be himself," they said, "if there was no such thing as courting?" And her Uncle Mathew that was the wisest man in their parts, and that was a schoolmaster in his young days, said to herself one day last winter: "Mona," he said. "Aren't you Mona? You are. I knew it. Very well then, Mona, let me tell you this: there's been courting, and there's been company-keeping since the first blackbird sat on the first bush and let the first shout of a song out of him! Remember that, my girl."

Every fellow and girl in the parish were company-keeping, no matter what the priest said.

"Have you got a boy yet?" the old ones were always asking a girl.

The blacksmith was always coming to the door of the forge when the children were coming home from school, and it was always the one word with him. "Did anyone get to steal a kiss off you yet?" And the men that were waiting for their horses to be shod would roar out laughing and some of them might let on to be going to make a run at you.

"I hate that old blacksmith," Mona said to her mother.

"It isn't right to say you hate anyone," her mother said, "let alone a fine upright man like James Farrelly, a man that never did an ounce of harm in his life." And he *was* a good man. Mona knew that now. He was head of his sodality. He was always in the back of the chapel, praying out loud, and wasn't a bit ashamed when people turned around and stared at him.

Company-keeping was no harm. The priest meant something else. Why couldn't he speak more particular? If he only gave an idea; only an idea. He should give people some idea.

Suddenly Mona's shoulders ached worse than when she first sat up. Her feet were freezing. The cold was awful. She was a terrible wicked girl, thinking bad of the priest. It wasn't his fault. How could he talk about such things in the chapel? It might be a sin to talk about them in the chapel. Sin was a queer thing. She never thought about it before. But now she did. Now she remembered what the priest said one time about the sinners that were walking the streets of bright cities with their sins creeping black behind them. What kind of sins, she wondered?

She had to close her eyes. The people knelt down but she stayed sitting up. She kept her eyes closed tight, because the light from the cold green glass of the windows scalded them. The starched whiteness of the curate's alb scalded them.

Jimmy said it was all right. He said every fellow did it, some time or another. That's what he said. And Jimmy never told a lie. That was one thing certain. Jimmy wore a medal too pinned on the inside of his trouser pocket. And one day in the graveyard when he stood on a wreath and broke the glass he took a shilling and he buried it in the grave. Jimmy was good. He said what they did was all right. But when he said it his voice was caught up with phlegm and when he put his head down in the hay she could hear him snuffling.

Maybe they oughtn't to have done it? But they didn't do it on purpose. They were only pushing and shoving and having fun.

Again a scatter of rain struck the window-panes and the cold voice of the curate struck through her stifling thoughts.

"It is the duty of parents and teachers to instruct children and servants and all those entrusted to their care."

In the pew behind her she could hear the wintry moaning of the hag, who had come in out of the rain.

"Sunday brings Sunday."

Mona felt a great fear growing in her heart when she thought of the way the priest's voice every Sunday, and the voice of the hag, and the voices of the fellows calling "How' you" from the wall were lashing on the year till it galloped, taking seven steps at a time. If she kept on feeling this queer way she would have no choice but to get up and go down the aisle and out of the chapel. And outside it would be colder. What would she do outside? If she cycled home to her own house she mightn't get back in time before the Mass ended and she might miss the doctor's car. And anyway there was next Sunday to face. If she felt worse today than she did last Sunday she might be worse again next week. And at home there'd be so many questions; she'd sooner die than face them. And Jimmy across the aisle in the men's side of the chapel would be sweating and wetting his lips if he saw her go out. He'd be scared. And people would see him. And it would all be talked over later on, in the chapel yard, when the people were straggling out from Mass. The old hag might have something to say, in a cracked voice for all to hear. She couldn't go out. That was all there was to it. She'd have to bear it.

Mona clenched her hands together. She'd bear it. And she'd pray as hard as she could that nothing would happen to her. She'd light as many candles as she could out of what was left of her pay after some was sent home to her father. She might, maybe, skip a week of sending money home and put such a blaze of candles all over the candelabra that the smoke of them would go up like the souls of the dead went up out of the tombstones. Prayer was an efficacious thing, the priest said. By prayer we avoid sin. She always did what the priest said. Her mother often told people that her Mona would cut off her right hand if the priest told her to do it. That was right. She'd cut off her right hand. She'd do it that minute, if it was any good. She'd do anything if only it would be that there was nothing the matter with her. She'd pray and pray and pray that in the lovely summertime she'd have red cheeks again.

"Sunday brings Sunday." If there was anything the matter she'd soon find out. The priest was still talking and the light was still glinting off his glasses. It wasn't his fault that Jimmy didn't know anything about anything any more than she did. It wasn't. Sure it wasn't? And anyway, it wasn't right to blame anyone for anything they didn't mean to do, least of all a priest. He didn't know how easy things could happen. He didn't know anything about the like of her or Jimmy, only seeing them in school and giving them pictures to put in their prayer books.

"Sunday brings Sunday." Where was that voice? Was Mass over? Mona couldn't see well, but she could hear feet moving and she could hear the hag's voice shrilling in her ear. The feet were the feet of the year! The year was coming! The year was rushing up the rutty gravelled yard. It was rushing in over the splintered wooden floor and grating on the flagstones where the dead priests of the parish were buried. It made a sound like the sound of a million feet, but it had only one blunt leg. She knew that. Ha! she knew that. She could see it even though she had her fists dug into her eyes. The year was a hobbled old hag! It was climbing over the pews to get to her! It was skipping the Mondays and skipping the Thursdays and hopping from Sunday to Sunday. The Sundays were a lot of lice-eaten pews. It didn't take long to hop over them. It didn't take long to hobble along when you were an old hag on a Sunday stick.

Sunday stick!
Sunday stick?
Who said that?
Who said that.
Who was sick?
Who was sick.

Sunday stick?

Sunday stick.

It wasn't cold now. It was hot. Nothing was cold any more. The wind beat a batter on the wooden door but with every batter rings of heat were sent up to her head. There was a scatter of pebbled rain on the window-panes but now no light glinted on the curate's glasses, because there was no light. The chapel was dark and getting darker every minute. The darkness was like water, and suddenly she was floating on it like the weeds that floated on the ditches. But the ditches were cool and green, and she flowed in some dark water that was dirty and yellow and warm like hay.

The Long Ago

Everyone was kind to Hallie. You'd be surprised at the number of young people in the town who visited her, and went for walks with her, and did little messages on her behalf. But, although she was always nice to them and offered them tea when they called, there were only two people in the town whose company Hallie really enjoyed. One was Ella Fallon, who used to be Ella White. The other was Dolly Feeny, who used to be Dolly Frewen. For Dolly and Ella and Hallie had all been girls together, and they had a great many memories in common. Their main bond was that Dolly and Ella had been in Hallie's confidence in the days long ago when all three of them were young, and Dolly knew for a fact, what other people took to be gossip, that in happier circumstances – and if it had not been for the intervention of a certain person – Hallie too would have been married like them, and have a home of her own. Dolly and Ella had read every note that had passed between Hallie and Dominie Sinnot. And they knew it was Dominie who had given Hallie the brooch which she always wore; a gold brooch with the word "Dearest" written on it in seed pearls. They both stoutly maintained that Dominie had once as good as told them, although not in so many words, that he would never marry any other girl but Hallie.

Ah well, that was all long ago, and Dominie at the time was only a law student, apprenticed to old Jasper Kane. And being young and innocent Dominie perhaps had not realized that an ageing solicitor would hardly make an offer of partnership to a penniless young apprentice unless there was more to the offer than met the eye. There was a string to it. And the string was Blossom – Jasper's only daughter.

Hallie never blamed Dominie, when he married Blossom, but she felt it no injustice to Blossom that a small spark of the truth should be kept alive and tended, particularly when poor Dominie lived so short a time.

"He would be alive today if it was you he married, Hallie!" Dolly said, one day, and Ella agreed. They were a great comfort to Hallie.

She felt she could speak her heart to them at any time. And indeed, shortly after Dominie's death, when an awkward situation developed with Blossom, Ella and Dolly took a firm stand in Hallie's defence. Why shouldn't she visit Dominie Sinnot's grave if she wanted? they cried. They knew all about the dream she'd had – three nights in a row – a dream in which Dominie had come to her, and in which he seemed to be trying to convey some message that she did not at first understand, until quite suddenly one day she guessed what he wanted. He wanted her to visit his grave! And promptly that very evening she went down to the cemetery and knelt beside the mound. She not only said a few prayers for him. She shed a few tears for him as well. And after that she went down to the cemetery every evening.

Those moments kneeling by Dominie's grave were the happiest moments of Hallie's day. But even those moments were sometimes spoiled by the appearance of Blossom draped to the waist in widow's weeds, and when Blossom arrived Hallie, of course, had to get up off her knees and move away. In fact she had to pretend she was visiting her own family plot – as if, like everyone else in the town, Blossom didn't know quite well that Hallie's parents had been laid to rest in the burial grounds of the old Friary before it was closed. No one had been buried in the Friary for at least a decade.

The situation could have been difficult for Blossom too, if matters had not settled themselves unexpectedly. Because a short time after Dominie's death Blossom married again. And unlike Dominie, her second husband was a big, assertive fellow who would not let Blossom out of his sight. She was always hanging from his arm. And since the main gates of the cemetery were kept locked except on the days of funerals, and the side gates were so narrow two people could not go through linked, Blossom soon gave up visiting the grave. She ordered a headstone to be erected, and never went near the cemetery again. The grave was all Hallie's after that.

Hallie soon had the grave a regular showpiece. A yew tree she planted back of the headstone did remarkably well. A box hedge she put inside the curbstone did not do quite so well, but Hallie took it up and put down a small privet hedge. People thought this behaviour a bit odd. There were raised eyebrows. And one or two unkind remarks were carried back to Hallie. But with Dolly and Ella to take her part she rose superior to all criticism.

"Don't mind what people say, Hallie," Dolly urged. "As for the

Kanes – their consciences can't be too clear about the way you were treated."

Those were the kind of remarks Hallie treasured.

The year that Hallie decided to buy a plot for herself in the new cemetery right beside the plot in which Dominie lay, people felt that she was going altogether too far. But again, Ella and Dolly took her part.

"We know how you feel," Ella said. "If things had gone as they should, we know where your coffin would go by rights – down into the same grave with Dominie!"

"I thought over it for a long time," Hallie assured her friends, "and I would not have bought the plot if Blossom had stayed a widow."

After that particular conversation, however, Dolly and Ella felt sadder for her than ever.

"She doesn't seem to realize that Blossom will have to be buried with Dominie anyway, whether she likes it or not," Dolly said. "A wife is buried with her first husband no matter how many times she marries."

"I hope nobody will tell her that," Ella said kindly. "Let her have what small comforts she can get."

Ella was always softer hearted towards Hallie than Dolly was, because, as far as these things can be known, it seemed that Ella was happier in her marriage than Dolly. Not that Dolly was dissatisfied; Sam Feeny was a man in a million. He was making money fast. He was buying up property hand over fist. And Dolly would have an easy life of it some day, although, for the moment, she had to fall in with his ideas about economy and thrift. The marriage was not the love-match of Ella and Oliver. Dolly had married Sam for security. And so it was a terrible blow to her when Sam was brought down with pneumonia one day and – putting up hardly any fight – was dead three days from the day he took bad.

Strange to say, it was to Hallie that Dolly turned. It was Hallie who held her together and gave her strength on the day of the funeral. No one would ever have imagined that an inexperienced spinster could have acted so tactfully, but it was she who, after the coffin had been got downstairs, put her arms around Dolly and persuaded her to control herself enough to go to the cemetery.

"Think of me," Hallie said. "When Dominie died I had to stand at the back of the crowd, like a stranger. It's different for you. You'll be standing at the lip of the grave, knowing no one has a better right to stand there."

Dolly recovered her composure at once.

"Poor Hallie," she said. "I never realized how you must have suffered that day." Her mind was taken off her own trouble for a few minutes. "Do you know, Hallie," she said, "I had forgotten until this minute, but now I distinctly remember that when Dominie's coffin was being lowered into the clay, Blossom was looking across the grave at the man she is married to today! He had only just come to town. I'm certain she was wondering who he was and already sizing him up! There were tears in her eyes, but there was curiosity in them as well." At the thought of Blossom's infidelity to Dominie, Dolly had braced up, and seen where her own duty lay. "Give me my hat," she said. "I mustn't keep the hearse waiting. Sam was always on time wherever he went. I won't delay him now."

Hallie was proud of the way Dolly behaved at the graveside. People were more impressed by her silence than they would have been by any amount of sobbing and screaming. Her behaviour was certainly most edifying by comparison with Blossom, whose screams could have been heard a mile away when the first sod thudded down on Dominie's coffin. Indeed Ella was astonished at Dolly's calm – and told her so. "I don't know how you did it, Dolly. I'd have broken down. I'd have thrown myself into the grave if it was Oliver – God forbid that the like should happen," she added tactlessly, and she hastily made the sign of the Cross. Dolly and Hallie exchanged glances. There are times when the silent heart grieves deepest, they seemed to say, each to the other.

After Sam's death it was Ella who was the odd one out, as Dolly and Hallie saw more and more of each other. Not that Dolly had much time to spare. She had two children and they took up a good part of her time. As well as that Sam's affairs were not in as good order as might have been expected – or desired – and his widow was in and out of old Jasper Kane's office every other day. There was even talk of a lawsuit. Nevertheless, it was undeniable that she had more free time than formerly, and it became an almost regular thing for Hallie and herself to go for a walk every evening after supper – just as they used to do in the long ago. No one could have known what those walks meant to Hallie. The thought of them bore her up through the long day, in a house that was empty and dark and cold, for nothing she did – no fire she lit, no light she burned – could bring back the warmth and brightness of the time when she was young. Young! Her faded face, and her faded hair, and her thin body that had dried up without giving out any of its sweetness, had been a bitter sight to her in her mirror for many a day. But somehow her ageing appearance did not trouble her as much after she took up her old companionship with Dolly. The days went quicker when there was something she could look forward to in the evenings. True, she, Dolly, and Ella had occasionally taken a walk together, even after the other two were married, but it was a different thing altogether to look forward to a walk every evening – regularly. It was, she told herself, just like long ago. And as she and Dolly strolled along the country roads in the soft twilight it sometimes seemed to Hallie that they were indeed back in that long ago. Walking idly along, sometimes softly humming a tune together in part time, it was so like when they were young! The evening skies were the same as ever, darkening away to the east, with a gleam still lingering in the branches of the western trees. There were bats striking through the dark air in fits and starts. There was the sweet sound of a little stream, that ran alongside the road, hidden by a high hedge from behind which came the same sound of cattle moving noisily in the rushy bottom. The same. The same. All around them the countryside was the same. The night sky was the same. And deep, deep down under the changed shape of their bodies, weren't they – she and Dolly – the same Hallie and Dolly of long ago?

More and more of the past was dragged back into their conversation as they walked and talked in the twilight.

"Do you remember the first day Ella put up her hair?" Hallie said one evening.

"Do I!" Dolly said. "It was a Sunday! In the chapel at last Mass! It fell down when she was genuflecting. I thought she'd die of embarrassment."

"So did I," Hallie said, and she laughed heartily, seeing Ella again in her mind's eye as clearly as she saw her that day – thin as a rod, with her toppling heap of pale hair, standing all confused halfway up the centre aisle, her cheeks flaming, not knowing whether to stoop and pick up her hairpins, or get into a pew as if nothing had happened, letting her hair hang down her back as it always had. She squeezed Dolly's arm. "Do you remember the day you first put up your own hair, Dolly?" she said.

E

"Will I ever forget it!" Dolly smiled as she thought of the day when she herself stood in her bedroom looking into the spotted mirror that reflected a saucy seventeen-year-old, her mouth filled with hairpins and a pile of chestnut hair caught on top of her head, while the rest of her hair rambled over her shoulder. She gave Hallie's arm a squeeze. "I'll never forget the day *you* put up your hair, Hallie," she said generously. "And I know there was someone else who never forgot it either."

"Who?" breathed Hallie, her heart fluttering. As if she needed to be told! Oh that day! Oh! Oh! Such a day. A Sunday too of course. She'd let her hair loose from its braids and piled it up on the top of her head, but all the way down the street to the chapel she was trembling with apprehension in case it might fall down like Ella's. And when she went into the chapel, although she did not turn her head to look in his direction, she knew that Dominie was kneeling just inside the door. And she knew he would be staring at her. If *her* hair had fallen down then what would she have done?

"Oh, what would I have done, Dolly, if my hair had come undone?" she cried. "At least Ella knew Oliver wasn't in the chapel the day hers fell down. He was laid up with a cold. How lucky she was: just think how awful it would have been for her if he had been there!"

"Oh, I don't suppose it would have mattered very much," Dolly said, indifferently. She was willing to talk endlessly about those days long ago, but she could not re-live them. And sometimes she wished Ella were with them. But Ella seldom got out in the evening. The children had to be put to bed, and after that she was usually tired. Dolly sighed. She understood why Ella did not want to come with them, whereas Hallie never understood. Hallie was always bemoaning Ella's absence, and regretting she was not with them. She got quite censorious at times. "Ella ought to get out in the evenings, if only for half an hour. Just for a change. Just for the fresh air." She wouldn't listen to any excuses from Dolly. "You have children too, Dolly!" she said.

"My girls are older than Ella's little people," Dolly said. "And anyway girls are able to do a lot for themselves."

"Why doesn't she come out after she's put them to bed?"

"But that's the only time she has alone with Oliver," Dolly blurted out at last, although she had regrets at once. Hallie unlinked her arm. "I should think she'd have seen enough of him by now," she said.

That annoyed Dolly. It was all she could do not to say something mean – to let Hallie see, for once and for all, that there was a big difference between a married woman and a spinster, and even a widow was not the same as a woman who had never had a man in the house at all!

But as soon as these bitter words came into Dolly's mind she suppressed them. After all, it wasn't fair to regard Hallie as an old maid. She had been the prettiest of the three of them, and she had a nicer disposition. If Dominie Sinnot had not been a worthless weakling, Hallie would have been married before either her or Ella. If it came to that, Hallie could have married someone else, even after Dominie married Blossom, if she hadn't remained so absurdly wrapped up in him. It really wasn't fair to call her an old maid.

"Don't walk so fast, Hallie," she said. "My shoe is hurting me." She was trying to pretend that it was she who lagged back, and not Hallie who had gone on ahead in a huff. "Isn't it chilly?" she added, as they drew abreast again, making this as an excuse for drawing Hallie's arm through hers again. And then, deliberately, she herself tried to feel critical of Ella. Ella should be more considerate. It was not very tactful of her to keep talking about Oliver all the time, considering poor Sam, and where *he* was now, poor soul. Ella and Oliver may have been nearer to each other in age than she and Sam, but that didn't necessarily mean their marriage was any happier. Love wasn't everything! But try as she might to turn against Ella, Dolly found herself echoing Hallie's regret that she was not with them on their evening walks. For one thing, the past to Ella – as to her – was a misty place, in which it was nice to let their minds wander, but which they knew they could never re-enter, whereas Hallie had never left it.

But they had reached the crossroads at which they usually turned back. Beyond this the road ran between tall trees, lonely and dark, and on the left somewhere – they weren't quite sure where – a man had once been done to death by thieves, or so they had always been told. One night in the long ago Ella had insisted that they should go further. It was a moonlit night, full of light and shadow.

"Oh, come on. Let's go down the ghosty road," Ella urged. "Come on." But they wouldn't go. She, Hallie, claimed to have a stone in her shoe, and Dolly flatly refused to go a step further, saying she was too scared.

"All right, go home!" Ella said. "I'll go by myself!" And away she went, with her sprightly gait, down the lonely road that was lit only in the centre where the moon played down through the branches of the trees, but dark and gloomy to either side where tangles of undergrowth cast their shadows. On Ella went, firm and straight, and fearless! And there they stood, feeling foolish at the thought that they who were two years older than Ella, had less spirit than she. But a few seconds after Ella had gone out of sight around the first bend of the road, they heard her calling to them and, next thing, she came flying back, her skirt held up with both hands and her silk stockings flashing. "Run, run!" she cried as she caught up with them, but they only laughed, because they knew that she had fancied her courage so great, her imagination had had to supply terrors to equal it. And ever after, when they came to that crossroads they used to tease her about that night. "How about going on another few yards?" they used to say, just to rattle her. Even after Ella married, Hallie tried to keep up the joke. "If we had Ella with us we might go a bit further," she'd say when they reached that point.

It was the kind of remark Hallie was always making – a remark that concentrated so much of the past in its essence, and Dolly didn't object as long as she didn't elaborate on it too much. But she always did. "I wonder if Ella really saw something that night or if her imagination ran away with her?" she asked this very evening as she and Dolly stood at the crossroads and looked down the ghostly road. "What do you think Hallie?" she said. "We must remember to ask her next time we see her." Unfortunately at that moment Dolly had been thinking of something quite different she herself wanted to ask Ella – a practical question about the future. She was having trouble filling in some forms that came in the post, relating to Sam's insurance policy and she was wondering if Ella could help her with them. She didn't reply to Hallie.

"What are you thinking about, Dolly?" Hallie asked peevishly, having seen that she was preoccupied.

"I was just wondering if Oliver has his life insured," Dolly said.

Hallie turned her head away. She wasn't interested.

However, if Hallie was not interested in what Dolly said that night, she had reason next day to recall Dolly's words. She ran down the street and knocked on her door.

"Wasn't it queer you should speak of Oliver the other night?" she said, breathless from running.

"Why? What did I say anyway?" Dolly asked.

"Oh, don't you remember?" Hallie was impatient. "You were wondering if he had his life insured."

"Well? What was queer about that?"

"But haven't you heard?" Hallie cried. "He's ill."

Dolly had an unpleasant feeling that Hallie was overstraining the coincidence.

"I don't see anything queer about that. What's the matter with him anyway? I suppose he has a cold? He's hardly likely to give anyone the benefit of his insurance!"

Hallie drew an enormous breath. "Oh, but it's not a cold, Dolly. It's more than that. The doctor doesn't know what's the matter with him. Yes! He's had the doctor. And a nurse. And there's talk of getting a night nurse. Ella is nearly out of her mind."

Dolly was still reluctant to believe it was serious, but she began to feel uncomfortable about having made that remark about the insurance policy. She was determined Hallie must be exaggerating Oliver's condition.

"Oh, I wouldn't mind Ella," she said scathingly. "Look at me. I was nearly out of my mind when Sam got ill." She had no sooner mentioned poor Sam, however, than she saw the look on Hallie's face, and her own face fell, thinking of where Sam had finished up. "Well," she said crossly. "If he is bad, we'd better go up there at once. Ella is no person for dealing with an emergency. Think of that houseful of children! Think of the turmoil! Oh! if anything should happen! Hurry! Hurry!" She grabbed her coat and together they hurried up the street to Ella's.

When they got to Ella's house Hallie and Dolly found they were not the only ones who thought it their duty to be there. It was Ella's mother who opened the door. She showed them into the parlour – a room that was rarely used and in which they had hardly ever before set foot. And on their way into the room they had to stand aside to let Ella's sister-in-law pass out with a tray. The parlour was crowded. And in the middle was Ella, sitting down like a visitor.

"Oh, Hallie! Oh, Dolly!" When she saw them, Ella's face lit up, and she tried to get to her feet but several people urged her back into her chair. She sat back again docile as a child. They saw that her poor face was as white as a sheet, and that she looked as if she did not know where she was or what she was supposed to do. It was someone else who provided them with chairs, and when the sister-in-law returned a few minutes later with fresh cups of tea, as she proffered them tea she pressed upon them also the information that Oliver's condition was grave. The crisis was expected any minute.

Hallie and Dolly felt awkward. They had come to help. To take charge of the children. To see that everything possible was being done for Oliver. And instead of that they were being treated like visitors. In other parts of the house they could hear people charging themselves with the tasks they had intended to undertake.

"Is the doctor with him?" Dolly asked, reluctant to stay in the background.

"The doctor has been here twice already," Ella's mother said. "He's upstairs with him now." Then she glanced at the clock and frowned. "He ought to be brought down for a cup of tea," she said and she turned away importantly, pausing only to whisper something to a cousin of Ella's sitting near the door, who promptly rose and followed her out of the parlour, closing the door.

"Can't we do something?" Dolly whispered to Hallie. "Did you say there was a nurse?"

"I believe so," Hallie said, "but I don't know if she's a proper nurse."

"What do you mean by that?"

"She's a cousin of Oliver's. They say she has some kind of a nursing diploma." She needed to say no more.

"A nursing diploma!" Dolly exclaimed contemptuously, but she had to lower her voice hastily because at that moment the so-called nurse put her head around the corner of the door, looking for someone who was not there. Then she went out again, and she too closed the door after her. But Dolly and Hallie had seen that although she wore a nurse's cap all right and a white coat, the coat was too short and under it showed a gaudy dress with a flowery pattern. But what they objected to most was that her long legs were covered with flashy flesh-coloured stockings, and stuck into small fashionable shoes with high heels.

"I don't think much of her," Dolly said. "Someone ought to send down for the district nurse." She stood up.

But just then the young nurse appeared again. This time she tiptoed over and whispered to the women on either side of Ella, who immediately began to assist Ella to her feet. Indeed this assistance was given with such vigour that, almost before Hallie and Dolly knew what had happened, Ella had been whisked from the room.

"The crisis!" Everyone whispered the same word at the same time, so the whisper ran around the parlour like a breeze. "The crisis!"

Up to then most people had been talking quietly, but now, subdued, they sat silent, straining to interpret the sounds from above. But where, formerly, there had been an occasional soft footfall, and the sound of an occasional voice, there was now absolute silence.

The silence lasted a long time. And the longer it lasted the more oppressive it became, until those who had occasion to move – to cross their legs, or open their handbags – did so with exaggerated care and self-consciousness. Once during this vigil, there was a short diversion when a child was heard outside in the passage, asking a question in a shrill voice. In the parlour several people started to their feet in dismay. But the child's voice stopped in the middle of a word, and then heavy footsteps were heard again, hurrying away. The child had obviously been snatched up and carried out of earshot. After that such stillness settled over the room, Hallie and Dolly were weighted down by it. On Dolly it lay so heavily her indignation could do no more than smoulder. But Hallie found it easy enough to yield to silence. Wasn't she used to it? One by one her thoughts began to drift away to their usual strolling ground: the past.

First she thought about Oliver, and of how strong and hearty he was long ago. It was sad to think of him, now, flat on his back, and helpless with strange women whispering and tiptoeing around him. Even the resentment she had borne against him for being best man at Dominie's wedding began to wear away. After all, he could hardly have refused. He had nothing against Blossom either, she supposed. He would have been best man for Dominie no matter who Dominie married. Poor Oliver! Was he really going to die? Did he know he was so low? When Dominie was dying, it was said he didn't know it. Even when they had brought the priest to him he thought the priest had just dropped in for a friendly chat. And he was unconscious when he was anointed. Would it have made any difference to her, she wondered, if Dominie had known he was dying? Would he have sent her any message? Suddenly a startling thought entered her mind. Perhaps Dominie had sent her a message. Perhaps Blossom had kept it from her. But at this point she pulled herself up. It was by never putting the strain of incredulity upon it that she had kept intact through the years the thin web of her romance. She had no doubt whatever that Dominie's last thoughts had been of her, but to think that he had expressed them would have been straining things too much.

Her mind returned to Oliver. Was he conscious, she wondered? Did he know that Ella was beside him? Not for anything in the world would Hallie want to deprive Ella of anything that might solace her in her sorrow, but if it should happen that Oliver was too far gone to recognize her at the end, then it was to her, Hallie, that Ella could turn. She would understand. After all, Sam had been fully conscious right up to the end. Hadn't his last words to Dolly been something about an insurance policy? Yes, it was to her, and not to Dolly, Ella would turn.

Hallie felt very close to Ella at that moment. After all they had both felt, at the time of Dolly's marriage, that there was something a bit too practical about Dolly's choice. Dolly had picked out Sam. There had not been the instantaneous, mutual attraction between them that there had been between Ella and Oliver, and between her and Dominie. She had never forgotten something Ella said the night before her wedding.

"Oliver will never have much money, Hallie," she said. "I'll never have things nice, the way I planned."

"That doesn't matter," Hallie had confidently answered.

Ella had pressed her hand. "I knew you'd say that, Hallie," she said. "You and Dominie wouldn't have cared about money either."

That was why it had hurt so bitterly, after Dominie married Blossom, to have to stand in the chapel and smile and smile when Ella and Oliver were married. That wound had never healed. It was strange, but even now when she'd sigh and say to Dolly that it would have been like long ago if Ella was with them she knew in her heart it wasn't really true. Things wouldn't have been the same. Because Ella would never have stopped talking about Oliver all the time. And it hurt. It hurt.

But now Oliver was ill and Hallie knew she mustn't bear resentment against him. He was ill, and maybe dying.

Just then the nurse threw open the parlour door again. "Where are the children?" she demanded to know. "I thought they were here." When she saw they were not in the parlour she withdrew her head, and shut the door with a slam. Those in the parlour exchanged glances.

"The children are wanted to say goodbye to him. He must be sinking fast."

A woman who was only distantly related to Oliver threw up her hands and burst into tears.

"Hush, hush!" the woman beside her murmured, not to silence her but to direct her grief into more suitable channels. "Poor Oliver is not the one to be pitied," they cried. "He's going to a better world. But think of his poor young widow. Think of her! Poor Ella!" And everyone in the room broke into the same refrain. "Poor Ella. Poor Ella." What in the world would she do now, with those young children and no father to look after them? "Poor Ella."

"Poor Ella. Where was she? She shouldn't be up there till the very end. Poor Ella. Had she any arrangements made? And the children. Where were they? They ought to be taken to a neighbour's, otherwise they'd be under everyone's feet!"

Everyone was aware of things to be done, and eager to undertake those tasks. No one could be expected to remain shut up in a small front parlour, when now, all over the house, in the kitchen and in the passages, there were people running back and forth, and running up and down the stairs, and people dragging articles of furniture across the floors. For the suspense was over. Oliver was sinking fast. The death rattle had been heard in his throat. Not a minute was to be wasted if everything was to be ready when death imposed a final and absolute decorum. Dolly, certainly, could not sit in the parlour a minute longer. She got up and ran out.

Hallie found herself alone at last. She had no urge to join in the tumult. Looking around her, she began indifferently to gather up cups and saucers and pile them on a tray, but she left the tray down on a side-table inside the door and sat down again, herself, by the dying fire. Poor Ella. It was strange to think that all three of them – Dolly, Ella and herself – had been left alone within so short a time. Dominie was only seven years dead – Sam less than a year. And now Oliver. She sighed. In various ways all three of them had been preyed upon by the years that once, far off on the horizon, had appeared like beautiful birds of paradise, laden with sweetness. The tears came into her eyes. She had been the first to feel Time's bitter beak and claw. She had been torn apart even before Dominie died. And, after he died, it was still a long time before the others suffered anything like what she had gone through.

But now they were all three alike again in their grief and loss as they
had once been alike in their hopes and dreams. Never, never would
she have admitted it before, but now she faced it, that in her heart
she had always resented the happiness the other two had known,
and she had missed. And that was why when she and Dolly talked about
their girlhood, it had secretly made her heart ache to think of Ella, snug
and warm between the four walls of her home, occupying herself by
attending to the needs of her children, and satisfying the demands
made on her by Oliver, her husband.

Oliver's demands upon Ella had always been very obvious. Whenever Hallie met her she was never able to stop and talk to them for
more than a minute or two. "I must get back. I have to iron Oliver's
shirt!" she'd say. Or some such nonsense. Even after Mass on Sundays he'd be waiting impatiently for her outside the chapel gate, and
she'd be in a hurry to join him. "I must fly," she'd say. "I mustn't
keep him waiting."

But now Ella too would be lonely. Now she would be glad enough
to go out walking with Dolly and herself of an evening. And whereas
she used to put the present before the past, now she too would begin
to put the past before the present. She would be willing and even
eager to talk about when they were young. Those golden days. That
leafy springtime.

For a moment as Hallie sat there in the stuffy parlour it seemed to
her that the leafy boughs of youth and springtime were about to form
a bower about her, when, abruptly she was recalled to her whereabouts
by a piercing scream. Oliver was gone!

Poor Ella. It was all over.

The next minute there were voices in the passage, among which
Hallie distinguished the voice of Dolly, who had clearly taken command.

"Bring her into the parlour," Dolly was saying. "And keep her
there." Then the door opened and Dolly and Ella's mother appeared
in the doorway with Ella between them. Ella was struggling to free
herself, but over her head the others spoke authoritatively to each
other – entirely disregarding her. "Keep her in here," Dolly ordered.
"Don't let her upstairs again. It's no place for her now. Is there any
brandy in the house? She should be given a sip of it, whether she likes
it or not."

Hallie stood up. She was dazed and disconcerted. And indeed

Dolly herself, who thought they were showing Ella into an empty room, was just as taken aback. "Oh, are you here?" she said, surprised.

But to Ella it seemed the most natural thing in the world to see Hallie standing there.

"Oh Hallie!" she cried, and where until then she had hung back protesting she now rushed forward and threw out her arms. "Oh Hallie! He's dead. Oliver is dead. He's gone from me."

Hallie came to life at that, and her arms flew out to enlace with Ella's. This was how they had always flung themselves upon each other in their tempests of girlish grief.

"Oh Hallie, Hallie, what will I do?" Ella cried, as she clung to her. And where she had been deaf to the others, she seemed willing and eager to listen to Hallie. Behind Ella's back Dolly made signs to Hallie. "See if you can calm her," she said out loud, feeling justified perhaps in disregarding Ella since Ella had buried her face in Hallie's bosom.

Hallie realized she was the centre of attention. They were all waiting for her to sepak. And after a minute, Ella, too, raised her head and looked up at her with swollen eyes.

"Oh, Hallie, Hallie! What will become of me? How will I live without him?" she cried.

All at once Hallie knew what to say. "Oh Ellie darling," she cried and she pressed her close. "Hush – hush. Time heals everything." Then her voice grew softer and more persuasive. "While you were all upstairs," she said, almost crooning the words, "I was sitting here thinking how lovely it would be when you, Dolly and I would be together again like we used to be. Like long ago."

But almost before she finished, Ella broke away from her, and began to scream again and to struggle to get out of the room again. Her mother had to take hold of her and try to pacify her.

"Don't mind her, Ella. She didn't mean it," she said. "She didn't know what she was saying."

What was the matter? What had she said? Hallie looked around for Dolly, but Dolly was staring at her with eyes that would take the heat out of the sun.

"Have you gone out of your mind, Hallie?" Dolly said. Hallie got more confused. "What did I say?" she cried. But Dolly pushed her to one side, and dropping down on her knees she put her arms around

Ella, and whispered something into her ear. Ella stopped screaming at once.

Hallie stared at them. She hadn't heard what Dolly whispered, but her eyes fastened on the hands of her friends, that were tightly clasped. And on their hands she saw their wedding rings. She knew then what Dolly had said.

A Wet Day

"How is your lettuce, ma'am?" asked the old parish priest. "I hear it's been bad everywhere this year." He paused to blow his nose, and then he looked around him. "Slugs!" he said sternly, before going on down the narrow garden path after my aunt. We hadn't room to walk abreast. We went in single file; the three of us. After a minute the old man turned around and looked back again. "Slugs!" he repeated, and it was only the fact that he put the word in the plural that kept me from feeling that this sturdy, blunt old man was calling me names.

"Our lettuce is very good this year, Father. Thank God," my aunt said as all three of us somewhat unconsciously turned down the sodden grass path that led to the kitchen garden. There, however, my aunt took a firm grip of my arm although it meant that both of us would get our ankles wet brushing against the box-hedge that bordered this path.

Father Gogan distrusted students and probably my aunt linked me in case I might take offence at some remark of his, although it is scarcely likely I would have shown my feelings if he did. But my aunt was always nervous when the local clergy called because she and I had had a couple of brisk arguments from time to time about one thing and another, and she was beginning to realize that in my estimate of a man's worth I did not allow much credit for his cloth. I had met some fine men in clerical clothes, but my respect for them had nothing to do with their calling. My aunt, however, had no use for my views on some subjects, sometimes going so far as to say she doubted the wisdom of my parents in sending me to the University at all. She maintained that it was there I got so many of the ideas she distrusted, although when she wasn't too angry to listen to me she'd keep interrupting so much she couldn't have heard more than half of what I said at any time. Cheap anti-clericalism – that was the phrase she most frequently used to batter her way through my arguments. Yet I believe that secretly she enjoyed our verbal battles and that they made

133

her feel she was fighting for the Faith. I could understand, of course, that she might not care to have outsiders hear my views. She certainly lived in mortal fear of my offending our old parish priest. That day in the garden, she wanted me close to her so she could squeeze my arm or nudge me, if I said anything out of place.

Just inside the kitchen garden there was a ramshackle fuchsia bush that hung out in an unruly way over the path and, since there had been a shower earlier, the bush was heavy with raindrops which sprinkled us all over as we passed.

"You ought to clip back that bush, ma'am," said the old priest. "Nothing can give a person a cold as quick as a wetting."

"I know that, Father," said my aunt deferentially, but she glanced at the fuchsia. "It looks pretty though, don't you think, when it's left untrimmed – so shaggy and unpretentious? On a sunny day I mean," she added hastily.

"On a sunny day!" The old man raised his eyebrows. "And when do we get a sunny day in this country I'd like to know? As far as I can see it's nothing but rain, rain, rain." While he was speaking he was angrily striking the bush with his umbrella and knocking the raindrops off it, and we knew that his thoughts were back in the days before his ordination – and before he got diabetes – when he hurried along the sun-blistered streets in Rome, wiping the sweat from his red young face.

He often told us stories about those days in Italy and those stories always had a glow of sunlight in them, that made up for the absence of humour. Listening to him we thought involuntarily of hot city pavements lined with barrows of melons and pawpaws and vegetable marrows – huge, waxy growths of red and yellow. We could imagine the young priest from Ireland in his black alpaca laying his hands on them, and smiling to find them warm, where at home they would be chill to the touch, with a mist of moisture on them.

It was extraordinary the way we thought of his youth every time we saw the old priest, because it was forty-five years – at the very least – since Father Gogan had last knelt to the Pope in Rome. And out of those forty-five years we ourselves had only known him for ten – the last ten – during which time he had been ailing. His duties as a parish priest put a great strain on him.

Father Gogan felt the cold intensely, and although his face was rosy-appled over with broken veins, it always looked blue and chilly. He looked particularly miserable on Sundays when, in his bleak, concrete church, he went through Mass perfunctorily, and gave out a hard dry sermon, his blackened silver watch in his hand, and his eye darting from one side of the church to the other according to wherever a cough or a sneeze escaped some incautious person. There was always some member of the congregation coughing or sneezing. Father Gogan used to say that he would like to preach a sermon one day on hygiene. He'd like to tell his people to cover their mouths when they sneezed and teach them to use their hankies properly and not to wave them about like flags – spreading germs. And he'd like to tell people who came in late to close the chapel door after them and not hold it open for someone behind them who was maybe still only half-way up the path. Next to a wetting, he maintained, false politeness was the cause of more colds being contracted than anyone realized. But he supposed sermons of this kind would be above the heads of his parishioners, and so when someone coughed he had to content himself with stopping in the middle of a sentence and staring at the offender, although the latter usually thought the old man was annoyed at the interruption. As if anything could interrupt the perfect machinery of Father Gogan's sentences. They ran smoothly in the tracks they had cut for themselves forty years before, when he was a careful curate, and had prepared his sermons beforehand with pen and paper.

It was remarkable the way he could pause and glare around the church – or even take out his handkerchief and blow his nose for a considerable time – before he finished a sentence, yet always go on at the exact place where he stopped, and never repeat as much as a preposition of what he had already said.

Once in a while in his sermons he'd drop a hint about the damp of the church, no doubt hoping that some confraternity would get up a subscription for the installation of a heating apparatus. The pious souls of our parish, however, thought that the cold of the chapel and the draught that came in under the badly hung door and, yes, even the splinter you might get in the knee when genuflecting on the bare boards of the floor, were all additional earthly endurances that enhanced the beauty of their souls in the eyes of the Lord. The last thing that would have occurred to them would have been to introduce any form of bodily comfort into the damp old church, although large subscriptions were raised every year for sodality banners, altar linen, vestments and new surplices for the altar boys, in spite of the fact that these things got discoloured and mildewed almost overnight in the damp, airless sacristy.

"It's a pity, you know," Father Gogan said one day, "that we Irish make no effort to counteract our climate. It's the dampest climate in the world. Damp. Damp. Damp. A most unhealthy climate to have to live in!" It was probably his constant talk about his health made my aunt feel great sympathy for him – trapped in a land where the days were mainly sunless and the nights seldom without frost. She often looked up at the sky and sighed.

"It looks like rain," she'd say. "Poor Father Gogan. This kind of weather is very injurious to him."

When the old priest came to call the conversation always centred on galoshes and leaking roofs and the advisability of wool next the skin. But my aunt's sympathy for him might not have exceeded mine were it not that she deliberately exploited the old man's frailty to gain merit in my eyes for his calling.

"The man is a martyr!" she'd say sometimes in the middle of lunch, almost taking the good for me out of our own well-cooked food. "Can you imagine having nothing for your meal but a soup-plate of cabbage?"

"Or rhubarb," I'd say with a shudder, because I did, at times, feel sorry for the old man.

"Rhubarb is not so bad," my aunt would say. She was inclined to be a bit vague at mealtimes, concentrating on pouring the melted butter over her fish, without letting it drip on the linen table mat, or some such occupation.

"Without sugar?" I'd say.

"Oh? Does he have to take it without sugar? Even rhubarb? Are your sure?"

"Of course I'm sure." And I'd feel obliged to remind her that he couldn't eat peas, or beans either. She tended to forget.

"You don't tell me! I thought he could eat any vegetable at all as long as it was a vegetable." And while I'd be explaining the difference between pulses and greens she would listen attentively enough. On these occasions I think she was quite pleased that I was going to the University and acquiring such general knowledge. But it distressed her to talk too much on the subject.

"Poor Father Gogan," she'd sigh. "How the rest of us can expect to reach heaven is more than I know." But here she might interrupt herself to lean back in her chair and call to Ellen, the parlour-maid, who would be standing discreetly behind the service screen waiting to change our plates, and ask if something – the cheese *soufflé* perhaps or the *soupe à l'oignon* – had gone back to the kitchen yet, because if not she might take a spoonful – just a spoonful. Then as she'd scrape the sides of the silver dish she might glance at me for a second and give me her undivided attention to ask if I was sure – absolutely sure – I, too, wouldn't have another spoonful? And when we'd get up from the table she'd never fail to send a message to the kitchen. "My compliments to the cook!" she would say devoutly.

If, however, after a conversation like that, the old parish priest happened to call, when we'd go out to the garden with him my aunt would urgently press him to take more and more lettuce, and more and more spinach and broccoli – even more sea-kale and asparagus – as a change from what he called the Eternal Cabbage. He could have had cabbage galore from us, of course, but he was supplied with that from every plot in the parish. It was on my aunt he counted to keep him supplied with vegetables more difficult of culture.

On the afternoon when he showed such solicitude for our lettuce the weather was at its dirtiest. And surely of all places on earth to feel the dismay of rain, a garden is the worst? The asters alone would depress the most steadfast soul, logged down to the ground, their shaggy petals splattered with mud. And as we went slowly along the path, printing it with our footsteps, we left in our wake great heaps of vegetables to be collected by Mike the gardener and put into the priest's car.

Mike the gardener was very fond of Father Gogan, and when the old man came to visit us he and Mike always had a chat.

"We must keep the old machine going, Mike. Isn't that right?" Father Gogan would invariably say.

"That's right, Father," Mike invariably answered. "Mind your health. It's the only thing that will stand to you at the finish."

"Perhaps you'd better throw a few more lettuces into the car, Mike?" Father Gogan might say then as an afterthought. And occasionally he might flatter Mike by asking his advice about the cooking or the preparation of a vegetable – a matter which I could see my aunt felt was not strictly speaking within the province of a gardener.

"While I think of it, Mike, may I ask you a question?" Father Gogan would say.

"Certainly, Father. Anything at all I can tell you!"

"It's about lettuce. Is there any way you'd recommend for keeping it fresh? My housekeeper says it ought to be kept air-tight, but it seems to me that dries it up. I have heard other people say you should put it in water, but when that is done it gets yellow and flabby. I thought maybe that you might have some knack for keeping it fresh?"

"I can't say I have, Father," Mike would reply. "But why do you bother trying to keep it fresh? Can't you always get a fresh bit from us here any time you want? There's always plenty. And you're always welcome to it."

Mike would speak from the bounty of his own heart, but he would look over the priest's shoulder as he spoke, and raise his voice so my aunt would hear. On these occasions she would give a nod of approval, and this nod was never lost on Father Gogan.

"You're working for a kind woman, Mike. There aren't many like her nowadays. She spoils us all. She spoils us all." But on this particular day I am speaking about he gave a sigh. "I suppose it's not right for me to let her spoil me though? Eh, Mike?"

"Ah! Why wouldn't she spoil you, Father? You of all people," said Mike. "Sure she loves giving you the few poor vegetables!"

"She does indeed. I know that, Mike. She does. Ah, isn't it grand the way Irish women treat their clergy?"

"And why wouldn't they treat them well, Father?" Mike cried indignantly. "Where would we be only for the priests?"

"You're right, of course, Mike," said the priest, but a little cloud came over his face. "Do you know, Mike, sometimes, all the same, I say to myself that I shouldn't be taking such care of myself – an old man like me. I'll sit down and eat a bit of steak tonight – I say to myself, what harm if it kills me? Amn't I near the end anyway? But then again I say to myself that it's everyone's duty to guard the bit of life that's left to them, no matter what happens, and to keep it from giving out till the very last minute."

At this Mike threw up his hands. "You've no call to talk of dying, Father. I never saw you looking better."

"Come, come, none of your flattery now, Mike," said the old priest, neatly rounding off the conversation. Turning then, he left the greenhouse and joined my aunt and myself who were waiting for him at a discreet distance – my aunt feeling that the old priest was in some way fulfilling his pastoral duty by these chats with Mike.

"Let him have his few words with Mike," she'd whisper to me, as she busied herself flicking slugs off the lettuce with an elegant fore-finger.

Father Gogan's conversations with Mike all had a remarkable similarity. Nevertheless, when he joined us the old priest repeated the conversation verbatim.

"Mike says it's up to all of us to keep going till the very last minute," he said, and he looked to my aunt for confirmation of this.

"Mike's right, Father," my aunt pronounced readily. "I've always heard it said we should try to tend our little flame of life to the end."

"I suppose so. I suppose so," the old man agreed happily, and we were about to move towards the drive where he'd left his car when suddenly he turned around and without a word of apology to us he bolted back into the greenhouse.

"Aren't you from somewhere around Mullingar, Mike?" we heard him ask.

"I'm from three miles the other side, Father."

"I thought that, mind you! Tell me – did you know a young farmer there by the name of Molloy?"

"I did, Father. I knew a young man by that name. A fine strong fellow, if I remember rightly."

"A big broad-shouldered fellow?"

"With reddish hair?"

"Red hair would be right."

"About twenty-five years of age?"

"That'd be him for sure," said Mike.

"Yes, that would be him all right," Father Gogan said, and we heard him give a deep sigh. "Well I hear he's dead, Mike," he said, shaking his head.

"You don't say?" Mike seemed shocked but in deference to Father Gogan he summoned up a rough and ready philosophy. "It just shows you can never tell the day nor the hour! Isn't that so, Father?"

Father Gogan gave another sigh, but this time it was a sigh in approval of Mike's sentiments and then he stepped out of the green-house and joined us again on the wet gravel.

"Forgive me, Father, but I overheard you talking to Mike," my aunt said solicitously. "You mentioned some young man who died. I hope he wasn't a relative of yours?" Her face was full of concern.

"No," said Father Gogan. "No. But it was a sad case." He shook

his head again and for a moment he looked doleful. Then he became
more cheerful. "Do you know something?" he said. "I'm a lucky man
that it's not me that is under the sod this minute, instead of that young
man."

"God between us and all harm!" my aunt cried. "Tell us about it,
quick!"

"I suppose you often heard me speak of my niece Lottie?" Father
Gogan said. "She's my sister's daughter, you know, and she comes
to see me once in a while. Every six months or so. She's a nurse up
in Dublin. Well, anyway, to tell you about the young fellow that's
dead – this Lottie got engaged to him a few weeks back. They were
planning on getting married next month. And now he's dead."

"Oh how tragic!" my aunt cried.

"Yes. Wait till you hear!" said the old man, looking back to make
sure that Mike was bringing out the trug of vegetables to the car. "As
I was saying," he continued. "They were planning on getting married
next month, and nothing would do Lottie but that I'd meet the young
man before the wedding. She wrote to say she was bringing him down
to see me. I suppose she had an eye to the wedding present, you know,
but however about that, I was expecting them last Thursday, and I
told my housekeeper to fix up a bit of dinner for them. I told her to
get a bit of meat and the like, as well as the dirty old cabbage and
rhubarb I have to eat myself. I told her to think up a bit of a sweet
for them too. She's a good cook, you know. Not that her cooking gets
any great strain put on it by me in the state of health I'm in lately!
But anyway – last Thursday she put together a nice meal. The smell
of it nearly drove me out of the house." Here the old man sighed
deeply. "And next morning when I saw her throwing it into the pigs'
bucket I could have cried. I could. That's a fact."

"Did they not come?" my aunt cried. And that was what I thought
as well.

"They came all right, but wait till you hear," said the priest. "It
appears the young fellow had a cold coming on, and driving down in
the car he must have got an added chill, because when they drew up
at the door of the parochial house the poor fellow was hardly able
to speak. And small wonder. The car was a ramshackle affair. I
wouldn't like to have gone down the drive in it, much less the journey
they had made. The niece was very upset. She was fussing over him
like as if they were married for years. Tea she wanted for him, if you

please! And right away – in spite of the fact that the dinner was about to be dished up in a minute.

" 'Don't mind about dinner,' said Lottie. 'He couldn't look at food anyway. Have you got a cushion?' A cushion if you please! 'Get him a pillow so, if you haven't any cushions!' she said, turning to my housekeeper – a woman who isn't used to taking orders, I can tell you – and pushing her out of the way she went over to the sideboard. 'Is there a drop of whisky here,' she said, 'or where will I look for some? I want to rub it on his chest.'

"By this time, ma'am, you can imagine – I was pretty well sick of her fussing – and I gave it as my opinion that the best thing she could do would be to take the young man back to Dublin as quick as possible where he could be given proper attention. But do you know what she said? 'What about the drive back?' That's what she said. And I saw in a flash what was in the back of her mind.

" 'The harm is done now,' I said. 'Another hour or so won't make any difference. A strange bed might be the death of him. Wrap him up warm,' I said. 'I'll lend you my overcoat.' It was my big frieze coat, ma'am, you know the one – I've had it a long time and it was getting a bit small for me – it's a good warm coat all the same. But Lottie was always one to fidget and fret. She said she didn't know what was the best thing to do. By this time I was getting very uneasy, I need not tell you. What on earth would I have done if she'd insisted on them staying? The whole house would have been upset. There's only one hot jar and that's mine. And where would I get blankets enough to cover a big fellow like that? To say nothing of the fact there's no one but the one woman to do everything and she with her hands full looking after me. And another thing! I could never have stood the excitement. There'd be talking till all hours. The doctor would have to be got and who knows but he might have to be given a meal too. Oh, I could foresee it all! I could foresee it all! I have to be careful at my age, you know. I have to have everything regular. I have to have peace and quiet. 'Lottie,' I said, 'if you know what is right, you'll take that man back where he came from this minute and get good medical care for him,' and as I was saying it, I was thinking to myself that if anyone knew what was right and what was wrong it ought to be her, with her hospital training. And sure enough there were no flies on her.

" 'I'll tell you what I'll do,' she said. 'I'll take his temperature, and

if he has no temperature I'll bring him back to the city and telephone
to the hospital. Of course, if he has a temperature it would be madness
to undertake the journey, but I suppose the doctor here is passable?'
While she was talking she was pulling out the drawers of my desk –
looking for the thermometer, you see – 'Where do you keep it?' she
said, turning round to me.

" 'I haven't one,' I said, catching on again quick to what was at the
back of her mind. She wasn't listening to me though.

" 'His forehead is very hot,' she said.

" 'Why wouldn't it be,' said I, 'with your hand on it?' I was making
a sort of a joke, you understand, but she didn't see the joke. The poor
fellow himself, sick as he was, saw it, and he gave a bit of a smile,
but it was a very weak and watery smile. He was very sick, I could see
that. Lottie all this time was rummaging through my few poor
belongings.

" 'Where did you say the thermometer was?' Lottie asked again.

" 'I haven't got such a thing,' I said. And, do you know, ma'am,
she was so shocked she could hardly speak.

" 'Every house should have a thermometer,' she said. 'It's a downright shame not to have one.' Then while she was giving out to me she
began to gather up rugs and pillows. 'As long as you haven't one, I
suppose I'd better not waste any more time but start getting him back
to the city.' She went over to the poor fellow. 'Do you feel able for the
journey back?' she asked, putting her hand on his forehead and frowning.

" 'I'm all right,' he said, not wanting to cause any commotion.
He was a nice lad. Very different from her altogether, I can tell
you.

" 'We'll come down another day, Uncle,' Lottie said then. 'I hope
you hadn't made a lot of preparations for us?' As if it wasn't a bit late
in the day to be thinking of that!

" 'I'll make greater preparations next time,' I said, not meaning it,
I assure you, but just to try and cheer up the poor fellow – he looked
so bad. She was wrapping him up in rugs and blankets and putting
him in the back of the car. I'd like to think I did cheer him up, because
I had a kind of a feeling that he knew he was worse than she thought
he was.

" 'I'll send you down a thermometer,' she shouted back at me as
they drove off down the drive. 'No one should be without one.' "

"That was true for her," my aunt interposed impulsively at this point, and I could see she was wondering if we ourselves had one to spare that she could give to him.

"I know that, ma'am," said the priest, "but all I can say is I hope she won't send one. You don't think a man like me would be without such a necessary thing, do you?" He looked at her sternly.

"Don't tell me you had one all the time?" my aunt said and I'll say this for her – she said it very falteringly.

"Three!" said the old priest. "I had three of them, no less, but I wasn't going to let on to her that I had. Not that *I* needed a thermometer to know how bad he was. I could tell by the feel of the young fellow's hand that he had a temperature! But I wasn't going to let myself in for having him laid up in the presbytery for a couple of weeks, as he would have been, you know, with pneumonia."

"Pneumonia!"

"That's right, ma'am. Pneumonia. Double pneumonia, I should say. He was dead the following Sunday. I was very sorry for the poor fellow. A nice lad. I repeat that. But I can't say that I was so sorry for my niece. It was very inconsiderate of her, as I think you will agree, ma'am, to come on a visit to anyone, bringing along a man that wasn't able to stand on his feet with a cold? People nowadays have no consideration. That's the long and the short of it: no consideration. After they drove away I sent down to the chemist's and got a bottle of disinfectant sent up and I sprinkled it all over the house. You can't afford to take risks. And even with all the precautions I took I still consider I am a very lucky man to be alive today. A man in my state of health could have been gone in the twinkling of an eye if burdened with a young fellow like that in the house, for maybe a month. And he might have died in any case – even without the journey back. Then think of the fuss! I'd have been put down in the grave along with him. There is no doubt in my mind whatsoever on that score."

Just then, however, there was a step on the gravel behind us. "Ah, here is Mike with my vegetables," he said. "Put the lettuce on the front seat, Mike, I don't want it crushed. Eat plenty of lettuce the doctor says to me at every visit!" Then the old man shook hands with us and got into his car. "I'm getting too old to be gadding about in a car," he said, smiling out the window at us, before he swung the car around and went off down the drive at a good lick.

My aunt and I looked at each other but for my part I thought the least said the better. "I'll go for a walk I think," I said. "I'll be back in time for dinner."

And when I came back from the walk I had temporarily forgotten about the incident. The air was very fresh after the recent rain, and a person would be apt to forget anything walking along a country road, listening to the birds: they'd tuned up again when they found the sky once more blue and clear. And when I came back I was hungry. I was looking forward to my dinner. When Ellen came in with a bowl of salad I hoped my aunt would not take too big a helping because I felt I could eat the whole bowlful. But what do you think? Before the girl had time to set the bowl before us my aunt rapped on the table.

"Take away that lettuce," she said. "We don't want any tonight."

I was going to protest when I caught her eye and held my tongue. We didn't mention Father Gogan or the big red-haired farmer from Mullingar – either then or since – but isn't it a funny thing, I have been on better terms with my aunt since that day. We get on better. And we have less fights about books and politics and one thing and another.

Brigid

The rain came sifting through the air, and settled like a bloom on the fields. But under the trees it fell in single heavy drops, noisily, like cabbage water running through the holes of a colander.

The house was in the middle of the trees.

"Listen to that rain!" the woman said to her husband. "Will it never stop?"

"What harm is a sup of rain?" he said.

"That's you all over again. What harm is anything as long as it doesn't affect yourself?"

"How do you mean, when it doesn't affect me? Look at my feet. They're sopping. And look at my hat. It's soused." He took the hat off, and shook the rain from it on to the spitting bars of the grate.

"Quit that," said the woman. "Can't you see you're raising ashes?"

"What harm is ashes?"

"I'll show you what harm," she said, taking down a plate of cabbage and potato from the shelf over the fire. "There's your dinner destroyed with them." The yellow cabbage was lightly sprayed with ash.

"Ashes is healthy, I often heard that said. Put it here!" He sat down at the table, taking up his knife and fork, and indicating where the plate was to be put by tapping the table with the handle of the knife. "Is there no bit of meat?" he asked, prodding the potato critically.

"There's plenty in the town, I suppose."

"In the town? And why didn't somebody go to the town, might I ask?"

"Who was there to go? You know as well as I do there's no one here to be traipsing in and out of the town every time there's something wanted."

"I suppose one of our fine daughters would think it the end of the world if she was asked to go for a bit of a message? Let me tell you they'd get husbands for themselves quicker if they were seen doing a bit of work once in a while."

"Who said anything about getting husbands for them?" said the woman. "They're time enough getting married."

"Is that so? Mind you now, anyone would think that you were anxious to get them off your hands with the way every penny that comes into the house goes out again on bits of silks and ribbons for them."

"I'm not going to let them be without their bit of fun just because you have other uses for your money than spending it on your own children!"

"What other uses have I? Do I smoke? Do I drink? Do I play cards?"

"You know what I mean."

"I suppose I do." The man left down his fork. "I suppose you're hinting at poor Brigid again?" he said. "But I told you forty times, if she was put into a home she'd be just as much of an expense to us as she is in the little house above there." He pointed out of the window with his fork.

"I see there's no use talking about it," said the woman. "All I can say is God help the girls, with you, their own father, putting a drag on them so that no man will have anything to do with them after hearing about Brigid."

"What do you mean by that? That is something new. I thought it was only the bit of bread and tea she got that you grudged the poor thing. This is something else. What is this?"

"You oughtn't to need to be told, a man like you that saw the world, a man that travelled like you did, a man that was in England and London."

"I don't know what you're talking about." He took up his hat and felt it to see if the side he had placed near the fire was dry. He turned the other side toward the heat. "What are you trying to say?" he said. "Speak plain!"

"Is any man going to marry a girl when he hears her aunt is a poor half-witted creature, soft in the head, and living in a poke of a hut, doing nothing all day but sitting looking into the fire?"

"What has that got to do with anybody but the poor creature herself? Isn't it her own trouble?"

"Men don't like marrying into a family that has the like of her in it."

"Is that so? I didn't notice that you were put off marrying me, and you knew all about poor Brigid. You used to bring her bunches

of primroses. And one day I remember you pulling the flowers off
your hat and giving them to her when she started crying over nothing.
You used to say she was a poor harmless thing. You used to say
you'd look after her."

"And didn't I? Nobody can say I didn't look after her. Didn't I do
my best to have her taken into a home, where she'd get proper care?
You can't deny that."

"I'm not denying it. You never gave me peace or ease about it
since the day we were married. But I wouldn't give in. I wouldn't
give in then, and I won't give in now, either. I won't let it be said
that I had hand or part in letting my own sister be put away."

"But it's for her own good." This time the woman's voice was
softer and she went over and turned the wet hat again on the fender.
"It's nearly dry," she said, and she went back to the table and took
up the plate from which he had eaten and began to wash it in a basin of
water at the other end of the table. "It's for her own good. I'm
surprised you can't see that, you, a sensible man, with two grown-up
daughters. You'll be sorry one of these days when she's found dead
in the chair – the Lord between us and all harm – or falls in the fire
and gets scorched to death – God preserve us from the like! I was
reading only the other day in a paper that came round something
from the shop, that there was a case like that up in the Midlands."

"I don't want to hear about it," said the man, shuffling his feet.
"The hat is dry, I think," he said, and he put it on his head and stood
up.

"That's the way you always go on. You don't want to listen to
anything unpleasant. You don't want to listen to anything that's right.
You don't want to listen because you know what I'm saying is true
and you know you have no answer to it."

"You make me tired," said the man. "It's always the one story in
this house. Why don't you get something else to talk about for a
change?"

The woman ran to the door and blocked his way.

"Is that your last word?" she said. "You won't give in?"

"I won't give in. Poor Brigid. Didn't my mother make me promise
I'd never have hand or part in putting the poor creature away? 'Leave
her alone,' my mother used to say, 'she's doing no harm to anyone.' "

"She's doing harm to our daughters," said the woman, "and you know that. Don't you?" She caught his coat and stared at him. "You know the way Marty Monaghan gave up calling on Rosie after dancing with her every night at the dances in the Town Hall last year. Why did he do that, do you suppose? It's little you know about it at all! You don't see Mamie crying her eyes out some nights after coming in from a walk with the girls and hearing little bits of talk from this one and that one, and putting two and two together, and finding out for herself the talk that goes on among the men about girls and the kind of homes they come from!"

"There'd be a lot more talk if the poor creature was put away. Let me tell you that, if you don't know it for yourself! It's one thing to have a poor creature, doing no one any harm, living quiet, all by herself, up at the end of a boreen where seldom or ever anyone gets a chance of seeing her. It's another thing altogether to have her taken away in a car and everyone running to the window to see the car pass and talking about her and telling stories from one to another till in no time at all they'd be letting on she was twice as bad as she is, and the stories about her would be getting so wild that none of us could go down the streets without being stared at as if we were all queer!"

"You won't give in?" his wife asked once more.

"I won't give in."

"Poor Mamie. Poor Rosie." The woman sighed. She put the plate up on the dresser.

Owen shuffled his feet. "If you didn't let it be seen so plain that you wanted to get them married, they might have a better chance. I don't know what they want getting married for, in any case. They'd be better off to be interested in this place, and raise a few hens, and make a bit of money for themselves, so they could be independent and take no notice of people and their gossip!"

"It's little you know about anything; that's all I have to say," said the woman.

Owen moved to the door.

"Where are you going now?"

"There's no use in my telling you and drawing down another stream of abuse on myself when I mention the poor creature's name."

The woman sighed and walked over to the fire.

"If that's where you're going you might as well take over these clean sheets." She took down a pair of sheets from where they were airing on the shelf over the fire. "You can't say but I look after her, no matter what," she said.

"If you remembered her the way I do," said the man, "when she was only a little bit of a child, and I was growing up and going to school, you'd know what it feels like to hear talk of putting her in a home. She used to have lovely hair. It was like the flossy heads of the dandelions when they are gone past their best. No one knew she was going to be a bit soft until she was toddling around and beginning to talk, and even then it was thought she was only slow; that she'd grow out of it."

"I know how you feel," said the woman. "I could cry sometimes myself when I think about her. But she'd be happy enough in a home. We could visit her any time we wanted. We could hire a car and drive over to see her, all of us, on a fine Sunday now and again. It would be some place to go. And it would cost no more than it costs to keep her here."

She didn't know whether he had heard the end of the sentence or not because he had gone out through the yard and was cutting across the field, with his ash plant in his hand.

"He was cutting across the field with the ash plant in his hand, when we were starting off on our walk," said Rosie, when she and Mamie came in to their supper, and their mother asked if they had seen their father out in the yard.

"He was going up to your Aunt Brigid then," said their mother. "Did you not see him after that?"

"That was three hours ago," Mamie said, looking worried. "He wouldn't be over there all this time, would he? He must be doing something for Aunt Brigid – chopping wood or mending something. He wouldn't be just sitting there all this time."

"Ah, you wouldn't know what he'd be doing," the mother said, and the girls looked at each other. They knew then there had been words between their father and mother while they were out.

"Maybe one of you ought to run over and see what's keeping him?" said their mother.

"Oh, leave him alone," Mamie said. "If he wants to stay over there, let him! He'll have to be home soon anyway to put in the calves. It's nearly dark."

But soon it was dark – very dark – and the calves were still out.

The girls had gone out again to a dance, and it was beginning to rain when Owen's wife put on her coat and went across the field herself, and up the boreen to Brigid's.

How can she sit there in the dark? she thought, when she didn't see a light in the window. But as she got nearer she saw there was a faint glow from the fire on the hearth. She felt sure Owen wasn't there. He wouldn't be there without lighting a lamp, or a bit of a candle! There was no need to go in. She was going to turn back, but it seemed an unnatural thing not to call to the door and see if the poor creature was all right.

Brigid was the same as ever, sitting by the fire with a silly smile, and not looking up till she was called three or four times.

"Brigid, did you see Owen?" his wife asked without much hope of a reply.

Brigid looked up. "Owen is a queer man," she said. That was all the answer she gave.

"So he was here! What time did he leave?"

Brigid grumbled something.

"What are you saying, Brigid?"

"He wouldn't go home," Brigid said. "I told him it was time to go home for his tea, but he wouldn't answer me. 'Go home,' I said, 'go home, Owen.' "

"When did he go? What time was it? Did you notice?"

Brigid could be difficult sometimes. Was she going to be difficult now?

"He wouldn't go home," Brigid said again.

Suddenly Owen's wife saw his ash plant lying on the table.

"Is he still here?" she asked sharply, and she glanced back at the door. "I didn't see him in the yard I didn't hear him."

"He wouldn't speak to me," Brigid said again stubbornly.

The other woman couldn't see her in the dark. The fire was flickering too irregularly to see by its light.

"But where is he? Is there anything the matter with him?" She ran back to the door and called out into the dark. But there was no answer. She stood there trying to think. She heard Brigid talking to herself, but she didn't trouble to listen. She might as well go home, she thought. Wherever he was, he wasn't here. "If he comes back, Brigid, tell him I was looking for him," she said. "I'll go home through the other field."

Brigid said something then that made her turn sharply and look at her.

"What did you say?" she said.

"I said to tell him yourself," Brigid muttered. Then she seemed to be talking to herself again, leaning forward towards the fire. "Why don't you talk?" she said. "Why don't you talk?" Owen's wife began to pull out the old settle bed that was in front of the fire not knowing why she did it, but she could feel the blood pounding in her ears and behind her eyes. "He fell down there and he wouldn't get up!" Brigid said. "I told him to get up. I told him that his head was getting scorched. But he wouldn't listen to me. He wouldn't get up. He wouldn't do anything."

Owen's wife closed her eyes. All of a sudden she was afraid to look. But when she did look, Owen's eyes were staring up at her, wide open, from where he lay on his back on the hearth.

"Owen!" she screamed, and she tried to pull him up.

His shoulders were stiff and heavy. She caught his hands. They were cold. She felt his face. But his face was hot, so hot she couldn't put her hand on it. She started back. God! Was he dead? If he was dead wouldn't he be cold? She wanted to scream and run out of the house, but first she tried to drag him as far as she could from the ashy hearth. Then suddenly feeling the living eyes of Brigid watching her, and seeing the dead eyes staring up from the blistered red face, she sprang up, knocking over a chair, and ran screaming out of the house and down the boreen.

Her screams brought people running out to their doors, the light streaming out each side of them. She couldn't speak but she pointed up the hill and ran on. She wanted to get to the pump.

It was dark at the pump, but she could hear people running the way she had pointed. Then when they had reached the cottage, there was no more running, but great talking and shouting. There was a smell off her hands and desperately she bent forward and began to wash them under the pump. But when she saw there was hair stuck to her fingers she wanted to scream again, only now there was a great pain gathering in her heart, not yet the pain of loss, but the pain of having failed; failed in some terrible way.

I failed him always, she thought, from the very start. I never loved him like he loved me; not even then, long ago, the time I took the flowers off my hat. It wasn't for Brigid, like he thought. I was only making myself out to be what he imagined I was. I didn't know enough about loving to change myself for him. I didn't know enough about it even to keep the love in him for me. He had to give it all to Brigid in the end.

He gave it all to Brigid, to a poor daft thing that didn't know enough to pull him back from the fire or call someone, when he fell down in a stroke. If it was anyone else was with him, he might have had a chance.

Oh, how had it happened? How could love be wasted, and go to loss like that? That was the way the tossy balls of cowslips they used to make as children were forgotten and left behind in the fields, to be trodden into the muck by the cattle and the sheep.

Suddenly she thought of the heavy feet of the neighbours tramping the boards of the cottage up in the fields behind her, and rising, she ran back up the boreen.

"Here's the poor woman now," someone said, as she thrust past the crowd around the door.

They began to make a way for her to where, on the settle bed they had laid her husband. But instead she parted a way through the people and went toward the door of the room off the kitchen.

"It's Brigid I'm thinking about," she said. "Where is she?"

"Something will have to be done about her now all right," someone said.

"It will," she said decisively, and her voice was as true as a bell. She had reached the door of the room. "That's why I came back," she said, looking around her defiantly. "She'll need proper minding now. To think she hadn't the strength to run for help, or pull him back a bit from the fire." She opened a door.

Sitting on the side of the bed, all alone, she saw Brigid.

"Get your hat and coat, Brigid," she said. "You're coming home with me."

The Small Bequest

It was generally understood that when Miss Tate died she would leave a small bequest to her companion, Miss Blodgett. There had never been any direct statement of the old lady's intention in the matter, but it was felt by their friends to be an understood thing. Meanwhile, of course, Miss Blodgett was getting an excellent salary, most of which she should have been able to put aside, because not only was her keep provided but, as well as sharing the necessaries of life with Miss Tate, she had full enjoyment of all the luxuries that the Tate family were continually bestowing upon the old lady: the sweets, the fruits, the magazines, the books. For Miss Tate, at eighty, was able only to appreciate the thought of the giver: the bodily appreciation of the gifts fell entirely to Miss Blodgett. As she herself often remarked, Miss Blodgett was just like one of the family. And indeed it was as such Miss Blodgett was always treated.

The Tates felt themselves greatly in Miss Blodgett's debt for her tireless devotion to Aunt Adeline, as Miss Tate was called by her family, young and old alike. It was twenty-seven years since Miss Blodgett had moved into the elegant house in Clyde Road, with her wicker suitcase and her tin trunk, and the Tates didn't know what Miss Adeline Tate would have done without her. Lord Robert, Miss Tate's eldest nephew, expressed the feelings of the whole family one evening after a visit to Clyde Road.

"What a good job it is," Lord Robert said, "that Miss Blodgett is only sixty. She's fairly sure of outlasting Aunt Adeline."

There had been a large family gathering in Clyde Road that afternoon, and some of the family were dining that night with Lord Robert. They all agreed with their host except Honor Tate, his first cousin, who, being a woman barrister, felt compelled to point out that, then, instead of Miss Tate, they would have Miss Blodgett on their hands.

"Oh, not at all!" said Lord Robert impatiently. "Aunt Adeline will see that Miss Blodgett is well taken care of after her death."

"How?" asked Lucy Tate, Lord Robert's youngest daughter.

"Don't be silly, Lucy dear," said her father. "You know it is under-stood that Aunt Adeline has made a substantial mention of Miss Blod-gett in her will."

"Oh, of course," Lucy was abashed. She blushed. "I forgot! The bequest!" She recalled at once that she had often heard her aunts and uncles mention Miss Blodgett's bequest. "Dear Aunt Adeline!" she murmured.

Miss Tate of course was Lucy's grand-aunt and not her aunt, but like all the younger members of the family she had grown into the habit of calling the old lady by the name she'd heard on the lips of her elders. Miss Tate was Aunt Adeline to all the family. None of them ever called her anything else.

It was quite disconcerting at times to hear some of the extremely young members of the family calling the old lady by such a familiar name. But it was even more disconcerting to hear Miss Blodgett calling all the family by their familiar names, although perhaps it was natural enough for her to do so, considering that she had known them all since they were in their cradles, and had dangled most of them on her knee with as much affection, and a great deal more energy, than Miss Tate had ever done. Sometimes, indeed, it seemed as if Emma Blodgett had never noticed that they had grown up, and, in some cases, even grown old. Lord Robert was always Robbie to her. The caustic Honor was still Honey. And I never heard her call Lady Elizabeth Tate-Conyers anything else but Bessie.

The Tates were an old family that went back for nine recorded generations of plain but prosperous people, who had, however, linked themselves all along the way with the best stock in the country. The root was a plain and sturdy natural growth, but successful grafting had resulted in the frequent breaking out of blossom. The family had rarely failed in any decade to show a famous belle, a great soldier, or a poet. When Miss Tate's nephews, nieces, grand-nephews, grand-nieces, and great-grand-nephews came to pay their respects to her on a Sunday afternoon, the drawing-room in Clyde Road was filled with a gallant company, of which the old lady might well be proud.

And Miss Tate was extremely proud of them all. So, too, was Miss Blodgett. Although, here again, when one heard Miss Blodgett familiarly chaffing with judges and peers, and scolding a bishop for having snuff on his cuff, it was a little surprising to recollect that she had originally joined the Tate household in a most humble capacity.

The only trace that still remained to indicate Miss Blodgett's original position in the family was that Miss Blodgett herself was never called by her Christian name. Miss Tate was the only one who called her Emma. The others delicately shrank from doing so in case it might seem to be taking advantage of her dependence. They felt too that this better emphasized the difference between her and Hetty, Miss Tate's old maid-servant. Hetty had been with the family for fifty years. She was a treasure too, but of course she was only a servant.

The first day I moved into the house next door to Miss Tate, I found two visiting cards lying in my empty letter-box. On one glossy white card was engraved the name of Miss Adeline Tate. On the other, which was equally white, if perhaps a little thinner, a little less glossy, the name of Emma Blodgett was printed by hand in pen and ink.

That afternoon I saw Miss Tate in her garden. It was some few days before I saw Miss Blodgett.

As a matter of fact, I was at first under the mistaken impression that I had seen both Miss Tate and Miss Blodgett, for there were two old ladies in the garden, and the two were dressed remarkably alike. Both wore long blue silk gowns, with tightly clipped bodices and hems weighted with rows and rows of braid. Both wore wide and delightfully dilapidated blue straw hats, wreathed – overpowered, you might say – with floppy silk flowers shaded from deep rose to pale pink, which the bees, that clouded around them like haloes, must have mistaken for real blooms. It is true that one of the old ladies was extremely elegant, and that the other was distinctly shabby, her gown having innumerable patches and darns, but nevertheless I think my mistake was pardonable. I ought perhaps to have guessed that the old heiress would give away her worn gowns to her servant, but how on earth could I have known that Miss Tate's fanatical affection for animals, birds, insects, and even slugs, was so great that on no account would she allow Hetty to come out into the garden in her cap and apron in case their white glare might startle them? Her beloved pets, the lapdogs, the tabby cats, and countless tame pigeons, wandered about the garden with as much composure as the ladies. Within-doors it was different. Then, with her blue gown hidden under an old-fashioned capacious apron, I would never have mistaken poor old Hetty for Miss Blodgett. Indeed, no two people could have been more dissimilar in many ways, although as a matter of fact in physique Hetty and Miss Tate were not altogether unalike. Both were small and frail, while, at the same time, agile and keen. And in Hetty's face, as well as in Miss Tate's, the flesh had thinned away with the years, and the bone below the flesh was seen to be fine and well chiselled. Miss Tate's face had, of course, the more delicate outline.

It was a pity Miss Tate had never married, a pity she had seen fit to discontinue the work of nine generations, for there could be no doubt that this charming old figurine was the result of careful selection and breeding. Yet, it was surprising to see how a generation or two of poverty and privation too could accelerate the pace of bone refinement, because there was undoubtedly something fine and compelling in old Hetty's clear and angular face. All the same, it was stupid of me to have mistaken Hetty for Miss Blodgett. And when I saw the real Miss Blodgett go down the steps into the garden a few days later, it was immediately clear that Hetty was the servant.

"Hetty," Miss Blodgett called out, "I forgot my sunshade. Run inside the house and get it for me."

And when Hetty, who had been putting some seedlings into the ground for Miss Tate, stood up to do the errand, she lowered her eyes deferentially while Miss Blodgett sailed past.

There could be no mistake this time. This could be none other than Miss Blodgett. When she got to the end of the garden I was amused to see her wag her finger at Miss Tate.

"Not so much bending!" she cried. "Not so much bending!" Then drawing up a garden seat, she again called out to Hetty, who was returning with the sunshade, and sent her into the potting shed for an iron foot-rest. "The grass is so damp in the garden," she said, as she settled herself plumply down to watch Miss Tate and Hetty continue dibbling in the seedlings.

Emma Blodgett was a big woman. She had a warm, friendly face; a very nice person, one would say unhesitatingly, but rather dull, perhaps even stupid. She was only about sixty, much younger than Miss Tate, much younger even than Hetty, but less active. Her plump face was perpetually flushed. She had a mass of grey hair, strong, straight, and unruly. Her figure was stout too, and she had a surprisingly matronly bosom for a spinster of her years.

Miss Blodgett also wore blue. As a matter of fact, she too was dressed somewhat similarly to Miss Tate, and yet there was some very great difference which I, from my study window, could see but could not at once define. First I thought it was a matter of the length of their gowns, but although like Miss Tate, Miss Blodgett wore her skirts longer than was fashionable they were not as long as Miss Tate's. Whatever impulse made Miss Blodgett disregard fashion had not been as strong as the old lady's, and was probably only imitation of her, for where Miss Tate's long blue hemline hung down to hide her ankles Miss Blodgett's stopped short a cowardly inch or two farther up from the ground, and revealed a pair of fat ankles with a tendency to swell, and possibly some other weakness as well, because Miss Blodgett wore thick blue woollen stockings even at the hottest time of year. It was impossible to tell what kind of stockings Miss Tate wore: no one ever saw Miss Tate's little ankles. But to go back to Miss Blodgett's dress again. As I said, I thought at first it differed only in length from Miss Tate's gown. Then I thought I detected a slight difference in the shade, and later still I thought it was a matter of age. But I soon dismissed these surmises, because Hetty's gown, although tattered and shabby, was in other respects exactly like Miss Tate's. It was not until the first day I went to take tea with the ladies that I discovered the difference between the three blue gowns. It was simply this: that Miss Blodgett's gown did not rustle! You know what that meant. It was blue. It was silky. It was cut to much the same pattern as the gown Miss Tate wore. But it didn't rustle. In other words, it was not quite the same quality. It was not real silk, not the genuine thing. And of course Miss Blodgett did not realize this at all.

"Look at Miss Tate," she said to me one day after we had become familiar over many cups of tea in their house and in mine. "Look at Miss Tate! She pays twice what I pay for the material in her gowns, and mine is exactly the same. No one could tell the difference. But the shop-keepers impose on Miss Tate. They know she has plenty of money. They don't impose on me! I'm well able for them!" Having triumphantly said this, Miss Blodgett begged me to have more cake, and as she went over to the table I heard the slight creak of artificial silk. Then, a moment later, Miss Tate delicately rustled across the room. Indeed, as my ear caught that rustle, which was as faint as a sigh, at the same time in a far corner of the room where Hetty was pouring out tea I heard another rustle, and if the rustle in Miss Tate's gown was like a sigh, the rustle that came from under Hetty's voluminous white apron was the echo of a sigh.

In time I became very friendly with the ladies in the house next door, but even before that I had become extraordinarily familiar with the sight of Hetty and Miss Tate in the garden.

The gardens of the houses in Clyde Road were large and secluded, and they were separated by high walls of cut granite, on which stone-crop and red valerian freely flowered. But from an upper window the gardens were not so secluded, and from my study I could see into every nook and cranny of my neighbours' gardens. The best comment I can make upon Miss Tate's garden is that from the first day I looked down into it I never bothered to look into any other. The others, like my own, were plain city gardens, with a plot of grass at the top and a few apple trees at the end. But Miss Tate's garden – well, I was hardly a day in Clyde Road when I realized I would have to change my study to the front of the house if I was ever to do any work. It was the most distracting garden I had ever seen.

In the first place, it was almost entirely given over to the old lady's pets, and everywhere on the small plot of lawn near the house, upon the grass and upon the green metal seats, and even raised on specially constructed standards, there were bowls of water of all shapes and sizes, wide and narrow, deep and shallow, to facilitate the different needs of bird, beast and butterfly. And although to either side of the grass plot there were small flower-beds, in them for the most part there bloomed only a few fragrant old flowers that were fashionable when Miss Tate was a girl: musk roses, heliotrope, lavender, and clove carnations. There were a few other flowers of unpretentious aspect, the names of which I did not know, but I afterwards found out were grown specially for the bees and the butterflies. Under my window there was a giant clump of catmint which was grown specially for the cats!

This grass plot with its border of flowers was, however, only one small fraction of the garden. The rest was planted with small flowering trees in which the birds and bees kept up a continual orchestration, the bees and pigeons supplying the bass, the blackbirds and thrushes breaking in with high trebles. These flowering trees, although fully matured, were of such a nature that, although as old as Miss Tate, like her they were frail and delicate even in their age. And in comparison with the plain old trees in the public park beyond our gardens they looked mere branches stuck into the ground on which had been tied paper flowers, pink and white.

Viewed from my study window, indeed, the whole of Miss Tate's garden looked as unreal but as entrancing as the miniature Japanese gardens that children used to construct long ago in shallow saucers, which, when finished, tantalized them with a longing to be small enough themselves to wander within.

Watching Miss Tate and Hetty in their garden, under the flowering trees, I myself was often tantalized with a desire to close my books and join them under those bloom-laden branches that seemed to be continually shedding either petals or fragrance, or fragments of birdsong.

It was at night, however, that Miss Tate's garden was most beautiful. Then the moon shone down in misty brightness over it, leaving its depths undisturbed and mysterious as the cold sea, but washing the tops of the miniature trees with light, and striking gleams from the glossy leaves as gleams are struck from the pointed wave. And in the middle of this misty moonlit sea the small white-painted glasshouse with its pointed roof seemed to float through the night like a silver barque of romance.

If ever a house was a harbour of happiness, it ought surely to have been the house looking over that blossom-tossed garden. Yet the first day I ever set foot in it I felt there was something wrong. There was some uneasiness in the air. There was some slight strain between Miss Tate and Miss Blodgett. But what it could be it was impossible to imagine, for seldom had two people more to give each other. On the one hand Miss Tate gave Miss Blodgett not only a home but a beautiful one, not only a salary but a bountiful one. While Miss Blodgett, on the other hand, was a perfect companion for Miss Tate. She not only ran the house, and supervised Hetty, but she had, it appeared, no friends or relatives at all of her own, and so even such time as she was supposed to have free for her own purposes was lavished also on Miss Tate, and occupied in doing errands and messages for her in town. In short, Miss Tate gave Miss Blodgett a share in everything she possessed, and made no distinction whatsoever between them, and Miss Blodgett, although she could only give Miss Tate her time and her interest and her care, gave them without stint and kept back not one morsel for herself.

Yet I felt there was something uneasy in their relationship. I felt it instinctively on the first day I took tea with the ladies, although I could not name it nor trace it to any cause. And when I became a habitual visitor seldom did a visit pass, however happily and pleasantly, without my getting at some time or another the feeling that all was not well. At some time or another I would see a little arrow in Miss Tate's blue eyes, and something sharp would shoot across the room. At first I merely felt a vibration in the air. But one day I actually saw it flash out: a little arrow of disapproval. I saw it flash out, yes, but I was no wiser afterwards. I still could see no cause for Miss Tate's sharpness. And when, afterwards, I pieced together the conversation of that visit, a more innocuous conversation could not be imagined. There wasn't a single remark that could have rasped anyone's nerves as far as I could see. And Miss Blodgett, who was helping Miss Tate to pick up a dropped stitch, had contributed to it only by smiles and nods, or by at most I am almost sure a single remark. Yet it was at Miss Blodgett that the arrow had been aimed.

There was only one grand-child to tea that day: Honor's eldest girl, Martha, one of the quietest of the family – a dull girl you might even say. Whenever Martha was there the conversation was always somewhat slow. The two ladies knitted, and the talk never ventured far beyond worsted and yarn. It is hard to recall an insipid conversation. But I took pains to recall every word in order to see why that little arrow had been sped from the bow.

Tea was over and Hetty was clearing the cups away.

"That's pretty wool, Aunt Adeline," Martha said, looking at the candy pink wool that Miss Tate was knitting.

"You saw it the last time you were here," said Miss Tate.

"Did I? Are you sure, Aunt Adeline? I thought you were knitting something blue last time."

"It's two years since I knitted anything blue," Miss Tate said firmly. "The last thing I knitted in blue was a scarf for your brother Edward."

"Oh, but this was only the other day, Aunt Adeline," said poor Martha, "and it wasn't a scarf for Edward; it was a shawl for Miriam's child."

Miss Tate looked up. So did Miss Blodgett.

"This is the same shawl," the two ladies said, speaking at the same time, and then Miss Tate said that she had been working at it for at least six weeks. "I'll never make a shawl again," she said. "It's boring."

Poor Martha put out her hand and drew over a corner of the pink knitted shawl.

"Such an intricate pattern!" she said, to cover her embarrassment. "You have wonderful patience, Aunt Adeline."

At this point – I remember it all exactly – Miss Tate dropped the stitch, and while she and Miss Blodgett were trying to take it up she did not catch Martha's last remark.

"What did you say, Martha dear?" she asked, when the stitch was safely back on the needle again.

"I said you have wonderful patience, Aunt Adeline," poor Martha repeated.

But Aunt Adeline did not hear the second time either. Now Aunt Adeline was not deaf, but she was decidedly nervous in case she might get deaf, and so, if for any reason she failed to catch something that was said, whether due to a noise in the room or an indistinctness in the voice of the person who spoke, or, as in this case, because she just wasn't listening, she always got flurried. The result was that the remark had to be repeated several times after that before she caught it. I often noticed that on such occasions Miss Blodgett was invaluable. She either repeated what had been said calmly and clearly, or, better still, she diverted Miss Tate's attention so that she forgot she had missed something. But on this particular occasion when Miss Blodgett came to the rescue, I, in my ignorance, thought it was her interference that annoyed Miss Tate, for it was right after Miss Blodgett spoke that I saw the arrow.

"Martha said you have wonderful patience, Aunt Adeline," Miss Blodgett said kindly. And she was just putting out her hand to rearrange a cushion that had slipped out of place behind Miss Tate's head when Miss Tate let loose the arrow.

"All old people are patient!" she snapped. "But the Tates were never patient before ninety."

Poor Martha blushed. But it was not at Martha the arrow was aimed. It was at Miss Blodgett. I saw it. I saw it go forth, aimed straight for Miss Blodgett's heart. But somehow it missed. Miss Blodgett sat as placidly as ever, smiling, and nodding her head in rhythm with the clicking of Miss Tate's needles. Perhaps the arrow had hit and splintered against the large cameo brooch that rose and fell on her big bosom. I don't know. Martha, however, was upset. She had not been quick enough to see the arrow, but she was not dull enough to be unaware that something was amiss. She thought, poor girl, that she was at fault, that she had said something to offend. Her eyes filled with tears.

The minute Miss Tate saw those tears she understood at once

what had happened. I thought I saw her give an angry look at Miss Blodgett's cameo brooch. Then she turned back with a gracious smile to Martha.

"Come, we will go into the garden, Martha my dear," she said. "Give me your arm. I must get a rose for my favourite grand-niece." The old lady was her sweet self again. Over me, too, she shed her graciousness. "Will you come with us?" she asked, turning toward me. "And I'll get a rose for you too." But at the door she paused. "Martha, like all the Tates, loves flowers," she said. Then she nodded in the direction of Miss Blodgett, who had turned away. "Miss Blodgett doesn't care about gardening," she said. "Miss Blodgett wouldn't know a rose from a cauliflower." And then flash went another arrow through the air.

But Miss Blodgett only smiled. She had not felt any prick this time either. Before she turned around I saw that her dress was fastened up the back with a row of little pearl buttons. I was not near enough to see if one of them was scratched or broken, but I think it could hardly have been otherwise.

"Oh, I don't mind gardens," Miss Blodgett said complacently, "but there are so many unpleasant things in a garden: bees and wasps, and ants and slugs. I'm quite satisfied to sit here at the window and get the sun through the glass." Smiling benignly, she went on with her knitting.

Miss Tate took Martha's arm, then mine, and we went out gossiping lightly. As if to make up to the girl, Miss Tate made an unusual fuss over her, picking her the best and most beautiful roses, and several times asking me if I saw any likeness between them.

She insisted on giving me a bouquet too, and as she pressed the bunch of red roses into my hand I felt that this charming old lady may have known that I saw that arrow speeding through the air, and wanted to divert my mind from what I had seen. In fact, when I was leaving, she kept me standing at the small green gate of the garden telling me how good Miss Blodgett was to her, and how much she was indebted to her dear companion.

"She has a kind heart. Not like the Tates. The Tates all have a bitter streak in them." She smiled at me then, and she smiled at Martha. But unfortunately Martha protested.

"Oh, Aunt Adeline! You're very naughty! Such a thing to say about us!" The poor girl! She was destined to be the cause of more trouble, for just then Miss Blodgett came to the steps leading down to the garden and overhearing Martha's remark she smiled at her with her wide benevolent smile.

"Did I hear you say Aunt Adeline was naughty, Martha?" she asked, and then before she said another word, there in the brilliant sunny air, with the birds singing and the bees humming as they went from flower to flower, Miss Tate let fly a third and dreadfully sharp arrow.

What was the meaning of it at all? I hugged my roses tightly and, saying good-bye, I went into my own garden greatly perplexed.

After that I saw the arrow several times, but only when I was near at hand.

At other times I would sit in my window and look down at Miss Tate and Hetty in the garden and think how gentle and sweet Miss Tate looked. And even when Miss Blodgett came out and the two of them took tea together under the trees, they presented a charming picture of peace, tranquillity and sweetness. They would sip tea, the two of them, and Miss Tate would perhaps call Hetty and pour a cup of tea for her, and insist on the old servant drinking it there and then, standing beside them at the tea-table with perhaps one of the lapdogs she had been combing caught up under her arm, or a bundle of weeds that she was going to burn at the bottom of the plot. On those occasions I saw no arrows.

Yet as surely as I went to tea with the ladies, at some point in the afternoon an arrow would pierce the air, and make straight for Miss Blodgett's heart.

I pondered a great deal over the whole thing. At first I thought there was some deep and serious reason for Miss Tate's antagonism to Emma Blodgett. Then a small incident occurred to make me veer around to quite the opposite opinion. Perhaps it was another case of the Princess and the Pea?

I had not called on the ladies for some days, when, on this particular afternoon, I went to their garden gate and pushed it open to pay them a short visit. They were going to take tea in the garden, and Hetty had just laid the tray on the wicker garden table. As I walked across the grass the old ladies were pulling up their chairs to the table, and Miss Blodgett had just relieved Miss Tate of a large catalogue at which they had both been looking. She threw it down on the grass underneath the table.

"Hetty, another cup," Miss Blodgett called out, and Miss Tate put one of the tabby cats down from its chair and invited me to take its place. Then as Hetty brought out a cup and saucer and turned to go back into the house, Miss Tate called her back.

"Hetty, will you please put on your hat and coat and go down to the hospital to ask how Mr. Robbie's baby is today," she said.

"Is the baby sick? In hospital?" I cried.

Lord Robert's son and namesake, young Robbie, had recently married, and there had been great excitement at the birth of his first son, Lord Robert's grandson, and another great-grand-nephew for Miss Adeline Tate. I was sorry to hear the infant was not doing well.

"The doctor says it won't live," Miss Tate said, when I begged her to tell me what was the matter with him. "There's something wrong with his spine. He was weakly from the start."

Miss Blodgett sighed sadly.

"Oh, dear," I said. I felt uncomfortable, and rose from my chair. "Perhaps if I hadn't come you would be going to the hospital? Please don't let me intrude. I only called for a minute. I'll call again another day."

But the ladies excelled each other in assuring me that I must on no account leave. Miss Blodgett rose to press me down into my chair again, while Miss Tate insisted over and over again that a few minutes before I appeared they were planning to send Hetty out with a note asking me to call.

"Because we just got a present of some rose geranium jelly that we want you to sample with us," Miss Tate said. "Sit down! Sit down!" And Miss Blodgett poured out three cups of tea and took the cover from the geranium jelly that its fragrance might tempt me.

I stayed. But I was uneasy waiting for Hetty to come back. She was a long time away. In fact, she did not come back until I was just leaving. I was letting myself out by the front door when I met her in the hall.

I looked inquiringly at her. "Is he better?" I asked eagerly.

Hetty was calm. "No, he's dead," she said. "But it was a good job I went up there." Then, with a remarkable compromise between deference and impatience, she prepared to pass me. "I must tell Miss Tate," she said.

I was confused. I tried to detain her. Surely she was not going to rush into the garden and blurt out the news like that? So bluntly?

"Hetty, wait," I cried. "Are you going to tell them at once?"

Hetty looked surprised. "What else would I do?"

"Don't you think you should wait a little while, and break it more gently to them?" I stumbled over my words. Had Hetty no sense? Couldn't she see what I meant? "If at first you said he was worse, and then later on suggested he wasn't expected to live, then perhaps they might be prepared for the shock and you could tell them the truth?"

But Hetty stared at me.

"What about the wreath?" she asked.

"The wreath?" I repeated.

Hetty looked at me impatiently. "Miss Tate will want to order it at once. She'll want time to decide what flowers to have put in it. She'd be most annoyed if she wasn't told in good time." Then, taking into consideration that I was, after all, a comparative stranger, the old servant paused to give me an explanation. "Miss Tate always sends a magnificent wreath to all funerals within the family," she said.

And with this the old servant hurried away. I stood uncertainly looking after her. I saw her run down the steps into the garden. I saw her go across the grass and I saw the ladies look up expectantly. I saw Hetty say something to them and I waited, holding my breath. In spite of what Hetty had said, I felt I might be needed. And I was on the point of going back to the garden, when I saw the two ladies rise excitedly to their feet. And in the soft, summer air Miss Tate's voice carried to me distinctly.

"The wreath! Quick! Where is the catalogue?" she cried. Hastily pushing aside the tea-table Miss Blodgett picked up the catalogue from the grass, the catalogue they had been scanning when I went in. It was a florist's catalogue, and even from a distance I could see the illustrations of wreaths and artificial bouquets, flowering crosses, and glass-domed immortelles. "Give it to me," said Miss Tate, putting on her glasses and stretching out her hand.

"Wait a minute," said Miss Blodgett, withholding it. "We marked a pretty one, don't you remember?"

"That's right," said Miss Tate happily.

I didn't wait to hear any more. I could see why it had not occurred to Hetty to break the news. The ladies had long since passed into that time of life when they were no longer capable of feeling the great emotions. Like children, their joys and sorrows were as real as other peoples, but were aroused by smaller things.

I stood looking back at them in their sunny garden for a few minutes longer, and as I did it occurred to me that whatever discord was between them must have sprung from something trivial. I decided to put them out of my mind, and not to let the matter bother me further.

This, however, it was impossible to do. From then on I never went into the house next door without feeling the familiar quiver in the air. The room might be filled with nieces and nephews. The talk might be gay and general and happy. But at some time or another I would see the little arrow in Miss Tate's eye. And at the most unexpected moment she would let it fly. Perhaps one of the young people would say something to her across the room, and Miss Tate, talking to another member of the family, would not hear.

"Aunt Adeline!" the young thing would call out again; and Miss Blodgett would step in.

"Aunt Adeline! Aunt Adeline! Lucy is calling you."

Miss Tate would look up. She never failed to hear Miss Blodgett. And, inexplicably, then she would let fly the dart.

"I hear! I hear!" Miss Tate would say. "It's nothing important, I suppose!" And she would glance very fiercely at Miss Blodgett. But to the young thing who had called her she would cross the room courteously and, sitting down beside her, she would listen to all the young thing had to say.

This, as a matter of fact, was a common scene. But one day when the drawing-room was crowded with a great many Tates, and their husbands and wives, their children and their betrotheds, there was a slight difference in the atmosphere. This time Lucy called out to her grand-aunt and Miss Blodgett drew Miss Tate's attention to her. But Miss Tate, who had been sitting beside me, stood up, and so fierce a light was shining in her eyes I positively trembled. I felt she was going to let loose a whole quiverful of arrows.

"Aunt Adeline! Lucy is calling you." That was all Miss Blodgett had said, but Miss Tate turned to Lucy and spoke quite crossly.

"I can't come now," she said, and she nodded to indicate me, as I sat behind her on the sofa. "I just promised our neighbour here that I would show here the family photographs."

I felt more uneasy than ever. This was the first I had heard of the promise. I saw, too, that Lucy was crestfallen at the snub. But Miss Tate was inexorable. She moved over to the mantelpiece, on which there were set out anything from twenty to thirty photographs in silver and filigree frames, showing a bewildering array of ladies and young girls, babies and young men, men with great, impressive beards and men so beardless they were like girls – small girls in frilly dresses and little boys in sailor suits. There were brides without number, in silks and lace. There were at least six men in uniform. There was Lord Robert in his wig, Lucy in a ball dress, Honor in her college gown – but it would have been simpler to say who was absent than who was present in that crowded gallery on the mantelpiece. Miss Tate beckoned me to follow her and took up the frame nearest to hand.

"That's my mother," she said, pushing the silver frame into my hand. But I had hardly time to glance at it when it was snatched away and another was pushed into my hand. "That's my grand-uncle," she said. "He would be the children's great-great-grand-uncle." Then she snatched back the great-grand-uncle. "This is a nephew," she said. "He was killed playing polo." One after another she rammed the silver frames into my hands, but snatched them away again almost as quickly, so that I had hardly time to do more than glimpse them. At first I strove to keep pace with her, tried to exclaim that the old ladies were charming, the young officers handsome, and the soldiers fearless and brave. But as frame after frame was rammed into my hands and snatched away again I became aware that behind this plan of showing me the photographs there was some hidden motive.

At last she came to the end of them.

"Well?" she said in a loud voice, and I saw her look across the room. She wanted everyone to hear. "Well, what do you think of that for a family?"

"They all have remarkably fine faces," I said awkwardly. It was true, although I must admit I felt embarrassed saying it out loud.

"But didn't you notice anything?" Miss Tate asked. I knew then that it was not my comment she wanted but an opportunity to make one of her own. "Didn't you notice how strong the likeness is all down the line?" She turned back and took down the great-grand-uncle again. "The Tates all had aquiline noses. The dead Tates had them. The living Tates have them." I looked around nervously, and, true enough, although I had not noticed it before, there was a large number of noses in the room, and they were all aquiline. But just then Miss Tate snatched up another frame. "Look at great-uncle Samuel's nose!" She snatched up another. And another. "Look at this nose. Look at that nose!" Then, putting down the last frame so carelessly that the young man in uniform who was looking out from it over his aquiline nose fell flat on his face on the marble slab, Miss Tate held up her little head. "Look at my nose!" she said triumphantly. Then in still a louder, clearer voice, that had by now caught the attention of the whole room, she repeated her first statement. "Yes, the Tates all have aquiline noses. And the men are all tall, and the women are all small. And" – here Miss Tate drew a deep breath – "we were always noted for our ankles." She turned swiftly to Lucy. "Pull up your skirt, Lucy, and show your ankles." She turned to Martha. "Look at Martha!" she said. "Martha, my dear, why do you wear such dark stockings? It's a shame. Dark stockings are all right for women with ugly legs." And then, to my astonishment, Miss Tate's little hand swooped down and lifted the hem of her own blue gown. "In my day," she said, "we might as well have had no legs at all, but I have the Tate ankles, too. Noses and ankles: that's how you can always tell a Tate!"

And then, deliberately, Miss Tate turned and looked at Miss Blodgett, and distinctly, as on the other occasions, I saw it flash out, that glance of hatred. And where did it fly? It flew of course straight for Miss Blodgett as she sat nearby, smiling complacently upon all the company, but it was aimed, of all places, at a point just below the hemline of the gown of imitation silk where Emma's fat ankles were comfortably crossed one over the other in their thick-ribbed brown woollen stockings.

All at once I understood.

And I think that Lucy, who was a sensitive girl, must have understood too, for she gave an embarrassed laugh.

"You're as vain as a young girl, Aunt Adeline," she said.

But Miss Blodgett did not betray the slightest upset. As a matter of fact she laughed heartily.

"That's good! Did you hear what Lucy said?" she cried, poking Miss Tate with the end of her knitting needle. "You're as vain as a girl, Aunt Adeline."

Aunt Adeline!

There they were, the simple words that had occurred in all the sentences I had analysed so unsuccessfully in my effort to try to find out what was poisoning Miss Tate against Miss Blodgett.

Aunt Adeline. Aunt Adeline? Everything that Miss Tate possessed in the world was at the disposal of Miss Blodgett, except one thing – the family blood. Miss Blodgett had no drop of it, and without it, and without the Tate nose and the Tate ankles, she was guilty of a grievous lapse every time she called Miss Tate by the familiar name reserved for the use of the Lucys and the Robbies.

I felt a pang of apprehension. I recalled the gossip I had heard about the small bequest. What if Miss Blodgett should jeopardize her chance of it? What if she should forfeit it?

I positively trembled. Why, Miss Blodgett, according to herself, was so much a part of the Tate family that most of her salary, lavish as it was, went in buying wool for the bonnets and shawls she was continually knitting for the Tate progeny and in small but frequent purchases of confetti and ribbons and good-luck tokens for the numerous Tate brides. Why! What a lot of money she must have spent on wreaths alone for the Tate corpses? She could hardly have saved a penny. She would be absolutely dependent on that small bequest.

Really, I felt so bad I took my leave shortly afterwards. And all that week the affair preyed on my mind. I began to dread going into the house. For every time Miss Blodgett addressed Miss Tate as Aunt Adeline I felt my heart freeze. Every time she said it I felt the small bequest was put more and more in jeopardy.

And so when, at the end of the summer, I was about to leave for the West of Ireland, as was my custom, I felt a certain relief as I said good-bye to the ladies. They came to the door to wave me out of sight. They seemed sorry to part with me. And Miss Blodgett had tears in her eyes. As I went down the steps from the hall door she linked her arm in Miss Tate's and called out after me.

"Aunt Adeline will miss you. Won't you, Aunt Adeline?"

Those were her last words to me before I set out. I didn't dare turn around. I simply could not bear to see the look in Miss Tate's eyes.

The following spring when I came back, the house next door was boarded up and for sale. A few forlorn pigeons hovered uncertainly on the eave shoot. A stray cat or two slunk in and out between the railings. These of course were not the regular pets that belonged to the house, but it was clear they had had claims on its hospitality and could not realize their claims had lapsed.

Miss Tate was dead.

There was no sign whatever of Miss Blodgett.

However, about a week after my return, as I was walking into town, I took a short-cut through one of those dreary intermediary streets that lie between the business section and the residential areas like Clyde Road but which have not yet degenerated into slums. Here fine old houses that had once been fashionable mansions stood forlorn, bereft of their elegant curtains, their gay window-boxes, and now their elaborate brass knockers were painted to save labour. The particular street through which I passed had been saved from complete degeneration by reason of the fact that several of the houses had been turned into offices and service flats, and the few that had remained in private hands had been retained by their owners at the cost of turning them into respectable boarding-houses.

And coming down the steps of one of the most precarious and ramshackle of these boarding-houses, who should I see but Emma Blodgett.

Dear Miss Blodgett! How glad I was to see her! I waved to her, and hurried across the street with hands outstretched. But even before I reached the other side I saw with a sinking of the heart that, although only a few short months had passed since I had last seen her, Miss Blodgett was decidedly shabbier in her appearance. Her clothes were clean and neat as ever, but she no longer had that sheltered look that all Miss Tate's household had had last summer, from Miss Tate herself down even to the sleek cats and the fat pigeons. Indeed, Miss Blodgett, at that moment, reminded me of the poor perplexed pigeons that I had seen clinging to the eaves in the empty house in Clyde Road.

Of course I did not pretend to notice any change, but I felt dreadfully upset about the poor thing, and feared that my worst forebodings about the bequest had been true. And yet somehow it did not seem like Miss Tate, dead or alive, to break her promise. I found it hard to see how she could have omitted Miss Blodgett's name from her testament when it was, as it were, an understood thing that it would be included.

"Dear Miss Blodgett!" I cried, and I sympathized with her on the loss of Miss Tate. And yet I felt a necessity to be guarded in my condolences. "So poor Miss Tate has left her garden?" I said, and I watched Miss Blodgett carefully as I said it.

But Emma Blodgett's eyes filled with tears.

"Yes," she said. "Poor Aunt Adeline!" And then she took out a small handkerchief that was not, alas, as spotlessly laundered as it would have been the previous year, but which, from the border of real lace that ran delicately around its hem, I took to be one of the many small treasures Miss Blodgett had amassed in her years at Clyde Road. "Yes," she said, and she blew her nose. There was no mistaking her sorrow.

I felt very much better. I felt I had been unjust to the memory of Miss Tate. Miss Blodgett's shabby appearance was due no doubt to the fact that she now had to be more prudent. She was living her own life now, and not the life of an heiress. And wasn't she justified in her prudence? Wasn't thrift a virtue if you were poor? If you had no home, but had to pay for every morsel you ate, as well as for the roof over your head, could you afford to be prodigal with your money? And, all those years when there had been constant talk about the bequest that Miss Tate was expected to leave her companion, had it not always been particularly stated that it would be a small bequest? Then something struck me. Goodness knows how small it might have been! It might have been a mere nothing; a paltry sum. Then a worse thought struck me. Perhaps it had not been money at all. How often old ladies and gentlemen of eighty or ninety have set such a value on small personal possessions that they have carelessly disposed of their impersonal millions on the advice of lawyer or vicar, to lavish all their attention on the disposal of some worthless trinket – a lock of hair, or an old watch – because, in these last sad hours of abnegation, they had set more value on it than upon all their money. Into this worthless object they feel they have distilled the essence of their lives, but unfortunately it is of no more value than a stone, and, like a stone, alas, not negotiable.

I looked hurriedly at Miss Blodgett, who was now weeping copiously, as between sobs she described Miss Tate's last hours to me.

"I was with her to the last breath," she sobbed. "I held her hand all the time. She clutched my fingers till the very end."

Here poor Miss Blodgett put out her hand and clasped mine in illustration of that last touching scene, but she was recalled swiftly from the bedside of her dead friend, as her eye and mine caught sight of a large hole in the finger of her cotton glove. She hurriedly withdrew her hand.

"Oh dear," she cried. "I must have caught my glove in something. It seems to be torn."

But the tear was not a new one. It had a frayed edge that told its own story. And irresistibly my eye travelled to Miss Blodgett's other hand. In the other glove too there was a hole – a slightly larger hole – and through it showed another finger, a finger which, alas, was not as immaculate as one would have expected. The fingernail was indeed decidedly grimy, and clearly showed that Miss Blodgett's landlady allowed her paying guest the privilege of doing out her own room, and blacking her own fire-grate.

I looked away hurriedly. But you know how it is. The eye is a most unruly member. Do what I might, it would rove back irresistibly to the hole in Miss Blodgett's glove. And where my eye went, irresistibly it seemed, Miss Blodgett's blue eye followed.

At last a point was reached at which I must either go away or one of us must make some telling remark. We had to lay the ghost of that torn glove that hovered between us interrupting our conversation, making us awkward and ill at ease.

It was Miss Blodgett who laid it.

"Poor Miss Tate," she said suddenly, and she held out her hand and frankly displayed the gloves. "Poor Miss Tate. How distressed she would be if she saw me looking so shabby!"

I didn't quite know what to say, but remembering that Emma Blodgett was probably friendless, with no one, perhaps, in the whole wide world to take an interest in her, I felt that I could venture a step further without danger of being thought vulgarly curious.

"I hope her death has not caused too great a change in your circumstances," I said, and then feeling that I had not handled the situation very well, I hurried my words. "I mean, I always understood that Miss Tate intended to arrange matters so that you should never want for anything after her death. You know? The small bequest!"

I spoke with my eyes on the ground, afraid to look up. But Miss Blodgett had dissolved into tears again, and lo! they were tears of love.

"Poor Aunt Adeline!" she said. "A small bequest? That was so like her, to underestimate every impulse of her dear, kind heart." She looked at me a little sternly. "You wouldn't call a thousand pounds a small bequest, would you?"

I was astonished; astonished. I had never thought about how much Miss Tate was likely to leave her companion, but I must admit I had hardly expected it to be more than a few hundred.

"Oh, Miss Blodgett," I said, putting out my hand again and taking hers, "I congratulate you!" But what, I wondered, was the mystery of the torn gloves?

Miss Blodgett withdrew her hand quickly.

"Congratulate me?" she asked. "Sympathize with me, you mean. There's nothing to congratulate me about. You see, I didn't get the money. And, what is more, it looks as if I'm never going to get it."

"What?" I was bewildered. Surely the noble and wealthy Tates were not going to contest this reasonable, if generous, bequest? Considering how much they must have shared among themselves, the size of the bequest – even if its size had surprised them – should have added to the family's pride in its own magnaminity. "Surely they're not going to contest the will?" I cried.

"Oh dear no." Miss Blodgett was shocked at the thought. "They feel worse than I do. In fact, Lord Robert is doing all in his power for me. He insisted on my getting the best solicitor I could get, and Miss Lucy Tate couldn't be surpassed for her kindness. They are all so kind to me, and so upset on my account. The Tates are like that, you know! The kindest people in the world. They think of me as one of themselves." She sighed. "And poor Aunt Adeline! She was the kindest of them all. I can only hope she is not looking down now and seeing all the trouble she caused, without realizing it, out of the goodness of her heart. For you see," and Miss Blodgett looked up at me earnestly, "it was because she was trying to be *too* kind to me that I lost the legacy." I didn't pretend to understand. Miss Blodgett hastened to explain. "Well, you know the way she always considered me one of the family. You know how she liked me to call her Aunt Adeline, just as if I was related to her in blood? You know all that, don't you? You could see it for yourself?" Miss Blodgett looked at me earnestly with her big obtuse face and her big stupid eyes filled with love and affection. I felt a great uneasiness gather again in my heart. I didn't answer, but there was no need, for Miss Blodgett rushed on. "Well!" she said. "Poor Miss Tate, when she drew up her will, put in a few words as a last message to me. I suppose she wanted to let everyone see my place in her affections. She wanted to let people see how close she considered me to her. And so," here Miss Blodgett forgot for a moment about Miss Tate as she was recalled to the dreadul weeks that had passed, spent mostly in a solictor's office, being questioned and brow-beaten, and for a moment she broke down and her poor lower lip fell open, and a tear, that was not for Miss Adeline Tate, but for poor Emma Blodgett, stole down her cheek. "And so, in the will Miss Tate designated me as her fond niece Emma. *'And to my fond niece, Emma,'* she said, *'I herby bequeath the sum of one thousand pounds.'* " Miss Blodgett spluttered. "A . . . a . . . a thousand pounds! And to think that I'll never touch a penny of it." She suddenly tucked her handkerchief into her sleeve again, and looked up at a clock on a church tower that showed between the high offices. The little gold wrist-watch she used to wear was no longer on her arm. "I am on my way down to the solicitor now," she said. "I have to go down every other day. They're doing their best for me. Lord Robert is most upset. And Miss Lucy too. Indeed, they all are extremely kind. But as for myself, I haven't much hope. You see, it would have been all right if poor Miss Tate had not tried to show me that last mark of affection. It would have been all right if she had left the money to Miss Emma Blodgett. That was what the solictor said. 'You are Emma Blodgett,' he said. 'Of that there is no doubt. But who is this *"fond niece Emma"*? There is no such person. There are fifty-four nieces, counting grand-nieces, and two great-grand-nieces, but none of them is called Emma!' " Miss Blodgett sighed. "It was perfectly clear, of course, to everyone that it was me that was meant. But" – Miss Blodgett's lips trembled again – "but what good is that to me?" She put out her hand. "I must be going," she said. "Those solicitors are very exact. They don't like to be kept waiting, although they think nothing of keeping others waiting. I'm often kept up to an hour there, and at the end I sometimes have to go away without seeing him. If an urgent call comes for him on the telephone, he has to attend to it. But his typist is very nice. She always gets me a chair." For an instant Emma brightened as she held my hand. "Do you know what I discovered the other day? The typist is a niece of Hetty's. You remember Hetty? Hetty was always very careful with her money, you know, and she educated all her brother's children. They all have good jobs. This girl in the solicitor's office is a very well-educated girl. She's very civil. And she's always very sorry for me if I have to go away without seeing the solicitor. 'Don't worry, Emma,' she says. 'Everything will be all right!' She's a very exceptional girl. Her name is Miss Hynes. Hetty's name was Hynes, you know."

I had almost forgotten to ask about Hetty.

"And how is Hetty?" I asked.

"Oh, Hetty is all right," said Miss Blodgett. "She's gone to live with her brother. They're glad to have her, of course; she has a nice nest-egg saved. And then, of course, Miss Tate left her a nice little sum too."

"And Hetty got it all right?"

Miss Blodgett's big, stupid blue eyes turned on me in surprise.

"Why, of course! Why wouldn't she get it? It was left to Hester Hynes. That was Hetty's right name. Hetty was nothing to Miss Tate. Miss Tate had no special feelings for Hetty. She just mentioned her name as a matter of course." Miss Blodgett had risen again for a moment to the height of the old days. Her bosom swelled. Her eyes gleamed. "Hetty was only a servant. She was nothing to Aunt Adeline! Well, I must be going. Sometimes, you know, I get tired of going up to the solicitor's, but I say to myself that Aunt Adeline will never rest in her grave until I have made the last possible effort to rectify her mistake." She put out her hand. "Thank you for your sympathy. I'll let you know how things turn out. Goodbye, my dear."

She turned away then, but I saw that the tears had gathered again in her eyes. I heard her mutter something to herself as I stood looking after the blue imitation silk dress, and the ample ankles in the thick woollen socks. I couldn't be sure, but I think what I heard was an exclamation.

"Poor Aunt Adeline! Poor Aunt Adeline!"

A Woman Friend

When the Inquiry was over, and he walked out of the Board-room, everything might have been the same as before – only for Bina. The whole thing had, in fact, passed off well. It hadn't been anything like the ordeal he had envisaged on the awful night the boy died, when he'd rushed around in panic to Baggot Street – rousing Bina in the small hours.

No positive blame had been attached to him at all. The charge of negligence was dismissed after the first five minutes, as soon as it was established that the boy would have died in any case. Possibly there had been some bungling on the part of the local doctor in charge at the County Infirmary who had sent the boy up for an appendectomy with nothing on his chart to indicate anything unusual about the case. There had not even been any indication that the case should be considered urgent, although, in point of fact, the boy was down on the slate for operation next morning. There would – as a matter of routine – have been a new diagnosis before he went on to the table, but by that time it would probably have been too late to save him by any means. This was fully agreed upon by all members of the investigation. Let it be said though that he himself could not escape a gnawing fear – even afterwards – that, for all his experience and all his skill, he might – he just might – have missed the, really quite rare, symptom which was the only indication of the boy's real condition. This, of course, would not have occurred to his colleagues in a million years.

And so, now, it almost seemed a stroke of luck that he had not been available when the hospital 'phoned him with that urgent summons – although when they finally did succeed in getting through to him, in the early hours of the morning, it had seemed disastrous to everyone that they had not been able to locate him earlier. That, of course, was due to the way the hospital staff behaved and also to his own unfortunate encounter with the boy's mother, when he'd met her as he ran up the hospital steps in the dawn, not knowing at the time that his patient was already dead. That encounter probably unnerved him

176

more than anything. It made him so vulnerable, and it was probably it which caused him to act so ridiculously later in Baggot Street, although, undoubtedly, there was something in what Bina maintained about his being run-down and overworked. If he hadn't been under a strain already he would hardly have been so apprehensive of an inquiry or so worried about its findings. Not with his reputation!

He ought to have had more confidence in that reputation. If anything it was higher after the investigation. There was such stress laid on his attentiveness, and in particular on his late-night rounds of the wards.

Admittedly there had been an awkward moment when he was asked why he had not been available to answer his 'phone after specifically stating he was going straight back to his rooms. The hospital claimed to have 'phoned repeatedly. But, at that point in the inquiry, seeing that opinion generally was favourable to him, he had taken a chance and asked if it was certain they were connected to the right number. There had been some technical flaw in the hospital switchboard that week and he recalled that fact at the right moment. And seeing that he'd scored a point he was inspired to ask if there could not have been some confusion in the porter's office: it was a fairly new fellow there. Had any of these things occurred to anyone? How was it they succeeded in reaching him later – in the early hours? Surely that was odd?

His defence at that point really boiled down to a counter-accusation against the hospital. Did it not enter anyone's mind – anyone at all – to send a messenger over to my rooms? In view of the seriousness of the situation? After all Fitzwilliam Square was not a hundred miles away! It would only have taken a matter of seconds and –

There was a sticky moment then, though, when the Chairman of the Medical Board interrupted: "And would they have found you in your rooms, Dr. Anderson, if they had done as you suggest?"

That was the climax of the whole thing. There was a hush of suspense. The Chairman, old Bates, must have thought himself exceptionally sharp. As a matter of fact you'd never think to listen to him that there had been some sort of a cloud over his past, although it certainly hadn't held him back. As a matter of fact, smart as the old chap thought himself, he had played right into his hands.

"Unquestionably," he answered; choosing the word carefully after a slight deliberation, which in itself curiously enough impressed the Board.

"Yes or no, Doctor, if you please!" old Bates snapped.

"Yes," he said then quickly and firmly.

"You understand you are on oath, Doctor?"

"Certainly – I mean, yes."

But his first answer had filled the bill to a nicety, because unquestionably if someone had gone around to the Square his car would have been noticed outside in the street. He had no scruples whatever on the score of that reply. If, after knocking on his door and getting no reply to the knock, the messenger had not wondered at the car being outside, he'd want to be a fool indeed. Surely he would automatically have looked into the car? And then, of course, all the subsequent bother and upset for everyone would have been avoided. Except for the boy of course. Well, no matter. Nothing, apparently, could have saved the boy. That was the main thing. And obviously when that had been made evident there was less stress laid on his failure to answer the 'phone. Integrity counted for something after all. It is quite possible that they would have believed him if he had told the absolute truth, ridiculous as it was, but that night – or early morning, rather – when he broke down in front of Bina, it seemed fantastic to expect anyone – even her – to believe he had fallen asleep on the seat of the car right outside his door! It was damn lucky he'd turned off the ignition. All the same, he felt a fool to think of it even now.

It was all very well for Bina to say it was the most natural thing in the world, but Bina was Bina and naturally she was prejudiced in his favour. She would have been that no matter what had happened.

"It was only to be expected, Lew," she said. "Thank God you had stopped the car. I was often afraid you'd fall asleep at the wheel on your way home from here some night."

He had often been afraid of that himself, and when he got into the car that particular night he was deadly tired. It was a wonder he reached Fitzwilliam; it wouldn't have surprised him in the least if, when he woke up, he'd found he hadn't started the car at all and was still outside the little hotel in Baggot Street. Only in that case Bina would have noticed. She never shut the door till he'd driven off, although he often urged her not to stand in the cold.

It was ironic to think that he had actually gone back to the hospital again after that to have another last look at the boy. Of course, that counted very much in his favour with his colleagues. Or did it? Might it not have shown too great a concern? No – only a proper concern, which was shown in any case by his having said he'd be available if they wanted him at any time that night. Oh, if only it had been outside the hospital he'd fallen asleep – before driving away. Surely, surely, then someone would have noticed the car there and had the wit to look inside? Specially knowing his habit? That cursed habit. It was in Baggot Street, of course, that he fell into the habit. Only there could he have got away with dropping off to sleep regardless of what company he was in at the time. It was there that it first happened anyway; not when he was a student, needless to say, but afterwards – years after, when he was qualified – on one of the rare occasions – all too rare indeed – when he had called, as he had promised, to see how Bina and her mother were getting along. Mrs. Cussen was still alive then. She was not even confined to her bed at the time either, because after she got the first stroke she still managed to get downstairs for a few hours and the two women spent the evening in their little hide-out in the basement after Bina got through with the work. But for some reason Mrs. Cussen wasn't downstairs the night he fell asleep in his chair. Bina was alone. She was getting him a cup of tea as a matter of fact, before he went back to his rooms, when, quite suddenly, he fell asleep. He could only have dropped off for the briefest possible time because one second she was standing in front of him with the teapot in her hand waiting for the kettle to boil and the next thing he knew she had made the tea and had poured him a cup. He had been as sound asleep as if he was stretched out on his bed.

Yet Bina had noticed nothing, which proved, of course, that it had been a quite natural sleep, with no affectation whatever. Not that night anyway, although when she realized he had been sound asleep she'd gone into such rhapsodies about what – instead of a lapse – she seemed to consider some sort of superiority in him – some exceptional self-control or will power – she'd ended by making him quite puffed-up about it. He knew, of course, that it was generally regarded as an indication of exceptional self-control for a person to be able at will to allow his mind to rest and so gather force to go on to greater effort – effort beyond the capacity of most, well no, say of some men.

But Bina went on so about it, she must have given him a complex. Certainly when it happened again – in the hospital the next time – and actually quite genuine then too, and he'd fallen asleep – briefly – again it was only for a few seconds – he had, at first, felt ashamed of it, still regarding it as a weakness. But recalling how Bina had been so impressed he'd seized his opportunity – and made a pretence of its being deliberate, claiming that his physical frame of itself had felt the need of a respite before undergoing the strain of operating. Some of his assistants – the young interns, for instance – thought it all rather theatrical – a bit of an act – but he ignored their raised eyebrows because, like Bina, the nurses were positively bowled over. And when, that day, he went on to give a particularly brilliant performance with the scalpel (he was quoting a staff nurse there) he let the subsequent exclamations of amazement pass. He actually basked in the admiration, and was not ashamed to do so either, knowing that there was always a sense of drama in the operating theatre. It kept the nurses in line, kept them tensed up, and on their toes. Anyway he could hardly have altered the interpretation they'd put on things, even if he'd wished. It was inevitable that an ambitious man – and he never denied that he was ambitious – would have realized the value of making a little weakness appear to be an attribute. It was a short step from that to cultivating it as a habit. Admittedly in time he did play it up a bit until it became an act – a gimmicky act.

The first time he could remember pretending to take one of those cat-naps, instead of its being a natural sleep, was outside the operating theatre. Everyone was ready, robed and scrubbed up, but at the last minute, almost as a joke, he had called everything to a halt, only for a second, of course, and sat down on a chair outside the theatre, closing his eyes. He only remained sitting for a second, but in that second he established his legend.

"Were you really asleep, Doctor?" one of the young nurses – a neophite – asked him in a whisper just after they went into the theatre and before the anaesthetist gave them the green light. He nodded. It was no time for lengthy explanations. And from then on even the theatre sister, even the matron, had been too favourably impressed for him to be able to dissuade them of their conviction. What man in his sane senses would interfere with his own legend? Wasn't it by creating legends that the great specialists impressed their own image of themselves upon their subordinates – and ultimately upon their patients? Ah but he had nearly paid dearly for his play-acting. It had nearly cost him his reputation. And that night when he rushed around to Baggot Street, and when he'd felt so beholden to Bina for her sympathy and good sense, he might, had he not been upset, have kept it in mind that it was partly her fault. For it was undoubtedly the eulogies Bina had gone into about his powers of concentration that had triggered off the whole thing. Actually – to be fair to Bina – he had never put on an act with her. When he'd sunk down into one of her shabby old armchairs and closed his eyes he used to relax completely – and often did go to sleep for a few minutes. He was always dog-tired when he called there. Perhaps indeed subconsciously it was when he was exhausted that he did drop in to Bina. It was always so homely there. And another thing – it was always pretty late when he got there. He never seemed to manage to arrive early, but it fitted in with Bina's routine as well as his own to leave it until after ten o'clock. At ten o'clock the little hotel stopped ticking. The hot water bottles were filled and put up in the beds. The maids were gone to their rooms and Bina was able to bring him downstairs to her little hide-out and take things easy herself for a few hours.

It was a hideous little room, stuffed and cramped with ugly pieces of furniture and actually smelling of damp, but he understood that it was for privacy Mrs. Cussen – and, later, Bina – had chosen to have their private room in the basement. Only down there could they manage to keep the hotel guests out of their lives. Even he himself was no longer staying in the hotel when he first set foot in it. It was almost impregnable. The stairs that led down to it were steep, narrow and dark. Moreover one's descent was blocked midway down by a green baize door beyond which only the most accustomed foot could descend in safety. And that by day! At night, when the light could only be switched on from below – and the bulb could never have been stronger than twenty watt – that stairs was as black as a coal hole. Then its privacy was inviolate. After eleven o'clock, when Bina made her last ascent to put the chain on the outer door and turn out the hall light, the little basement room might as well have been a cave tunnelled under a mountain.

Once down in that little cave, sunk into the battered armchairs, one on either side of the fire, Bina and her mother had things so arranged that they seldom had to stand up again until they stood up to go to bed. Everything was to hand. They even had a little tin kettle – specially small to fit on the bars of the narrow parlour grate – so they could heat the water for their own hot bottles or make a cup of tea for themselves if they felt like it. They even – and this always made him smile – they even had an old grey woollen sock hanging on the knob of the tongs to catch hold of the handle of the kettle. It was a man's sock, he noticed one night, with amusement. It might even be an old sock of his own after all those years. He had left a lot of odds and ends behind him when he was shifting to consulting rooms in Fitzwilliam, because it wasn't as if he were leaving them in ordinary lodgings; he knew Mrs. Cussen and Bina would care for anything belonging to him, and that he could take his time about picking them up. He'd be dropping in to see them often. Or so he thought. He'd promised faithfully to do so, knowing it would mean a lot to them.

It had been a break leaving the little hotel. But he knew he couldn't afford to let the grass grow under his feet. It wasn't as if he were buying a practice. His high marks in the finals – second place – gave him the right to set up in Fitzwilliam, but he knew he would have to put up his plate straight away before he was back-numbered. He set up without delay, in the thick of the established men. Nothing very grand – just the usual thing: reception room and consulting-room on the ground floor, with private accommodation in another part of the house. His rooms were by no means posh in those days, but he had had a good eye for what was "the thing", and his rooms were much the same as the rooms of the other specialists. Indeed they were just what he had envisaged they would be when he was a student taking note of everything about the top men in his profession. There was a coldness that characterized these men at the top, and everything belonging to them – their manner, their voices, their hands, but above all their rooms, that were never more than moderately heated. He used to think there was an air of touch-me-not about their furniture, with its high cold gloss. If one touched a table-top, one was apt to be overcome with shame at the way a ring of mist would spread out from under one's hand and then as suddenly contract again, almost as if the highly polished wood shrank repulsed from the contact.

Well! He had the same cold mahogany now in his own reception room, but it did not mist or shrink from his hands, because his hands were no longer hot and moist. He was fully acclimatized to professional life.

Anyway he was very seldom in his rooms for long. And as for sitting down! As he said to Bina one night, he hardly ever sat down in an armchair except when he dropped into Baggot Street to see her, which although not often, he had had at least the good grace to do so oftener after Mrs Cussen died and Bina was on her own.

It was true he seldom relaxed elsewhere. When did he get a chance to sit down? He was in the operating theatre from nine to eleven every morning, and after that he had his clinics. A good part of the afternoon was spent in the wards. From three to six he saw private patients, and then the night visits began. He had only himself to blame for the latter, of course. In the beginning of his career – whether from ambition or from conscientiousness he could not say – although he was inclined to be a bit scrupulous in his early days – he had formed a habit of paying a late visit to the hospital before he went to bed every night.

They were a mistake, those late rounds. On the other hand they had helped to establish a reputation for him. The staff, of course, in a short time became so accustomed to having him drop in around midnight that they counted on his coming, and decisions that should have been the province of the house surgeon or the matron, or even of the nurses in many cases, were deferred instead to him. It meant, in the long run, that everyone shifted his or her responsibility onto his shoulders, day and night. And the worst feature of it was that, as time went on, they all lost sight of the fact that his nightly attendance was voluntary. It would have seemed like neglect of duty if he failed to put in an appearance.

But he didn't mind. It was all part of the price he had been prepared to pay from the start. *Per ardua ad astra*. He hadn't forgotten that motto when he got to the top like some of the other fellows that had qualified with him. It wasn't enough to get to the top: you had to stay there; and as far as he could make out, to stay there meant ruling out a lot of things that other men took to be theirs by right.

So many of his contemporaries had fallen back into mediocrity for the sake of bodily comfort. It was usually marriage of course. Almost without exception his contemporaries had made indifferent marriages. They never seemed to consider whether or not a girl would make a suitable doctor's wife. And what had determined their choice? As far as he could see, it was nothing more than propinquity or contiguity; they had almost all married their receptionist, or their secretary, or a pretty nurse.

There were notable exceptions of course. The wives of the men who were ambitious like him and who went on to specialize were very different from the wives of those who were content to become general practitioners. He used at one time to think the specialists' wives were a special breed. But when he made inquiries he was surprised at the humble origin of most of them. As a matter of fact Mandeville's wife, just like Bina, was the daughter of a small hotel-keeper, but the hotel was in some seaside resort, Kilkee or Tramore, and that made a difference he supposed. Because you couldn't imagine Bina ever turning into a Mrs. Mandeville. Not that he was criticizing Bina. On the contrary, he had always had the highest opinion of her. He often wondered that she never married, and felt she deserved better than the lot that seemed to have fallen to her. She ought to have had someone to provide for her as she got older. But she was very unambitious. She never made any effort in that direction, in spite of the fact that it was mostly elderly, and often eligible, men who stayed in the little hotel. Bina got on well with them too, and had plenty of chances to get to know them because although Mrs. Cussen didn't like keeping permanent boarders – nor Bina herself either – it came to almost the one thing in the end because the same people came there month after month.

It was only because he had got the soft side of Mrs. Cussen that they had taken him – because they never kept students. And never, under any circumstances, did they keep medicals. But once he'd got in he knew he was in clover and he made up his mind he'd stay there by hook or by crook until he was qualified.

They didn't know he was a medical at first. He'd got around Mrs. Cussen with a doleful story about a digs in Grantham Street where he had to stuff his sock in a broken window and put the floor-rug over him in his bed at night. She was a motherly soul and that touched her heart. She agreed to let him stay for a few weeks. And then when she saw that he was sober and earnest she consented to keep him as a permanent. She was shrewd, that was it – and she knew he was bent on getting to the top, and she admired him for it. She began to take an interest in him. He landed on his feet there and no mistake. If it wasn't for the way she and Bina had minded him all those years, he'd hardly have done so well.

That was a thing people didn't take into account, that in a man's early years he needs minding. Poor Mrs. Cussen couldn't have minded him better if he were her own son. She never let a night pass without sending Bina up to him with a cup of hot milk before he went to bed.

He'd want to be very ungrateful to forget what they did for him.

And he hadn't forgotten. He hadn't gone back to see them as often as he ought after he left and went to Fitzwilliam, but they were understanding people. And they were always glad to see him when he

did call. It was really pathetic the welcome he got the first night he
went back.

"It's not you!" Bina cried, looking at him as if she could not believe
her eyes. "Come on downstairs," she cried, and she brought him
right down to the basement – for the first time – right into their little
private room, going before him sideways down the stairs like a crab in
order that he might have more light to pick his steps, or so he thought
at the time. It may just have been that she didn't want to miss a minute
of him. She hadn't taken her eyes off him.

"You've put on weight," she said. "And may I admire your new
suit?" It was like old times. It warmed his heart the way she called
down to her mother. "It's Dr. Lew, Mother!"

That was another thing. From the moment he qualified they stopped
calling him Lew and began to call him Dr. Lew. As a matter of fact
their entire attitude towards him changed subtly after he moved to
Fitzwilliam. And mind you, he appreciated it. They helped him to
realize his own importance. It wasn't as if they were any the less
friendly or kind towards him. It was just that they knew the difference
between intimacy and familiarity – particularly Bina. Now and again
Mrs. Cussen used to be a little bit free with him.

"You're working too hard," she'd said one night. "You're not the
young dog you were when you were here, you know." He thought
that was a bit over-familiar at the time, but he knew it was motherliness
that was behind it. She was so proud of him. That was it. She admitted
it. "It isn't because you're a big pot that we're proud of you, you know,"
she said. "We're proud of you because of all the good you do for the
poor; isn't that right, Bina?"

He laughed.

"Is she codding me, Bina?" he asked, to hide his gratification.

But Bina was twice as proud of him.

"You don't hear all the nice things *we* hear about you," she said. It
was Bina who stuck his picture up on the mantelpiece, and when he
remarked on it she was not a bit put out. "Indeed, it's about time you
gave us a proper photograph," she said, "and not have us put up with
that old stickyback we found in your room after you were gone."

Bina never hid her regard for him. She had no sense of propriety. He
often noticed that. When her mother got the second stroke and wasn't
able to come downstairs any more – and later when poor Mrs. Cussens
was dead – Bina still brought him down to the little room in the

G

basement, and it never seemed to cross her mind that it was in any way peculiar to be alone with him down there until all hours, as they were many nights.

That was just like her, of course, unself-conscious.

It was curious all the same that she never thought of him in any other light than that of an old friend. Of course, that was the light in which he saw himself, too, but once or twice when he was sitting in the little room with her it had crossed his mind that it wouldn't be too bad at all if, instead of having to get up and go out into the cold, to his cheerless rooms, he could sit there opposite her until it was time to stand up for good. The thought didn't excite him, of course, but that may have been because he never thought of it as anything that could still happen – only as something that might have happened.

There they would have sat, he thought, married or single, in just the same way, with him yawning every other few minutes and Bina gently accusing him of working too hard.

She never minded whether he talked or not. He could just sit there in front of her like a pig with his legs stretched out, not saying a word if he didn't want. She never made any demands on him at any time, not even the smallest.

How then had the picture altered so quickly – in a few minutes, you might say, on the night that boy died? That was what he could not understand, no matter how often he went over the events of the night.

Of course, he had been very upset. That was why he had made straight for Baggot Street. And Bina had looked so different when she came down to the door. For one thing she was in her nightdress, and for another she was without her glasses.

She had heard his knock and come down herself to the door. The maids would have been afraid, thinking it could be some drunk who had come to the wrong door.

"My God, Lew, what is the matter?" she cried.

"Let me in," he said roughly. "I'll tell you then."

He wanted to get in off the street, the vacant dawnlit street that had accentuated the unreality of his situation. But to his astonishment she hesitated.

"I'm not dressed," she said.

Then under his withering look she stepped back and let him enter. Did she think he was fool enough to be affected by the sight of a woman in her nightdress?

"I don't think this is the first time I saw you in this elegant garment," he said cuttingly, because even in his upset state his eye had taken in the stained and faded condition of the old woollen dressing-gown she had bundled about her. But, curiously enough, although he spoke so sharply he didn't really mind the dirty old dressing-gown. It reminded him of when he was staying in the place and made it seem more natural for him to have come back there when he was in trouble. His nerves were all on edge though. "For God's sake don't keep clutching it like that; you're not naked under it, are you?" he said. He knew she was far from being naked. Under the woollen thing, as far as he could make out, she had some other preposterous garment. Could it be flannelette? He didn't think there were still women who wore such garments. It was like what his mother used to wear – God be good to her – when she'd come in to him in the middle of the night if he wakened in a nightmare. He knew just how it would feel, warm and moist. He knew just the way it would smell, stuffy and sweet. Oh, with what relief he used to bury his head in those stuffy flannelette folds. For a moment he had had an almost overpowering longing to bury his face in Bina's bosom. But at that point he was still in command of himself and knew he couldn't do a thing like that. And in any case it was enough to be with her – someone he knew, someone who was not a stranger.

"Oh, Bina," he said, and he covered his face with his hands. "I'm in such trouble." But they were still standing in the hallway, and he felt uncomfortable. He glanced up the well of the staircase. If there was anyone else awake in the hotel his voice would easily carry up to them. "Let's go downstairs," he said, and he motioned towards the basement steps. But Bina held back. For a minute he thought that she was looking at him queerly, and blinking. Since she wasn't wearing her glasses perhaps she thought he had drink taken? He had never before seen her without her glasses, although he used to wonder what she would be like without them, and he remembered thinking, once, that if she had married her husband would have seen her without them: it would have been one of their first intimacies. And he had felt in some way sorry for her, as if over and above the pitiful exposure of her sex she would have been submitted to an additional indignity. But he was wrong in thinking that she had doubted his sobriety. She had only delayed to run into the dining-room and snatch up a glass and a decanter.

He had to stop her from pouring it out.

"No – please," he cried, impatiently. "They might smell it off my breath."

It wasn't until then that she realized there was something very seriously wrong. The extraordinary thing was that she jumped at once to the conclusion it was the boy.

"Is it that boy you were telling me about last night; the one you were dropping in to see again before you went back to Fitzwilliam?" He nodded. He couldn't help being touched, because he himself hadn't remembered telling her anything at all about the case. But he must have made some reference to having an appendectomy for the morning. "Is he – dead?" she asked quietly. He nodded. She said nothing for a moment or two. "My poor Lew," she said then. He almost burst into tears. That was what you might call a friend. Her loyalty was such that she didn't wait to hear what had happened: she was on his side at once. It was so different from the hostile attitude at the hospital. "Surely you're not blaming yourself, Lew?" she cried. "You often said yourself that there is no such thing as an unsuccessful operation – that the damage is done long before the case comes onto the table – that the operation can only attempt to remedy matters."

At that point he couldn't help being a bit edgy with her.

"You've got it wrong," he said abruptly. "I didn't get time to operate."

But she wasn't one to waver.

"Do you mean they didn't get you in time? Why, that was criminal negligence!"

He winced. "It wasn't their fault," he said impatiently. "They tried to get me on the 'phone repeatedly. Can't you let me tell you, Bina, and not keep interrupting me?"

But she wasn't listening to him.

Her face was white.

"You were sick, Lew?" she cried, and she made a start forward almost as if she were going to put out her arms to him, but she stopped short of it.

"No, no, there was nothing the matter with me," he said. "At least not in the ordinary sense of the word." He paused and took a breath. "I was asleep, Bina – outside the house – in the car!" If telling her was hard, how would he ever tell the Board? It sounded so incredible, so foolish. "If I was in the house I'd have heard the 'phone, but I was outside in the car asleep. I must have closed my eyes for a minute when I got to the kerb, and the next thing I knew it was morning – morning! – and the telephone was ringing; but although I got the door opened in time to answer, it was only to tell me they couldn't get any pulse."

At the thought of the way he felt when he had wakened, cramped and frozen, on the seat of the car, and staggered into the house to take up the receiver to hear the consequence of his lapse, he gave a violent shudder.

"You mustn't let it upset you, Lew," she said quietly. "Think of all the hundreds of lives you've saved. Think of that!"

She still didn't seem to understand the full seriousness of the situation.

"You don't seem to realize, there'll be an inquiry," he said sharply.

"Do you mean you'll be blamed?" She looked so bewildered as to appear actually stupid. "How could they possibly blame you? If it was anyone's fault it was the fault of the hospital – yes, I mean it – you're grossly overworked there – you know it – I told you so a hundred times. I'm always saying it. So was poor Mother. I used to say to her, 'I hope they're grateful, that's all–' "

She was so vehement he stared at her in surprise. It was true what she said; he was overworked. Many a time he had had to acknowledge it when in her mother's time they were all three sitting around the fire, so cozy, so warm. Oh, those evenings were so happy. Would such evenings ever come again?

"You don't understand, Bina!" he said. "This could be the end of me. A man in my position has so many enemies; people are so jealous, you know nothing about it. They're only watching for you to make a false step and they come down on you."

It was true, and as he said it, involuntarily as a wave of nausea, the longing came over him again to press his head into the soft moist flannelette bosom at which he was staring. But Bina's practicality was like cold water.

"What kind of talk is that?" she said. "I'm surprised at you. Have you no confidence. I must say that I think you ought to have a little more faith in the people at the hospital, too, if it goes to that!" He couldn't help admiring her. She built him up. "Inquiry indeed!" she scoffed. "I'll tell you what there ought to be: an inquiry into when you last had a holiday! I'm surprised at you, Lew. You'll be ashamed of yourself when you think things over. You'll find there will be no inquiry at all; or if there is, it will be only a formality." She was so matter-of-fact. Indeed just then she looked up the well of the stairs. "I thought I heard someone stirring," she said. "It's getting on for seven. The maids will be getting up. It wouldn't do for you to be seen here. And anyway you're not shaved. Are you going back to the hospital? Because if you are I think you ought to go around to Fitz-william first and shave and have a wash. You look a bit the worse for wear. Take a look at yourself." She nodded at the little diamond of mirror on the hall-stand.

He did look bad. There was no doubt about that. It sobered him to think that he had to go out into the street in that condition. He didn't want to go.

"I'd better get back I suppose," he said, half-heartedly.

"That's the spirit," Bina said, and she opened the hall door.

Instantly, when the door was opened, his reluctance to go out vanished. In fact he felt eager all at once to get away. There was a stuffy night odour in the little hotel and out in the street the air was fresh and untouched. He felt stifled every minute he remained within. But he could not rush out abruptly. After all, he had wakened her up out of her sleep and it was too late now for her to go back to bed. She would be on her feet all day. She was fagged-looking even now, he saw with compunction. And, of course, she was not as young as she used to be. Suddenly he wanted desperately to be kind; to show his gratitude. She had done so much for him in the bad half-hour that had passed. Perhaps she was correct in thinking everything would be all right? He was inclined to see things in a different light by then himself. But there was no doubt things had looked black to him when he had first come knocking on her door. Only for her – well, candidly, he didn't like to think of what might have happened. She had helped him to live through the worst hours of his whole life.

"You're a good friend, Bina," he cried, from the bottom of his heart.

She was pleased. He could see she was pleased. But that wasn't enough for him. He had to let her see how he felt. "I wish there was something I could do for you, Bina. Isn't there anything I could do for you?"

But what needs had she that he could satisfy?

"Take care of yourself, Lew," she said quietly. "That's the best thing you can do for me."

It was inexpressibly touching. He was bowed down with humility in the face of such unselfishness.

"I will," he said simply.

He stepped out into the air. Then he turned and put out his hand. She took it.

"When this is all over, Lew, I hope you'll take a good holiday."

Now that was something positive she was asking of him. He owed it to her to treat it seriously.

"I'll do that, Bina," he said, emphatically. "I promise. When this thing blows over I'll take a good holiday." It was quite an idea; he needed a rest. Not just for a few days, either, but a decent holiday. He might take a few weeks off and a trip over to the Continent. He looked across the rooftops in the direction of the coast. This would be just the time of year for it too. He took a deep breath. He felt better with every second that passed. It was hard to think that he had been so rattled. He hoped they had not seen in the hospital how rattled he was. If so, the sooner he got back there the better, to let them see him in his new frame of mind. "Well, Bina – thanks again." He went down two steps.

"You won't forget the holiday?"

"I won't forget," he said. He was standing on the pavement below her looking up. By then he desperately wanted to get away. "But you'll see me again before," he added. Surely she didn't think that he would be casual enough to go away on a holiday without calling to thank her if only for her kindness?

And yet it was just what he'd be likely to do to her – unless – unless? Just as he was about to walk confidently away, this word arrested him. Unless? Unless what? Supposing she was too confident, supposing he'd allowed himself to become too lulled into confidence by her? Supposing things went badly for him? He'd be back to her soon enough then! He had told her she was a good friend. She was more than that; she was the only friend he had. If things went against him, and he had to pack his bags, he'd have to have someone to go with him wherever he went. He'd never be able to start all over again without someone to help him. He'd never build up a practice again in a new place – alone.

But Bina was closing the door. "Bina!" He felt if that door closed he would be all alone in the world. He ran up the steps. "Will you be here all day, Bina?" he cried.

"I suppose so," she said absently, and glanced back over her shoulder. The maids would soon be getting up and coming downstairs. "Why?"

"I might be back," he said. But he didn't feel safe in leaving it at that. He'd have to go the whole hog. "Wait a minute, Bina. Don't go. I want to ask you something. Will you come with me – on the holiday, I mean?" It gave him some satisfaction to see how stupefied she looked. He hadn't been walked into it anyway: it was his own doing. "Will you marry me, Bina? No matter what happens – no matter how things go with me?"

It was the only thing he could do. You couldn't ask any woman to wait, and see how things went; even a person like Bina.

The only pity was that there had never been any question of things going badly. If he had kept his head he would have known that everything would be all right. It was only a little cloud that blew up in a clear sky, and after a few days it had blown over. And afterwards everything would have been the same as ever – only for Bina. Not that he was altogether sorry. And he did badly need a holiday.

The Long Holidays

"You may as well call me Dolly," said Dolly, whenever she was being introduced. "Everybody does. It's silly really, now I'm a grown-up woman; but what can I do?" And she'd laugh – a little dolly laugh. For the most part, people were relieved when she herself mentioned her size. They felt at liberty to utter the exclamations that rose to their lips the moment they set eyes on her tiny little figure, her tiny feet and hands, and her tiny tiny waist.

"I have a friend who can span my waist with one hand," Dolly said, and presumably the friend was a gentleman.

Dolly had lots of gentlemen friends. Just to look at her made men feel big and strong. Unfortunately she had the same effect upon ladies; she made them feel big and strong too, so she had not many lady friends. This didn't matter to Dolly, however, because Dolly didn't care much for ladies anyway. They always seemed to be jealous of her, although most of them had so much more of everything than she had: more hip, more middle, more bust. Dolly was frightened of them, really. She made it a point never to be alone with them, but sometimes she got cornered, in the ladies' cloakroom, and it terrified her the way they seemed to pen her up, and pluck at her.

"How do you ever get things to fit you?" they'd cry. "Fancy having to have everything made or altered!"

The married ones were the worst. "I suppose it's *deliberately* you never got married?" one of them whispered into her ear one day. The implications of this seemed so enormous, yet at the same time so undiscoverable to Dolly, that she was frightened to death for weeks. Because, of course, it was not deliberate at all.

So when the Major came along, Dolly had no hesitation, on any account whatever. With the Major at her back – even metaphorically – she wasn't half as frightened of other women as she used to be, and she didn't mind any more when they exclaimed at her size.

"You should see me beside my fiancé," she'd say. "I'm like a real doll beside him," and opening the beak of her little handbag she would take out a snapshot.

There she was, on the left of the picture, as small as ever, in a long white dress and a big white hat, with a parasol on one arm, and the Major on the other, although, considering the size of Dolly, and the size of the Major, who was six feet one in his socks, it might have been more exact to say it was a picture of the Major with Dolly on his arm. One usually associates the lesser as belonging to the greater. There are exceptions, of course, as one can see by the *Tatler,* which invariably has at least one photograph of a little man in white ducks and topi holding up by his side some mighty monster of land or sea. And the Major was definitely Dolly's trophy.

Even in our hour of glory, however, we have our detractors. And some people wondered if Dolly would have captured the Major so readily if he hadn't been a widower with a small son on his hands. But Dolly seemed to take Vinnie in her stride.

"He's only a baby," she said, "hardly eleven! I'm longing to give him the comforts of a real family life. I haven't met him yet, he's away at boarding school – but I'm looking forward wildly to when he comes home. I bet I'll turn out to be a born stepmother!" She turned to the Major. "Has he a tuck-box, darling?" When she heard the boy did not have one the first thing she did after she and the Major were married was buy a big box, and off she went to the station with it strapped to the back of the little red car the Major had bought for her. And after that there was hardly a day she didn't drive to the post office to despatch a postcard or a bundle of comics.

The postmistress was deeply touched by this devotion. "You won't feel till you'll have him home for the holidays, ma'am."

Then, two days before the holidays, Vinnie got the mumps!

Dolly was so disappointed, the Major had to keep reminding her that the next term was a short one. When that term came to an end, however, there was another disappointment. It appeared that Vinnie's house-master had planned to take a party of boys to Switzerland, and it seemed wrong to deprive Vinnie of the chance of going. It seemed a pity to disappoint the young teacher too, he was so madly keen. The young man had never been abroad before, and this was a great chance for him, because a travel agency was sponsoring the trip, as an advertisement, and issuing free travel vouchers to any teacher who succeeded in rounding up twenty boys. The young man might never get another chance, because the whole thing was an experiment, and might easily be a dismal failure. Boys were so troublesome, always getting into mischief, and liable to every kind of misadventure – illness, accidents, God only knows what! Anything might happen! And, of course, if anything did happen to one of the kids that would be the end of the scheme as far as the travel agency was concerned.

"In Vinnie's case," the Major said, "the ups and downs will be a good thing. Good for his character. We simply cannot refuse to let him go. We must be firm, though, when it comes to the summer holidays, because he'll probably be asked to stay with people. When I was a little chap, other chaps were always inviting me to stay. My mother used to be furious: she hardly ever saw me."

"Surely you didn't stay with people for the summer holidays," said Dolly. "Not the *long* holidays? Who could possibly want another person's child around the place for three months – particularly in the dead of summer? I'm sure we can count on having Vinnie home. In fact, I'm going to start making preparations right away."

The Major couldn't but be proud of the way Dolly threw herself into these preparations. Every day she seemed to have a new suggestion for making the boy's holidays enjoyable. "We'll get his room repapered," she'd cry one day. And the next day she'd want to know if he had a bicycle? "If not we'll have to get him one at once," she'd declare. "And what about a fishing-rod? And roller-skates? Or is he too small for roller-skates?"

"Too big, I think, my dear," the Major said. But Dolly felt one was never too old to have fun.

"What else can we get him?" she cried.

Every day there was fresh excitement; it was a regular plan of campaign. One day, about a fortnight before Vinnie's arrival, the Major's eye fell on the little silver calendar on Dolly's desk. He was deeply touched. For the date on which Vinnie was expected home had been singled out by Dolly from all the other dates in the month, and ringed around with red ink, till it stood out like a military target. And the days that lay between her and her objective, like cities in the path of an advancing army, had been heavily scored out, devastated, sacked.

Looking at that calendar, the Major was ashamed of how little he personally had done to prepare for his son's homecoming. But what was there left to do? Dolly seemed to have bought the boy everything under the sun.

Suddenly the Major got a brain-wave. Boxing-gloves!

The boxing-gloves had to be ordered, and they didn't arrive until the day Vinnie himself was due. And by that time Dolly was suffering from nervous exhaustion. When she saw them on the hall table she shuddered.

"Ugh! Aren't they ugly!"

She couldn't get them out of her mind all day. Like human hands, big and bloated – abnormally big – they floated before her as she rushed around putting last-minute touches to things. In the end, a morbid fascination made her pick them up and examine them. She put them down hastily.

"I never really saw a pair before," she said. "Not so close." She shuddered again.

"I had no idea they'd upset you like this. I wish I hadn't got them," the Major said.

Dolly told him not to be silly.

"The boy has to have them," she said, but a far-away look came in her eyes. "It would be different if it were a little girl." And, then, a few minutes later, to the Major's distress, when they were upstairs taking a last look around Vinnie's room to see that nothing was missing, she sighed. "It would have been much easier to get a room ready for a little girl – and so much more fun. I'm sure that if I had had a child of my own it would have been a little girl – because I'm so small," she added quickly, when the Major turned a hurt eye upon her. "Let me see," she said dreamily. "I'd have pink wallpaper instead of that bright blue – it's too bright, I think, don't you? I'd have little white ruffles – "

But the Major had to cut her short. It was time to go to the station to meet Vinnie.

The minute Vinnie jumped out of the train, Dolly got a start. He was so big. He rushed up to them like a young bull.

I'll scream if he puts his arms around me she thought when she saw how he grabbed at his father.

And just then the Major made things worse.

"Shake hands nicely with your mother," he said.

"Don't you think he ought to call me Dolly?" Dolly cried. People might think he was her real son! And her mind revolted against such an error. It would not be seemly for people to think she was his mother

– this great lump of a boy. Already she thought she'd seen a woman on the platform snigger. "Let's hurry home," she said, anxious to get out of the station.

The drive home was far from pleasant though. Vinnie was sitting on the back seat but he kept leaning forward and breathing down her neck all the way.

And such facetiousness!

"Thanks for the lift," he said, as he bounded ahead of them out of the car and up the steps to the house.

"We'll have to draw his attention to the foot-scrapper," the Major said placatingly, when they saw the muddy tracks on the parquet floor.

"I think it would be better to draw the attention of the cobbler to his boots," Dolly said, because the floor was scratched as well. "Oh, never mind," she added resignedly, "we may make it less noticeable with sandpaper. Oh dear! What was that?"

There was such a crash.

It was only Vinnie's door banging, as he went out to the toilet, but after he had come out and gone in a second time, and come out again, and gone back to his own room, Dolly began to realize she might as well get used to doors banging.

"Better call him down for his sandwiches, dear," she said to the Major. It being late afternoon and near suppertime, she had cut some sandwiches and covered them with a napkin so that she wouldn't have to set the table twice. But what a quantity of sandwiches the boy ate! To begin with, he took two at a time, and he let half of the filling fall on the carpet. It would have been far better to have set the table.

Well, I'll know next time, Dolly told herself.

Long before suppertime came around, however, Dolly began to think that no woman's memory could possibly store so many precautionary plans for the future as were necessitated by Vinnie's conduct. And, of course, one would always have to deal with unlooked-for accidents that couldn't possibly be foreseen.

She had to admit that the boy was willing enough to please her. He even suggested taking off his hobnailed boots every time he came in through the hall door, though why he couldn't use the back door she did not know!

It was on one of these occasions, when he was crossing the hall in his bare feet, that Dolly noticed the peculiar marks his stockinged feet had made on the floor – wet and sticky, like paw marks.

"Are your feet wet, Vinnie?" she called after him.

"How could they be wet?" Vinnie looked at her with surprise. It was a warm summer day. Then he looked at the marks on the floor. "Maybe it's sweat!" he said.

Dolly turned aside hastily. It was too near suppertime to let one's mind dwell on such a thought.

Then, just as they were sitting down to supper, with the soup in front of them, the Major gave a sniff. Although it was evening it was still very warm, and the odour of food hung heavy in the air, the odour of food and – yes – of something else.

"Peculiar smell, isn't there?" the Major said.

Dolly glanced at the window.

"Something outside, I dare say. Something dead in the wood, perhaps? Shall we shut the window?"

But when the window was shut the smell was worse.

Vinnie tried to be helpful by sniffing harder than anyone.

"That's enough," the Major said at last.

They ate in silence for a few minutes, and then suddenly Vinnie put down his soup spoon.

"Perhaps it's my feet that smell?" he said helpfully.

"Is that meant to be a joke, young man?" the Major asked icily.

It was not a joke.

"Don't they have any regard for personal hygiene in that school?" Dolly said faintly, addressing herself to the Major.

But fair was fair: Vinnie wasn't prepared to let his school be maligned. He hurried to correct a false impression.

"It's not my feet, it's my socks," he said, and he turned to Dolly aggrievedly. "I told you in a letter that we have to pay out of our pocket-money for getting our socks washed. They don't go on the bill like shirts and things. A woman in the village does them whenever we want. Some fellows don't get theirs done at all, she charges too much – threepence a sock. It's a bit thick, isn't it?"

Dolly turned to the Major.

"Please, dear!" she said. "Do something!"

Vinnie was sent off at once to change his socks.

"Take a pair of mine if necessary," the Major shouted.

Vinnie wasn't long changing.

"This calls for a fresh start I think," he said, as he sat down, and he took a second helping of soup; a much larger helping than the first.

"You're spilling it," Dolly said, as he carried his plate from the sideboard to the table.

"Only a small drop," said Vinnie.

The meal continued.

It was in the middle of the custard and apple that Dolly saw the warts.

"How did you get those disgusting things on your hands, Vinnie?" she cried, and taking out her handkerchief she put it to her mouth. "Look at them," she said impatiently, pointing them out to the Major. "Around his thumb. You must be blind if you can't see them. And there are more on his wrist, under the strap of his watch. I never saw anything so unsightly in all my life. Really! It does seem odd that something wasn't done about them if the school is as good as it's said to be."

The Major examined the warts.

"I must say they are not a pretty sight," he said, "but I don't know that it's fair to blame the school. At a certain age boys are inclined to get warts, I believe – and some people say they are contagious, too, which makes it more difficult to control them. Indeed, I seem to remember having heard it is nearly impossible to get rid of them. You simply have to wait till they go away of their own accord. There isn't any really reliable cure."

"Nonsense," Dolly said. "That's all superstition – and ignorance. I'll bring him down to the dispensary first thing in the morning and get them treated with caustic."

Vinnie was the only one still eating while this conversation was going on, but he was evidently closely following what was being said. Ramming a last piece of cake into his mouth, warts or no warts he wiped his mouth clean with the back of his hand.

"Will they charge for taking them off?" he asked with great interest.

"Only a few shillings," Dolly said. "You'll have to go down there two or three times. I don't think the caustic removes them at once; it withers them away gradually. But anyway the cost is unimportant."

It was not unimportant to Vinnie.

"Oh, shucks!" he said. "I wouldn't waste good money like that if I were you! I'll get them off when I go back to school. Can't think why I didn't have them done before the holidays! I can get them off for nothing! There's a chap in the lower form that takes them off for everybody – he gets them off right away – first go – you don't have to go back to *him* – and all you have to pay him is do his sums for him every night for a week. A week a wart – that's his charge."

Then and there he began to calculate how many weeks' sums he'd have to do for this warts.

"Seven weeks!" he said, partly in dismay, partly in awe.

In spite of herself Dolly was interested.

"How does he do it?" she asked, as she took up her fork again.

Vinnie looked surprised that she should have to be told.

"Bites them off – how else did you think?" he said, and then he looked at the Major. "What's the matter with her?" he asked.

For Dolly had rushed from the room.

She didn't come down any more that evening, but next morning, when the Major was passing her desk, he noticed that the little army of black numbers on the calendar was once more on the march. This time it was the date of Vinnie's departure that had been singled out as the objective. And in the vast desert of days that had yet to be traversed before that objective was achieved – only one day had passed. Unlike the short, quick campaign that had just been concluded, however, this new campaign would be a long-drawn-out affair, lasting the whole summer. And the forecast gave it for hot.

An Akoulina
of the Irish Midlands

Akoulina was not her name, of course, although oddly enough it might
have been a diminutive of it: Lena. Nor was there any exterior resemblance between my Lena and Turgenev's beautiful peasant girl in
The Tryst, who stirs the heart so deeply in that brief scene in the
birch glade when, like her pathetic bunch of cornflowers, she is trodden
underfoot by the affected Victor Alexandritch.

My Lena was far from beautiful. It was because she was so plain – I
had almost said ugly – that she first attracted my attention. On other
visits to the small country hotel where she worked as a waitress I had
found the servants all so neat and attractive I had come to think it a
perquisite of the guests to be attended on by pretty maids. And on this
particular occasion, as I was being driven up from the station in the
one and only hackney car, I was in fact wondering how on earth the
proprietors were able to persuade those good-looking girls to bury
themselves in such a backwater. I assure you it was a little hole of a
place, not particularly pleasing from a scenic point of view, and provid-
ing only middling quality fishing and shooting. Its charm for me lay
in the very fact that it was quiet and unfrequented. But what suited a
retiring person like myself was hardly likely to suit a lively servant girl.
What, for instance, did these girls do for male companionship? Except
for the hackney driver, whose dour but handsome profile was visible
to me in the little mirror on the side of his vehicle, there was, so far as I
knew, no other eligible young man in the locality. And upon him
various chambermaids and parlour-maids had pronounced judgment.
Some of them had confided in me that they thought him too stuck-up
for anything. They said he thought nobody was good enough for him,
and were all agreed there was no use wasting time on him. Indeed I
had seen for myself that he was unassailable. I had watched several
girls make unsuccessful tilts at him. Thinking of their shapely figures

and their fresh, pert faces, I wondered at his powers of resistance. He certainly seemed to have set himself a high standard. A confirmed misogamist?

Imagine my surprise, therefore, later that evening, when I saw my brave hackney driver standing under a tree on the avenue, to be joined after a few minutes by Lena. A Lena to whom he proudly offered his arm. A Lena who seemed to take his favours quite for granted! She was natural and easy with him, linking her arm in his and looking happily up into his face. In the course of the next few days I was in fact to learn that this complete lack of self-consciousness was one of Lena's pronounced characteristics. Another was the eagerness with which she threw herself into whatever was the matter of the moment. The first time she waited on me at table I had been struck by her vitality. Everything she did was done with tremendous energy. If she did but pull out your chair, or flick a crumb of bread from the table-cloth, you were aware of a force of life in excess of that which would, in a like instance, be exhibited by another person. And when she was engaged in something that was of special moment to her this vitality became tumultuous. Her little body then seemed a perilously fragile vessel to contain such strong fluid. In those moments her small face, at other times so plain, became irradiated by something that was a very good substitute for beauty. I would go so far as to say that anyone who saw her in one of those moments would be likely ever after, to be blind to her physical defects, in the same way that foreigners, having once seen our insignificant thrush burst upon a sudden into song, can never again look with indifference at that drab, dun-coloured bird. Thenceforth their every pinion is implicit with melody. So with my Lena. And lest you think this image far-fetched, I must tell you that, like the song-bird, Lena had a beautiful voice.

My room was at the head of a service-staircase leading down to the kitchens and pantries and half-way down these stairs there was a small still-room where Lena spent a good deal of her time. One day I was startled by a glorious voice rising up from this little cubby-hole, and after that I always left my bedroom door ajar to catch snatches of her singing, for, although with her irrepressible energy she was for ever flying up and down the stairs, and darting in and out of rooms, she always came back to her little pantry, like a bird come back to the bough. And once there she always broke involuntarily into song. Believe me it was heavenly sweet.

Do you know the thought that crossed my mind? I thought that He who made her, and watched over her from above, seeing how radiant had grown the soul that He had encased – would it be irreverent to say inadvertently? – in so awkward a body, must have leant down and given her that glorious voice, to be another vehicle for her soul's expression.

Anyway, taking all with all, when I got to know Lena better, I was less surprised than I had been at first by her having attracted the attention of the handsome Andy Hackett. He went up in my opinion. Instead of being a contemptuous scorner of pretty girls he must be a connoisseur. One who knew a good thing when he saw it. He must have discernment, discrimination, depth. He'll marry her too, I thought, as I looked out of my window at them, going down the avenue every evening arm in arm.

I was surprised, however, one day, when happening to take a short-cut down the service-stairs which we guests were not supposed to use, I heard someone sobbing in the little pantry on the landing. Surely it could not be my Lena? But who else? None of the other servants used that little closet, and as I glanced into it, I saw – like a signature proclaiming it to be her private place – a pair of cheap silk stockings hanging to dry on the hot pipes, and they were the hideous apricot colour – sold no doubt for flesh-colour – which my poor Lena greatly favoured. I put my head around the door.

It was Lena. When she saw me she crouched back behind the door, and began at once to excuse herself.

"Oh, sir! I didn't know there was anyone about at this hour. Nobody ever comes in here. It's my little pantry, and I . . ."

Feverishly she wiped away her tears with the tail of her apron. But her grief, like all her other emotions, was profound, and in the short time she had been crying it had ravaged her face. Never had she looked plainer, and I couldn't help thinking of her handsome swain, and of how incongruously she would at that moment have paired with him. Had they had a tiff, I wondered?

But no: that was not it.

"Oh, well, if you haven't lost your beau, I can't see what you have to cry about, my dear," I said. "As you know, my room is at the front and every evening when I see you going off with him I think how jealous all the other girls must be of you!"

But if I expected her to pick up, to preen, I was disappointed.

Instead, she looked up at me with her whole heart – her whole soul – in her eyes.

"What good is that when we can't get married?" she cried. But before I had time to ask the reason she proffered it. "On account of my religion, sir," she said.

So they were not of the same religion? That was something I hadn't expected. There must have been five or six hundred in the congregation that met every Sunday in the big Catholic church on the hill behind the hotel, and less than twenty in the little Protestant church at the foot of the hill.

Perhaps it was because the little Protestant church had a lonely look about it that I jumped to the conclusion Andy was the Protestant, for he too had always struck me as lonely. He didn't seem to have any family. He slept in a loft over the shed where he kept his hackney car. Thinking that his conversion would embarrass no one but himself, whereas Lena had her family to consider, I patted her reassuringly on the shoulder.

"Oh, you'll convert him, Lena," I said, and showing how complacently I had accepted the local colloquialism for conversion, I trotted it out glibly. "He'll turn with you Lena," I said. "You'll see. He'll turn."

But Lena looked at me sorrowfully.

"Oh, sir, you don't understand. It's not Andy that's the Protestant. It's *me*."

Why, of course! How could I have forgotten? Lena did not live in at the hotel. She lived with her family in the basement of the Protestant church. I had several times seen her scuttling down the vaulted steps to those underground quarters where the family lived. I had even suspected that her family might be indebted to Lena for their habitation, bad as it was, and held it perhaps in token of her services in the choir. How could I have forgotten! I used to think of the little family as a family of church mice when I'd see them disappearing into their dark hole! But I knew there was a serious housing shortage in the locality, and no church mice could have had a greater dependency upon the Church Body than Lena's people! I realized she and Andy were in an awkward situation. And when, at that moment, down from the big chapel on the hill, there rolled the deep tones of the Angelus bell, Lena started to sob again, bitterly.

"I'd love to be a Catholic," she sobbed. "I think it's a lovely religion.

All the candles they burn! And the lovely smell of incense that comes out the door when you're passing. And the singing! I often stood outside – even before I met Andy – especially of a winter evening when it was dark and I wouldn't be seen, and I listened to the singing. It was just like a concert. And I thought how I'd love to be in there in the crowd, matching my voice with the voices of all the other people, singing out free and not minding whether they were in tune or not! Not like our church, that's always nearly empty with no music only a wheezy harmonica and no voice but mine wavering up to the rafters. Oh, I always wanted to be a Catholic. Yes, even before I met Andy."

But I was hardly listening. I was thinking hard.

"Couldn't you get married and each keep your own religion?" I asked, knowing that mixed marriages, although frowned upon, were not unknown in Ireland. Admittedly they were difficult to arrange, but by no means impossible.

I'll never forget the way she looked at me.

"Oh, but I wouldn't want to be of a different way of thinking from my husband," she said. "In a real marriage the man and the woman ought to agree on everything. Surely God would not want them to differ – specially about Him?"

"I see," I said humbly. But to achieve this divine harmony, which Church – I wondered – would be the one to cede? "Well, I hope things will come out right for you somehow, Lena," I said, lamely, as I prepared to leave.

Despair, however, had gripped Lena in its vice.

"It will never come right," she said. "Andy will never turn."

"Well, then, it looks as if it will have to be you!" I said. "You'll have to put your own interests before your family, no matter what!"

Lena only sobbed louder.

"That's what I say to Andy. Doesn't the Bible tell us to forsake all others? To cleave unto each other? Doesn't it, sir?" she said. But suddenly it was as if there was a Third Person there with us in the little pantry – One who spoke more wisely than I and to whom Lena was listening. She dried her eyes. And at once I felt unwanted – or at least unneeded.

"Well, Lena," I said from the door. "Whatever about the future, take my advice and enjoy the present. I'll be watching you from my window this evening as usual and I hope I'll see you smiling and happy again."

"Thank you, sir," she said. Then, with the courtesy which was second nature to her, as I was going on down the stairs she came to the door and although I could see she was still in the grip of some inner excitement – she called after me. I was touched by the consideration of her words. "You won't see me this evening, sir," she said. "Today is my half-day and I'll be meeting Andy early. We're going for a walk in Bellinter Woods."

I myself had no idea of going near Bellinter Woods that afternoon. I was a most unwilling witness of what took place there. That I should happen to have been upon the scene at all was the merest accident. It rained heavily after lunch and I was later than usual taking my own afternoon airing. It started to rain again before I was ready to turn back, and there being a small wood at one side of the road I climbed over the ditch to take whatever refuge its leafy trees might offer.

I had no idea that such a small wood was dignified by a name at all – no idea that it was the trysting place of Lena and her swain. But I was actually thinking of the girl as I stood under the dripping trees looking out at the veils of rain that dimmed the landscape and made it seem nearer than it actually was to evening. Where was she, I wondered? It was a pity the weather was wet for her well-earned half-day.

As far as I was concerned the only good thing about this second shower was that it did not look as if it would last long – unlike the earlier downpour. And indeed, after a few minutes the clouds began to break, and patches of blue showed through the beech boughs overhead. Soon it would be only in the woods that rain still fell, dropping not from the sky but from the drenched leaves. And just then, as if to show the resilience of nature, at my feet a blade of grass that had been pressed down with the weight of the rain shed of a sudden its crystal burthen, and sprang upright. Next minute, darting out of their green tunnels in the undergrowth and scattering drops from their glossy wings, the birds began to fly about again and sing. And at the same time, everywhere, the air breathed forth a gentle exhalation from a million fresh-washed leaves.

I was about to make my way out to the road again when I became aware that someone was climbing over the ditch, as I had done earlier, and was coming into the wood. Instinctively I drew back with the slight start of the heart one experiences in a lonely place when another human being unexpectedly appears. Given a second to gather myself together I would have stepped forward, and declared myself – but the person who, next moment, came into fuller view was none other than Andy Hackett. Due no doubt to my conversation with Lena that morning, I felt an unaccountable awkwardness at sight of him, and drew back.

He would pass on in a minute or two, I thought, and then I could make my way out without a direct encounter. Meanwhile I might profit by taking another and closer look at him in view of what Lena had told me about him and their problem.

To my consternation, however, the young man approached to within a few paces of where I stood, and, looking at his watch, leant back against a nearby tree although its mossy bark was sodden. I looked around – behind me the undergrowth was too dense to penetrate. To get out on to the road again I would have to make my presence known and that I was more reluctant than ever to do. Would it not seem to Lena that I had come to Bellinter Wood intentionally knowing it was to be the place of their tryst? I was pondering unhappily on my predicament when I heard a twig crack underfoot again. I saw that Lena herself was approaching, her red cap bobbing up and down.

Having failed to make my presence known at the start, I was now properly trapped. I could only hope that, having met, the young couple would move away together. And I was confirmed in this hope by the fact that hearing her coming through the trees Andy had removed his handsome back from the tree which was so embarrassingly close to where I was standing – and had gone forward to meet her.

But good heavens! What had happened to her? I almost cried out myself at the sight of her, and Andy certainly did. She looked a fright – a positive fright! To begin with she was wet to the skin. But that wasn't all. The red dye from her cap had run in the rain and unknown to her had gone in streaks down her cheeks. As I said before, I nearly betrayed myself with a cry of surprise. But Andy's loud exclamation was less of surprise than annoyance.

"Are you out of your mind, Lena?" he cried. "Why didn't you shelter till that shower was over? You know I'd have waited?"

But even as he spoke, he must have seen, as I had done, that Lena was soaked to the skin. Her condition was wetter than could be accounted for by having been out in that one relatively short shower. Had she fallen into a river she could hardly have been more sopping. Water was actually dripping from her clothes, and forming a little pool on the earth around her. Yet under her saturated cap, between the wet coils of her hair, heavy as cables, her face was – if you can believe it – radiant.

"Oh, Andy, I was soused long before that shower!" she cried, and it was clear that her condition was in some odd way a cause of pride to her. Ignoring Andy's concern, she pulled off her cap and began to shake it. "Wait till you hear!" she cried. "I suppose I ought not to have gone when the day turned out so bad, but I'd made up my mind, and I wasn't going to be stopped by a sup of rain. Then when I was so wet already there was no sense sheltering from that last shower, was there?"

"But where were you?" the young man asked, bewildered.

Before she answered, Lena caught his hands in hers and careless of the fact that trickles of water from her cap had begun to stain and spot his suit she looked up at him with such intensity of feeling that I realized – with a sinking heart – such love could never be matched.

"Oh, Andy, I couldn't stand it any more. I couldn't wait any longer. After all, it was up to me! You couldn't do it for me, I know, or else you'd have done it long ago."

Did the young man draw back nervously? I thought he did, but I couldn't be sure, and in any case my eyes were on Lena's glowing face.

"I don't know what you're talking about, Lena," Andy said, and his voice was cagey, I thought, but Lena didn't seem to notice.

"I'm talking about us, Andy," she said. "I mean about me – and my religion. I know you were afraid my people would be mad with me if I changed over with you. And they will! But suddenly this morning I saw everything in a new light, and I knew I oughtn't to care what anyone would say – only you. So – " she paused before the tremendous revelation – "so I went to the priest and told him all about us. I did!" she cried triumphantly, seeing an expression come over her young man's face which she took to be incredulity. "I told him everything. And," she added proudly, "he said I had done the right thing. He's going to start instructing me tomorrow evening. He would have given me my first instructions right away, this afternoon, only I was so wet." She laughed. And, although two more drops of dye from her cap ran, one after the other, down her face, she sighed contentedly. "He said I must have been in earnest to come out on a day like today! He said he hoped it wouldn't be raining tomorrow." Then, plunging her hand into the front of her blouse, that was so wet it was pasted to her skin like tissue-paper, she pulled out a small booklet printed on cheap paper, which, like everything else about her, was nearly destroyed by the rain. "He gave me this," she cried. "Now will you believe me? It's a Catechism. I'm to learn the first chapter tonight, and he'll hear me it tomorrow night!"

Oh, my poor Lena! Why did you misread the first look that had crossed the face of your lover? Why did you not hear what he had to say before you produced your wretched, sodden treasure? Because this time the expression which came on Andy's handsome face was unmistakable. His every feature was distorted with rage.

"You little fool!" he cried. "How dare you go behind my back and do a thing like that? You know I told you to wait! That everything would work out right in the end! Didn't I tell you that? Didn't I?" For me – as an unwitting onlooker – the moment was one of such intolerable pain I could not bear to look at Lena's face, and it was with some relief I heard Andy's voice change again. "There's no need to look at me like that, Lena," he said. "Don't cry! Please don't cry." I knew then that she was crying and I was glad to see that her tears had upset him. "You know I'm only speaking the truth, Lena," he said. "God knows I ought to be prepared for anything by now – the way you dash about without thinking – but it's a bit thick to find you were so concerned about yourself and not giving any thought to me! What will your family have to say about me? Tell me that! You don't suppose they'll believe you acted of your own accord – do you? They'll think it was me put you up to this. Oh, Lena – how could you do it?"

Then, at the thought of how opposed to his wishes her action had been, the last vestiges of Andy's anger diluted into self-pity. "Oh, Lena, you've spoiled everything," he said. "How can I ever face your people again? How can I ever set foot in their house? What will they think of me – they that often said they hated people that were two-faced?"

Andy's misery was so abject, my first anger against him – and my contempt – began to lessen and I tried to tell myself how much it must have meant to him, a loner, an outlyer, to have been admitted into the intimacy of a real family, even one as poor and humble as that little family of church mice. And indeed as my thoughts ran on, Andy must have been thinking along the same lines. Indeed, thinking perhaps that his place in the family of man was threatened, if not lost, by Lena's foolhardiness – ignoring her grief again – he leant back against the wet bark of the tree, and gave way to tears himself. Yes, tears.

I think it was his tears that reached Lena, where his words must have been almost meaningless to her.

"Oh, Andy, Andy, I didn't know you'd feel this way. I thought it was only for my sake you didn't want things brought to a head. I thought – I thought–"

But whatever she thought was so at variance with what had in fact happened, the poor child could not bring herself to put her thoughts into words. However, after the first impact of shock, with characteristic impetuosity, she caught his hands again.

"I'll go back to the priest," she cried, her woe momentarily eclipsed by this new devotion. "I'll go back and tell him I've changed my mind. He won't say anything to me. He was a nice old man. He warned me it was not a step to be taken in a hurry, only he saw I had my heart set on it." With every word, now, her face was brightening. "Oh, Andy, stop looking like that at me!" she cried. "Everything will be all right."

Andy's peace of mind was not to be so readily restored, however. A frightened look still haunted his eyes.

"It won't be as easy as you think," he said, despairingly. "Did you mention my name to the priest?"

Lena hesitated.

"I had to mention it, Andy," she said contritely.

"Well, there you are! If he finds out it was me who put you from going on with your plans, he'll make it hot for me, I can tell you. Oh, Lena, Lena, whatever made you do such a thing? It's no use saying you'll undo it – it's too late. The harm is done."

"But nobody knows only the priest, Andy, and he won't tell anyone," Lena cried, and I don't think she spoke from any knowledge of sacerdotal secrecy but only from a reading of the old priest's face. "I *know* he won't."

"Oh, I daresay he won't," said Andy, half-heartedly. "But how do you know someone didn't see you going into the parochial house? People in these parts can put two and two together, you know!"

For a moment, Lena looked frightened herself, but only for a moment.

"I'm sure no one saw me, Andy. I looked around, and there was no one on the road, and I ran up the steps and knocked hard so I'd be let in quick. I'm sure no one saw me. And anyway, who'd know me over there?"

"Over there? What do you mean?"

"Oh, but, Andy, you didn't think I'd go to the priest here in the village, did you? I went across to Kentstown where I wouldn't be known. That's how I got so wet."

But before she had finished, I saw that this new piece of information had worked wonders upon Andy.

"Why didn't you tell me that at the start?" he said. "That puts everything in a different light. The priest over there didn't know you! He's probably forgotten your name already, much less mine. You say he's an old man too, so he's hardly likely to come over here looking for us. There's one thing no priest likes, and that's poking his nose into another priest's business." Where he had been so dejected, Andy was now elated, but then his spirits flagged again. "It's a wonder he didn't tell you to go to the priest in your own parish?"

Lena wondered too – for the space of a second.

"Oh, but I haven't a parish priest," she cried then, triumphantly. "I'm still a Protestant!"

"Oh, that's right. Good, good. Couldn't be better," Andy cried. "He'll never find out who you are! You don't need to go back near him at all."

"Oh, but I wouldn't want – "

Andy looked at her sternly.

"Isn't it time you gave up doing what you want yourself all the time – without any regard for me? Haven't we had enough trouble already through you not consulting me? You do as I say, Lena. Unless you don't care about what I say?"

"Oh, Andy, how can you say such a thing? You know I only did this because – "

But tears had welled into her eyes again, and this time they were not the same as the tears she had shed when he first upbraided her: they were softer, sweeter tears, and in them was distilled the very essence of love. They finished her sentence for her.

"Now, don't start crying all over again," Andy said gruffly, and he put his arm around her with a clumsy kindness. At the same time he looked up at the sky that was now a clear expanse of unbroken blue.

"Come on," he said. "It's going to be a fine evening. Let's not waste any more of it." His grip on her waist had tightened, and an altogether new look came on his face. "Where will we go?" he asked, and without waiting for her answer he peered towards where the leafy undergrowth was as sheltered as a chamber, close and secretive, and he began to breathe heavily. For the first time something of the intensity so habitual to Lena animated his face and lit his eyes. "Let's see what it's like further on, in here," he said. "We never went further than this."

Taking her arm he pulled her roughly after him and went to break a way through the dense underwood. But as he was about to part the bushes his eyes fell on the little paper-covered Catechism that she still held in her hand. "Let's get rid of this, though," he said, and taking it out of her hand he tore it into pieces and threw the scraps on the ground. "Your name wasn't on it, was it?" he stopped to ask, before, with his heel, he pounded them into the ground. "Come on," he said then. "What's the matter with you?"

"Nothing," said Lena, unconvincingly.

"Oh, I know what you're thinking!" Andy said. "But you're wrong. We'll be married all right, Lena, some day, but we'll have to go about it with a bit of common sense." He gave her a playful jerk in the ribs. "Come on. Trust me. I won't let you down. Things will work out right in the end. I promise!" Leaning closer to her, his voice grew thick and hoarse. "There are more ways than one of killing a cat. I won't have your family turned against me. If we let things take their natural course, you'd never know, they might be glad enough to see us getting married one of these days, no matter what sacrifices had to be made."

His arm had tightened so convulsively around her waist it was impossible after that to tell whether he led her or whether of her own free will she disappeared with him into the depths of wood.

Released from my captivity, and feeling cramped, I stood for a moment longer under the trees before going out to the glade where the lovers had stood, but when I looked down at the ground I saw the bits of torn paper in the mud. I remembered the nosegay of cornflowers that Turgenev found on the forest floor when Akoulina had fled. And I thought of how he picked up the nosegay and treasured it. Needless to say, I did not pick up the torn scraps of the Catechism. Nor did I see

Lena again. I left the hotel next morning before the servants came on duty. The night porter gave me a cup of tea and I walked to the station, where I had a long wait for the first train. But I often thought of her, and of the flame that burned in her heart. I wonder, but now will never know, how long it was before that flame was quenched.

My Molly

What I couldn't understand was why my Molly took it so badly. We were only six months in the town at the time.

Most people were upset, of course. Why not? There wasn't a day in the past forty years that old Sam was not to be seen, sitting in the window of his shop turning the wheel of his old sewing-machine. He was like a sticky-back of himself pasted on to the window, if you know what I mean. It wasn't that he didn't look real, with his red face, and his bright blue eyes – the exact colour of the veins in his cheeks – and his big fibry eyebrows. It was just that you couldn't imagine him doing anything else: eating, sleeping, anything – only sitting there!

It was a shock to hear that one day he was gone. Yes: like that. Like a snap of your fingers! No, I don't mean dead. People die every day, likely ones and unlikely ones! No: gone, that was all! Took his hat, put it on his head, and lit out: no one knew where.

It wasn't nice, to think of an old man like that – like Sam, I mean – wandering about somewhere, maybe out of his mind.

Still I couldn't see why my Molly took it so badly. Not that I understand her that well. All unexpected she is: my Molly. She's not a bit like what you'd think from looking at her. Most people think she's delicate, just because she's so small, I suppose. But, you should see the work she does! Her being so pretty gives people a wrong opinion of her too. Flighty, that's what she looks. My own mother used that very word when I first told her we were getting married. And you should hear what my father said. "You'll hardly get a family out of that little girl," he said. That was the worst guess of all. We have five already, and no signs of stopping. Not for many a day yet I'd say. Lack of money is the only thing that would stop *that*. And money never troubles my Molly at all.

"Don't worry," she's always saying. "Did you ever know anybody to starve yet in this country? Something will turn up, you'll see!" She believed a lot in luck.

But I always feel that luck isn't something you get hanging on a bush – especially good luck. Some people attract it. Molly did. She had tact, too, Molly had – or so I was told. A funny kind of tact it seemed to me. I used to think tact meant always doing the right thing, but after living with Molly I began to think it was more like always doing the wrong thing and no harm coming out of it, but only good. Do you know what I mean?

They're hard to understand, people like my Molly. Even when you're married to one of them for ten years, there are still times you can't make them out. Take her and old Sam. If it was anyone else in the town but Molly who went on like she did I'd say she was putting her sorrow on – just for show. But there's no show about my Molly – outside of her looks, I mean. Her looks are showy, I know, but that was God's doing, not hers. She's true to the bone, my Molly.

Yet, there she was the day Sam vanished with the tears running down her face. The news that he was missing went round the town early. Then at midday the radio gave out an announcement about him. Anyone who had seen a person answering to his description was to go to the barracks and give in the information. Molly started to cry again and all the kids began to bawl with her, although they didn't know what they were bawling about.

"Now look here, Molly," I said. "I've had enough of this. Don't carry on like that. I don't suppose you ever spoke to the poor fellow?" Well! You should have seen the look she gave me!

"Is it me?" she cried. "Me that has been doing business with him every other day of the week for the past three months."

Business? With a saddler? My Molly?

"Oh, I beg your pardon, Molly," I said. "I didn't know you'd taken up hunting!"

That was a good joke, you know. You'd only have to look at us to know our social standing. Not that I believe much in class, but in a small town in Ireland you may not make any distinction between yourself and those below you, but you have to allow for the people above you making distinctions between them and you.

"I suppose you think you're funny," Molly said. "It was to get him to mend the straps of the go-car I first went in to him." I don't mind admitting I was mortified.

"You don't mean to tell me you brought that battered old go-car in to be mended by a man like Sam?" I said.

Saddlers aren't two a penny in Ireland any more, and I was ashamed to think of my Molly getting the like of Sam to mend an old strap. If only you could see the go-car, you'd know how I felt. It wheeled out every one of our children in turn, and it was second-hand in the first place. But Molly knows no limits when she's bent on good for me or the family.

"He was so kind," she said, and she began to cry again. "He came out into the street and knelt down and undid the string" – you can imagine how I winced at that – "and when the strap was sewn he came out and put it on for me. Oh, I can't tell you how kind he was. And he told me to come back to him any time I wanted it done again. 'Don't wait till you get let down, my dear,' he said. 'Step in any time you have a spare minute and I'll put a stitch in it that will hold it together a bit longer.' Which I did! He always did it there and then for me, he never charged me anything. I forgot to tell you that! It wasn't that I appreciated, so much as his manner. You'd think he'd have no time for the likes of me compared with his usual customers? But it was the other way round! 'There's a lot of the horse in themselves,' he said as they'd stamp off with their saddles and bridles, 'the bad points, I mean.' Wasn't that a queer thing for him to say, and his trade depending on them? It showed how he trusted me. He liked having me come in and out. It was a change for him. He liked talking to me. In a way, I wasn't surprised when I heard he was gone! From things he said to me now and then, I think he had a notion of doing what he did for a long time past–"

"Molly!" I cried. Was there more worry to come? "You're not keeping anything from the police, are you? What kind of things did he say?"

"Oh, only just one thing and another," said Molly in her vaguest voice.

"Tell me one!" said I.

"Well," she said, "there was one morning he was out in the street with me, putting the strap back on the go-car – when it broke again – a flight of birds went across the sky over our heads. I don't suppose we'd have noticed them only the baby chirped. Lying on their backs, babies see all kinds of things we never look at – birds and trees and the sky itself. Sam and I looked up at those birds."

" 'Queer creatures, aren't they?' Sam said. 'I often think it must be very tiring to be always flying about like that. Isn't it a curious thing, now, that if one of those little birds was to fall down here in the street, you'd have a crowd around it in a minute – a crowd as big as a football match. It'd be a nine days' wonder!' And here he looked at me with his little wrinkled-up face, and I knew he was going to say something important – important to him anyway. 'That's not the wonder at all, though,' he said. 'The wonder is that they keep on flying!' "

"Well? Go on, Molly!" said I.

"That's all," said Molly.

I didn't know whether to be relieved or annoyed. There was no need to go to the police with a rigmarole like that, but how did it show he was going to disappear? Only Molly could figure that out.

"I hope the poor old fellow is all right anyway, wherever he is," I said. "Perhaps he'll arrive back as suddenly as he went – like the last time." I thought Molly mightn't have known Sam had once before done the same thing – it was over twenty years before we came to the town – but Molly knew all about it. That's why she was so upset.

"I think it's a shame the way people are letting that influence them," she said. "Just because they made fools of themselves the last time is no reason to think the same thing is going to happen this time."

Now, I could not help feeling there was something to be said for people being a bit cautious this time – specially the Gardai. Sure anyone can make a mistake. And the Sergeant was on holidays at the time. It was just that there was something unlucky about the way things happened. The whole town was leaning over the bridge watching the drag-net, the Gardai yelling and making themselves officious – I believe the young fellow in charge forgot his dignity altogether and rolled up his trousers legs – forgetting they were government property, I suppose – and waded into the river up to his middle. Another of them let his cap fall into the water, and away it floated, with all the kids in the town throwing stones after it. It was a great moment altogether, I believe, when the cap went over the weir, and a rousing cheer went up from every man, woman and child on the bridge. Undignified though. And that's what the Superintendent concluded.

To think that it was at the height of all this, I'd say myself – wouldn't you? – that it was likely at the very moment the cap was going over the weir that old Sam got off the bus in the Market Square, and the Square as empty as if it was up for auction! And when the fun was over below at the river and everyone came back up to the Square,

H

there was his sticky-back pasted to the glass again, the same as ever. No wonder the Gardai were lepping mad.

"It'll be hard to get them to drag the river this time," I said.

"There may be no need for that," Molly said coldly. "There are some people who claim he was seen in Dublin. Did you hear that? Did you not hear about the car? The Sergeant gave it out that on account of the rumours of his having been seen there a car was going to be hired, and that he was going to ask for volunteers to go up to Dublin and comb it out well before any more time was lost."

"Well, isn't that a great idea?" I said.

"Do you think so?" said Molly, doubtfully. "It's all depending on who goes in the car." Then she sighed. "They'll have a grand free trip to Dublin, anyway, whoever goes." Suddenly she sat up very straight. "Do you know! I have a notion of going myself!" she said.

"Is it you?" I cried. "What hope would the like of you have of finding him? A little bit of a thing like you isn't fit for traipsing the streets of Dublin. It wouldn't be fair to take up a seat that might be taken by someone able and fitter than you – "

She gave me a look.

"It's because I don't like to see good money go to loss that I'd go! Don't you know poor Sam is dead!" she said. "And here now is all that money going to loss on a hired car to Dublin. Dublin: a place I haven't been in these two years, me that loved it so much, and me that badly needs a bit of change, as Sam himself said only a few days ago. I didn't tell you at the time because I knew we couldn't afford it, but this would be a great chance of an outing, wouldn't it? I think I will go!"

"Would you do any looking at all for him, Molly?" I asked. "I mean any *real* looking for him."

Well, if you saw the kind of look I got then!

"Shame on you," she said. "Shame on you! Do you think I'd go gallivanting off on a trip like that if I thought there was the smallest chance of his ever being found? As you said yourself, I'd be a poor hand at sifting and sieving through the streets of Dublin. If I thought there was the smallest chance of him being found, it's you I'd make go in the car; not me. I do hope it will be fine," she cried, and she ran over to the window and looked up at the sky. "There's so much I want to get done. I'll get new vests for the boys – there's hardly a stitch left in their old ones – and I'll get some hair-ribbon for the girls –

you can't get the real good stuff in a country town, and it doesn't cost any more – there might even be a sale. And I'll bring your suit to be cleaned – " But here she bit her lip. "I'd better not bring the suit; it might give me away," she said.

"What about the parcels coming home?" I asked.

"Oh, I'll get them made up very small, or I'll get the things sent by post. I'll do something anyway – don't worry." But she was a bit worried herself. "Maybe I ought to content myself with looking at the shop windows – or I might go out and get a breath of sea air. That was what Sam probably had in mind. He was always saying he wished I could get the taste of a good sea breeze – I'm sure that's what he'd wish I'd do. I didn't tell you, but I was dreaming of him last night; that's why I'm so sure he's dead. I forget what it was about – you know the way it is with dreams, they're so daft – but it was something to do with the sea. He must have been trying to put it into my head to go in that car! Sure he *must* be dead when he's able to put things in my way like that, don't you think? The Lord have mercy on him!"

The car left for Dublin the following Saturday. According to Molly it was an uneasy car-load. If only you could hear her taking off the Sergeant's voice: she's a great mimic, Molly.

"Now before we start," said the Sergeant, "I want you all to bear in mind that there are two purposes in this trip. The first is to find the person in question, but the second is to take particular note of the circumstances in which you find the person, if it should happen the person is found. By that I mean it is particularly important to the law to know if there is anything unusual, anything irregular that is to say, in the behaviour of the said person, if and when found. It cannot be overlooked that this person might try on a certain trick he played before and the State cannot allow irresponsible people to be a source of expense to the force, and a disturbance to the public."

"You don't mean you'd have him committed?" Molly cried. It was all she could do not to say she was glad he was dead! "Well, I hope you're not the one to find him, Sergeant, if that's what you'll be thinking about, instead of trying to make things easy for him. Or you either!" she said, turning her head to the fellow on the seat beside her, because who was he but another Garda who she thought had the same thing in mind as the Sergeant. He had a face as long as a fast, this other Garda.

"Ah, go easy on the poor fellow, ma'am," said the Sergeant. "It's promotion he's after. He didn't know I was coming, any more than I thought he was!"

"It's my day off," said the young fellow sourly. "I don't have to ask leave of anyone for what I do on my half-day."

"Oh, so it's in a civilian capacity you're coming, is it?" said the Sergeant, and he gave another wink at Molly. "Ah sure, I wronged you, man. In that case you wouldn't be eligible for promotion at all; but sure it's in heaven you'll get your reward. It's true to say it's hard to judge any man! Isn't that so, Captain?"

The Sergeant it seems – to give him his due – was doing his best to make the jaunt as pleasant as possible for all concerned, but the other two occupants of the car were, up to that, a sort of a dead-weight: the Captain and Miss Muggins. The Captain was one of the old gentry, and who was the other but Miss Muggins, sister of the local member of the Dail, a die-hard who got into the Dail because of a slogan he invented after the Troubles. *"We didn't go half far enough!"* That was the slogan. It meant we oughtn't to have left the odd ninepin, like the Captain, standing, but burnt them all out like rats. I can tell you, in spite of his laughing and joking the Sergeant must have been uneasy between the two of them. Molly wasn't. Let dog eat dog was her slogan.

The Captain was civil enough at first, and didn't say much, but after a while he spoke up.

"Excuse me, Sergeant," he said then. "An interesting point occurred to me. It's a matter of general interest only, of course. But what is the position of a person that is – what's this you said? – committed, is it? – in regard to his debts, I mean?"

The Sergeant sat up.

"An interesting point, Captain," he said, "but do you mean in regard to money owed by the person to another person or persons, or do you mean the money owed to this person by another person or persons?"

That's the Sergeant's way of talking: it's maybe meant to bother people, but the Captain got his meaning all right, and so did Molly. Molly, you see, knew about the Captain owing Sam a lot of money, because Sam had told her. It wasn't only the saddles and bridles either. He'd got a few quid in hard cash out of Sam from time to time by simply walking into the shop and asking for it, and telling Sam in a lordly way to put it down on the bill. Oh yes, Molly knew all about it. Sam told her one day that if the Captain had the income on all the money he owed him, then that gentleman could pay cash for everything to the end of his days, and need no more credit!

What puzzled Molly was whether the Captain was hoping Sam was alive or dead. She couldn't be sure which. The Sergeant's way of talking had him strayed, as it was maybe meant to do.

Molly said she'd have given anything if Sam himself could have seen the Captain sitting there, looking like the rest of us for once in his life, instead of letting on he wasn't the same breed of bird at all, and every one knowing it all only a matter of feathers.

They were nearly in Dublin by this time.

"Where will we start?" said the Sergeant.

It was then that Miss Muggins came into the picture.

"If you've no objection, Sergeant, I know where I'll start! Whatever about the rest of you, I'm not wasting my time looking in unlikely places!"

"Commendable, ma'am!" said the Sergeant. "But I hope you are not by any chance in possession of special information that you failed to pass on to the proper quarters?"

Miss Muggins drew herself up.

"I should think, Sergeant, that as my brother's sister I would be fully aware of my duties in that and all matters of civic responsibility. The knowledge I have is based entirely on what you might call my private insight into the character of the missing person."

Now it was very hard on Molly to hear that one sitting there referring to Sam as This Person. She nearly lost her temper and said outright that it was no wonder Sam jilted her long ago – which was what everyone said. Only it wasn't really true. It was just gossip. There was never anything between them. Sam had told Molly all about it. But Miss Muggins had something in for him all the same.

The Sergeant wasn't born yesterday, though.

"I'd have you know, ma'am," he said sharply, "we do a course of psychology in the Depot, and we take character into consideration too – at all times!" He was having a dig at her there. "Now tell me this, ma'am. I seem to remember hearing that, in a manner of speaking, you and This Person – ?"

"Oh, that's what *he*'d like thought," said Miss Muggins. "And," she added, "I don't mind admitting that if it weren't for certain things I

discovered we would doubtless have come to a settlement, because he
was very persistent. And he ought to have had a tidy sum in the bank
if it weren't – " and here she shot an unexpected glance at the Captain –
"if it weren't for him being taken advantage of by certain people."

The Sergeant saw the glance.

"Ah, I think you have a spark of the old feeling for him still, Miss
Muggins," he said, trying to be playful.

Miss Muggins wasn't one for playing.

"Not a spark!" she said. "And, what is more, I go down on my
knees every night and thank God for what I was spared. Oh, women
can be terribly deceived in a man. There was everyone in town linking
our names, and envying me, I'm sure, and the next thing they knew
it was all broken off, and no reason given. Indeed, there were some
that were bad enough to think it was broken off by him. If only they
knew! But I am a conscientious woman, and I kept my lips sealed on
what I found out. I wasn't going to take away his character – no matter
what the cost to my own reputation."

"Commendable, very commendable, ma'am," said the Sergeant
again. "Of course, there is a time and a place for everything, and I
suppose you feel that the present circumstances are such that – "

"That's just what I felt, Sergeant. And I got my brother to get me
certain information." She rummaged in her bag and took out a piece of
paper.

"May I see it, ma'am?" said the Sergeant, and he stretched out his
hand and took it. "But it's only a list of streets," he said, and his face
fell.

"That's all," said Miss Muggins, with some asperity. "But I think
it ought to be your business, Sergeant, to realize the kind of streets
they are – unfortunate streets, if I might say so! Unfortunate streets!"

Now you'd think my Molly wouldn't know what was meant by that,
would you? But she was quicker than the Sergeant to get the meaning,
and she was about to fly at the Muggins one!

"Easy now, easy," said the Sergeant. "We can neglect nothing, my
dear. But perhaps we had better all separate and meet at the end of the
day."

"Put me down at the Pillar," Molly said coldly, and she left it at
that.

Oh, but she had a great day. She got all the shopping done, and she
managed to put on most of the things she bought, like as if she was

going through the Customs: a pair of pyjamas for me, and the kids'
vests, and I don't know what else. She must have looked a bit peculiar
if you looked close, but sure no one saw her as things happened,
because, you see, in spite of doing all the shopping, she kept it in
mind to get that breath of sea air Sam was always recommending to
her, and in the afternoon she hopped on a train and went off to
Dun Laoghaire for a dander down the pier.

The weather, by the time she got there, wasn't as nice as it was in
the morning. It was getting chilly. There was sun all right, but it was a
cold, grudging sort of sun. And there was nobody on the pier. All
the same, Molly thought she might as well walk out to the end of the
pier, because it's nice out there the way it's sloped off gradually so
the waves wash in across the flat stones like they do on the sands, not
bashing against the rocks like they do at the sides of the pier. So on
she went, and the wind nearly dragging the clothes off her, till she
came in sight of the end.

Well, there's no use making a mystery out of nothing! Who do you
think Molly saw standing down at the edge of the water but Sam!
The very one. But it was the way he was standing that got Molly. She
didn't have time to think how odd it was him being there, because it
was so odd the way he was standing. He was in his bare feet. Worse
than that, he had taken off his pants and was standing there with
nothing but his shirt on him. Do you know, the first thing Molly
thought was that he was like our own children when she'd be getting
them ready for bed at night, and they'd run out on the landing, and
start walking around, and them in no condition to appear before
anyone but their mother. Anyway, to cut things short, she ran up to
him. And she had him dressed again in jig-time, and no harm done.

"Were you out of your mind, Sam, to be standing like that?" she
said. And, by the way, there now is a good example of her way of
saying the wrong thing at the right time.

"I suppose I was, Molly," said Sam. "I was thinking of how I used
to paddle when I was a child."

"Well, you're no child now, Sam," said Molly. "And, what's more,
it might be all right to go paddling on Sandymount Strand, or beyond
at Dollymount, but you wouldn't paddle far out there." She drew
him back a bit more from the edge of the water. "Don't you know it's
deep enough there to take the mail-boat, and sometimes it comes in
close enough to skin the lighthouse! Paddling indeed! If you didn't

go straight to the bottom, Sam, you'd be taken up and put into an asylum. How would you like that?"

"Oh, I wouldn't like it at all," said the poor old fellow, and he started to cry. "Do you know, Molly, that's what I'm always thinking will happen to me in the end. When I'm sitting in the shop all alone, I often think that's what will be the end of me, God help me!"

That nearly broke Molly's heart altogether. She knew she'd have to do something for him.

"Come on out of that, Sam," she said. "I know what will be the end of you. There'll be no more living alone for you. Sure God never meant any of us to be alone till we're boxed up in our coffins. Haven't we plenty of room for you in our house? And you can pay us a few shillings if you like – just so as not to feel under a compliment to us! How would you like that?"

He liked it well, I needn't tell you. And we liked having him too. It wasn't for long anyway, God help him.

And we didn't lose by it either, except that the Sergeant had his nose in the air for a while, and the others were lepping mad, because, you see, Molly didn't go back to the Pillar at all, and the car – with the lot of them sitting in it – was there till nearly midnight waiting for her. She took Sam home on the train. Sam paid the fares. He had plenty of money in his pocket. You should have seen the cakes and buns they brought back with them as well.

We all had a share in Molly's day out, you might say.

There was only one cloud over the day for Molly. She left her hat behind her on the pier. I suppose it floated off on the waves, like the Garda's hat floated over the weir – only there was no one to give it a cheer. It was a new hat, too.

"Ah well – it didn't suit me anyway," she said.

Didn't suit her? And she only after buying it!

What I sometimes wonder is, will I ever understand her: my Molly?

The Living

"How many dead people do you know?" said Mickser, suddenly.

Immediately, painfully, I felt my answer would show me once more his inferior.

"Do you mean ghosts?" I said, slowly, to gain time.

"No," said Mickser, "I mean corpses."

"But don't they get buried?" I cried.

"They're not buried for three days," Mickser said, scathingly. "They have to be scrubbed and laid out and waked. You're not allowed to keep them any longer than that, though, because their eyes go like this." Here he put up his hands to his eyes and drew down the lower lids to show the inner flesh swimming with watery blood. "They rot," he explained, succinctly.

"Mind would you fall, Mickser!" I said, hastily, thinking he might let go his eyelids if he had to steady himself on the gate-post.

We were sitting one on each of the big gate-posts at the school-house that was down on the main road. We were supposed to be sitting there watching the cars coming home from the Carlow and Kerry football finals. But it wasn't much fun. As Mickser said, it was only the family man that came home straight after a match. The real followers, the enthusiasts, didn't come home till near night; or near morning, maybe! And they were the only ones it was any sport to watch.

"Those ones have no drink taken," Mickser said contemptuously of the cars that were going past at the time. "It's great sport altogether when the drunks are coming home. Passing each other out on the roads. On the corners, mind! But your mammy wouldn't let you stay out long enough to see them."

It was only too true. It was a wonder she let me down to the road at all. You'd think she knew there'd be no fun in it. She had a terrible dread of fun, my mammy. She always saw danger in it.

"You can go down to the school-house and look at the cars coming home if you're careful. And mind yourself!" she said to me. "Keep well in from the road! And another thing! Don't sit up on that high wall the way I saw you doing once."

That was why we were up on the gate-posts, although they were much higher than the wall.

"Gate-posts isn't walls," Mickser had said definitively.

That was Mickser all over. You could count on him to get you out of anything. But he could get you into anything too! You never knew where a word would lead with him. This talk about dead people seemed safe enough though.

"How many do you know, Mickser?" I asked, fearful, but fascinated.

"Oh, I couldn't count them," Mickser said, loftily, "I bet you don't know any at all."

"My grandfather's dead."

"How long is he dead?"

"He died the year I was born. On the very day after," I said, having heard this told as a matter of importance by my mother to many, many people.

"Bah!" said Mickser. "You can't count him. If you could, then you could count your great-grandfather, and your great-great-grandfather, and your great-great-great-grandfather and – " but he stopped enumerating them, as a more vivid denunciation of my foolishness occurred to him. "Isn't the ground full of dead people? People that nobody knew?" He pointed down below us to where, through the nettles, the clay under the wall showed black and sour. "If you took up a spade this minute," he said, "and began digging down there, or anywhere you liked, you'd be no time digging till you'd come on bones; somebody's bones! Oh no!" he shook his head; "you can't count people you didn't see dead, like my Uncle Bat, that was sitting up eating a boiled egg one minute, and lying back dead the next. He's the best one on my list though," he added, magnanimously. "I saw him alive and dead. Most of them I only saw dead, like my two aunts that died within a week of each other. Everyone said it was a pity if they had to go it couldn't have been closer together so they could have made the one wake of it. But if they did I might have to count them as one. What do you think?" He didn't wait for an answer though. "How many is that?" he asked.

"Only three," I said, and my heart rose. He mightn't be able to think of any more.

Not a chance of it. He looked at me severely. He was a bit of a mind-reader as well as everything else. "I want to pick out the good ones for first," he said.

That overwhelmed me altogether.

"Ah sure, Mickser," I said, frankly and fairly, "you needn't strain yourself thinking of good ones for me, because I never saw one at all. One of my aunts died a year ago all right, and they had to take me to the funeral because they had no one to leave me with, but they wouldn't let me into the house till the funeral was ready to move off. They took it in turns to sit out in the car with me."

"And what was that for?" Mickser looked blankly at me.

"I don't know," I said, in a grieved voice, but after a bit, in fairness to my mother and father, I felt obliged to hazard a reason for their behaviour. "Maybe they thought I'd be dreaming of it in my sleep. Not that it did much good keeping me outside because I dreamt about it all the same. I kept them up till morning, nightmaring about coffins and hearses!"

"Did you?" Mickser was genuinely interested, but baffled, too, I could see. "Coffins and hearses?" he repeated. "What was there about them to have you nightmaring? It's corpses that give people the creeps." He looked at me with further interest – with curiosity. "I wonder what way you'd take on if you did see a corpse!" Suddenly he snapped his fingers. "I have it!" he said. "There's a wake being held this very day in a cottage the other side of the town."

"Mind would you fall, Mickser!" I cried again, because there looked to be every danger of it with the way he was hopping about with excitement.

"Do you know the cottage I mean?" he asked. "It's at the level-crossing. Do you know the woman in it: the one that opens and shuts the railway gates? Well, her son is dead. Did you know that? Did you ever see him?

"A big fellow with red hair is it?"

"That's the one! She used to have him sitting outside the cottage most days on a chair in the sun. He was a class of delicate." Mickser tapped his own pate. "Up here," he said. "Did you know that? Well, he's dead now anyway. He died this morning. Isn't it a bit of luck I was put in mind of it? This is your chance of having one corpse, anyway, for your list. But we'd want to get there quick," he said, jumping down off the gate-pier, into a clump of nettles below, without minding them any more than if he was a dog. "We'll have to get down there before the crowds start coming. They'll be glad to see us then no matter who we are, because they're always glad to see the first signs of people arriving, after the cleaning and scrubbing they've been at all night. And they love to see children above all – at first, that is to say. 'Look who we have here,' they'll say." He mimicked a woman's voice so well I nearly fell off the pier myself. " 'Bless their little hearts,' " he went on. " 'Come in, children. Sure there's no prayers like the prayers of a child.' Up they bring you straight to the bed, and down they put you kneeling beside it where you can get a good gawk at everything. Oh, but it's a different story altogether, I can tell you, if you leave it till late in the evening. They're jaded tired by then, and you haven't a hope of getting inside the door. 'Out of this with you, you little brats.' That's all you'll hear then. 'This is no place for children – out of it, quick!' They'd take the yard brush to you if you didn't get yourself out of sight double quick. So we'd better get up there immediately. What are you waiting for?"

I was hanging back for more reasons than one.

"I was told to stay here," I said.

"You were told not to be climbing, too," said Mickser, as quick as a lawyer. "So you can't say you were doing what you were told, anyway. Not but it's doing all you're told to do that has you the way you are this day, knowing nothing about anything. Come on out of that, and I'll show you what's going on about you, or if I don't, I dread to think how you'll end up in the finish. Sure fathers and mothers are the worst people in the word to depend on for finding out the least thing. They're all out for keeping us back. I've proved that many a time with my own ones. And there's yourself! To think they wouldn't let you see your own aunt laid out! I know it wouldn't be me that would be done out of a thing like that. And what's more, you oughtn't to put up with it either. You ought to tell them there'd be no nightmaring or carrying-on about corpses if you were let get used to them like me. Are you coming, or are you not?"

It was a sweet, mild afternoon as we set out for the edge of the town to where the level-crossing was, and the small, slated house to one side of it. It was very familiar to me when I was a bit smaller and my mother used to take me for a walk out of the town to get the country air. We often had to wait for the gates to be opened for us, although the train had already thundered past.

"What is the delay?" my mother would ask impatiently.

"I have to wait for the signals, ma'am," the woman in charge of the gates would say. "You can pass through the wicket gate if you like, ma'am, but that's none of my responsibility."

"Oh, we're in no hurry," my mother would say hastily – in order no doubt to give me good example.

But there was no need to warn me about it. I had heard Mickser say he put a halfpenny on the line one day and the train made a penny out of it. I had no fancy for being flattened out to the size of a man. And anyway, I used to be very curious about the big, white-faced boy that was always to be sitting in the little bit of garden outside the house on a chair; a chair brought out of the house, not one you'd leave outside like we had in the garden at home.

"Does she take it in at night?" I asked.

"Of course she does," said my mother, in a shocked voice; but she must have thought I meant the boy. "Please don't stare," she'd say to me. "Why do I always have to tell you the same thing?"

Only when the gates were opened, and we were crossing over the rails, would she let on to see him for her part. It was always the same.

"How is he today?" she'd ask the woman.

And the woman's answer was always the same too.

"Poorly," she'd say. At times – but rarely – she'd add a few words. "It's a great cross to me, but I suppose God knows what he's doing."

"We must hope so anyway," my mother would say, piously, and she'd step over the rails more quickly till we were on the other side. "How is it," she'd say testily to me, "those gates are always shut no matter what time of the day we want to pass?"

And now, today, for the first time in my life, the railway gates were wide open.

"Do you think they might have forgot to close them on account of the wake?" I said, hanging back nervously as Mickser dashed over the shining tracks. But in the middle of the line he stopped and looked back at me.

"God knows it's high time someone took you in hand," he said. "You're nothing but a sissy. What harm would it be if they did forget? Haven't you eyes? Haven't you ears? And if it comes to that, haven't you legs? Come on out of that!" But before he went on himself he looked up and down the line. "We're the first here," he said, looking ahead again towards the cottage. "They're not finished yet," he said, expertly sizing things up.

To me it was as if the little house had been washed down from top to bottom like I was washed down myself every Saturday night, and not only was the house immaculate, but the bit of garden outside it was the same, neatened and tidied, and the big stones around the flower-beds to keep back the clay from the grass were whitewashed every one. It was a treat: the stones bright white and the clay bright black with not a weed to be seen out of all the weeds there used to be everywhere. But the chair wasn't out!

"We're too early, maybe," Mickser said, and he sidled over to a window to one side of the door. I couldn't see near as well as him, being behind him, but I saw enough to open my mouth. What with white counterpanes and white tablecloths and white mantelcloths and white doilies, the place was got up like the chapel at Lady Day. And, in the middle of it all, like a high altar, was a big bed with a counterpane as white and glossy as marble and —

But Mickser didn't let me see any more. He pulled me away.

"I don't think they're ready yet," he said. He seemed to be losing his courage just as I was finding mine. He put his hands in his pockets and sauntered towards the door. "There now, what did I tell you?" he cried, as we barely missed getting drenched to the skin by a basin of slops that was sloshed out the door at that minute. He looked at me. "Did you ever go down the line?" he asked, suddenly. And I knew he'd let up altogether on going to the wake.

"I'm not allowed to walk on the line," I said. I was bent on seeing that bed better, and what was on it. "Let me get a look in the window anyway," I said, and I skipped over the flower-bed and pasted my face to the glass. What did I expect to see? I don't know. Not the full-grown man that was carved out on the bed, hard as stone, all but his red hair. The hair was real looking, like the hair on a doll. "Hey, Mickser. Give me a leg-up on to the window-sill?" I cried, getting more and more curious and excited.

"Are you pots?" said Mickser. "If they came out and caught you up on that window-sill you'd be clouted out of here with one of those stones," and he gave a kick to one of the big white stones, leaving the black track of his boot on it.

"A true word if ever I heard one!" said a voice. And a thin bit of a woman in black came round the gable-end with her sleeves rolled up and no smile on her, I can tell you. "Out of here with you!" she shouted. "This is no place for you!" Just the very thing Mickser claimed would not be said to us. But before we had time to get out of the flower-bed another woman came running out of the front door – and this time it was the woman herself that had charge of the railway crossing.

"It's not right to send anyone from the door of a dead-house," she said, dully.

"Hush now: they're only gossoons," said the other one.

"He was only a gossoon too," said our woman. "Only a child; that was what the priest said to me many a time. Not that he ever had any childhood, any real childhood." She lost her dull look for a minute and a livelier look came into her face. "Isn't that strange? I never thought of it before, but he was like an old man when he ought to have been a babby; and he was nothing but a babby when he ought to have been a man. I did my best, but it was no use. And you can't do everything, isn't that true? He'd have liked to have other children to keep him company, but they wouldn't understand."

We weren't sure if it was to us or the other woman she was talking. I wanted to say that I'd have kept him company, only I didn't know if my mother would allow me. That didn't sound very polite though, so I said nothing. It was good I didn't say anything, because I think it was to the other woman she was talking.

"There now! There now!" said the other woman. "Isn't it better God took him before yourself anyway?"

"I used to pray He would," said the woman, "but now I'm not sure I was right. Wasn't it the unnatural thing to have to pray for anyway? Don't all women pray for the opposite: to die before them and not be a burthen on them? And wasn't it a hard thing to have to bring him into the world only to pray for him to be taken out of it? Oh, it's little you know about it, and if there was a woman standing here in front of me, and she had the same story as me, I'd say the same thing to her. Isn't it little anyone knows about what goes on inside another person?"

She was getting a bit wild looking, and the other woman began dragging at her to get her back into the house. "Hush now, you'll feel different as time goes on."

"Will I?" said the mother, looking wonderingly at the other one. "That's what's said to everyone, but is it true? I'll feel different, maybe, sometimes when I look at the clock and have to pull off my apron and run out to throw back the gates. I'll feel different, maybe, when some woman stops to have a word with me, or when I have to take a jug and go down the road for a sup of milk. But in the middle of the night, or first thing when the jackdaws start talking in the chimney and wake me out of my sleep, will I feel different then? And what if I do forget?" Suddenly she pulled her arm free. "I'll have nothing at all then! It will be like as if I never had him." At that she put her hand up to her head and began moaning.

Stepping behind her back, the woman that wanted to be rid of us started making signs at us to be off with ourselves, but it was too late. The dead fellow's mother started forward and caught us by the hands.

"We must make the most of every minute we still have him," she cried. "Come inside and see him." She pushed us in the doorway. "Kneel down and say a prayer for him," she commanded, pushing us down on our knees, but where her voice had been wild, now it was wonderfully gentle. "He was never able to pray for himself," she said, softly, "but God must listen to the prayers of children if He listens to nothing else. I used to long for him to be able to say one little prayer, and I was always trying to teach him, but he couldn't learn. When he'd be sitting out in the sun on his chair, I used to show him the flowers and tell him God made them. And do you know what he'd say – ?" She gave a little laugh before she told us. " 'Who's that fellow?' he'd say! And he'd look around to see if He was behind him! But the priest said God would make allowances for him. I sometimes think God must have a lot to put up with no more than ourselves. That's why we've no right to complain against Him."

But I wasn't listening. When she put us kneeling down, I put up my hands to my face and I started to say my prayers, but after a minute or two I opened my fingers and took a look out through them at the man on the bed. I was a bit confused. Why was she saying he was a child? He was a man if ever I saw one! Just then the woman swooped down on me. She saw me looking at him. I thought she might be mad with me, but it was the opposite.

"If only he could see you here now beside him," she said. She leant across me and stroked his hands. And then she began to talk to him, instead of about him. "Here's two nice little boys come to see you!" she said, and her eyes got very bright and wild again. "He never had another child come into the house to see him in all his life. He never had another child as much as put out a hand and touch him. Isn't that a lonely thing to think?"

It was indeed, I thought. I wondered if it would be any use me shaking hands with him now. And it might be she saw the thought in my eyes.

"Would it be asking too much of you to stroke his hand?" she said, and then, as if she had settled in her own mind that it wouldn't be asking much at all, she got very excited. "Stand up like good boys," she said, "and stroke his hands. Then I won't feel he's going down into his grave so altogether unnatural. No – wait a minute," she cried, as she got another idea, and delved her hand into her pocket. "How would you like to comb his hair?"

I was nearer to the head of the bed than Mickser, but Mickser was nearer than me to the woman, and I couldn't be sure which of us she meant. I wanted above all to be polite, but against that I didn't want to put myself forward in any way. I stood up in any case so as to be ready if it was me she meant. She was taking a few big red hairs off the comb. Mickser stood up, too, but it was only to give me a shove out of his way.

"Let me out of here!" he shouted, and sending the woman to one side and me to the other, he bolted for the door. The next minute he was flying across the lines.

And me after him. I told you I wanted to be polite to the people – the dead one included – but after all it was Mickser brought me, and it wouldn't be very polite to stay on after him. Not that he showed any appreciation of my politeness. He was very white in the face when I caught up with him, and I thought maybe there was something wrong with him.

I was full of talk.

"Well! I have one for my list anyway, now," I said, cheerfully.

"I suppose you have," he said, kind of grudgingly I thought, and then he nearly spoiled it all on me. "That one oughtn't to count by rights. He wasn't all in it when he was alive; he was sort of dead all along!" He tapped his pate again like he did the first time. "Up here!" he added.

I thought about that for a minute. "He looked all in it there on the bed!" I said, stubbornly.

But Mickser didn't take well to talking about him at all. "I've had enough of corpses," he said.

You don't know how sorry I was to hear that. I had been wondering when I'd get a chance to go to another wake.

"You're not done with them altogether, are you, Mickser?"

"I am," Mickser said flatly. "Come on back to the main road. The cars are coming along good-o now. Can't you hear them? Some of those boyos have a few jars in them, I'd say, in spite of the wives." He looked expertly into the sky. "There'll maybe be a fog later on, and in that case they'll all be coming home early – even the drunks. Come on!"

"Ah, you can go and watch them yourself," I said. "I'm going home."

The truth was I was too excited to sit on any wall for long. I wanted to go home because there were a few things I wanted to find out from mother, if I could bring the talk around to the topic of corpses without letting on where I got the information I had already.

As I ran off from Mickser across the fields for home I felt that I was a new man. The next time there was a funeral I felt sure there would be no need to leave me sitting out in a car. I felt sure they would all notice a change in me when I went into the house.

"Wipe your feet, son," my mother cried out to me through the open door of the kitchen, the minute I came in sight. She was scrubbing the floor. "Not that you'd be the only one to put tracks all over the place," she said, and I could see what she meant, because there, in the middle of the floor, was my brother's old bike, upended, with the wheels in the air, resting on its saddle, and he busy mending a puncture. Or perhaps it was my father she meant? Because he was sitting the other side of the fire with his feet in a basin of water. It must have been my father she meant, because she lit on him just then. "This is no place for washing your feet," she said. "There's a fire inside in the parlour. Why don't you go in there and wash them? I haven't got room to turn around with you all."

"The parlour is no place for washing feet," my father said quietly, and he pointed to the bike in the middle of the floor. "When that fellow's done with that bike you'll be glad to have a bit of water on the floor to swish out the mess he'll have made. Why don't you make him take it out in the yard?"

My mother sighed. She was always sighing, but they weren't the kind of sighs you'd heed. They were caused by something we'd done on her, all right, but they were sighs of patience, if you know what I mean, and not complaint.

"Ah, it's a bit cold outside," she said. But she turned to me. "Here, you, son," she said, and she picked up my satchel and shoved it under my arm. "Let you set a good example and go into the parlour and do your homework in there by the nice fire."

But I wasn't going into the empty parlour.

"Dear knows!" my mother said with a sigh. "I don't know why I waste my time lighting that fire every evening and none of you ever set foot in there until it's nearly night. I only wish I could go in and sit by it. Then I'd leave you the kitchen and welcome."

But I think she knew well that if she was to go in there that minute it wouldn't be many minutes more till we'd all be in there along with her: myself and my satchel, and my father with his feet in the basin, and the old bike as well if it could be squeezed in between the piano and the chiffonier and all the other big useless pieces of furniture that were kept in there out of the way.

"Ah sure, aren't we all right here," said my father, "where we can be looking at you?"

"You must have very little worth looking at if you want to be looking at me," my mother said, in a sort of voice I knew well sounded cross but couldn't be, because she always stretched up when she spoke like that, so she'd see into the little mirror on the mantelshelf and she smiled at what she saw in the glass. And well she might. She always looked pretty, my mother, but she used to look best when we were all around her in the kitchen, annoying her and making her cheeks red and she fussing around trying to keep us in order.

"Mind would you catch your finger in the spokes of that wheel!" she cried just then to my brother.

"Mind would you catch your hair in it, my girl," said my father, because as the kettle boiled and the little kitchen got full of steam, her hair used to loosen and lop around her face like a young girl's. And he caught a hold of her as if to pull her back from the bike.

"Let go of me," she cried. "Will you never get sense?"

"I hope not," said my father, "and what is more, I don't want you to get too much of it either, girl," he said.

"Oh, go on with you and your old talk. Before the boys and all!" she cried, and then she tried harder to drag herself free.

"She's not as strong as her tongue would have us believe, boys," said my father, tightening his hold. And then he laughed. "You'll never be the man I am!" he said, and this time it was my mother herself that giggled, although I didn't see anything specially funny in what he'd said.

Indeed at that very minute, in the middle of tricking and laughing, my father's face changed and it was like as if he wasn't holding her for fun at all, but more like the way he'd hold us if he had something against us.

"You're feeling all right these days, aren't you? You'd tell me if you weren't, wouldn't you?" he cried. And then, abruptly, he let her go, and put his hands up to his head. "Oh, my God, what would I do if anything happened to you!"

"Such talk!" said my mother again, but her voice sounded different too, and although she was free she didn't ask to move away, but stood there beside him, with such a sad look on her face, I wanted to cry.

And all the things I had wanted to ask her about the poor fellow at the level-crossing came back into my mind. But I didn't feel like asking her then at all. And do you know what came into my mind? It was a few words of the prayer we said every night of our lives.

". . . the living and the dead . . ." Over and over we'd said them, night after night, and I never paid any heed to them. But I suddenly felt that they were terrible, terrible words, and if we were to be kneeling down at that moment, I couldn't bear it: I'd start nightmaring, there and then, in the middle of them all, with the lamps lit, and it in no way dark.

But the kettle began to spit on the range, and my mother ran over and lifted it back from the blaze.

"How about us taking our tea in the parlour?" she cried. "All of us. The kitchen is no fitter than the backyard with you!"

And in the excitement I forgot all about the living and the dead. For a long time.

Bridal Sheets

I declare to God, I'd liefer be inside washing the corpse with them, thought Peigin, as she caught the sound of tittering from the women in the room beyond the kitchen. She – God help her – had to sit all night in the kitchen with Brede – the new-made widow. Peigin sighed, and for a moment the sound of the sigh drove out the sound of the sea that, else, was ever and always sounding in her ears, as it washed the four shores of the island. Then she gave another baleful glance at Brede.

"Ah wisha, will you quit saying we none of us know what you're going through," she said. "Sure – isn't losing one's man a common class of sorrow altogether in this, or any other island of the western wave? Doesn't the sea get them one and all in time?" Then she turned away in disgust from sight of the other young woman. But after a minute she looked back at her. "I wonder would it be because you came here from the inlands, and you not used to the way of the sea with a man, that you're taking on this way?" she asked.

For the man that was being readied for his wake in the inner room had brought Brede with him, when he came back from Bohernameen, up in the middle of Ireland, along with the other islanders that weren't eejits enough to be taken in for ever by a foolish government scheme, even though they'd been eejits enough to be taken in by it at the start.

The scheme had had a two-fold purpose: to assist the islanders, and to spread the blas – blas being the word used to describe the true flavour or taste of the Gaelic language on the tongue of native speakers. The idea was to coax the native speakers up to the rich counties of Meath and Kildare, and give them twenty- or thirty-acre holdings of the fat pasture-lands up there – with a new cement house thrown in – and all for no more on their part than putting this blas of theirs on the tongues of their neighbours.

The trouble was that when the islanders got up to the midlands they found it wasn't only the blas the people up there were lacking: the people up there didn't have one word at all of the Gaelic. And if the

237

islanders themselves weren't quick to pick up a few words of the English their tongues might have gone idle in their heads. When, into the bargain, they found that the people in the midlands looked upon them as land-grabbers – and worse – they upped and made back for the island before the grass would get time to grow over the stones again in their bits of fields that they had worked hard to clear, and before the thatch would start to sprout and rot on the roofs of their mud cabins. As far as they were concerned, the scheme was a dead loss altogether, unless maybe some of them someday might take it into their heads to drift over to Boston or Philadelphia, where they might make use of the bit of English they'd learned. Indeed, those cities seemed a lot nearer than Bohernameen to them when they were safely back on the island, looking out from the shore of an evening, with only the waves of the Atlantic and nothing more between them and America.

Ruairi Og was the only one of the islanders who might be said to have got anything out of Bohernameen, and all he got was Brede. But to listen to him boasting about her for the four short months he had with her anyone would have thought she was the wonder of the world in the way of a wife.

Looking across at her now though, sitting lumpish by the fire, and moaning, Peigin began to think a man might maybe pick a good wife in the midlands, but he'd do well to look no further than the island if it was picking his widow he was! She put her fingers in her ears. Brede was at it again. Such a hullabaloo!

"Ah quit it, Brede," she said. What ailed her at all, she wondered, any more than any woman in a like case? But as the sound of the sea stole into the room again she looked at the widow more kindly. "Is it the sound of the sea ails you, Brede, seeing you're not used to it?" she asked.

Brede looked indignantly at her.

"You must think it takes little to ail me. Is it the sound of the sea?" she said. "I put no heed on it no more than back home in Bohernameen, when they used to put on plays in the Town Hall, and a fellow back of the stage would have a fistful of peas in a corset box and he rolling them up and down to let on it was the sound of the waves. Oh no, it's not the sea! There's more than that ailing me, I can tell you, and none to know it. None to know it. I said it once and I'll say it again. And what is more you'll not stop me saying it, Peigin."

"I'll not, I'm afraid," Peigin said dejectedly, and she was silent for a few minutes, but she soon looked up again. "I might think you had cause to carry on if there was a babby on the way, Brede, but sure that isn't the case with you." She sat up. "Or could it be the case without you knowing, do you think?"

"It could not, thank God," said Brede flatly.

Peigin crossed herself. Does God ever get used to being thanked for queer things? she thought. Then another notion took hold of her. Could it be the opposite of that altogether? she wondered. Ah but sure a person had only to think of the fine strong man Ruairi Og was, to know he could handle any woman, and that there'd be no holding back from him. For that matter, what could it be but love that brought them together, seeing as how no one had ever seen anything on Brede's back from the first day she set foot on the island to this mortal minute. And as for the sheets that she'd given the women for laying out Ruairi Og, weren't they a holy show altogether, mildewed and yellowed and mended in twenty places? They looked very like the sheets that were put over and under Ruairi's poor father that died in the same way: sheets that were in the house when Brede came to it, and many a long day before that. Peigin sighed. It would be a poor wake, what with the sheets and with poor Ruairi being a bit over-long in the sea before he was found.

"Is it worried you are he was so long in the water, Brede?" she asked suddenly, meaning, if so, to tell her the island women were a great hand at readying up a corpse in such cases.

But Brede turned up her nose.

"One hour in the sea or three days in it, what differ?" she said. "A man is a queer sight after! Back home in Bohernameen, even if a man were to fall into a bog-hole, he'd come out of it still looking like a man. Did I ever tell you," she said, brightening, "about a man back home that my grandfather used to know? He fell into a bog-hole one night after taking a few drinks too many – God help him! Well, his people never heard of him more. It was thought he was gone off to America, because he had sold a heifer that morning and the price he got for it was the exact fare to America in those times. And then one day about forty years afterwards there was a body found in the same bog, and who was it but the same man, and – here's the best of it – looking like as if it was only that day he was after falling into it. Preserved like a Pope of Rome, he was. They only guessed it was him by the make of his clothes – he had a swalley-tail coat on him and frieze trousers – and by a big turnip of a watch chained across his chest."

" – and it still ticking, I suppose?" said Peigin, who had begun to have her doubts.

Brede gave her an indignant look.

"It's the living truth I'm telling you, Peigin, and that very same man is above in the Museum in Dublin this minute in a showcase for all to see."

"For all to gawk and gape at him? Glory be to God, how can you call that a good thing to happen to a man?" said Peigin. "Well, it's true to say tastes differ!" She stood up impatiently. "I wonder if those women inside would like a cup of tea?" she said. "They say there comes a terrible drought on a person scouring a corpse." She let down the kettle two notches lower on the crane over the flames. "I'll step to the door and ask them"

When Peigin opened the door of the inner room though, the women inside peered out past her at Brede.

"Is she still taking on the same way?" one of them whispered. "Ah sure, God help her," she added. "It's my belief they know nothing at all about death up there in the middle of Ireland. Do you remember her telling us a story once about her own grandfather that was sitting up by the fire with them one night, and with the laughing and talking it was a couple of hours before they found out he was dead? Someone gave him a nudge to move over so they could pull nearer the fire, and down he came on the floor like a jug off the dresser! Now wasn't that the unnatural death! Think of that compared with the grand death of an island man, standing up in his boat, maybe, one minute, and those in the boats alongside him shouting to him across the wind, and his womenfolk, maybe, watching him from afar off on the shore, and the next minute he's gone from their sight, with one wash of a wave, and his currach floating empty as a cockle-shell on the water. Sure that's what you might call a decent death. Only how could Brede see it our way, she being used only to inland ways? But, tell me, did you say the kettle was boiling? There's a terrible drought on us. Not but we'd suffer anything sooner than be out there in the kitchen with her, like you, Peigin, having to listen to her moaning and groaning."

But at that moment a gap of brightness came between the two pieces of sailcloth that were pinned across the window for curtains. The sun was rising. One of the women ran over and pulled down the sailcloth.

"Glory be to God for the grand day that's going to be in it after all the storms," she cried. "And maybe the seed herring will be in on the tide? Oh look, they're in already. Look at them tangled in the weeds on the shore. The waves are swelling with them. The pier is stuck all over with them, and they glinting like the sun itself! Oh, isn't it a great pity the men have the grave to dig and can't be out with the tide!"

"Oh, but the grave was dug an hour back," Peigin cried. "I heard the step of the men on the shingle and I knew what was on foot but I didn't say anything." She looked back at Brede. "Not but they are grand graves, the island graves." Suddenly, with a warm impulse, she ran over and put her arm around Brede. "They are grand graves altogether, Brede. Not like the cold black clay you have over on the mainland, but fine white sand only, and it lifting on the wind in a way would put you in mind of the soul itself streaming back to its Maker. And if your eye should chance to fall on an odd bone, it's rusted red with the salt of the sea, so's you wouldn't think it was a common man at all was in it, but a man of bronze or of gold itself!" As she was speaking, another idea struck her and she sprang to her feet. "Maybe you were never down there, Brede? How would you like to run down now, this minute, and see the grave for yourself? Because I can tell you you'll not see it properly later with all the crowds that will be pushing and shoving to get near the edge when the coffin is going down. Come on! That's what we'll do! We'll run down there now and see it in the first sparkle of morning. Where's your shawl, Brede? Let you get it and come."

"I don't know where my shawl is," said Brede dully.

It wasn't a very eager response but it was enough for Peigin. The next minute she had the shawl found, and thrown over Brede, and twisted around her, and had her out the door and facing down the boreen to the shore. But on the threshold she paused and called back to the women within.

"Now you'll get a chance to have your cup of tea in peace and quiet," she said. Then she caught up with Brede again. "Glory be to God! Such a morning!" she cried, as she felt the cool air on her face. It was as fresh as the slap of a wet sheet on their hot faces. "Come on, Brede," she urged, and without letting go of her she started to run down the boreen, dragging her with her. "Glory be to God!" she cried again when they came in sight of the sea, not hid now by any humps of land.

Away it stretched blue and flat except for a few light ripples near the shore and a small break of spray around a solitary rock far out from the land. "Come on. Come on," she cried again, and she started to run downward towards the sea-edge.

As the two women ran along the rutted boreen, one minute they'd lose sight of the sea and the next minute it would rise up again till it was as if the island was a ship pitching and tossing in the blue.

At last, they came to the graveyard that was marked off from the rest of the sandy shore by a loose wall of big round stones, set unsteadily one on the other. Peigin hopped nimbly over the wall without knocking one stone.

"Mind yourself," she cried, as two big stones clattered down around Brede, and she only after putting a hand on the wall. "Don't you feel better now that we're here?" she asked, after she'd fixed up the gap. She straightened up and drew a big deep breath. It was a grand thing after the long night to be out in the morning air, and, sure, if the sea brought death, it brought life too. The whole coast glittered with the seed herring. And it wasn't only fish that was in plenty. She gave a little laugh unbeknownst to Brede, thinking of the big barrel of drink there was like to be at the wake that night, if any was left from the barrels that were floated in on the tide from the French trawler that went down beyond the Point. "Aren't you feeling better now, Brede?" she asked again.

"Why would I feel any better now than before?" Brede demanded. "Oh, it's easy seen you know little of what I am feeling, Peigin, or you wouldn't ask that question." Lumping down on the wall, she knocked off a few more stones. "Do you know what I think? I think it's little you know about death at all in this island! And how could you? The way it comes leppin' at you, out of a wave, like an eejit creature would lep out from behind a bush, putting the heart across you with fright before you'd know rightly what was in it at all! Ah, but it's a different thing entirely up with us, up in the middle of Ireland, the way it can come gentle into a house, with no one seeing it at all, maybe, for a long while, and then maybe one person will see it, and one person there and maybe the man it came for, often the last one to see it! But by that time the house is full of neighbours and kinsmen with not one of them giving him anything but looks of love, so that all can know their last looks back from him will be looks of love, too. Not like this place! Why here, it's, maybe, in a fit of anger a man will cleave down through the shingle, and he not looking back even when he pushes out the currach into the little waves and steps into it! And you left with that black look for his last look at you in this life."

But Peigin could bear no more.

"Oh, Brede, Brede," she wailed, thinking now at last surely she knew what ailed her. "Was that the way it was with you and Ruairi?"

Brede turned in pained surprise.

"It was not," she said sharply. "And if that's what you thought, let me tell you you're as far away as ever from knowing!"

If Peigin's pity had flared up sudden, it died down sudden too.

"Ach, I've heard that once too often," she said. "If you want us to know what ails you, then why can't you tell us?"

But Brede had an answer to that too. "Would I be believed if I did tell you, Peigin? That's the thing! Would you believe me yourself, Peigin? Would you even as much as remember the big trunks I had, and I coming here, and they part of my story? It wouldn't surprise me this minute if you'd forgotten all about them trunks, in spite of it being only four months ago, and in spite of Ruairi having to get the lend of another ass as well as our own to carry them from the pier for fear our own ass would be kilt with the weight of them. Maybe you have forgotten that entirely?"

"Oh, but I have not forgotten it, Brede," Peigin cried. "And why would I? Wasn't it our ass that you got the lend of that night? To tell you the truth I was always wondering what was in them trunks, Brede!"

"What do you think would be in them?" asked Brede.

"Ah sure, how would I know?" said Peigin.

At this Brede gave a big sob.

"That's true for you. How would you know? How would anyone know? All the finery and style, all the dresses and all the caps, and all the gloves and all the scarves and all the buckled belts and all the bits of ribbons for my hair that were in those trunks. It was no wonder they nearly broke the back of our ass. How would anyone know what I brought and not one soul on this island ever to see a stitch of them on me. Oh, isn't it me that is steeped in sorrow!"

Peigin stared at her. It was true that for the four months Brede was on the island no one had ever seen her in anything but the one old brown skirt and the one old black jumper that was on her at that minute. Indeed it was one of the reasons that it was thought Ruairi must have married for love surely, when his bride had brought no more clothes with her than what she had on her back.

"But if it was finery you had in the trunks, Brede, why did you never wear them?" she cried, wonderingly.

"Ah, well may you ask! Isn't that what I'm asking myself ever since the first minute Ruairi was brought in to me stiff and dripping wet on the boards. To think he never saw anything but these old rags." She began to sob again – loudly.

Peigin could think of nothing to say for a minute.

"Ah whisht, Brede," she said then. "Sure you're forgetting your wedding day? Didn't he see you that day?"

Brede looked coldly at her.

"I can see you're not in mind of the day was in it when Ruairi and me married – the wettest day ever came out of the sky. And do you know the time we were married? Seven o'clock in the morning! And didn't we have the long journey back here to make the same day? And on top of that Ruairi always telling me about crossing the bay and how it would be maybe, with the boat rocking and rolling, and if my stomach wasn't right, that it's sick I'd be and leaning out over the deck all the way?" She paused. "Were you never on that boat, Peigin?" she asked sternly. "Did you never see poor creatures with their stomachs turned inside out, and it no use their leaning over the deck either, with the wind blowing back against them, destroying their whole front!" She paused again. "Well?" she demanded. "How would you like to be wearing your best blue coat and skirt in a like case? And it a light blue too that would show up stains something awful!"

"I wouldn't like it at all, Brede," Peigin said emphatically. "And was it destroyed they were on you?"

"It was not," said Brede. "Do you think I'd be that foolish as to have them on me?"

"Oh, but you brought them with you, didn't you? You didn't leave them behind in Bohernameen, did you?" Peigin cried. She thought she was beginning to get a glimmer of what Brede was trying to tell her.

"Of course I brought them with me! But suppose it was you had a fine blue coat for your wedding, and you didn't get to wear it on that day, wouldn't you be only belittling it to wear it on a common ordinary day?"

Peigin considered this.

"How about Mass of a Sunday?" she asked.

"At home in Bohernameen, yes – maybe," said Brede. "But after one look around the chapel here on a Sunday and seeing all of you with only shawls on you, I made up my mind that it would be out of place to be dressed up in a new outfit that had the pleats still tightened down with the tailor's tacking. I know the way it would be taken – that I was putting myself up to be better than my neighbours. And you know it too, Peigin Mac. Don't you wear a shawl to Mass yourself? You'd probably be the first to point your finger at me and my finery. Aye, and specially at my hat, with the brand brass pin through the brim!"

"Oh, Brede! And you had a hat too? Not blue like the dress!"

"And why not? I like things to match other, although, to tell you the truth, the hat was a shade lighter than the coat. But then, of course, it went with my gloves and my bag."

"Your bag and your gloves? Oh, you must have looked gorgeous, Brede!"

"When?" snapped Brede. "Amn't I after telling you the kind of day it was! Black as night when I was going down to the church! And then the long train journey to Galway – four hours I'd have been sitting on those pleats – and after that the dirty old boat to get out here – and you know yourself what came after that – the cottage full to the door with all of you waiting for us and the men stotious drunk by the time we got here without waiting for the proper drinking to begin at all. Oh, that night! I was jaded. If I had my good dress on me, I would have slipped into the room and changed out of it, in order not to have it rendered a rag in no time with sweat alone! And there was one thing Ruairi forgot to tell me, that there'd only be oil lamps here. Sure, whatever call a woman might have for wearing her finery outside of the house, she'd have no call for it at all inside with the smoke and the dark. That was the first land I got! And I knew well it wasn't only that one night but it would be the same every night, and maybe it would be that I'd never get a chance to wear one stitch of all the style was in my trunk. And—"

"You didn't have more things, Brede?" Peigin interrupted her in amazement.

"You don't think I brought the trunk half empty, do you? Do you remember the size of it? More did you say? Hadn't I three pairs of shoes alone, leaving out of count the black patent leather ones I was planning to wear at the wedding! Instead of that, the first thing I did the day after I got here was to go down to the shop and buy these." She stuck out her feet with the coarse pair of men's boots that were all anyone had ever seen on her. "One look at what you call roads hereabouts and I knew that was the end of my wearing fine shoes! I never took them out of the trunk!"

"Ach, Brede. I don't believe you. I bet you were always putting them on at night, for Ruairi, and the two of you talking about what it would be like if you were living in the midlands, where you could show them off to all! Oh, if it was my Lorcan I swear he'd be out with a pick trying to level the boreen, and lighting fires on the big stones of a frosty night and throwing water on them in the morning to crack them so he could dig them out of it, and make a fit causeway for me to be minching down it alongside of him of a Sunday and he showing me off to all! Oh, men are devils for style, though they don't like to let on to it. What did Ruairi think at all of you not being able to wear your shoes?"

But at this question Brede began to sob again.

"Didn't I know I was right in saying you knew nothing at all of what I was suffering! Sure, Ruairi never saw them, Peigin. Isn't that why I'm eating my heart out. I was always thinking I'd get a chance to wear them – that we'd go over to the mainland maybe – or we'd take an excursion train up to Dublin perhaps – and I'd give him a surprise when I'd take them out. But you know what happened!"

"Do you mean to say he never saw them at all?" Peigin cried. "Oh God help you, you're right. I didn't understand. But I do now. Oh God help you, you poor creature." And here Peigin threw her arms around the widow and she too started to sob. But after a while Peigin dried her eyes. "Come now, Brede," she said, and she tried to seek out some little way of consoling the other. "Don't take on so. You're making things out worse than it was, I'm sure. Think back! There must have been some things he saw – if it was only some little bit of ribbon for your hair or –" But suddenly her face lit up. "Ach sure there must have been lots of things he saw if you come to think of it! And things no one else saw but him too! I'm sure you had gorgeous shifts when you had so much room for carrying them over here in that big trunk! If it comes to that, what does a man care about hats and shoes? I don't believe they could tell, five minutes after, what it was we had on us and we standing beside them at the altar! And why would they? It's not for them a woman is got up on that day of all days, but for show! It's different altogether when they're alone together at last, the two of them. You know what I mean? It's only then they begin to see what they've got." A flush came into her face and she lowered her voice. "Ah sure God help them – you'd feel sorry for them really, wouldn't you: they get such a thrill out of seeing a bit of a shift, or a thing you'd wear inside next to your skin. You'd have to laugh at them if you didn't feel so sorry for them. But God help them, you can't blame them – from the time they're out of petticoats themselves, people are always telling them not to look here and not to look there and to keep their hands off this, and their hands off that, and slamming doors in their faces and asking them to turn the other way! Even when they start courting it's not much better, with the girl going behind a tree or a haycock if she only wants to straighten the seams of her stockings. Sure it's a great excitement for them the first night they can look all they like at woman, shift or no shift – you know what I mean, don't you?" she asked. "Not like us. Sure there's no mystery about men for us. I was washing my father's underpants as soon as I was able to stand over a basin of water, and sewing buttons on them ever since I could thread a needle. But it's different for men – sure you know it is, Brede, so why can't you console yourself? Come now, let you forget about the blue dress, and the coat, and even the shoes and the buckles. It wasn't those things that Ruairi was wanting to see when the two of you were alone together at last."

At last Brede spoke.

"Didn't I tell you I was jaded tired that night?" she cried. "Didn't I tell you my eyes weren't used to the oil lamps? It was as dark as dawn in that cottage. Who'd think of getting into anything good in that smoky little hole of a room?"

"You mean you never wore your good shifts either?" Peigin gasped.

Brede nodded her head.

"How was I to know that I'd never get a chance to wear them for him at all?" she cried, and she began to rock from side to side, as a new aspect of her sorrow occurred to her. "Oh what will my mother say when she hears I never put on a single stitch of all the things she went to such trouble to have right for me, getting them taken up and let down, and let down and taken up, till I was sick of the sight of them. My poor mother!"

"Ach, bother your mother! It's Ruairi not seeing them I mind," Peigin said.

"Him too, of course," said Brede. "But my mother is the one most to be considered. Wasn't it she paid for them? And the things in the other trunk as well. The other trunk was never unpacked either."

"You hadn't other things, had you, Brede?" Peigin cried. It was hard to believe she could have had anything else. "What else could you have, Brede?" she cried.

"Ach, what do you think?" Brede said impatiently. "What would any bride have in her other trunk but her bridal sheets?"

But Peigin could only stare. "What in the name of God are bridal sheets?" she asked at last.

"Well, Peigin Mac, if it was back in Bohernameen I was at this minute and I to be asked that question I'd be staring at you for a week! But seeing that I've lived here now for four long, dark months I can easily see that it would be a waste of time entirely for a bride in these parts to be having anything fancy in the way of sheets for her marriage bed, with nothing but dirty old oil lamps good only for filling the room with smuts! I don't wonder at you knowing nothing but sheets made out of flour-bags split up and sewn together and hardly hemmed at all and the name of the mills not bleached off them! But oh, it's cruel to think of the way I was planning to take the sight out of Ruairi's eyes with the sheets I had for our wedding bed – made by my own hand. Those sheets were the talk of the parish back in Boherna-meen. And when I'd finished embroidering them and put in the last of the lace medallions insets – cutting the cloth from the back so the lace would show up – and washed them and ironed them – well! – everyone in the parish had to see them before they went into that trunk. And to think they never came out of it! Oh! Oh! Oh! I told you before and I'll tell you again, there's not one woman on this island ever had a sorrow like mine."

And at last Peigin felt that this might be true.

"Oh, Brede!" she cried. "How did you put up with us at all? She threw her arms around her again. "Oh God have pity on you," she cried. And when over Brede's shoulder she caught sight just then of the currachs strung out on the line of the sky, and looking as safe as if they were only painted in a picture, she felt that the sorrow which always and ever menaced herself and the other island-women was a bearable sorrow, and not to be compared in any way with the queer sorrow of Brede. "God help you, Brede. Sure we didn't understand. Oh, aren't you the unfortunate woman entirely! Did you say he never set eyes on any of the style at all? – not even the sheets?"

It was a terrible sorrow indeed, she thought, and how could such a sorrow be borne?

But suddenly she gave a cry.

"Oh, Brede. Sure nothing is so bad it can't be worse. Why in the name of God didn't you tell me this sooner?" She threw a wild glance up at the cottage. "Are they finished drinking the tea, do you think? Have they gone back to laying him out yet, do you suppose? Look! There's a fresh bit of smoke coming up the chimney – they're after giving the sods a poke; it must be that they're boiling up the kettle again to put more water in the pot. I told you there's a great drought to be got out of working on a corpse. Oh God be praised we may be in time! Come on, quick. Isn't it good you told me! You've a chance yet to make up entirely for everything. We'll get out them sheets and have him laid out in them." But she paused here for a moment and looked curiously at the widow. "Isn't it a wonder you didn't think of it yourself, Brede! Talk of his wedding night! Won't poor Ruairi be the proud man looking down from Heaven this night and seeing himself lying in such grandeur! And God knows he'll be fitter and abler to see them looking down from above tonight than he'd have been on the night of his wedding – for sure he had other things on his mind to distract him on that night. Oh come on, Brede! Hurry, will you! I can't understand how you didn't think of it yourself! Do you remember that time you were saying the sheets you gave them were a bit yellow. Glory be to God, I didn't like to say it then, not knowing you had any better, but they were as yellow as the bill of a gander. Oh well, isn't it great that you don't have to disgrace the poor corpse after all. Come on, quick!" she urged, lepping along herself, not seeing Brede was hanging back, until she called after her.

"Peigin, hold your whist a minute," Brede called. "Isn't linen a terrible cold cloth to be laying him in? Did you think of that?"

Peigin stopped. Then she gave a laugh.

"Will you ever learn, Brede! This is one night in the poor creature's life he's not going to heed the cold, God rest him. Come on." And she started off once more.

But they'd only gone a short way when Brede stopped again.

"Peigin, I was thinking of something else. Linen is terrible easy

I

creased. Did you know that? I declare if it wasn't for the medallions and the fancy stitches I'd say that common sheets would look better on him in the long run!"

Peigin stopped.

"Well, to tell you the truth, Brede, like you said yourself a while back, I can't say I ever saw any sheets but ones made out of flour-bags. What's the differ, anyway?"

"Ah, there's a great differ, Peig," said Brede. "Linen is a very soft class of cloth. You know the test for linen, I suppose?"

"I don't then," said Peigin humbly.

"You don't? Well, come over here," said Brede, and going over herself to a stone wall she selected two stones on the top of it with her eye. "Say this stone is made of linen," she said, pointing to one, "and say this stone here is made of an old flour-bag. Well now, if you were to wet your finger – like this – and put a spot of spit on this stone here – the linen one – and if you were to do the same then with that one there – the one that's not linen – you'd know the differ at once, because the spit would soak into the linen, but it would hardly soak into the other one at all. Here! I'll show you," she cried, and spitting on her finger, again she dabbed first one stone and then, spitting on her finger again, she dabbed the other one. "Oh, but I forgot, they're only stones," she cried impatiently, as the spits stayed winking and bubbling on the two stones alike. "No matter, I was only trying to show you that linen's a queer stuff altogether. I often wondered why there's so much thought of it. It may be all right for tablecloths and the like, but it's a poor stuff for sheets, at any time. I think maybe we ought to leave things as they are, Peigin, because after a few hours those sheets would be a proper show, all creased and crumpled!"

"Do you say?" said Peigin, and it was clear she was dejected for the minute. But the next minute she gave a laugh and a sort of skip of joy. "Ah, but we're forgetting – sure it isn't as if the poor creature in the bed will be twisting and turning. Sure he'll have no carry-on tonight that would put creases in sheets. Ah, Brede, you'll never learn anything about corpses, that's my belief. You're only looking for trouble where there's none at all. Come on, and let you hurry too, for if we're late and he's laid out already, you'll have cause then to be sobbing and moaning, having lost your one chance of making up to him for everything –" And this time she caught Brede by the sleeve and gave her a pull.

But Brede pulled back.

"Tell me one thing, Peigin," she said. "Do they bury the sheets along with the corpse?"

"Is it bury good sheets? Are you cracked or what?" cried Peigin, shocked. "Why would they do that? What about all the corpses to come after? It's not every house can say it'll only have one corpse, like your house, or two at the most – if you stay on the island, which I don't suppose you will? Of course the sheets are not buried," she said, and then she stopped dead as a new aspect of the situation struck her: "unless you want it that way," she said. "But we can decide that later. That is if we are in time at all."

They were in time.

"Oh thanks be to God," cried Peigin when they went in the door and she saw the women were only after standing up from their tea, and were wiping their mouths. She turned to Brede. "Tell me quick where you keep them, Brede!" she cried, and she turned back to the women. "She has grand sheets for laying him out," she told them. "Her bridal sheets. I'm dying to see them." She turned back to Brede. "Where are they, Brede?" she said. "Get them out quick and give them to the women." Brede went into the room and pulled out a trunk from under the bed, but the catch seemed to be rusty and she was a long time trying to get it open. While she was struggling with it Peigin turned back to the women. "I suppose it will take you a while to change the sheets," she said. "I think I'll run home, if you don't mind, any of you, and make sure my fire isn't gone out. I might make a small cake of bread, too, while I'm at it, because there isn't a bit in the house." She threw a smile to Brede. "Let you not fear, Brede. I'll be back early before the wake starts so I'll see them medallions!"

"Well, Peigin," said the women. "Let you go quick if you're going. And let you come back quick too, because maybe when you come back you might let us slip home for a while as well before the crowds of the world arrive?"

But at this point, all of a sudden, Brede came to life – or leastwise she became more lively than anyone had ever seen her.

"The lot of you can all go if you like," she cried. "It's all the same to me. You needn't think I'll mind being alone. Isn't it the last time I'll ever be with him! Wouldn't it be only right to leave us alone together for a while?"

The women stared at each other. Was this another custom they had up in the midlands? "What do you think, Peigin?" they asked.

"Ah sure, there's no knowing," Peigin said, as she went to the door. "We may as well humour her," she whispered. "When you've all done and you've the new sheets under him, couldn't you slip away one by one, and whoever is last could maybe stand at the door till I round the Point, and then that one could slip away too. I wouldn't be leaving her alone really, but only letting on to it."

"That's a good idea, Peigin," said one of the women. "Let you go now. And, as we said, let you hurry back. We'll get the corpse into the fine sheets. Have you got them, Brede?"

Peigin, however, was a bit longer at home than she thought she'd be, and when she rounded the hill she saw the last of the women standing at the door of Brede's house straining her eyes outward. Peigin beckoned her to start but the woman waited.

"I was kept a bit longer nor I reckoned," Peigin gasped.

"Ah, don't worry yourself," said the older woman. "As long as you're here now, it's no matter what kept you. We've everything done. We have the poor man wrapped up in the fine linen sheets. And God help Brede, I'm beginning to feel sorry for her. She must have meant what she said about wanting to be alone with him, because even before I saw you coming she wanted me to go, God help her, and in the end she nearly pushed me out of the room, and she went in herself, and shut the door! And after all, isn't it true what she said that it's the last time she'll ever have him to herself!"

"It is true," said Peigin. She was still out of breath from running. "God help her," she added fervently. And indeed these same words welled up in her heart again when the woman left and she stepped into the cottage and ran across the kitchen to rap on the door of the room with the corpse. "God help you, Brede," she said. "Can I come in? I'm in dread of not getting a look at the sheets before the whole island is down on top of us. I know you'd like to be alone with him, but if I get one gawk of the lace medallions I'll sit out here in the kitchen and leave him to you till the first of the mourners gets here."

She pushed open the door. But on the threshold she stopped.

"What in the name of God are you doing, Brede?" she screamed. For there was Ruairi, and he turned over on his face. And there was Brede and she pushing one of the old yellowed sheets under him. And on the chair beside the bed, creased and limp, where she'd dragged it from under him, was one of the bridal sheets with its big dollops of embroidery and its big round medallions of lace. "What in the name of God are you doing, Brede?" she cried again. But she knew. And Brede was too busy anyway to turn round.

"Mind your own business, you!" Brede said. "And go back to the kitchen. I don't want the whole island in on me before I'm ready!"

The Mouse

Leila was not my real aunt at all. I only called her Aunt Leila from affection. She was a dear friend of my mother. They were girls together. Not, I gather, such very great friends at all, but when my father died and my mother came back to her home-town, the friendship developed. Aunt Leila being an old maid, you see, and mother being a widow they were in greater need of each other's company than when they were young and supported by their hopes and dreams.

They saw a certain amount of each other, of course, even in their young days, because they were the only three girls in their town who went by train each day to a convent school in Galway. They had a pass on the railway, the three of them: my mother, and Leila, and Mina.

Mina was never at any time a friend of my mother's. Indeed, they disliked each other. My mother said so straight out one day to Leila.

"I never liked her, Leila. I never could understand what you saw in her."

And Leila sighed.

"It just was to be, I suppose," she said, and her face was so sad that later, when she had gone, I asked my mother about it.

She hesitated for a minute.

"Well, there's no reason why you shouldn't know – what little there is to know. You see, Leila was going to be married one time, to a most suitable person too, and then – well – no one knew exactly what happened, but one day he eloped with Mina. Leila behaved wonderfully. Nobody ever heard her say a word against either of them. Not a word. Can you imagine that! Wouldn't you think she'd simply have to unburden herself to someone? We may not have been bosom friends in those days, but she could have told *me*. Yet their names never passed her lips. It was very strange. The whole town was a hive of gossip. Everyone wanted to know what had happened, but all they could make out was that there was a bit of an estrangement between Arthur and Leila, and that he was seen talking to Mina a few times, but no more than that. Nothing to explain them eloping – Mina and

Arthur, I mean. They went to Dublin and got married there. Poor Leila: even now it seems hard to believe it really happened."

"But why didn't she marry someone else?" I cried. "She must have been very good-looking."

"She was! She was absolutely lovely; a most striking face, as you can still see, but unfortunately, as she said to me recently, *she didn't know it*."

I didn't see how that counted for anything.

"Oh, it made all the difference in the world," my mother said. "Why, even that awful Mina, who was hardly to be called pretty, even in the commonest way, was so well-read about her own looks she'd have known how to show herself off to advantage if she were to be laid out dead! Oh that one! She was good-looking, I'll admit: but there was a lot of trickery to her looks. Whereas Leila had a kind of unregarding beauty that was there *all* the time, no matter whether it was being shown up or not. If she paid any heed to it, she could have dazzled people. Not that I think she would have liked dazzling anyone. She was the kind of person that you would have to put something into before there'd be anything to get back from her, if that's not beyond you to understand? That was what Arthur did, you see. We all thought it a great bit of luck when he turned up. Everyone noticed the change in her when he began to walk out with her. We all saw suddenly that she had a beautiful face, and we hadn't realized it. But it wasn't everyone would have acted on her like Arthur, and that's why it was so terrible when that awful Mina got mixed up with them. Only for her, they'd be happily married today, like me – like I was, I mean."

"All the same, it's a wonder she didn't marry someone else," I said quickly, "if she was so good-looking."

"You poor child," said my mother, "you don't understand. She couldn't possibly have married anyone else. They were made for each other, she and Arthur – made for each other! It was like your father and me! You might as well say I'd have married someone else if *he* had jilted *me*."

I'm afraid I took this avowal lightly, I wouldn't say there was a lot to choose between mother and Mina when it came to having boys, just that mother was a nice girl, and Mina – well, of course, I didn't know her, but she didn't seem nice. Whereas Leila – ah, yes, I felt, she was the kind who might easily give her heart once and once only.

"You see, Arthur was a bit of a stick really," my mother went on.

"At least, that's how he appeared to us at first. I don't think I told you that I used to know him too, long ago, when we were going in and out to school on the train every day. There were three of us girls – I told you that – but there were five boys as well, although they travelled in a separate compartment. They were always dashing against us on the platform when we were waiting for the train and pulling our plaits and jeering at us – just showing off! But they never really mixed with us all the same. They wouldn't be caught dead in the same compartment as us. I remember once one of them was late – I do believe it was Arthur! – and he came running on to the platform as the guard was locking the doors, and what did the guard do but open the door of our carriage and shove him in on top of us. Oh, such laughing – we nearly died laughing – but when Arthur saw it was our compartment he wrenched open the door again and jumped down on the line, although the train was moving. He nearly broke his neck. And the stationmaster was fit to kill him, and, needless to say, he missed school that day. But he'd suffer all and more besides rather than have the indignity of travelling with us girls. He was always sort of shy. Not but that the others would have acted the same, and some of them were a long way from knowing the meaning of shyness. There was one big fellow – I forget his name, but if you knew what Mina told me – " But here mother stopped. "Looking back on it," she said, "I suppose Mina could have made up that story, or the half of it anyway. But I know there was something gentler about Arthur than there was about the others, although, to tell you the truth, I don't remember much about him. He was only a short time going in and out on the train. He wasn't living in the town, you see, only boarding with people – distant cousins I think – who lived in a big house on the outskirts. His own people were abroad, or something – I don't remember – but in any case he went back wherever he belonged after a bit – I forget where – somewhere in Enniskillen, I think – not that it matters. And he went clean out of my thoughts, and out of Leila's too, I'm sure, because it was only a coincidence that he came back to the town later. There must be dozens of branches of the Ulster Bank in the Twenty-six Counties! But there you are! It was to our town Arthur was sent. Can you blame us for thinking it was Fate? And when we heard Leila's mother was going to take him as a paying guest, well, anyone could guess what would happen! To begin with, they were both Protestants – did I tell you that? And then they were both the moody type – quiet, and happy to say nothing if they weren't pressed. They were great readers, too – both of them. I like a good book myself, but if I take one up I can't put it down – it's the story I'm after, you see – but I often saw Leila take up a book – any book! – and start reading it – anywhere – in the middle or near the end – anywhere, just for the sake of reading! And he was the same. Such books as he had in his room – stacks of them – Leila took me in one day – not a novel among them – would you believe it? And he was finished his studies at that time. It wasn't compulsory I mean, if that's what you're thinking. Not that Leila thought it remarkable. It wasn't to show me the books she took me into the room, but for some other reason, which I forget, but looking back now I think it might only have been for the pleasure of going into his room. Would you believe it? I think she'd have been too shy to go into it alone, and he away on his holidays in Enniskillen! That was Leila! It wouldn't be Mina's way, I can tell you. And talking about books, do you know I only saw Mina with a book in her hands on one occasion, and it turned out to be one that, when you opened the cover, wasn't a book at all but a cigarette box! You couldn't imagine two people more unlike than Mina and Arthur. But Leila and he looked sort of alike. I noticed it right away, a few days after he came to the town, when I saw them in the street. Don't laugh. Why shouldn't people be alike outside if they were alike inside like those two?

"Arthur was good-looking too, in an odd way. I would even go so far as to say that, like Leila, he was also the kind, too, who was better looking than you'd think at first sight. I know if he had half the notions about himself that some men have he'd have put more oil in his hair for one thing, and not have it sticking up like a sweeping brush. Most people saw the shock of yellow hair on him before they saw what good features he had. I remember Mina laughing the first *she* saw him. That was the funny part of it. Mina didn't think anything of him at first. We were all dying to see what the new bank clerk would be like, and of course Mina – trust her – was the first to clap eyes on him. 'Towpate: that's what we'll call him, girls,' she said, when she came back from some trumped-up message to the bank. She didn't even recognize him, or know she'd ever seen him before in her life. And when she heard Leila's mother was taking him as a paying guest, she pitied Leila. 'Isn't it a shame,' she said to me, 'that when Leila's mother took it into her head to have a lodger, that she didn't get somebody eligible? Because, you know, Leila will never marry – she'll be an old maid for certain – unless some man is thrown at her head. There'd be some hope for her in propinquity!' She was very well up, Mina. But it wasn't propinquity that brought Arthur and Leila together, because I suppose that implies only a physical attraction, and really I sometimes thought that was one thing they didn't have at all! It would have come in time, of course. Oh, it would have come for certain when they were married, which would have made everything perfect, but I don't think it was there then – unfortunately for Leila – " Here my mother stopped. "I wonder if I ought to be talking to you like this at all," she said, dubiously, "but then, you young people nowadays seem to know all that's to be known about everything without ever being told!" She sighed. "Anyway, that's all that's to the story, so there's no harm done."

"You mean you don't know what happened?"

I never felt more let down in my life.

"I told you she never mentioned his name," said my mother, with asperity.

"But perhaps Mina – ?"

"As if I'd demean myself by talking about it to *her*," said mother. "Anyway, who'd believe her version?"

"Do you know something, mother?" I cried suddenly. "You ought to ask Leila what happened. Ask her *now*!"

"Are you out of your mind?" said my mother. "When I kept my mouth shut at the time, I'm hardly likely to bring it all up again now, when she's probably forgotten it, or so one would hope."

"She's not forgotten it," I said. "You'd know by a certain look in her face. Oh, mother, it was wonderful of you not to have said anything to her then – at the time, I mean – but somehow I think it's almost unkind never to refer to it *now*. You see now, it's all she has – or ever will have – that romance. And even if it never came to anything in the eyes of other people, it might comfort her to feel her life wasn't always empty and cold. Oh I *do* think you ought to bring it up some day. It would be like talking about the dead – you said it yourself about father – the dead are only really dead when they are no longer remembered by the living. It may be the same with Leila. You might put more reality into her memories."

"I never thought of that," said my mother. "And after all, there *was* a good deal of reality in it. Arthur *did* love her, I know that for certain. And he never loved Mina – I told you that, didn't I? – the marriage was an awful failure. I haven't heard anything about them for a long time. They left the town after a short while, but I knew from the start it could never work out. So maybe, in a way, Leila ought to be made to feel she had more than Mina in the long run. Oh, the past is a queer place surely! I think, sometimes, it's like what we're told to believe Heaven is like, with no marriage, and no giving in marriage only love. I mean the bodily memories die away and all you remember is the love. If it weren't for that, the pain of love would be unbearable. I hadn't so much more than Leila myself when all was said and done. But Mina had less than either of us. You're right about talking to Leila. I will."

And I knew she would. So, that evening, when I was out for a ride on my bicycle and I passed mother and Leila pacing slowly along a country road, I didn't get off the bicycle, but just waved because I knew they were deep into it. Indeed, mother gave me one of her flashing blue glances that conveyed all, and more, than she wished to convey.

It was a beautiful evening. I cycled for miles, but I wasn't really going anywhere in particular, and there was only the one road back, so I had to pass them a second time – whether I liked it or not. They were still walking up and down when I passed the second time. I was a bit embarrassed, but I don't think Leila noticed me at all. Mother saw me all right, but the look she gave me wasn't at all the same as earlier in the evening. Even flying past on the bicycle, I could see she was impatient, not only with Leila, but with me. The evening was coming down and it was chilly for spring. Mother was probably cold, I thought, walking up and down the road, and so slowly too.

When she did come home, about an hour later, her hands were icy. And she was inclined to be irritable with me.

"Well I hope you're satisfied," she said. "I'm two hours listening to her. And what about? I'll tell you! About nothing! All about nothing!" She threw off her coat crossly and began to fill the kettle for a cup of tea. Then suddenly she put down the kettle, and left the tap running. "Look here! You wouldn't think Leila was a bit – a bit strange, dear, would you? – from thinking about the past too much?"

"Hadn't you better tell me what happened first?"

"But that's what I'm trying to tell you: nothing happened. Only Leila thinks the nothing was something! Oh dear, it was so hard to follow her, and she went on and on, once she started, and my shoe was hurting, and it was getting cold, and I don't see that it did any good, one way or another. Not that I'm sorry I spoke to her, because you were right about how precious those memories were to her, and I could see that my remembering them did make a difference to her. She said so. She said she sometimes found herself doubting that there had ever been anything between her and Arthur. She began to wonder if she had only invented the things he said, just to fill up the terrible vacancy in her heart. As if she was getting queer, she meant, I suppose. I was so glad to be able to reassure her. Because, of course, everyone knew how Arthur loved her. 'It was plain to be seen in his eyes when he looked at you, Leila,' I told her. 'And he was so manly about it, walking along the roads with you, right from the start, where another fellow would be afraid of getting his name up with you.' The tears came into her eyes when I said that.

" 'Oh those evenings,' she cried, and she lifted her head – you know how lovely she can look even now – and it was like as if the same sweetness was in the air for her still. 'Oh those evenings,' she cried. 'We were only getting to know each other then; talking about the books we'd both read and the places we'd like to see if we could travel and that kind of thing.'

" 'Just the same!' I said, 'it was manly of him, to be so open about you; and later in the summer, when you *really* were caught up with each other, it impressed everyone the way you still walked out together in the daylight, and sat down on a bank by the side of the road where everyone could see you together, although you weren't engaged really, were you? I mean, you hadn't a ring from him, had you? There was something very innocent about you both.'

" 'Too innocent maybe,' Leila said quietly, and then she started to talk in earnest. 'Mina passed that same remark, once,' she said, quickly. 'Only Mina had an ugly way of saying things, and yet, do you know, I often wondered afterwards if she was trying to warn me: warn me against herself I mean. It was one day she met us on the road.

" 'You two don't deserve to live in a town like this,' she said, 'with all the little lovers' lanes and shady paths there are! I know where *I*'d go if I was spooning.' I remember she looked queerly at us: at me in particular. I think it was that day she first got interested in Arthur. After that we met her once or twice in about the same place, and she was always alone, and that wasn't like Mina. She'd stop when she came to where we'd be sitting, and she'd sit down on the bank on the other side of Arthur, and sometimes she stayed with us till it was nearly time to go home. 'I mustn't spoil sport,' she'd say then. I always thought that was a vulgar expression – that it was downright common – but there was more than commonness in it when Mina said it that day. I think she was sneering at me. But maybe I'm wronging her. Another day she said it was well for us to be so innocent. 'Have you nothing to hide at all?' she said. But we hadn't. And even now, even the way things turned out, I'm still glad we were like that, and that Arthur felt like that about me – wanting it to be all out in the open. Yes! I'm glad, or I would be only for one thing. Only one thing! I used to think that if we were the kind that wanted to go down lonely lanes or climb through the hedges into the quiet of the fields Mina wouldn't have come on us, and she wouldn't have been able to hang around the way she did! I suppose if I'd got time I'd have shaken her off, but I got no time. It all happened so quickly. Mina only joined us a few times really, and even when she did, although it was two or three times running, it was all still less than a week – first a Thursday and then a Friday, and then the Saturday. It was the Saturday I felt really hurt, because we were out for the whole afternoon. I thought she'd see that that was different from our little walks in the evenings, when we went out as much for the air as for anything else. And as a matter of fact we weren't sitting on the side of the road that day either. Do you know the first field outside the ramparts, with the little stream running through it? There are stones from the rampart fallen into the water, and when it's sunny the water sparkles and sings going over the stones. It still does. But it was heavenly that afternoon. The wall was down in a couple of places, and we'd climbed over and sat down by the stream. I may have had it in the back of my mind that Mina wouldn't see us if she passed. Not that we weren't plain to be seen from the road, but I thought she mightn't think of looking across the wall. But we weren't settled rightly when I heard her voice.

" 'Can I come in?' she cried, as if it was into a parlour she was coming. And the next minute she flounced across the field and flopped down beside us.

" 'I hope the ground isn't damp,' she said. 'My mother told me never to sit on grass without something under me. Give me that book, and I'll put it under me.'

" 'Oh no, you won't,' Arthur said, snatching it away. He had a great respect for books. 'Anyway, the grass is dry, Look at us sitting on it.'

Then he looked at her and laughed. 'I must say I didn't think, though, that you were the kind of girl that would heed her mother's warnings.'

" 'Oh, not all of them!' said Mina, and she laughed and Arthur laughed again. 'Anyway,' she said, 'my mother died when I was ten, so she didn't have time to warn me about everything.'

"Arthur laughed again. I never heard him laughing just like he did that day. But I was glad. Although it was his seriousness that I liked, I loved to see him laughing too – of course when he felt like it, which wasn't often I must say. Even then, sitting there with Mina and me, he soon got serious again.

" 'My mother died too when I was ten,' he said.

" 'Then you're in the same boat as me!' said Mina, but I don't think he heard her.

" 'I only remember one thing about my mother,' he said. 'When she came to say good night to me, I used to hold up my face to be kissed, and then I used to hold out my wrist to her. "Do the mouse! Do the mouse!" I'd say, because sometimes – not always – she used to put her hand up my sleeve and run her fingers over the inner side of my wrist where the veins are – pretending her fingers were little mice-feet.' Suddenly he pulled back the sleeve of his coat, and tugged at his cuff and bared his wrist. 'I never forgot it,' he said. 'I don't know what age I was, but I hardly remember anything else about my mother; even what she looked like.'

"That was all he said about that, and we talked about other things. It was such a warm, soft day. Arthur lay back in the grass, looking up at the sky, and we two sat on either side of him. I think I did most of the talking. Mina was quieter than usual, I remember that well. I remember almost everything about that day like as if it was a painting, and I was outside it, instead of in it. There was a man with an ass and cart came down to the bank of the stream where we were sitting, with a big barrel to fill for the cattle grazing inside the ramparts. Well, I suppose anyone would remember a thing like that, but I remember every detail of it: how, when the barrel was filled, and the man was leading the ass up from the stream, the wheels of the cart rocked, and little silver drops of water were tossed up into the air, and they seemed to hang in the air for a minute, like a spray of tremble-grass, before they fell back into the barrel. Fancy remembering that all those years! And then, just close to Arthur's face once, where he was lying back in the grass, a little black insect – at least it must have been black, but it glinted green and gold in the sun – a little insect you'd hardly see, it was so small, started to climb up a blade of grass, a thin green blade, and then, just when it was near the tip, the blade bent and down it splashed into the meadow again.

" 'Oh dear,' I exclaimed, and the others looked startled. 'It was only an insect,' I said.

" 'I hope he doesn't crawl into my ear,' Arthur said. But he wasn't greatly worried, and he threw back his arms over his head, his hands palms-upwards. Perhaps it was the way they were palms-upwards that put it into Mina's head to do what she did. Perhaps it was me talking about the insect that made Arthur start and sit up. But anyway, all of a sudden he sat up, and began to rub his wrist. 'Something stung me,' he said crossly.

"Mina laughed.

" 'It was only me,' she said, and she leant over him. 'I only did this,' she said, and she dabbled her fingers in the air over his wrist: not even touching him at all this time. 'I was doing the mouse,' she said.

"That was a Saturday. We all walked home soon afterwards, and the following Monday they ran away – Arthur and Mina. And I never mentioned their names again to anyone; till now. I never told anyone about the mouse either, because I don't really see what it had to do with their running away, do you? And yet it must have had something to do with it.' "

My mother had stopped talking suddenly. She looked at me.

"Did you ever hear such a rigmarole?" she said. "Could her mind be affected: that's what I want to know! Or can *you* make anything out of a story like that?"

I thought I could. But I said nothing.

Loving Memory

"The child of a ghost – who'd marry me?" Alice said bitterly. She was fifteen then, but even before that she knew she'd never marry. Years before her mother died she knew it. Alicia's children were branded even then – the love-birds' children!

"Now for the love-birds' tray," old Ellen used to say, after she'd given the children their meal. She'd heave a sigh and get to her feet again.

There was a fiction kept up in the house that it was only their mother who had her meals brought upstairs, but their father was always nipping into the china cupboard and taking down a cup and saucer. "Put mine on the tray too, Ellen. I have a few things I want to discuss with my wife."

"You'd think they'd get enough of each other sometime or other, wouldn't you?" Ellen would grumble, as she steadied the tray on her knee at the foot of the big dark stairway. "Love-birds; a pair of love-birds."

"Does that mean we are love-children?" Alice asked earnestly one day. She was the oldest. She was nine then.

Ellen gave a laugh. "If they heard that!" she cried. "Where did you learn the like? Do you know what it means?" She laughed again, and then she looked soberly at them. "You're no such thing," she said. "No such thing." The children looked at each other. Were they something still more odd? Ellen looked at them more kindly. "Ah, don't worry your heads, children. Love is the same as anything else in the world: it's all right in its own place – *and* in moderation."

The children looked at each other. *That* they knew. Overhead they could hear their mother's feet tapping back and forth across her room. If only she didn't hog it all – the love, they meant. "There are some houses," Ellen went on, "and the love is thrown about like a thing of no value. But never mind," she added consolingly, "houses like that are very untidy – *very* untidy." The children nodded. They knew. Their house wasn't littered with love. "And noisy," Ellen said. That, too, they knew. Love didn't thunder like a cataract down their staircase. It was all kept stored in their mother's room, and only their father had the key. "And to think," said Ellen, "that when he was a young fellow, no one thought he'd ever marry, much less take to it like another man would take to drink."

It was a fact that when he was a young fellow Matthias Grimes was so shy of love he was a reproach to the town. It was a great town for love – in its way. And the Grimes' parlour was what you might call the Temple of Love. Matthias had two sisters, and they were a great draw. Their father was dead and their old mother was bed-ridden for so long the girls had their own way in everything and no interference. They were both good-looking girls, and Nell had a lovely touch on the piano. Minnie had a voice, or at least an ear. From the street you'd think it was a dance-hall to hear the laughing and the singing and the thumping on the keyboard:

> I love you and *you* love me,
> I'm for you, and *you*'re for me.

The two Grimes sisters were older than Matthias – even Minnie, the younger one, was a good eight or nine years older than him – but they looked like two schoolgirls, the way they wore their hair looped over one shoulder. All the same, they were a long time about getting married. But that was the great thing about the parlour. There was no knowing what a word could do, or where it might lead. And no one had to plough a single furrow. Courtship was a sort of co-operative effort.

"Oh, I'm sorry, Eddy," a girl might say, over-emphatically, if her loop of hair brushed into a fellow's face as she bent to turn a sheet of music. But it would be one of the other girls who would reply.

"No need to be so sorry, Nell! I'm sure he loved it." Then she might turn to Eddy. "Isn't that so, Eddy?"

And what would Eddy say? It hardly mattered. One word was enough to send innuendoes echoing through the room.

"Do it again, Nell, till we see how he likes it!"

Lightly, loosely, couples were linked together till a fine mesh of compromise was woven around them.

"Your hair is nice tonight, Minnie – what did you do to it?"

"My hair! It's a show! It's always awful when I wash it – it's far too thick!" The girls would all protest – it being a convention among the girls that their hair was too long, too thick, or too silky, just as their skin was always too fine, or too delicate; a convention that was never accepted by the men.

"Oh, come now, you're looking for compliments."

"From whom, I'd like to know? Not you!"

"And why not? Do you think I'm not good at paying compliments?"

"It's not a question of being good at it. It's a question of – "

" – of what?"

" – of the consequences!"

"Oh, so that's it – you think I'm afraid of the consequences. Well, suppose you were mistaken about that?"

"But I'm not!"

"I wouldn't be so sure if I were you!"

Meaningless, idle, leading nowhere, the banter went on inconsequentially until, almost by a slip of the tongue, a remark more pointed than the usual would be acclaimed as a kind of public proposal. Then, but not till then, could a couple claim the prize of the parlour: the right to sit on the sofa behind the door.

This sofa was really only an outsize armchair, but big enough for two people. Its particularity lay in the fact that whenever the parlour door was opened or shut – even for a minute – the sofa went into total eclipse. Only a hug at most, or a squeeze, would be covered by this eclipse, but it was enough to stop the piano and turn the singing into whistling and cat-calling. In a way that nook behind the door was a symbol of love as understood by the town. The nearer a couple got to marriage the more they were given cover, till finally marriage itself came down like a snuffer over their flame.

It was on this point – as to where love got private – that Matthias fell foul of the town. He had always been awkward as a boy. He had been sent away to school more to get him out of the way than anything else, until he was old enough to take over the business, which was kept going by the sisters. When he came back from Newbridge, however, he seemed more awkward than ever. He couldn't be got into the parlour for all the tea in China. And one evening, when his sisters and their friends tried, for a dare, to drag him in there, it's certain he'd have made away naked if they hadn't let go before his clothes parted from him.

Matthias used to spend the afternoons and evenings mooning about the ramparts that ran brokenly round the town. These ramparts dated from King John's visit to Ireland, but for years they had been put to practical use as boundary walls of the business premises and the old family residences that made up the town proper. These old premises all had big wild gardens at the back, and of them all the Grimes' garden was wildest and most overgrown. It was used only for tossing out crates and cardboard cartons from the packing house, and actually these did not look as bad as might be thought, they were so quickly grown through and grown over by nettles and convolvulus. Sticking up among the spiked nettles away at the far end of the garden was a butt of a tower that had once been a watch-tower on the rampart. Here Matthias used to sit for hours. A flight of broken steps led up to the tower from the inside, and there was a drop of fifty feet on the outer side, so that it was like a belvedere or gazebo for viewing the countryside.

It wasn't much of a view. Nothing but flat fields of thin grass stretched away to all sides, marred at many points by ugly concrete bungalows. These bungalows were held in great contempt by the Grimes girls. Because of the size of the Grimes' premises, which had originally comprised three separate buildings, it was not unreasonable for Nell and Minnie to expect that the partitions that had been knocked down by their grandfather could be put up again by Matthias to provide accommodation for them if need arose. This would widen the field of eligibles for them, and take in bank clerks, government officials, and school inspectors, who earned decent enough salaries but had no houses, and were forced to reside in the Central Hotel. After all, a small part of the house would do for Matthias. The part occupied by the old lady would do nicely for him when she passed away.

For it was somehow assumed that Matthias would remain a bachelor, although at this time he was still in his early twenties. Apparently, however, it was only of love's preliminaries that Matthias was shy, for in the spring of his twenty-fourth year, and no more than one month after the old lady finally died, Matthias not only met someone to his liking, but within two weeks had asked her to marry him. Furthermore, he had named a day for the wedding on a date which gave him exactly six weeks to make and carry out his plans and bring his bride home. It had all come about so unexpectedly. Matthias had had a touch of bronchitis after his mother's funeral and had been persuaded to go to the Spa Hotel in Lisdoonvarna. He stayed away only four days because there was a commercial traveller he wanted to see on the fourth day and he had to get home, but the following Sunday he hired a car and drove over there. The Sunday after that he hired the car again. Then, just as his astonished sisters were beginning to smell a rat, he broke the news and told them his plans: his plans for them. He had bought them one of the new bungalows outside the town, and he expected them to install themselves in it before the wedding.

That night there was such consternation in the parlour there wasn't a single note struck on the piano.

"But what is she like? Do you mean to say you never saw her?" Eddy Troddyn cried. "And her name? You've told us nothing!"

Nell and Minnie hardly knew her name.

"He speaks of her as Alicia," said Nell doubtfully. "It's a form of Alice, I think."

"Then why isn't she called Alice, I wonder?"

The sisters didn't know.

"I always think Alice sounds a bit youngish," Minnie said.

"But isn't she young?" they all cried.

"Oh, I suppose she must be," said Minnie, but somehow vague doubts about the bride had formed in everybody's mind.

"Oh, well, we'll soon see her, I suppose," said Eddy Troddyn. "When is he bringing her over here? You'll have to meet her before the wedding."

A day or two later, however, Matthias announced that he was not bringing Alicia home until after the wedding, which – for sentiment sake – was being held in Lisdoonvarna, Alicia having no real home or family connections.

"After they're *married*? What good will that be?" cried the crowd. "All the fun will be over then!"

Not a cuddle, not a squeeze would anyone have seen. Cold fish that he was, no better might have been expected from Matthias. But what of the girl? Had she no spark at all in her? Could she be older than him? Could it have been a made-match? No one ever denied he was eligible.

"I bet she's years older than him!"

The girls were more disparaging than the men. The men were inclined to look on Matthias with a new respectful curiosity.

"She may be a good business woman. And she may have a bit of money too!"

Alicia had no money, though. Nell and Minnie could have told them that. Six weeks from the day she met Matthias, Alicia was to have gone out to America to an aunt of hers, who had sent her the passage money. Matthias made her send back the money, and the day named for the wedding was the day she was to have sailed, because she had given notice for the day before that in the millinery where she worked, and lived in. This was a clear indication that she had no money. On the other hand, some thought it gave an indication of Alicia's age.

"She can't be so old at all," someone cried. "They only want young girls in America."

"Wait a minute: I've an idea!" Eddy Troddyn cried. "Where are they going for the honeymoon? If she's old it will be Dublin. If she has a jog in her at all it will be Tramore or Kilkee!"

The really incomprehensible news, however, had not been divulged. "I didn't tell you," said Nell, flushing. "He says they're not having any honeymoon. They're coming home after the wedding."

"Nell! Are you raving?" There was pandemonium in the parlour. "You're joking!"

Nell and Minnie were not joking. It was no joke at all to get rid of the rubbish of years in six weeks, and pack into a box of a bunaglow. A honeymoon would at least have given them a bit more time. Oh, that bungalow! Their only hope was that they might not be long in it, but the coming of the bride to the house in the market-square gave to the whole removal a touch of dowagerdom.

"If you ask me," said Nell, "she can't wait to get her hand into the till!"

Grasping? That could be another explanation. Elderly? Ailing? Money-grubbing? There was no end to the speculations about Alicia. Starting straight into marriage without a honeymoon was like starting into Lent without Shrove Tuesday. And for Minnie and Nell and their friends it would be goodbye to the fun in the parlour!

"We'll miss those nights at the piano," said Eddy.

"You'll be more than welcome in the bungalow," Minnie and Nell cried in duet.

"If only it wasn't so far out from the town," Eddy wailed. "And is it true you won't have the piano? We heard it wouldn't fit into the bungalow. Is that so?"

It was so. A sadness fell on the room. It was hard to think that all the swaying and singing around the old piano was already nearly a thing of the past. And each evening the sadness deepened till the last evening of all arrived. That last evening a real effort was made to be light-hearted, but it was only when everyone was out in the street going home, and the door was safely shut on the Grimes' household that the one really good laugh of the evening was raised. "I forgot to tell you all – I know the bride's secret," said Eddy. Putting out his arms he drew them all into a ring. "She has a wooden leg," he whispered. They had to race away up the street so as not to let the laughing be heard by those inside. Yet it was just as well they had a bit of fun that night because there was a kind of embarrassment over all the town the next night. The Grimes sisters came home from the wedding on the afternoon train but they went straight out to the bungalow. The bridal pair were not coming till the late train. Unfortunately, apart from the evenings in the Grimes' parlour the only regular pastime in the town was going down to the station to see the late train pass through from Dublin and maybe get an evening paper from the stoker or the guard. But it didn't seem nice, somehow, to go down that evening, so there wasn't a soul on the platform when Matthias and Alicia stepped off the train.

It was a fine night, but the moon had not risen, and the streets were dark. They encountered no one as they walked up from the station to the market-square. And the house, when they came in sight of it, was dark, because Matthias had given orders that no lamps were to be lit in the parlour.

"I hate that parlour, Ellen," he said vehemently. "I'm going to speak to a contractor and see about having it let in with the shop."

"Very good, sir," Ellen said, but it flustered her, and she wondered if she was to prepare the big parlour upstairs that had never been used in her time except for rooting geranium slips.

"Oh, no need; no need," said Matthias. "A fire in the bedroom will be enough: we'll be tired out."

The flicker of this fire on the ceiling was, therefore, all the light that could be seen from the old house as Matthias unlinked his arm from Alicia to let them in with his own key. Ellen hadn't heard them coming. She didn't even know they had arrived and gone upstairs until her niece told her. The niece had seen the light in the big oblong window as she was coming down the street to see if Ellen needed a hand. As she got nearer to the house indeed the window got brighter and brighter, as if one after another every lamp in the house had been carried into the room. There was never such illumination in the market-square, and although the blind was drawn, there was a golden oblong larger than life traced out on the pavement below.

"How did they get in without my hearing?" cried Ellen, rushing towards the stairs. But Matthias met her on the stairs. He was half-way down.

"Can I have a glass of milk, Ellen?" he asked.

"Is it for yourself?" said Ellen, taken aback.

"No. For her," said Matthias.

"But surely she's going to have something more substantial than that after the journey?"

"We had a meal on the train," said Matthias. "We're not hungry. If you give me the glass of milk I'll take it up to her, Ellen."

"Am I not going to see her at all?" Ellen cried.

"Tomorrow," said Matthias gently, and he smiled to himself as he took the milk from her and went up the stairs.

Ellen went back to the kitchen where her niece was still waiting to see if she'd be needed.

"There must be some truth in what was said about her," Ellen muttered dejectedly. "She must be older than him – a lot older!"

"Oh, I wouldn't say that!" cried the girl. "I saw her shadow on the window-blind when I was coming down the street, and it wasn't an old-looking shadow at all."

It was, in fact, a very young shadow. And it darted like quicksilver over the blind, while, down in the street below, at wing with it, went the shadow of the shadow, looking so agile and living a thing the heart would flinch to step on it.

Before the couple were home ten minutes, everyone in the town had stolen a glance at that oblong window. It stayed lit up for about twenty minutes, and then it went dark. Rebuked, those who were looking up looked down. But not for long. With a pinging sound that was heard all over the square, the ivory knob at the end of the blind-cord spanked against the window-pane and the blind was let slap up again. Then, with a rattle of dry putty, the big window sash was thrown up and a young woman put out her head.

"Such a night!" she cried loudly and youngly. "Come and see, Matthias!" And leaning her elbows out on the sill she waited for him to come and lean out with her. Together they contemplated the night for all the world as if they were on a balcony in some Italian resort.

Now, this was not what the town had been led to expect. They'd been told there would be no honeymoon – not that it was to be spent brazenly before their eyes in their own town. After all, it is not only the couple concerned that a honeymoon safeguards. Friends, relations and acquaintances are entitled to a like protection.

As the night wore on, the oblong window, lit or unlit, magnetized the town. It could only be hoped that daylight would bring the couple to a sense of decorum.

And the next day was a Sunday.

"Well, Ellen?" Nell and Minnie asked, stopping to talk to their old servant when they met her on the way to Mass. (It was a fine day, and it was a nice walk in from the bungalow, but how would it be on a wet day?) Ellen pursed her lips. "Breakfast in bed!" she said cryptically. "I hope that won't be kept up for long."

"For her, of course?"

"For both of them," said Ellen, "sitting up together like a king and a queen!"

A few paces further along the street, old Ellen met Eddy Troddyn and he had more enquiries.

"She's young after all, I hear? How about her looks?"

Ellen could not deny that the bride had looks. "Take care she's not too good-looking, though!" she added. "I found out one thing. It was her doing they didn't go away on any honeymoon. She told me when I went up with the tray – straight out in front of him, too. She said she wanted to spend her first night in their own—" she faltered. "I'll spell it," she conceded, "in their own b-e-d! There!"

It was felt by Ellen – it was felt by all – to be, at the very least, an *unnecessary* remark.

Then, just in time for late Mass, Matthias and Alicia themselves appeared in the street – linked. And linked they went in through the chapel gates. Only to take holy water and genuflect did they unlink.

"It's a wonder she didn't link him all during Mass!" said one.

"It was bad enough the way they kneeled so close up to one another!" said another.

But it was those in the gallery had a really good view of them. "Do you know where she had her hand? In his pocket!"

Clearly there was going to be a scandal. It was scandalous enough to think that he was not going to let her set foot in the shop. Who did he think she was? – the Queen of Sheba? Ah well – it was felt – he'd soon change that tune.

But on Monday morning the contractor started breaking down the wall between the parlour and the shop, and not only was Alicia kept out of the shop but she spent most of her day out of sight upstairs. From the start this gave her a remote air, like a lady in a tower. But if Alicia spent her day up in a tower, Matthias spent the best part of his day on the stairs, going up or coming down. Almost the only time they were both to be seen downstairs was when Alicia came down to go out for an afternoon walk, which, wet or fine, the pair took every day of the year.

Those walks! Linked like lovers, every afternoon they set off out of the town and round the rampart-walls, seemingly aware of none but themselves.

"There's only one thing will put a stop to their gallop," said Ellen. "One of these days she'll learn there are more uses than one for a bed."

But four births, and two miscarriages, took place in the big bridal bed, and from them Alicia emerged more precious to her husband than ever.

Not one of her children was like her. Fragments of her charm, particles of her enchantment had been scattered among them. The eyes of one, the hair of another, might occasionally be compared with hers, but not one of the children could ever hold a candle to her. And Alice, who had been named after her, resembled her least of all.

As the years passed Alicia's fraility made her even more different from her children. And every year Matthias got more insistent that she keep to her room and rest for most of the day.

"Put another cup on the tray, Ellen," he'd say, as he dodged in from the shop, and put his foot to the stairs.

"Nothing at all about me lugging these heavy trays up there!" said Ellen grumpily. "You'd think she'd get tired of looking at the one wallpaper all day long."

Ellen had a name for Alicia's bedroom. She called it the love-nest.

Alicia somehow suggested bird images all the time. She was given to wearing bird feathers, as it happened. She had a hat with a blue quill that quivered when she walked, and she had another with the whole wing of a bird on the brim: not only the stiff fan feathers, but the little bone that bends back, like an elbow, plumed with down.

Above all, she was bird-like in her urge to fly up to her room all the time, as a bird returns unremittingly to its nest.

Poor bird: she never made her nest in the heart of her children, that is certain. Every afternoon her children could be seen upstairs in the big parlour standing at the window when their mother and father were setting out for their famous afternoon walk.

Their parents were never late. At four o'clock exactly the door opened and they stepped into the street. There was a short delay, while Matthias turned to shut the door, and Alicia caught back the small brown muff she wore on a silver chain around her neck, and which, when it dangled out from her, seemed to draw them apart. Then Matthias shoved his outer hand into his outer pocket, and with the other linked Alicia fast. Her free hand she pushed into the muff, and by pressing closer to him she was able to push in also the arm he held. But because the big granite sill of the upstairs window was as broad as a parapet these preliminaries were hidden from the children, and so when the pair below stepped off the kerb there seemed to be a precipitance about them that could only be compared with the precipitance of swallows leaving their nests under the eaves when, with a rush of wings, they quit one element and effortlessly enter another – infinitely more familiar.

Off they went then up the street, and Alicia's muff – that now hung down between them – seemed to fasten them tight to each other like a small padlock. That muff – when seen like that from a distance – had the solidest look. Yet, when they came back, and Alicia took the chain from around her neck and laid the little muff on the table in the hall, it was seen in all its frailty. It was not made of any sturdy fur, but of hundreds of marabou feathers so soft and light that for a long time after she laid it down it trembled and shivered.

"Come and put away Alicia's muff," Matthias would order the children, as they came timidly down the stairs, for the muff was kept down in the hall in a special box, like a pet.

It was always as Alicia that he spoke of her, even to the children. They could not recall a single time that he had called her mother except on the awful day he brought her back early from their walk.

The children weren't expecting them. They were not at the window. They only heard the voices down in the hall, their father's and Ellen's. They ran and looked down the well of the stairs. It was when he looked up and saw them that Matthias dropped the Alicia.

"Your mother isn't well," he cried. "Come down and carry up her things."

For Ellen had taken off their mother's coat. And her shoes! She was only in her blouse. And she had been put sitting on a chair in the hall: not the hard oak chair that was always there but an old wicker chair brought out of the kitchen. Her head was thrown back. From the stair-head a cold north light poured down, and lay whitely on her face and on her hair that glistened with sweat. The children were scared and they started to run down the stairs, but before they got to the foot of the stairs Ellen and Matthias had decided to try and get their mother up to her room, and so the children were right in the way.

"Out of the way – out of the way," Matthias shouted, and, terrified by the tone of his voice, the children stitched themselves to the wall.

"Wait! Let me breathe. Let me rest," Alicia whispered weakly, and at the same time her beautiful eyes came to rest on the children. "Speak gently – to them," she said, with a gasp, and before she attempted another step she closed her eyes with the effort of taking the step upward, and the sweat from her wet hair ran down her face like tears. Suddenly, she opened her eyes again, very wide. "My – muff –" she said, each word separate and distinct, "don't – let – it – get stepped on – in the – fuss."

The fuss was near an end, though, whether she knew it or not, and whether Matthias did; or Ellen.

"How will he live without her?" That was the question everyone asked when word went round the town that Alicia Grimes was dying. And even on the day of the funeral concern was centred not on the children but on Matthias. No one took any notice of them as they stood around the grave, up to their necks in black. How would Matthias take it? He'd start to drink! He'd go out of his mind! He'd follow her to the grave within the year!

"The children won't be any consolation to him," Ellen said openly in front of them. "He'd see them all put down if it would bring her back!"

Yet Matthias actually took it fairly well – in the beginning. After the funeral he let himself be led out of the cemetery willingly enough. But the truth may have been that he had in his head, even then, the idea that was to sustain him. That night he went down to the kitchen where the children were all gathered together around Ellen not knowing what to do. He had an armful of catalogues and leaflets in his hands. "You're not too young," he said stiffly and formally, "to help me choose a memorial for your mother. Come here, please."

They gathered eagerly around him. It was a relief to have something to do. To the smaller ones it was as good as a game, going through the pictures of tombs and headstones.

"Oh, look at this one, Father!"

"Too big – it's vulgar-looking!" said Matthias.

"There's a nice one, Father – with doves!"

"Too small – it's insignificant. And not enough room for the inscription."

By bedtime they hadn't settled on anything.

"Not that there's any great hurry," said Matthias, as he put away the catalogues. "Better be sure than sorry."

The next night they went over the catalogues again, but once again their father found nothing to his satisfaction. The night after that they had several new catalogues that he had had sent by post. Scrolls, crosses, urns, tablets: every kind of shape was considered. "Nothing worthy of her!" he cried in despair. "Nothing to do justice to her. I want something striking, that will catch the eye the moment people enter the cemetery. In that way we'll make sure she isn't forgotten. Even people who did not know her will ask who she was and want to hear about her."

The prospect of erecting a really striking memorial gave him such pleasure; it didn't seem to matter that he couldn't find a suitable one.

"Would you think of a Pieta, Father?"

"Too impersonal!"

"A weeping angel?"

"Only for infants."

"Oh, I know, Father," Alice cried one day. "How about a stone casket?"

Her father seemed to like the idea, and his face lit up for a minute, but then he shook his head. The children couldn't help feeling sorry for him when he gave his reason for turning down that idea – even Alice felt sorry for him.

"It would be very heavy over her," he said.

In fact, Matthias was beginning to despair of finding anything suitable in the catalogues.

"I think I'll walk down to the cemetery," he said to Alice. "I might get an idea walking around and looking at the graves."

It seemed a good idea. He was pale from sticking in the house. He missed his afternoon walks.

Alice ran to get his hat and coat.

"It'll be a nice walk for you, Father."

He looked better when he came back. She was glad to see he had more colour in his face, and more life in him.

"It was a good thing I went down there," he said. "There's something we hadn't thought of at all – it's really amazing the way different materials withstand the weather. I didn't know marble was so easily stained! After a few years it gets yellow and streaky. I think we may rule out marble!" he said decisively. "That leaves only limestone and granite. Now granite I know is excellent on a fine day; the mica sparkles in the sunlight. But I wonder how it stands up to rain?" He glanced at the barometer. "If it's wet tomorrow I'll go down there again and take a walk around. I'd like to see what effect the rain has on it."

"But people don't visit the cemetery on a wet day, Father," Alice said.

"What about a day there is a funeral?" Matthias said sharply. "Funerals are not postponed for a shower. And when people are there they look around them and cannot avoid seeing what's to be seen. Let's hope there will be a shower tomorrow."

It was downright wet next day. Matthias went off early with his umbrella.

Granite was ruled out when he came back.

"I have some more information that will surprise you," he said animatedly as Alice helped him off with his coat which was soaking wet. "Limestone too can look very depressing in the rain. It gets a very dark, saturated appearance. I must admit that marble comes off best in the wet. Rain gives it a great gloss. Yes; there's more to be said for marble than I thought at first. And one mustn't forget that it can be re-polished if it gets stained! We must admit that in its favour," he said warmly.

He was greatly exhilarated. That seemed to have settled the matter for the moment; but the next day, having left for the cemetery early in the afternoon, he returned hastily after a few minutes.

"Have you got a tape-measure, Alice?" he asked. "I've just realized there must be a proper proportion between the stone and the plot. This is a science in itself," he said importantly, as he set off once more. He came back in high spirits. "I'm glad I thought of that nicety," he said, giving Alice back the tape-measure. "I'd like to think her grave would never be completely cast into shade by the stone!"

It was a nicety indeed. Alice could hardly appreciate it. Yet finer niceties still were to be considered.

"I wonder if shadows cast by the moon are the same length as those cast in sunlight?" he asked her suddenly one evening.

"Oh, Father! The cemetery is locked at sundown."

"Not locked," he said gently. "The gates are only closed over."

Alice knew then that he'd been down there some of the evenings when she'd thought he'd gone around the ramparts. She began to worry vaguely about him. It wasn't as if Alicia was only a few days dead. The weeks were passing, and the months. If in the start he had gone more often than was wise it might have been supposed that by now he would have been going less often. The opposite, however, was the case. This was a passion that was taking possession of him. Like his love, his grief too seemed to grow without diminish.

"Stay at home for once, Father," Alice pleaded one evening. "Don't go down there tonight, please."

"On such a night?" he cried, amazed at her request. "It's a beautiful night for a walk, and later there will be a moon."

"Then, I'll come with you," Alice said firmly.

"Not *with* me – I can't be delayed – you can follow me down if you like," he murmured, slyly. He was out the door before she could get her coat.

It was a few minutes before Alice was ready to follow him. He was right about the night. It was good to be out on such a night. It had been what Ellen called a "pet" evening: that is to say, although it was not summer, but late spring, yet an unexpected sweetness had come in the air for so early in the year. It was already dusk, but a number of small stars could be seen if you peered into the heavens. They were not the hard white stars that sharpen a sky, but a vague scattering of little lights, soft and warm looking, as if they belonged to a human world.

Because it was such a pet evening, a gang of children were still playing in the streets, and although now and then a woman came to an open doorway as if of a mind to call them inside, she would hesitate, and only look out bemused, unwilling to grudge them the last vestiges of the magic moments.

Down near the cemetery there were more children. It seemed late for them to be out, because the road near there was dark with trees. As Alice went nearer she could hear their high-pitched voices, and when she got close she saw they had climbed upon the cemetery railings and were sticking their heads between the bars. They were chanting some silly song.

When they heard her coming they stopped. And she fancied that when they saw who it was they jumped down sheepishly from the railings and fell silent. The silence was as silly as their silly singing.

"Is my father inside?" she asked them sharply.

The question acted like magic to free their tongues.

"He's over there, miss. Beside the grave," they cried.

They were all willingness, all helpfulness, all eagerness. One of them rushed to open the gate for her.

"Would you like us to go in with you, miss?"

She remembered that unaccompanied children were never allowed into the cemetery. They wanted a chance to get in there.

"No," she said. "I've only come to fetch home my father," she said.

They nodded their heads sagaciously. When she went to pass through the gateway, though, they still blocked her way. And when they asked her another question she couldn't tell at the time if it was asked slyly or innocently.

"Who does he be talking to in there, miss?" they asked.

Alice hesitated.

"Himself, I suppose," she said, trying to be frank with them, but she saw they received her explanation dubiously. "You should be at home at this hour! Your mothers will be looking for you."

There was indeed someone calling at that moment, further down the road.

"Child – ren!" said the voice. "Child – ren!"

It carried well, that voice. In the air, it seemed to change into an unrelated sound, inconsequent like the cuckoo's call.

Alice listened for a minute and then went into the cemetery, which was curiously bright in the moonlight because no trees were allowed to be planted in there as roots were troublesome when a grave was being dug. And even without the light of the moon there was a

whiteness everywhere – the whiteness of the marble slabs and gravestones.

"Father, you must come home," Alice called to her father, who
stood beside Alicia's grave. "You're carrying this thing too far. You
can't make her live for ever, no matter what you do. And after all, she
was only an ordinary woman. She wasn't an Egyptian queen!"

Alice's voice, in spite of herself, was harsh and bitter. Yet, when her
father answered, his voice was gentle and conciliatory.

"For ever is a long time indeed," he said sedately. "But I'd like her
to be remembered as long as possible! Don't wait for me! I'm watching
for the moon to shine out full. I have a few more measurements to
take."

Alice stood irresolute.

And then the moon shone out more bright than ever, so bright
that the trees on the other side of the road threw a great mass of
shadow over half the graveyard. But at the edge the shadow was
serrated. Each young leaf cut out its own sharp shape. And she could
count every pebble of the gravel. Here and there a pebble, larger than
the others, cast a pebble of shadow, and the path was dappled.

Then the woman's voice called out again as she stood there, the
woman away in the dark, and Alice in the light.

"Child – ren – child – ren!"

As Alice listened the voice fell to earth. Then, after a minute, it
came again, but nearer, and now it was a purely human voice.

"Children? Where are you?" Was there a giggle in the dark high
grass inside the gate? "I hear you. I know you're there," the woman
cried. "Come along home at once. You'll answer for this! Don't
make me come and get you. Do you think I don't see you?" The
last feint was so feeble, even to the woman herself, that in another
minute she raised her voice again in a high, timeless note. "Child – ren!
Child – ren!" The giggling this time was ill-concealed; and somewhere
near a fat bottom flopped down into the moist grasses. "Oh, you
devils," cried the woman. "Stay out all night if you like! But you
know what will happen."

Alice thought she too knew. She waited for the age-old threat by
which Ellen, as evening came down, had got her and her sisters
and brothers in from the dark corners of the garden. When all the
other threats had failed, Ellen used to warn them that Mad Mary would
get them. Who was Mad Mary? Was she a real person? Or was there

a Mad Mary in every town, a puppet in the prop-box of bogeys and bugbears with which exasperated parents scarified their offspring when they themselves were at the end of their own nervous energy? She smiled.

And so she was actually smiling when the threat was finally flung out.

"Stay out, so – " the woman said, "and see what'll happen! Have you forgotten Alicia Grimes? Oh-ho, you haven't! Alicia Grimes will get you! Alicia Grimes will get you!"

K

The Yellow Beret

"Two murders in the one night? In Dublin? Nonsense! Maybe it's the same one they're talking about?" Mag looked at her husband in mild disbelief.

"How could it be the same?" Don said. "Wasn't the other one down at the docks? Do you never read the papers?"

"But two murders in the one night!" Mag knew that the note of doubt in her voice would annoy him, but she couldn't help it, so, to please him, she peered across the breakfast table at the newspaper in his hand. But without her glasses the sun made one blur of everything on the table – plates, napery, and newsprint – and waywardly her mind went back to her own concerns. She'd soon have to call Donny. She glanced up at the mantelpiece to see if the entrance card for his examination was still propped in front of the clock, so he couldn't possibly forget it when he was going out. Then she looked around the room to make sure there was nothing else he was likely to forget – his fountain-pen, or the key of his locker in the College.

But all the time she was vaguely aware that Don was critical of her lack of attention. She'd have to make some comment.

"I hope we're not going to have a wave of crime!" she said.

Exactly the wrong thing to say. She had only revealed the full extent of her heedlessness.

"Wave of crime!" he scoffed. "I told you there was no connection between the two crimes. You're as bad as the newspapers." He sounded irritated. But as he read on down the long columns devoted to the two crimes he became more amiable. "It's a disturbing business," he conceded. "It will have a very upsetting effect on the public, I'm afraid!"

Well, here was something Mag could discuss with a genuine interest and liveliness.

"I don't see why! Why anyone should be upset – ordinary people like us, I mean. There's always a reason for these murders! Don't tell me they come out of a clear sky! I see no reason why anyone should be concerned at all about them – beyond feeling sorry for those involved, of course! Take that girl at the docks. I'm sure what happened to her was only the end of a long story!"

"Not necessarily," Don said curtly. "As a matter of fact they're looking for a Dutch sailor who only went ashore a few hours before the murder – "

"But he knew her from another time, I suppose? And – "

"Not necessarily," said Don again.

Mag reddened. She hadn't understood that it might all have happened in that doorway: not only the murder, but . . . well . . . it all.

"Oh!" she said, repulsed. Then her voice quickened. "Oh, Don. Let's not talk about it. Let's not even think about it. You know how I feel about that kind of thing."

It was not so much a feeling as an attitude. She had made it a point to draw a circle, as it were, around their home, and keep out all talk of violence and crime. She had always tried to let their son feel he lived in a totally different world from the world where such things happened. Don't talk about it. Don't think about it. That was her counsel to him – and to herself as well.

It wasn't as easy to practise as to preach, though. Last evening, although she had only caught a word or two about that girl who was strangled on the docks, yet she could not get the thing out of her mind all night. Although she had never been out to the Pigeon House where it happened, and had only seen the long sea wall from the deck of the B. & I. Boat – seen it sliding past as the ship pulled out past the Alexandra Basin into the bay – yet she kept picturing the place as if it were a place she knew well.

Through the cranes and ships' rigging one could see the wide wharf narrowing into a place with no human habitation; nothing but coal-yards, and warehouses, and the Power Station of Pigeon House itself, its windows lit by day as well as night with a cold inimical light. Then the wharf narrowed again until it seemed only a promenade for birds, with bollards here and there splattered with glaring white droppings; and where in places steps led down into the water they seemed senseless, more than half of them under water, wobbly-looking and pale, and when a wash of water went over the top steps it lay on them thin as ice.

It was here she pictured it happening. Not at the edge near the steps, but back from them, where, in an abortive bit of wall, an iron gate stood giving entrance or egress to nowhere. She could distinctly picture that gate, reinforced top and bottom with rusty corrugated iron – cut in jags along the top as if with giant pinking-shears.

How could a gate-way she had never seen be so vivid in her mind? Even now, in the sunny breakfast-room, with Don across the table from her, she felt the picture forming again in her mind. But this time there was a man in the picture. A Dutch sailor. It was him: the murderer! Who else could it be? Bending downward, in the gateway, with his back to her, she saw him, as clearly as she saw the gate in which he stood. His clothes – a faded blue shirt – his hair – a carroty red – were as plain as if he were standing in front of her in the flesh. She could not see his face, but he could not stand there for ever. In a minute he would have to straighten up and turn and get back to the densely-peopled streets and lose himself in the crowds, and she would be forced to look at him face to face. And when she saw his face – ah, this was the terror – it would, she felt certain, be a face well known to her.

What was the meaning of this vision? There had never been anything psychic about her.

Desperately she closed her eyes to blot it all out – the wharf, the gateway, the figure – but against her closed lids they formed again, more clearly. And then – as she knew he must – the man turned, or half-turned rather, because only his eyes turned towards her; his face and head remained partly averted. His head, indeed, seemed fixed in an implacable pose as if he had no power to move it, and yet in another sense it was all movement, a strange and terrible inner motion. Every cell of skin and hair and membrane seemed to vibrate. His coarse orange hair quivered, and his fibrous beard, while the enormous white whorl of the one ear visible to her seemed as if it was still evolving from its first convolution. And not only the face but the very air around him seemed to whirl and spin until it, too, was all spirals and oscillations. She went rigid with tension.

Then the white whorl of that ear brought her back to her senses. Van Gogh! The self-portrait! Relief left her so limp she slumped down in her chair. What a fool she was! She glanced at Don, glad he was not always able to read her mind. Yet – wait! Why did Van Gogh come into her mind? Could there be any reason? And what did the real murderer look like?

To think that he might at that moment be walking the streets of Dublin! Oh heavens! she could see him again. This time he was standing on Butt Bridge, leaning over the parapet and staring down the river. Terror swept over her.

"Did you say the other murder was in Dublin, too, Don?" she asked sharply.

"Still trying to link the two? I tell you, there was no connection between them, Mag. The other poor creature – " he nodded down at the paper – "the other poor creature was the soul of respectability – "

"The other victim was a woman too? You didn't tell me!"

"An elderly spinster," said Don, as if not altogether corroborating her statement. "A school-teacher, I think it said." He bent and looked for verity to the paper. "Yes, a school-teacher living in Sandford Road. Respectable enough address! Over fifty, too!"

But Mag rushed over and grabbed the paper out of his hand.

"Over fifty? Oh, no, Don! No! Why didn't you tell me? That's terribly sad. I didn't realize. I thought it was another of those ugly businesses. Why didn't you tell me it was so sad? The poor creature!"

Don stared at her.

"What's sadder about her than the girl on the docks?" he asked.

But Mag had got her glasses and was gathering up the pages of the paper. "Where is the front page? Was there a picture of the poor thing?"

"I don't think so," said Don. "There was a picture of that girl, though! She was only seventeen. A lovely looking girl. Now that was what you might call sad! Oh, I know the sort she was, and all that, but she was so young. She had her whole life ahead of her. There's no knowing but she might somehow have been influenced for good before it was too late. And anyhow," he said limply, "the other poor thing – " he shrugged his shoulders, not bothering to finish the sentence. "She can't have had much of a life. Can't have had much to look forward to in the future! Lived alone. Kept herself to herself. An odd sort apparently. Say what you like – it wasn't the same as being seventeen!"

"Oh, stop it, Don. I can't bear it. You don't understand. To come to such an end after a lifetime of service." Mag was poring over the paper. "Yes! she was a teacher. To make it worse she was a kindergarten teacher – oh, the poor thing. I can't bear to think of it. The head was battered in – with a stone, they think – and bruises on the neck and back."

"Not a sex crime, anyway," Don said, facetiously Mag thought.

"Oh, Don, how can you? There's no question of anything like that! She was over fifty! Fifty-four. And several people have already come forward, voluntarily, to testify to her character. She led the most normal, the most regular life and – "

"Nothing very normal or regular about wandering the streets in the small hours!"

"Oh, you didn't read it properly." Mag consulted the paper again. "She was found in the small hours, but it was done before midnight. They haven't given the pathologist's report yet, but the police put the time between eleven and twelve. She wasn't found earlier because the body was dragged into someone's front garden."

"Nice for those people!" Don said.

"Oh, Don, how can you joke about it? Do you realize that if she had been left in the street there might have been a spark of life in her when she was found? As things were it seems she wouldn't have been found at all until daylight only a couple coming home from a dance happened to step inside the garden hedge."

"Nice for them too!" Don said irrepressibly. "Sorry, Mag, sorry! I feel as bad as you do about it, but you never take any interest in murders, and to hear you carrying on about these women – "

She pulled him up short.

"Don't speak of them in the same breath!" she said coldly.

But he was looking down at the paper again.

"Oh, look, there's more about it in the late-news column. They're looking for any information that may lead to the recovery of a yellow beret believed to have been worn by the victim earlier in the evening."

Mag pressed her lips together.

"The unfortunate girl! She little thought when she was putting on that beret – "

"It wasn't the girl! It was the other woman."

"The elderly woman? Are you sure? A yellow beret? It sounds more like what a young girl would wear, surely?"

"The old girl must have fancied herself a bit, it seems."

"Oh, Don, I asked you not to take that tone again, please. Please! I'm certain it was simply a case of some thug attacking her in the hope that she might have money on her. He probably didn't intend anything more than to stun her, but maybe she screamed, the poor thing, and he got frightened and hit her again to keep her quiet. Maybe he didn't realize he'd killed her at all."

"Then why did he drag her into that garden?"

"Oh, I forgot about that."

But Don had had enough of it. He glanced at the clock. "You forgot something else! How about calling Donny?" he said, and he went out, got his hat and coat in the hall, and where he stood put them on.

"Oh, he has plenty of time yet," Mag said, and she followed him out into the hall. But she looked up the stairs. "All the same, I'll go up and call him before I do anything else." At the bottom of the stairs, however, she turned. "Don't go till I come down," she said, quite without reason. Or was it, she thought afterwards, that even then, at the foot of the stairs, a vague uneasiness had already taken possession of her? Had she, all morning, been unconsciously aware of a sort of absolute silence upstairs, different altogether from the merely relative silence when the boy was up there, but asleep? Certainly half-way up the stairs when she looked through the banister rail she was outrageously relieved to see that her son's bed had been slept in, although he was not in it.

"Oh, you're up?" she cried, talking to him, although she wasn't sure whether he was in his room or not. He could be behind the door, perhaps, taking down his clothes from the clothes hook? Or in the bathroom? "Where are you?" she called, when she saw he wasn't in his room. She went to the door of the bathroom. "Are you in there, Donny?" she asked from outside the bathroom door. "Where are you?" she called out then sharply, still addressing herself to him. But when she leaned over the banisters to see if he could have gone downstairs – to the kitchen perhaps – without their noticing him – it was to Don she called. "Is he down there, Don?"

"Why would he be down here?" Don had come to the foot of the stairs. She thought there was an uneasy note in his voice. Then he too started up the stairs.

"Why are you coming up?" she cried.

She must have begun to cry at that point, because Don shouted at her.

"Stop that noise, for God's sake, Mag! The boy probably stayed out last night. But what of it? I wish I had a pound note for every time I stayed out all night when I was his age. I'd be a rich man now if I had! He has you spoiled; that's all! There's some perfectly reasonable explanation for his staying out!"

"But he didn't stay out. He was in bed when I brought up his hot jar last night!"

Don seemed taken aback by being reminded of this.

"He's gone out somewhere then, I expect," he said, "that's all."

"Where? And when? I was down early. There wasn't a stir in the house. I didn't hear a sound till I heard you!"

Together they stood stupidly, one above the other, in the middle of the stairs.

"He must have gone out during the night then," Don insisted.

"But why? And why didn't he tell us he was going out?" Mag demanded. "He knows I'm a light sleeper. He knows I never mind being wakened. Many a night, before his other exams, he came into my room and sat on the end of the bed to talk for a while if he couldn't get to sleep."

"Well, come downstairs anyway, Mag," Don said, more gently. "There's no use standing up here in the cold. He hasn't done this before, has he? No! You'd have told me, of course. And he didn't have a sign of drink on him last night, I suppose?"

"Has he ever had?" she flashed.

In spite of the anxiety that was creeping over him too, she saw that Don was irritated by her righteous tone.

"Look here, Mag," he said, "it wouldn't be the end of the world, you know, if he did take a drink! We can't expect to keep him off it for ever. Moderation is all we can demand from him at his age."

But Mag set her face tight.

"I'll never believe it of him," she said. "Not Donny!"

"Well, how else are you going to account for his behaviour now?"

"Maybe he thought of something he wanted to look up before the exam," she said desperately. "You know Donny! If it was anything important – anything for his exam – he'd think nothing of getting up and dressing and going out to quiz some of his pals about it. Not like other fellows that would be too lazy and would chance leaving it to the morning! Donny would never chance anything."

That was true. She saw Don had to acknowledge it.

"Yes," he said, "but in that case he'd have been back in an hour or so."

"Unless he stayed talking, wherever he went!"

"He would have telephoned!"

"In the middle of the night?"

They looked at each other dully.

"You don't suppose . . . that he might have met with an accident or something?"

"Funny, I never thought of that," his father said.

Yet, now, to both of them it seemed an obvious thought.

"Hadn't we better do something?" said Mag.

"Like ring the hospitals?" Don went over to the hall table where the 'phone stood. There, he hesitated.

"Which hospital ought I to ring? Street accidents are usually brought to Jervis Street Hospital, I think, but I don't suppose they are brought there from all parts of the city. I suppose all hospitals have casualty wards. I wonder where I ought to try first?" Suddenly his hesitancy left him, and confidently he put out his hand to take up the receiver. "I know what I'll do, I'll ring the police. That's the thing to do. They must get reports from every hospital." He turned to her. "Did he have his name on him, I wonder? Or any form of identification?"

When she didn't answer he looked up. Her face had gone white. He put down the 'phone. "Don't look like that, Mag," he said. "I'm sure he's all right. It was only to reassure you that I was 'phoning at all. We've got a bit hysterical, if you ask me. I think we should wait a while longer before doing anything. He'll breeze in here any minute, I bet. Wait till you see. And look here, Mag, let me give you a bit of advice. When he does come back . . ."

But he saw that she was in no condition for taking advice.

"Don't ring the police anyway," she said.

It was the way she said it, dully and flatly, that made him feel suddenly that whatever had come into her mind to trouble her was out of all proportion to his own vague fears.

"You're not keeping anything from me, are you, Mag?" he asked, sharply.

"Oh, no," she cried. "It's just that I don't think we ought to draw attention to him in case – "

"– in case he got himself into some scrape or other? Is that it? What scrape could he get into?" he asked, stupidly.

"Oh, I don't know," she said, "but it seems a bad time to draw attention to him – with all this going on . . ."

It was an exceedingly vague and formless reference to what they had been discussing at breakfast, but he got her meaning at once, and his face flushed angrily.

"You can't mean that! You just don't know what you're saying!" he said. "Your own son!"

"Oh, don't go on that way," she cried. "You didn't wait for me to finish. Listen to me!"

But he wasn't listening then, either. He was just staring at her.

"Oh please! Please!" Mag said wearily. "I only meant that he might be innocently involved, drawn into something against his will, or even accidentally, and afterwards perhaps been afraid of the consequences. That was all I meant!" Then she looked sharply at him. "What did you think I meant?"

In sudden enmity each probed the other's eyes for a fear worse than his own.

"Might I ask one thing?" said Don at last bitterly. "Which of these killings is the one in which you think my son is involved? Battering in the head of an old woman? Or the other one?"

"You know right well the one I mean!" Mag snapped. "How could he be involved in the other? Nothing on earth could justify killing that poor old creature."

Don gave a kind of laugh.

"Well! You women are unbelievable. So you consider the poor girl on the docks was fair game for any kind of treatment! Bad luck if it should end as it did – bad luck for the man, that is to say!" He turned away as if in disgust, but the next minute he swung back vindictively. "Tell me one thing," he said. "Just how did you think that anyone could be innocently implicated in a business like that? Your son, for instance!"

"I don't know," cried Mag. "It's not fair to take me up like that. I didn't say I thought anything of the kind. I was only frightened, that's all. Any woman would be the same. Many a time when we were first married, if you were late coming home, I'd be looking at the clock every minute and imagining all kinds of things."

"About me?"

"Oh, you don't understand! What comes into one's mind at a time like this has nothing at all to do with the other person. It doesn't mean one thinks any the less of him. It's as if all the badness of the world – all the badness in oneself – rushes into one's mind, and starts up a terrible reasonless fear. I know Donny is a good boy. And I know he wouldn't harm anyone. But he might have been passing that doorway –"

"Down at the docks, on a dark night? It was raining too, the paper said."

"Well, how do we know what might have brought him down there? How do we know where he is any night he's out, if it comes to that? He could have been passing that way just at the wrong moment, and maybe seen something. Then, who knows what might have happened!"

"But you forget he came home last night, Mag. You saw him yourself, or so you said. You said you went up and said good night to him like you always do, and gave him his hot bottle?"

Mag said nothing for a minute.

"Don," she said in a low voice. "There's something I didn't tell you because it seemed silly, but last night wasn't quite like other nights. His light went out as I went up the stairs. He had put it out although he heard me coming. I didn't mind it at the time – well, not much – and I tried not to be hurt – I told myself his eyes might be giving him trouble after studying so hard all the week. So I said nothing but went into the room without putting on the light and he put out his hand and took the hot bottle from me – in the dark. It wasn't quite like always."

"Oh, now you're splitting hairs," Don said, impatiently. Yet, Mag could see he was carefully considering what she'd told him. "I think there's something you ought to get straight in your mind, Mag," he said then, slowly, "even if he were to walk right in the door this minute. You've got things wrong. It's just possible that a young fellow like our Donny might on occasion have some truck with a girl like that poor girl that was strangled without its being necessarily taken that he'd be mixed up in her murder, but he couldn't be mixed up in her murder without it necessarily being taken that he had some sort of truck with her! Get clear on that!"

Mag's mind, however, had unexpectedly cleared itself not only of that, but of all her other senseless fears as well.

"Oh, I'm sure we are being ridiculous," she cried. "There's bound to be some simple explanation. Look, Don! If it makes you feel better, dear, go ahead and ring the police." But when he said nothing she put out her hand timidly and laid it on his sleeve. "What do you really think, Don?" she said.

"I don't know what to think, now," Don said, roughly. "You've succeeded in getting me into a fine state." He moved over and stood at the window. Then all of a sudden he gave a loud guffaw. "Well,

well," he said, in an altogether new tone of voice. "They didn't hang him yet anyway: he's coming down the road!"

"Oh thank God. Let me look. Where is he?"

Mag ran to the window, and then, when she had seen her son with her own two eyes, she ran towards the door.

"Mag!" Don's voice was so strident she turned back, but when their eyes met they were instantly at one again and could seek counsel from each other.

"What will I say to him?" she asked quickly.

"Let him speak first," Don said, authoritatively.

What they didn't realize, either of them, was that it would be Donny who, with his sunny smile, would speak first as always – with his smile that was always so open, and had such a peculiar sweetness in it.

"I suppose I'm in for it!" he said, light-heartedly. "Or perhaps you didn't miss me? I thought I'd be back before you woke up." When they didn't answer, he reddened slightly. "I meant you to come down and find me as fresh as a lark instead of like most mornings, trying to get my eyes unstuck." He turned to Mag. "Were you worried, Mother. I'm sorry. I'll tell you how it happened. I hope you weren't too upset?"

Mag was flustered.

"Well, it was mostly on account of your exam, Donny – " she said, vaguely, glancing at the pink card. "If it was an ordinary morning . . ."

Donny glanced at the card too, and also at the clock. He went over and took up the card and put it in his pocket. "I mustn't forget this. It's a good job I came home. I'd have forgotten it. I wasn't going to come home at all, but go right on to the College, only for thinking about you and how you might worry."

"It was a bit late in the day to be worrying about us then," said Don.

"I know," cried Donny. "But I ought to have been home hours ago, only I got a blister on my heel. It hurts like hell still. I ought to bathe my foot, but I don't suppose I've time. If it wasn't for thinking you'd have been in a state about me I could have washed my foot in the lavatory down at the examination hall. But then I'd have had nothing to eat, and I'm starving." Seeing some unbuttered toast, he picked it up and rammed it into his mouth.

"Oh, that toast is cold," cried Mag. "Let me make some more."

But Don brought his fist down on the table.

"Toast be damned," he said, and he turned to Mag. "Where the hell was he? Isn't that what we want to know?" He swung back towards his son again. "Where were you? You don't seem to realize – your mother was nearly out of her mind."

"Oh, Don, what does it matter now!" cried Mag – "as long as he's back, and everything is all right."

For everything was more than all right now. The absent son had been unknowable and capable of – well – capable of anything. The real Donny, standing in their midst, was once more enclosed within the limits of their loving concept of him.

But Don could be stubborn.

"How are we so sure everything is all right?" he snapped. "My God, Mag, but you have a short memory!" He turned to Donny. "It's a queer thing to find a person has got up out of his bed in the middle of the night, and taken himself off somewhere – God knows where – without as much as a word of explanation. Why didn't you tell your mother where you were going? You know she's a light sleeper. And you knew you needn't have been afraid of waking me. I never hear a sound once I finally drop off. Why didn't you do that? Why didn't you come in and tell us what was going on?"

"Oh, Don, don't upset him," Mag cried. "Look at the clock. He can tell us at supper tonight, and – "

"But there's nothing to tell!" Donny cried. "It'll all sound foolish now. I only meant to go out for a few minutes in the first place, but the night was so fine – "

"Are you trying to tell us you just went out for a nice little walk?" said Don. "In the middle of the night?"

Missing the ironic note in his father's voice, Donny turned round eagerly.

"Not a walk! I had no notion of taking a walk. At that hour of the night! I only intended stepping outside to get a breath of air." He turned back to Mag. "I couldn't sleep after I went to bed. You know how it is before an exam! Well, after I was a while tossing about, I knew I'd never sleep. I knew the state I'd be in for the exam, so I got up and dressed. I thought that after a mouthful of fresh air I might look over my notes again for a bit. But as I said – when I stepped outside I was tempted to take a few steps down the road. It was such a night! You've no idea. I just kept walking on and on, till I found myself nearly in Goatstown! I was actually standing on Milltown Bridge before I realized how far I'd walked! And there were the hills across from me when I leant over the bridge – and somehow they seemed so near and – "

"You didn't go up the hills?" Mag couldn't conceal her astonishment.

"Well, as far as the Lamb Doyle's," Donny said proudly. "I'd have liked to go on further, up by Ticknock, but it was beginning to get bright – not that it was really dark at all, but day was breaking – you should have seen the sky – I'd like to have stayed up there. But I had the old exam to think about, so I had to start coming down again. Oh, it was great up there: I felt wonderful. I'd been going a bit hard at the work in the last few weeks and everything was sort of bunged up in my brain. Up there, though, I could feel my mind clearing and everything falling into place. But I don't suppose you understand?" he said, suddenly aware of their lack of comment.

"If only you'd come to my door, son," his mother said.

"As if you'd have let me go out if I did, Mother! You know you'd have got up and come downstairs, and insisted on cups of tea, and re-heating jars and re-making beds. You'd never have let me out! But that breath of air, and the exercise, was just what I needed. I felt great! The good is well taken out of it now though, by all this fuss!" He looked accusingly from one to the other of them.

Mag turned to Don.

"Now! What did I tell you! He could have explained everything at supper."

"Let's have no more of it so," said her husband, and he took up his brief-case. "All I'll say is, it's a pity he didn't cut short his capers by an hour or so, and save us all this commotion."

"I told you, I got a blister on my heel," said Donny, indignantly. "I would have been back hours ago only for that."

Mag had forgotten the blister. "Oh! Let me look at it, son," she cried. "The dye of your sock might get into it. You could get an infection. We'll have to see that it's clean and put a bandage on it. Sit down, Donny, son," she said, and as he sat down she sank down on her knees in front of him like she used to do when he was a little boy and she had to tie his shoe-laces for him.

"Wait till you see the bandage that's on it now," said Donny. "I came down part way in my bare feet – as far as Sandyford, where the bungalows begin – but people were stirring – milkmen, bus conductors, and that class of person – going to work, and I had to put on the shoes, but I wouldn't have got far in them only I found something to pad my heel. This!" he cried, and he rolled down his sock and pulled it up – a bit of sweat-stained, blood-soaked felt. "What's the matter?" he cried, as he saw Mag's face. Then he saw Don's. "What's the matter with you two?" he cried.

Was it the texture of the cloth? Was it the colour? What was it that made his parents know, instantly, that the bit of felt had once been part of a woman's beret?

"Why are you staring at me?" Donny cried. He looked down at the bit of stuff. At the same time he shoved his hand down into his pocket and brought up the rest of the beret. "I felt bad about cutting it up," he said, "it looked brand new, but I told myself that – as the old proverb goes – somebody's loss is somebody else's gain.

Mag and Don were staring stupidly at him.

"I suppose it wasn't all a yarn you were spinning us, was it?" Don asked at last. But he answered his own question. "I suppose it wasn't," he said, dejectedly. And he walked over and took up the paper. "There's something you'd better know, boy," he said, quietly. "You evidently didn't see the morning paper." He held it out to him, pointing to one paragraph only.

Donny read quickly – a line or two.

"Is this it, do you think?" he asked then, with a dazed look at the bit of yellow felt.

"That's what we want to know," Don said. "Where did you get it?"

"I told you! I picked it up in the gutter, somewhere about Sandyford Road. Oh, do you think it's it?" he cried again, and letting the pieces fall he ran his hands down the sides of his trouser legs, as if wiping them. "Why didn't you tell me when I came in first?" he said, looking so pathetically young and stupid. Mag began to laugh, odd, gulping laughs.

"Don't mind me, son," she said, between the gulps. "I can't help it." She didn't see the warning look Don gave her. "It's from relief," she said.

Donny looked at her. He had not missed his father's look. Ignoring her he turned to Don.

"What did she mean?"

"Nothing, boy, nothing," said Don. "We were a bit alarmed, you must realize that. You wouldn't understand, I suppose. Some day you may. Parenthood isn't easy – it induces all kinds of hysterical states in

people at times – men as well as women!" he added, staunchly, taking
Mag's arm and linking them together for a minute. "I mean – " he
said, but suddenly irritation got the better of him. "Anyway you've
only yourself to blame," he snapped. "We were beside ourselves with
anxiety – almost out of our minds. We were ready to think anything."

Donny said nothing for a moment.

"You were ready to think anything? But not anything bad?" He
turned to Mag. "Not you, Mother? You didn't think anything bad
about me? Why, you know me through and through, don't you, like –
like as if I were made of glass. How could you think anything bad
about me?"

"Oh, of course I couldn't," Mag cried. And she longed to deny
everything – words, thoughts, feelings, everything – but all she could
do was show contrition. "I was nearly crazy, Donny," she cried.
"You don't understand."

"You're right there! I don't understand," said Donny, and he
slumped down on a chair. After a minute, apathetically, he began to
pull his sock on over his grimy foot. "I'd better go to my exam," he
said.

"Your exam!" Don shouted. "Are you joking? Well, let me tell
you, you can kiss good-bye to your exam. Don't you know you'll have
to account for that beret being in your possession, you young fool?
You don't think you can walk into the house with a thing like that –
like a dog'd drag in a bone – and when you've dropped it at our feet
walk off unconcerned about your business?" Suddenly Don, too,
slumped down on a chair. "Oh, weren't you the fool to get us into this
mess! You and your rambles! If you were safe in your bed where
you ought to have been we'd have been spared all this shame and
humiliation."

Shame? Humiliation? Mag thought all that at least was over. Don
gave her a withering look.

"We'll be a nice laughing-stock!" he said. "I can just see them reading about this in the office. There'll be queer smirks." He looked at
Donny. "And I'd say your pals in the University will have many a good
snigger at you too. To say nothing of what view the University
authorities may take of it. And they might be nearer the mark. It's not
such a laughing matter at all. It's no joke being implicated in a thing
like this. There's no end to the echoes a thing like this could have – all
through your life! People have queer, twisted memories. They won't

remember that you were innocent: they'll only remember that your name was mentioned in connection with a murder – no matter how innocently. I'd take my oath that from this day you're liable to be pointed out as the fellow that had something to do with the murder of a woman." In a flash of involuntary malice he turned to Mag. "They'll probably get things mixed up, seeing both murders were the same night, and think it was in the other one he was involved."

Donny didn't catch the last reference. He was thinking over what Don had first said.

"God help innocence, if everyone is as good at distorting things as you!" he said, angrily.

"Well, it's no harm for you to be shown what can be done in that line," said Don, a bit shamefaced, but still stubborn. "I'd be prepared to swear you'll want your wits about you when you're telling the police about it. They'll need a lot of convincing before they believe in your innocence – or your foolishness, as I'd be more inclined to call it. It isn't as if you only saw the thing, or picked it up and hung it on the spike of a railing, as many a one would have done – as I'd have done, if it was me! It isn't even as if you picked it up and put it in your pocket and forgot about it, as maybe another might have done. But oh no! You had to cut it up in pieces! How will that appear in the eyes of the police? And I must say I wouldn't like to be you when it comes to telling them about the blister on your heel! As if you were a young girl with feet as tender as a flower! Those detectives have powerful feet. You couldn't blister them with a firing iron! I tell you, you'll wear out the tongue in your head before you'll satisfy those fellows' questions." He put his head in his hands. "Oh, how did this happen to us?"

Mag ran over to him.

"Don! I can't understand you!" she cried. "You didn't take on this bad when we thought – "

Don glared at her. "It wasn't me thought it, but you," he cried. "And if it was now, I'd know better what to think. He's only a fool – that's clear."

But Donny stood up.

"I may be a fool, but I'm not one all the way through," he said quietly, calmly. "How is anyone to know – about this? It was hardly light when I picked it up. There wasn't a soul in sight. And if no one knows, why should I go out of my way to tell about it? It was up to the police to find it anyway. Isn't that what they're paid for – paid for by us and people like us? Whose fault is it if they don't do their job properly? There must have been any number of them in that vicinity last night, with flashlights and car-lights and the rest of it. If the beret was so important, why didn't they make it their business to find it? Why was it left for me to find? And why should I neglect my business because they don't do their business right? Here – I'm going out to my exam!"

"Oh, but, son," cried Mag, "you could call at the station – or 'phone them – yes, that would be quicker – 'phone them – and tell them you found the beret, but that you have to go to your exam."

Donny sneered.

"A lot they'd care about my exam. They'd keep me half the day questioning me, like Dad said."

"Not if you explained, son. You could say you'd be available in the afternoon."

"As if they'd wait till then for their information, Mother! No – I'm going to the exam."

"Oh, son! Time might be of the greatest importance!" She ran over to him. "Oh, Donny! You don't understand. Even if you were to miss your exam – think of what this might mean – it might lead to their finding whoever did it!"

"It could as easily lead them astray," Don said quietly. "I know them – they could lose more time probing Donny than would find twenty murderers in another country. It might not be as bad as it seemed at first, Mag, for him to do as he says: keep his mouth shut!" He stooped and picked up the two pieces of felt and stared at them.

Donny put out his hand.

"Give them to me," he said. "I've got to go." Almost absently, he fitted the two pieces together for a minute till they made a whole. "I'll see later what I'll do," he said. Then he looked his father in the face. "But I think I know already," he said.

Hastily, Don took up his brief-case again.

"I'll be down the street with you, son," he said. "We have to consider this from every angle." At the door he turned. "Are you all right, Mag?" he asked.

Mag wasn't looking at him. She was looking at Donny.

"Don't look at me like that, Mother!" Donny said. "Nobody's made of glass, anyway. Nobody!"

The Becker Wives

When Ernest, the third of the Beckers to marry, chose a girl with no more to recommend her than the normal attributes of health, respectability and certain superficial good looks, the other two – James and Henrietta – felt they could at last ignore Theobald and his nonsense. Theobald had been a bit young to proffer advice to them, but Ernest had had the full benefit of their youngest brother's counsel and warnings. Yet Ernest had gone his own way too: Julia, the new bride, was no more remarkable than James's wife Charlotte. Both had had to earn their living while in the single state, and neither had brought anything into the family by way of dowry beyond the small amount they had put aside in a savings bank during the period of their engagements, engagements that in both cases had been long enough for the Beckers to ascertain all particulars that could possibly be expected to have a bearing on their suitability for marriage and child-bearing.

"And those, mind you, are the things that count," James said to Samuel, now the only unmarried Becker – except Theobald. "Of course every man is entitled to make his own choice," he added with a touch of patronage, because no matter how Theobald might lump the two wives together, the fact remained that Ernest had taken Julia from behind the counter of the shop where he bought his morning paper, whereas his Charlotte had been a stenographer in the firm of Croker and Croker, a firm that might justifiably consider itself a serious rival to the firm of Becker and Becker. But Theobald ignored such niceties of classification. In his eyes both of his brothers' wives came from the wrong side of the river, as he put it, and neither of them differed much – in anything but their sex – from Robert, the husband of Henrietta. Robert had been just a lading-clerk whom James had met in the course of business, but since it had never been certain that Henrietta would secure a husband of any kind, the rest of the family – except Theobald of course – thought she'd done right to jump at him. Theobald had even expected *her* to make a good marriage. But once Robert had been raised from the status of a clerk to that of husband, it had been a relatively small matter to absorb him into the Becker business.

The Beckers were corn merchants. They carried on their trade in a moderate-sized premise on the quays, and they lived on the premise. But if anyone were foolish enough to entertain doubts about the scale and importance of the business conducted on the ground floor, he had only to be given a glimpse of the comfort and luxury of the upper storeys, to be disabused of his error. The Beckers believed in the solid comforts, and the business paid for them amply.

Old Bartholomew Becker, father of the present members of the firm, had built up a sizeable trade by the good old principles of constant application and prudent transaction. Then, having made room in the firm for each of his three older sons, one after another, and having put his youngest son Theobald into the Law to ensure that the family interests would be fully safeguarded, the old man took to his big brass-bound bed -- a bed solemnified by a canopy of red velvet, and made easy of ascent by a tier of mahogany steps clipped to the side rail -- and died. He died at exactly the moment most opportune for the business to be brought abreast of the times by a little judicious innovation.

In his last moments, old Bartholomew had gathered his sons around him in the high-ceilinged bedroom in which he had begot them, and ordering them to prop him upright, had given them one final injunction: to marry, and try to see that their sister married too.

The unmarried state had been abhorrent to old Bartholomew. He had held it to be not only dangerous to a man's soul, but destructive to his business as well. In short, to old Bartholomew, marriage represented safety and security. To his own early marriage with Anna, the daughter of his head salesman, he attributed the greater part of his success. He had married Anna when he was twenty-two and she was eighteen. And the dowry she brought with her was Content. By centring her young husband's desires within the four walls of the house on the quayside, Anna had contributed more than she knew to the success of the firm. For, when other young men of that day, associates and rivals, were out till all hours in pursuit of pleasure and the satisfaction of their desires, Bartholomew Becker was to be found in his countinghouse, working at his ledgers, secure in the knowledge that the object of his desires was tucked away upstairs in their great brass bed. And as the years went on, the thought of his big soft Anna more often than not heavy with child, sitting up pretending to read, but in reality yawning and listening for his step on the stairs, had in it just the right blend of desire and promise of fulfilment that enabled him to keep at the ledgers and not go up to her until he'd got through them. In this way he made more and more money for her. Anna might not take credit for every penny Bartholomew made, but she was undoubtedly responsible for those extra pence, earned while other men slept or revelled, that made all the difference between a firm like Beckers and other firms in the same trade. It was inevitable, of course, that the more money Anna inspired her husband to amass, the more her beauty became smothered in the luxury with which he surrounded her. Yet, on his death-bed, his memory being more accurate than his eyesight, it was of Anna's young beauty that he spoke. And reminding her of their own happiness, he laid on her a last injunction to be good to his sons' wives. He made no mention of how she should conduct herself towards a son-in-law, no doubt fearing it unlikely such a person would put in an appearance. Anna gave the dying man an unconditional promise.

Theobald therefore had his mother to contend with as well as his brothers when he objected to each of his sisters-in-law as they came on the scene.

"Have you forgotten your father's last words, Theobald?" Anna pleaded, each time. "How can you take this absurd attitude? What is to be said against this marriage?"

"What is to be said in its favour?" Theobald snapped back.

And on the occasion of Ernest's engagement, when Theobald had put this infuriating question for the third time, his mother had been goaded into giving him an almost unseemly answer.

"After all," she said, "the same could have been said about your father's marriage to me!"

That, of course, was the whole point of Theobald's argument, although he could not very well say so to Anna. Surely he and his brothers ought to do better than their father: to go a step further, as it were, not stay in the same rut. It was one thing for old Bartholomew, at the outset of his career, to give himself the comfort of marrying a girl of his own class, but it was another thing altogether for his sons, whom he had established securely on the road towards success, to turn around and marry wives who were no better than their mother.

"No better than Mother!" Henrietta was outraged. She could

hardly credit her ears. She had the highest regard for Charlotte and Julia, but a sister-in-law was a sister-in-law, and the implication that either of them could be put on the same plane as her mother was unthinkable. "No better than Mother!" she repeated, her voice shrill with vexation. "As if they could be compared with her for one moment. I'm shocked that you could be so disrespectful, Theobald."

But Theobald was always twisting people's words.

"So you do agree with me, Henrietta?" he said.

"I do not," Henrietta shouted, "but you know very well that both James and Ernest would be the first to admit that no matter how nice Charlotte and Julia are they could never hold a candle to Mother. They've said as much, many many times, and you've heard them."

It was true.

On his wedding day James had stood up, and putting his arm around his bride's waist and causing her to blush furiously, he had addressed his family and friends.

"If Charlotte is half as good a wife as Mother, I'll be a fortunate man," he said.

And Ernest, on *his* wedding day, had said exactly the same, giving James a chance to reiterate his sentiments.

"My very words," James said, and all three wives, Anna, and the two young ones, Charlotte and Julia, had reddened, and all three together in chorus had disclaimed the compliment, although old Anna had chuckled and nodded her head towards the big ormolu sideboard, laden with bottles of wine and spirits and great glittering magnums of champagne, from the excellent cellar laid down by old Bartholomew.

"I never heed compliments paid to me at a wedding," old Anna said. They all could see though that she was pleased and happy. But just then, happening to catch a glimpse of her youngest son between the red carnations and fronds of maidenhair fern that sprayed out from the silver-bracketed epergne in the centre of the bridal table, Anna leant back in her chair, and lowered her voice for a word with James who was passing behind her with a bottle of Veuve Cliquot that he didn't care to trust to any hands but his own. "For goodness' sake, fill up Theobald's glass," she said. "It makes me nervous just to look at him, sitting there with that face on!"

For Theobald sat sober and glum between Henrietta and Samuel, where he had stubbornly placed himself, thereby entirely altering the arrangement of the table, and causing the bride's elder sister and her maiden aunt to be seated side by side. Theobald had flatly refused to sit between them, and it had been considered unwise to press the matter.

"I would have made him sit where he was told," Charlotte said to James, when he came back to her side after pouring the champagne and she had ascertained what Anna had whispered to him. "Theobald is odd, but he'd hardly be impolite to strangers."

"I don't know about that," James said morosely. "Don't forget the way he behaved at our wedding. He wasn't very polite to – " James stopped short. He'd been about to say "your people" but he altered the words quickly to "our guests".

"Oh, that was different," Charlotte said. "That was the first wedding in the family."

James wasn't listening though. He was trying to read the expression on Theobald's face as, just then, his youngest brother turned and spoke to Henrietta. Henrietta frowned. What was the confounded fellow saying *now*?

It was just as well James could not hear. Theobald was on his hobby-horse. "The joke of it is, Henrietta," he said, "that for all their protestations to the contrary, both James and Ernest would get the shock of their lives if anyone saw the smallest similarity between their wives and our dear mother."

"Well, there are differences of appearance, of course," Henrietta said crisply. "No one denies that." She always felt that in every criticism of her sister-in-law there was an implied criticism of Robert, and she was annoyed, but on this occasion she was ill at ease as well in case Theobald would be overheard. He hadn't taken the trouble to lower his voice.

"My dear Henrietta," he exclaimed. "You would hardly expect our brothers' wives to wear spectacles and elastic stockings on their wedding day and take size forty-eight corsets, would you? Give them a little time. For my own part I'd like to think my wife would have something more to depend upon for attraction than slim ankles and a narrow waist."

Yet, even Theobald could hardly have foreseen the rapidity with which his sisters-in-law lost their youthful figures. The punctual pregnancy of Julia coinciding with the somewhat delayed pregnancy of Charlotte made both women look prematurely heavy, and there was something about their figures that made it seem they would never again snap back to their original shape. Indeed, since both of them thought it advisable to conceal their condition under massive fur coats, soon there wasn't a great deal – unless you were at close quarters – to distinguish one from the other of the three Becker wives.

After their confinements, of course, Charlotte and Julia regained some of their differentiating qualities, but even then, due to having followed the advice of Anna and adopted such old-fashioned maxims as "eating for two" and putting up their feet at every possible chance, neither their ankles nor their waists would ever be slender again. Now, too, Charlotte and Julia felt entitled to accept freely the fur capes, fur tippets, and fleece-lined boots that they had been a bit diffident of demanding when they were dowerless brides. Indeed as the years went on, they came to regard these things more in relation to the effect they made upon each other than to the effect upon their own figures, so that when finally Anna passed to her last reward, and the fallals and fripperies she had won in happy conjugal contest with Bartholomew were dispersed among her three daughters, it seemed at times that instead of passing from the scene Anna had been but divided in three, to dwell with her sons anew. And nowhere was their resemblance to Anna as noticeable as when, in accordance with a custom first started by Bartholomew, and strictly kept up by James, the Beckers went out for an evening meal in a good restaurant. But whereas formerly Anna had sat at the head of the table, comfortable and heavy in furs and jewellery, there were now three replicas of her seated on three sides of the table.

Henrietta, Charlotte, and Julia. There they sat, all three of them, all fat, heavy, and furred, yet like Anna, all emanating, in spite of the money lavished on them, such an air of ordinariness and mediocrity that Theobald, when duty compelled him to be of the party, squirmed in his seat all the time, and rolled bread into pellets from nervousness and embarrassment. Yet he had to attend these family functions. One had to put a face on things, as he explained to Samuel, who came nearest to sharing his views. After all, although it was for the benefit of the family that old Bartholomew had made a lawyer out of his youngest son, Theobald was not without a return of benefit. His practice was mainly dependent on family connections and he just couldn't afford to ignore family ceremonial. But it went against the grain. Indeed, ever since he was a mere youth of sixteen or seventeen Theobald had nurtured strange notions of pride and ambition, and when to these had been added intellectual snobbery and professional stuffiness, it became a positive ordeal for him to have to endure the Becker parties. In Anna's time, a small spark of filial devotion had made them bearable. Without her it was all he could do to force himself to go through with them. But once at the party, however, he could at least make an effort to keep control of the situations that sometimes arose. With a little tact it was possible to gloss over the limitations of the others.

"Not there, Henrietta!" Just in time he'd put his hand under his sister's elbow and shepherd them all to a quiet corner of the restaurant, whereas left to themselves they would have made straight for a table in the centre of the room. "How about over there?" he'd murmur, and guide them towards a table in a corner behind a pillar, or a pot of ferns.

It was not that he was ashamed of them. There was nothing of which to be ashamed. Indeed, the Beckers were the most respectably dressed people in the restaurant, and they were certainly better mannered than most. Moreover, one and all they possessed robust palates that almost made up for their hit-and-miss pronunciation of the items on the menu. And James, who as the eldest was always the official host, was more than liberal with tips to the waiters. Nevertheless, Theobald was ill at ease and cordially detested every minute of the meal.

"Are you suffering from nerves, Theobald?" Henrietta asked one evening, frowning at the disgusting pellets of bread all round his plate. She was the one who was most piqued at being led to an out-of-the-way table. "I don't know why you had us sit here. The table isn't large enough in the first place, and in the second place we can hardly hear ourselves thinking, we're so near the orchestra."

The table was in a rather dark corner, behind a potted palm, and it was indeed so near the orchestra that James had to point out with his finger the various choices from the menu, in order to come to an understanding with the waiter.

"I wanted to sit over there," Henrietta said, indicating an undoubtedly larger and better placed table, but just then the orchestra reached a lightly scored passage, and overhearing his sister, James looked up from the menu.

"Would you like to change tables, Henrietta?" he asked. "It's not too late yet: I haven't given the order."

Theobald shrank back into his chair at the mere thought of the fuss that would accompany the move. Charlotte and Julia were already gathering up their wraps and their handbags and scraping back their chairs. His left eye had begun to twitch, and the back of his neck had begun to redden uncomfortably.

"Aren't we all right here?" he cried. "Why should we make ourselves conspicuous?" In spite of herself, Henrietta felt sorry for him.

"Oh, we may as well stay here, James," she said, settling back into her chair again and throwing her fur stole over the arm of it. "We can't satisfy everyone, although I must say I don't know what Theobald is talking about when he says we'd make ourselves noticeable, because I for one can't see that anyone is taking the least notice of us!"

There was a thin, high note of irritability in his sister's voice that made Theobald more embarrassed than ever. Under the table he crossed and uncrossed his long legs, and took out his handkerchief twice in the course of one minute, as he tried in vain to disassociate himself from them all. The paradox of his sister's words suddenly came home to him. She'd put her finger on what was wrong with them. His discomfort came precisely from the fact that there was no one looking at them. They were the only people in the whole restaurant who were totally inconspicuous. Around them, at every other table, he saw people who were in one way or another distinguished. And those whom he did not recognize looked interesting, too. The women stood out partly because of their appearance, but mostly because of their manner which was in all cases imperious. The men were distinguished by some quality, which although a bit obscure to Theobald, made itself strongly felt by the waiters and where the Beckers often had a wait of ten or even twenty minutes between courses, these men had only to click their fingers to have every waiter in the room at their beck and call. As well as that, most people seemed to know each other. They were constantly calling across to each other, and exchanging gossip from table to table.

Yes, it was true for Henrietta. No one was taking the slightest notice of the Beckers. In that noisy, unself-conscious gathering, the Beckers were conspicuous only by being so very inconspicuous. It was mainly because they liked to stare at other people that the Beckers went out to dinner. Theobald looked around the table at the womenfolk, at his family. There they sat, stolid and silent, their mouths moving as they chewed their food, but their eyes immobile as they stared at someone or other who had caught their fancy at another table. There was little or no conversation among them, such as there was being confined to supply each other's wants in matters of sauces or condiments.

As for the men, Theobald looked at his brothers. They too were unable to keep their eyes upon their own plates, and following the gaze of their wives, their gaze too wandered over the other diners. They had a little more to say to each other than their women, but the flow of their conversation was impeded by having to converse with each other across the intervening bulks of their wives.

Theobald bit his lip in vexation and began to drink his soup with abandon. He felt more critical of them than usual. Was it for this they had dragged him out of his comfortable apartment – to stare at strangers? He was mortified for himself, and still more mortified for them. Such an admission of inferiority! And why should they feel inferior? So far as money was concerned, weren't they in as sound a position as anyone in the city? And as for ability – well, money like theirs wasn't made nowadays by pinheads or duffers. James was probably the most astute business man you'd meet in a day's march. There was no earthly reason why his family should play second fiddle to anyone in the room.

"Look here!" Theobald roused himself. As long as he was of the party, he might as well try to put some spirit into it. He leant across the table. "I heard an amusing thing today at the Courts," he said, determined to draw the attention of his family back to some common focus. To help his own concentration he fastened his eyes on a big plated cruet-stand on the table. His story might gather up their scattered attention and make it seem that they were interested in each other, that they had come here to enjoy each other's company, to have a good meal, or even to listen to the music: anything, anything but expose themselves by gaping at other people. "I said I heard an amusing thing at the Courts this morning," he repeated, because his remark had passed unheard or unheeded the first time, the gaze of all the Beckers having at that moment gone towards a prominent actor who had just seated himself at an adjoining table. But Theobald's simple ruse seemed doomed to failure. Only James appeared to be listening.

"I didn't think the Courts were sitting yet," James said. "I didn't know the Long Vacation was over." In Theobald's story he displayed no interest at all. He had done no more than, as it were, listlessly lift his fork to pick out a small morsel of familiar food before pushing aside the rest of what was offered.

Theobald did not know for a moment whether to be amused or annoyed. It might perhaps be an idea to try and make a joke of their inattention. If only he could rouse them to one good genuine laugh, he'd be satisfied. If only he could gather them for once into a self-absorbed group! But how? Just then, however, to his surprise he found Charlotte had been attending to what James had said.

"Of course the Courts are sitting," she said, and the glance she gave her husband had an exasperated glint. Theobald was about to meta-phorically link arms with her and enlist her as a supporter, when she leant forward to reprimand her husband. "How could you be so stupid, James? Didn't you see the Chief Justice and his wife in the foyer when we were coming in here tonight? You know they wouldn't be back in town unless the Supreme Court was sitting." But after another scathing glance she turned the other way, and this time leaning across Theobald, she caught Henrietta's sleeve and gave it a tug. "They're sitting at a table to the right of the door, Henrietta, if you'd like to see them. She has a magnificent ring on her finger. I can see it from here. And that's their daughter in the velvet cloak. What do you think of her? She's supposed to be pretty."

Theobald's story was not mentioned any more that evening by any-one, least of all by himself, and he had the further mortification of knowing that it was due to his abortive attempt to tell it that Henrietta and James, the least curious of the Beckers, and the least given to gossip, were craning their necks all during the meal to see the Chief Justice's wife and daughter. As if they were a different race of beings! Some species of superior animal which they – the Beckers – were kindly permitted to observe.

And those were exactly the words he used, later that night, when he and Samuel were walking home. Being unmarried, they were the only two of the Becker men who were at liberty to walk home from these gatherings. James and Ernest, and Henrietta's husband, had to hire cabs to convey their wives to their abodes.

Samuel and Theobald were in rooms, but not of course in the same locality – Samuel thinking it advisable to reside near the business, and Theobald feeling that for the sake of his practice he had to live further out in a more fashionable area, although he admitted that at times it was inconvenient.

"A good address is essential to a man in my position," he said. It irritated him that he had to explain this so often to the others. Samuel was the only one who understood. He had even made mention once or twice of doing likewise. For the present, however, Samuel was all right where he was. As bachelor's quarters his rooms were quite comfortable.

The two brothers walked along the streets talking without great interest, but with a certain affection, and looking down as they walked at the pavement vanishing under their feet, except when, intermittently in the patches of pale light from the street lamps they raised their heads and appeared to look at each other, giving the impression that they were attending to what was being said.

Samuel had enjoyed his dinner. He was also enjoying the walk home. The streets late at night had an air of unreality that appealed to him. Like limelight the moon shone greenly down making the lighted windows of the houses appear artificial, as if they were squares of celluloid, illuminated only for the sake of illusion. He hoped Theobald wouldn't insist on dragging him back to reality. But he might have known better.

"Did you see them tonight, Samuel? Did you see them staring at the Chief Justice and his wife? Did you see the way they were turning around in their chairs?"

"I didn't notice particularly," Samuel said. He still hoped to hold himself aloof. High up in a window on the other side of the street a light went out. What was going on up in that room? What unknown people were intent on what unknown purposes? Vague curiosity stirred in him.

Theobald was relentless. "What do you mean?" he fumed. "You were as bad as anyone yourself."

Samuel reluctantly lowered his eyes and looked at his brother and sighed.

"What harm is it to look at people?" he asked mildly.

Theobald came to a stand. "You know the answer to that as well as I do, Samuel," he said. "You know it marks people off at once as coming from a certain class, to stare at anyone who has raised himself the least bit above the common level. It's tantamount to acknowledging one's own inferiority, and I for one won't do that." All Theobald's pent-up vexation of the evening threatened to break over the head of the defenceless Samuel. "How is it no one ever stares at us when we go into these places? Isn't there a single one of us distinguished enough in some way to attract a little attention from others instead of our always being attracted to them?"

Samuel did not reply, not knowing whether it was wiser to reply or to remain silent. Theobald's words might be no more than a protracted exclamation, and a reply might provoke an argument. As they walked on a few more paces in silence it seemed as if he had followed the wisest course. But when they were passing under another lamp-post Theobald stood again.

"I'll never get used to it," he cried.

This time Samuel was genuinely caught. "To what?" he asked, taken by surprise.

But it was only the same old pill in another coating.

"To the poor marriages they made," Theobald said, and of course he was talking about James and Ernest. Samuel sighed. He was into the thick of it. "It makes me sad every time I think of them," Theobald went on. "I don't feel so bad about Henrietta, but I hate to think of the chances our brothers let slip – with their positions and their looks, and above all, with their money. Think of the opportunities they had. They might have made excellent marriages. Instead of that – what did they do?" Unable to find words caustic enough to answer his own question, Theobald made a noise in his throat to indicate the greatest of contempt. Then he put out his hand and patted Samuel on the shoulder. "The only hope we have rests in you, old man," he said.

Except for the fact that Theobald was younger than him, which gave an unpleasant sense of patronage to his brother's words and gestures, Samuel felt flattered. He immediately paid more heed than the Beckers normally paid to Theobald. This did not mean he approved of Theobald's nonsense. He was just vaguely titillated by his brother's confidence in him, though there was something about his brother's attitude that he still didn't like.

"When your time comes, Samuel," Theobald said, "I hope you'll do a bit better for yourself than the others. I hope you'll have some aspiration towards a better social level."

That was it. *That* was the undertone Samuel disliked. He had not been able to put his finger on it before. All this talk about lifting themselves up to a higher level implied a criticism of their present level which was decidedly disagreeable to him.

"Look here, Theobald," he said. They were passing under yet another lamp-post but it was he this time who came to a stand. "I don't know what you're talking about, and I don't know what levels *you* want to reach, but personally I don't think there is anyone in this city, whatever his position, with whom *I* am unacquainted. Why only this morning I was talking to Sir Joshua Lundon over a cup of coffee and –"

Samuel was trying to speak casually, but as he uttered the baronet's name his voice rose to a higher and thinner note, and his eyes bulged slightly with the strain of trying to appear indifferent. He drew back a pace or two on the pretext of clearing his throat behind a large grey silk handkerchief heavily monogrammed in purple silk to match the silk clocks that ran up the outer sides of his grey lisle socks: he was the most elegant of the Beckers. But he was smart enough to know that the only time their younger brother's views were acceptable to any of them was when the fellow managed to get hold of one of them separately – as now – because while they were all unable to apply his counsels and criticisms to themselves, they came within reasonable distance of agreeing with him when discussing each other.

And, of course, in the present case Samuel felt sure there could not possibly be any personal application intended. Unless Theobald was using the past of the others as a future warning to him, who, though he might have the elegance, had few other attributes of the real dyed-in-the-wool bachelor. Samuel indeed entirely lacked the stamina of the successful bachelor, and at the time of this late night walk with Theobald, he was almost at the end of his tether. So he was at one and the same time drawn towards the dangerous topic of matrimony and anxious to skirt it. He felt, however, that his reference to the baronet had been particularly clever, because it might serve to draw Theobald out in his views without leaving him, Samuel, open to direct examination. Yet when he saw the look that came on Theobald's face, he had an uneasy feeling that he had made a false move, and he was about to be out-flanked.

"Yes," he said nervously, repeating his words, as if having taken up a poor position he felt it was best to dig himself in – "Yes, Sir Joshua Lundon. He came over and sat down at my table. We had a most interesting talk."

But whereas on the first occasion he had looked at Theobald as much as to say "What do you think of that?" he now looked at him as much as to ask "What can you say against that?"

Theobald, however, had another most irritating habit, learned no doubt from his profession. He kept people in suspense before replying to their simplest remarks, thereby giving his own words a disturbing preponderance.

"My dear Samuel," he said at last, "I have no doubt but that you have often sat down with people as notable – and I hope a lot more interesting – than old Sir Joshua. One meets all kinds of people in public places."

Under Samuel's heavy chin a blush began to spread. That was a confounded insinuation. No doubt it was another trick of the trade. No Becker had ever been bred to such cute ways. Not that he, Samuel, couldn't summon up certain wiles if needed and beat the damn fellow at his own game. He knew very well what was implied. And he'd give an answer in the same wrapping.

"Curious – that's just what Sir Joshua was saying to me only today," he said, as casually as possible. "He was remarking on that very thing – the promiscuity of persons one meets with when one ventures into public places. 'As a matter of fact, Becker,' he said to me, 'I'm always delighted to see you, or someone like you, with whom one can suitably sit down when one is forced to come into this kind of place.' "

As he spoke, Samuel's confidence returned, and he felt there was no small skill in the way he parried the laywer's thrust. He even felt for an instant that the Old Man could as readily have sent him, Samuel, for the Bar as the younger brother. Now, of course, after a number of years, training told, but if it came to native wit and natural aptitude he believed he would be prepared to cross swords with Theobald any day. Why Theobald was as good as eating his words. Listen to him!

"I didn't think you knew the baronet so well," Theobald was saying. And in spite of Samuel's efforts to twitch it away, a look of gratification stole over his face. This was almost an apology. He felt he could afford now to be magnanimous about the whole thing.

"Oh, yes, yes. I've known him a long time," he said. "I'd like you to meet him – I must arrange something some day. You might come and have a meal with me in the city?" He looked at his younger brother. The fellow appeared to be thoroughly deflated. Oh, how Samuel wished that James or Ernest could see him. "Yes," he said, intent on enjoying his position, "as a matter of fact I have had it in mind for some time to make you two acquainted. The baronet might be of some assistance to you. And I think he'd be glad of a chance to do me a favour because I don't mind telling you I have obliged him in a number of ways over the years."

"Thank you, Samuel," Theobald said, and Samuel could hardly credit the look of humility that he thought he saw on the other's face.

But all at once he felt a twinge of uneasiness. Surely there was an excessive quiet in the tone of Theobald's voice? Yes, undoubtedly there was. And what was he saying? However suave it sounded Samuel was on the alert.

But Theobald was only thanking him.

"Thank you, Samuel," he'd said. "I'd like that very much indeed." Then he paused. "I have often thought that Lady Lundon looked more intelligent than the old man. I'd be most interested in making her acquaintance. For when shall we arrange?"

For one moment Samuel measured eyes with Theobald and thought of taking refuge in dissimulation, saying that he would drop him a line when he had arranged something. But at the thought of the calculating way he had been led into this conversational trap, his temper so got the better of him that dissimulation was impossible. A feeling of positive hatred for Theobald rose within him, and he felt a vein begin to pulse in his forehead, and his jaw to twitch involuntarily. He was only too well aware of these distressing indications of ill temper, and his awareness did nothing to ease them.

The young cur, he apostrophized. He was well suited to the Law. A fox to the snout. He himself could do nothing but bark out the truth.

"If it's Lady Lundon you want to meet you can get someone else to introduce you," he said sourly. "I only know the old man."

This, of course, was what Theobald was waiting to hear. He met the explanation with one simple word.

"Ah!" he said. Just that, no more. "Ah!" The vein in Samuel's temple throbbed more violently, but Theobald put out his hand and patted him on the shoulder. "Take it easy, Samuel," he said. "I'm sorry for baiting you, but it gets to be a habit with us fellows at the Courts, I'm afraid."

As he patted his brother approvingly, however, Theobald looked anxiously at him. How the chap shook when he got agitated! But when Samuel relaxed again into his usual complacency, Theobald abruptly withdrew his hand. "You did rather ask for it though, old fellow," he said.

They had reached the street in which Samuel resided and had slackened pace to lengthen the time at their disposal, for in spite of a customary invitation to do so, it was not a practice for the brothers to accept hospitality from each other on such occasions. Tonight, how-

L

ever, Theobald wanted a little more time with Samuel to say something important he thought ought to be said.

"For heaven's sake let's drop the pretence, Samuel," he cried. "Don't try to pull the wool over my eyes with your social contacts in public places. Of course, you don't know Lady Lundon, or anyone like her if it comes to that, and if you did you'd keep your mouth shut about it or the rest of the family would be living vicariously on your relationship." Dropping his normal tone, Theobald affected a thin, high and wholly unnatural tone, instantly recognisable to his brother as the voice of their sister-in-law Julia. "Oh, Lady Lundon," he mimicked. "Oh yes. Oh yes. I haven't met her myself yet, personally, but she's a great friend of Samuel's. I believe she is a charming person – simply charming – and most unassuming. I understand she is a very friendly person, and so simple – just like anyone else in fact."

Theobold as he imitated her was so like Ernest's wife that Samuel had to smile in spite of himself. And some of his resentment left him.

"Isn't that true?" Theobald asked, although he had not actually formulated a question.

"Well – up to a point I suppose it's true," Samuel said, knowing what Theobald meant.

"Of course, you understand I have nothing against them," Theobald said, and in spite of a certain ambiguity in his use of the pronoun, it was possible to tell by the derogatory tone of his voice that Theobald was referring to his sisters-in-law. "In fact," he said more explicitly, "Julia is a very decent sort really. Those socks she knit for me last winter look as if they'll never wear out, although the colour is a bit drastic, but all the same she meant well and poor Charlotte isn't a bad sort either. It's only a pity James and Ernest didn't do a little bit better for themselves."

Samuel couldn't let this pass.

"They're happy!" he protested weakly.

"Happy! Well, I should hope so!" Theobald said with a flash of contempt. "That's all they considered at the time, their own comfort and pleasure. If they'd been let down about that I wouldn't know what to say. But happy or not, I still maintain, and will do so till my dying day, that it's a pity their wives hadn't a little more to recommend them."

"It is certainly regrettable that not one of them – Robert included –

had a single penny to bring into the business," Samuel said with a sudden burst of animation.

"There you are!" Theobald was delighted by Samuel's agreement, although as a matter of fact he himself had not been thinking of his in-laws' lack of money when he'd spoken of their limitations. But it was so encouraging to have someone agree that they did have limitations he let this pass. "There you are!" he repeated. "Why, it's ludicrous to think we tolerated it – that no one said 'boo' at the time. In proper levels of society there is some kind of control in these matters: not that I approve altogether of too much interference. In fact interference ought not to be necessary if a family is brought up to an understanding of its obligations, its duties." He frowned. "I must, of course, say in defence of James and Ernest that we ourselves were not brought up to have that understanding, but –" He stopped and looked Samuel straight in the eye. "– but how is it, then, that you and I came to have the proper outlook?"

Whatever disparity might still have been between the two brothers was blasted away by this shattering bolt of flattery.

"Oh well," Samuel said modestly, "people can't all be alike, I suppose."

"I suppose not," Theobald agreed, but more curtly, and he turned aside in case he would laugh out loud at the foolish look on Samuel's face, although it was not indeed a laughing matter, and he felt he was to be congratulated on the evening's conversation. If he had been too late to do anything about the marriages of his older brothers, he believed that at least he had made an impression on Samuel.

There were as a matter of fact two special reasons why Theobald was glad to think he had influenced Samuel. The first was that he had sensed for some time past that the citadel of Samuel's celibacy would not continue to stand much longer, and that he had spoken just in the nick of time. The second reason was that he himself had begun to engage his mind with plans of his own in a certain interesting direction, and he did not want to have any more mediocre connections to have to drag out into the light.

"Well, goodnight, Samuel," he said abruptly.

They had reached the foot of the steps that led up to the old Georgian house where Samuel still resided in single dignity. Taking a last look at him, Theobald congratulated himself again on having said his say so determinedly. Then having watched his brother admit himself into the house he started to saunter on his way, giving himself up, with more ease of mind than he had done for some time, to the joys of contemplating his own plans – plans which, by the way, he told himself, he would shortly have to divulge to the family.

Before, however, Theobald had time to divulge anything to anyone, Samuel's capitulation had taken place.

" – and I was guided a great deal by you, Theobald, in making my choice," Samuel said, turning to his younger brother with a special courtesy after he had made the announcement of his forthcoming marriage to the rest of the family. "I was greatly impressed by that conversation we had the other evening."

"Did you hear that, Theobald?" Henrietta cried, her face purple with excitement. All the Beckers – bar Theobald – loved weddings. There was nothing they enjoyed more, unless perhaps christenings. "Did you hear that? Samuel says he was largely guided by you in picking his bride."

"Is that so?" Theobald said morosely. "Well, all I can say is that he wasn't guided very far!"

"Theobald! What do you *mean?*" Henrietta cried, but she didn't wait for him to answer. "Really, there is no understanding you at all," she said. And indeed it seemed that there was not, because unlike the rest of them Samuel was marrying money. He was in fact marrying a great deal of money. He was uniting himself to Honoria, only daughter of the elder Croker of the firm of Croker and Croker, which was the only other firm of corn merchants in the city which might be said to be in any way comparable in size and importance with the firm of Becker and Becker. Although, as James had quietly expressed himself, there was not much point in making speculations as to the relative importance of the two firms since now undoubtedly there would be an amalgamation between them, Honoria being the sole heiress to Croker and Croker.

"Perhaps you didn't understand that, Theobald?" Henrietta said, willing to give him another chance to alter his extraordinary attitude.

But Theobald understood. He understood everything. He shook his head sadly. It was the rest of them that did not understand. To them it seemed that Samuel had scored over him in a way that would protect them for evermore from what they regarded as his notions.

"This will silence Theobald for good and all," James had said earlier in the day, when as the head of the family he had been given an intimation of what Samuel planned before it was announced to the others.

"Did he get any hint of it at all?" Charlotte had asked eagerly, when it was whispered to her. "I'd give anything to be there when he's told."

That was what they all wanted to know – what Theobald would say.

What would Theobald say? What would Theobald do? The question went from lip to lip all that day as one after another the Beckers passed on a hint to each other of the felicitous step Samuel was taking. Julia alone refrained from this eager questioning because Theobald, she maintained, would have nothing to say now. Samuel had cut the ground from under his feet.

And that was exactly what Samuel himself felt he had done.

"He may not come out with it," Samuel said, "but I'd dearly like to know what's in his mind."

And although Samuel got a shock when he was told what Theobald *had* come out with, he did not let his younger brother's words rankle because he felt that in cases like this one always had to make allowances for a certain amount of jealousy.

Only when he was alone with Honoria did Samuel allow himself to brood over Theobald's reaction.

"Theobald is your youngest brother, isn't he?" Honoria asked. To an only child the Becker family seemed at times bewilderingly large. "I heard something or other about him, I think," she said, "but I can't remember exactly what it was – Anyway I'm dying to meet him."

"You'll shortly be meeting them all, my dear," Samuel said. "James is giving a dinner for that purpose I understand." Then suddenly remembering the last dinner party James had given, and his walk through the empty streets afterwards with Theobald, he frowned. "I hope James will agree to giving it in his own house," he said. "It would be more suitable than in a restaurant, don't you think?"

"Oh, I don't know so much about that," Honoria said, and she seemed disappointed. "I love eating out," she said. "I love looking at the other people. Father and I go out for dinner occasionally, just for that alone – to look at people. We went out last evening and, Samuel, you'd never guess who was sitting at the next table to us – Father knows him slightly – Sir Joshua Lundon. Father whispered who he was to me. And Lady Lundon was with him. Oh Samuel, she was so nice. Just as simple as could be! She ordered the simplest food too, just like you or me, or anybody else."

Where had Samuel heard that before? Familiar and unpleasant echoes sounded in his brain. Had he himself not said something like this to Theobald recently and been promptly and severely shown his error?

"It would be more suitable for us to meet in James's house," he said, and he resolved to insist on it.

When Samuel mentioned the matter to James, James agreed – if reluctantly.

"Very well," he said. "I'll tell Charlotte and we'll arrange for some night next week. All right?"

It was more than all right. It was perfect. For once the whole family was in accord in its preference for the betrothal celebrations to be as private as possible. For once their attention was focused fully on themselves. There was not one member of the family but wanted to witness Theobald's reaction to the wealthy bride-to-be. Their interest was centred on their own affairs for another reason too. Was there not a growing rumour that Theobald himself was about to introduce a new member into the family? And might it not be possible that in the intimacy of Samuel's party there could be further disclosures made? The hearts of the Becker women beat faster at the thought. The girl that was good enough for Theobald! How they longed to see her.

Who was she? What would she be like? Above all, would she live up to Theobald's own lofty notions? Not one single member of the family but was sorely tempted to hope she would not. And this, from no more unworthy motive than the common one of self-preservation. It would be such an ease to everyone if Theobald's mouth could be shut once and for ever.

And as the rumour grew this ungenerous feeling grew with it until finally the nearest any of his sisters and brothers could go to letting themselves believe Theobald's principles were inviolable was to disbelieve the rumour entirely.

"It can't be true," Henrietta declared flatly on the morning of the day James and Charlotte were giving their little dinner for Samuel and Honoria. "I don't believe it!"

"Well, I do!" Charlotte said. "And so does Julia."

"What about you, Robert? What do you think?" Henrietta asked, because Robert had come along with her to James's place to see if they could give a hand in the last-minute preparations.

"I must say I'm inclined to believe the rumours," Robert said with a grin he couldn't seem to control.

"Why don't you ask Theobald straight out, Henrietta?" Charlotte said slyly.

"That's just what I intend doing," Henrietta said. "I'll make a point of asking him the very next opportunity – that is to say the very next time I'm alone with him."

It was therefore rather unfortunate for Henrietta that a few minutes later, having volunteered to collect a few pot plants in town for Charlotte and having left Robert behind to attend to some hitch in the lighting arrangements, who should she run into – right outside Charlotte's door – right under the windows in fact – but her younger brother. There was nothing to do but take a rush at him.

"Is it true, Theobald?" she demanded, and she actually put out her arm to bar his way as if she feared he might bolt off.

"Is what true?" Theobald asked coldly and looked at her even more coldly. "Are you feeling all right, Henrietta?"

For the life of her Henrietta could not bring herself to speak any plainer, but feeling forced to say something she took refuge behind further obscurity.

"Well, if it *is* true," she said, "all I can say is I hope you'll do as well for yourself as Samuel."

Then, telling herself she had done what she proclaimed she would do, Henrietta threw a triumphant glance up at the windows of the house behind her, feeling pretty sure that Charlotte would be watching them from behind the curtains. She was so carried away by a sense of her own courage she wished Charlotte could have heard her, as well as seen her.

It was perhaps no harm that her sister-in-law had not heard, because Theobald did not seem to understand what she'd been driving at. Or did he? Really, he was impossible. No one could ever tell what he was thinking. Henrietta stared at him to try and figure out what was in the back of his mind. But the next minute she stepped back in alarm. Theobald's face had begun to work as if he was going to have a fit.

"What's the matter, Theobald?" she cried.

"The matter!" Theobald, although he had calmed down again, still looked very peculiar. "Pray tell me, Henrietta," he said then, "in what way you consider our brother Samuel has done so well for himself?"

Henrietta simply did not know what to make of him. Who were they talking about anyway? Him or Samuel? She'd been under the impression that she was unearthing information about *him*.

"Well," she said, taken aback, "Honoria has plenty of money."

"Money!" Theobald positively sneered at the word. "What does money matter? To Samuel anyway! What does he want with any more than he has already? Money, my dear Henrietta, is not the only thing in this world."

Was it not? Henrietta allowed herself to have mental reservations in the matter, but for the moment she was concerned with a less general aspect of what was being revealed. Very quickly she came to a decision. If there was any truth in the rumours about Theobald, well then it looked very much as if *his* intended was penniless. But Theobald was still ranting on about Samuel.

"I never thought he'd be so short-sighted," he said. "He's making a worse mistake than any of you."

Henrietta had swallowed too many of these jibes to object to one more, and anyway she was just beginning to think she might draw him out a bit after all.

"How is that?" she asked faintly.

"Oh, can't you see!" Theobald cried impatiently. "What difference does it make to Samuel whether he has thirty thousand or fifty thousand. It isn't more money Samuel needs: it's less. And that applies to all of us."

"Less?" The daughter of the Beckers felt faint at the suggestion.

"Exactly," Theobald said. "I thought Samuel would have had the wit to forget about money for once and try and acquire some of the things of which this family stands in such sore need."

"And what are they?" Henrietta gaped.

Theobald fixed her with a cold eye.

"Social position for one thing, and distinction for another; preferably the latter. But instead of that Samuel turns up with this mediocre Croker person. As I said before, he's made a worse mistake than any of you. What did the rest of you do? – Well, to put it bluntly you did no worse than keep within, whereas Samuel has widened, the circle of our mediocrity."

In his vexation Theobald made several extravagant gestures, that to Henrietta appeared most unseemly in the street, but when his arms fell suddenly to his sides she felt still more uneasy about him.

"Tell me," he said in a low despairing voice, "I expect this girl has a horde of relatives? How many of them do you think there will be at James's tonight?"

"Only her father, I think," Henrietta said quickly, "and maybe an old aunt, but the aunt is deaf." The question had made her very anxious. "Why?"

"Because," Theobald said, "I was thinking that if there weren't too many Crokers there, tonight might be as good a time as any for the family to meet my Flora."

"Flora?" Henrietta said stupidly, and then with a rush of blood to the head, she realized that this Flora, whoever she was, must be the living embodiment of the very rumours she had been trying to run to earth. "Why, Theobald," she cried, "is her name Flora? I mean is it true? What I mean to say is we heard a rumour but –"

"That's all right, Henrietta," Theobald said, cutting her short, and he allowed her to find and briefly hold the hand she was vaguely feeling for, as her words stumbled and tumbled over each other. Her muttered incoherence was painful to him, and it was painful too for him to have to watch what he took to be her embarrassment, knowing that Flora would call it gaucherie.

But Theobald was wrong, for although Henrietta was confused, her confusion came, not from embarrassment, but from trying to do two things at the one time: to talk, and to think. She was thinking furiously. Apparently whatever attributes this Flora of his might possess, she, Henrietta, must be right in assuming that untold wealth was not one of them. Flora certainly couldn't claim to be the heiress that Honoria was. How far therefore was it wise – she was thinking in terms of worldly wisdom, of course – to make use of the party given in honour of Honoria to introduce into the family another prospective bride who could, money apart, if Theobald's prognostications were true, put poor Honoria's nose out of joint? Was it even fair? And above all, was she, Henrietta, to be the only one to know of the bombshell that her young brother was planning to throw into their midst that night? If so, the responsibility was just too much for one pair of shoulders. Should she tell him so? Decidedly she would have to tell him.

These were the thoughts that were running through her head while actually she was shaking his hand in felicitation.

"Of course I'm longing to meet her, Theobald," she said, when she regained her hand. "I'm just wondering if tonight is the proper occasion for introducing her to us?"

"Why not?" Theobald said. "She has to meet you sometime."

Memories of certain scathing remarks Theobald had made about

Robert still rankled with Henrietta, and they bred a sudden vicious hope in her mind. Was he ashamed of this Flora?

But she was quickly and in fact rudely shown how wrong she was. It was not of Flora Theobald was ashamed.

"I'll have to get it over some time or another," he said. "It's something that will have to be faced sooner or later, and anyhow I'm sure Flora will make allowances. It is always people like her who are most understanding when it comes to the shortcomings of others."

Henrietta swallowed quickly, and took a deep breath. Was it possible Theobald had accomplished the feat he expected of himself? She swallowed again. All the more reason, then, to protect poor Honoria from the hazards of a comparison.

"All the same, Theobald," she said firmly, "I think it wouldn't be nice – for your Flora, I mean – to introduce her to us casually like that. I think we ought to wait and talk to James and get him to name a definite evening for the purpose. It's nice to be formal about these things don't you think?"

She spoke so primly Theobald threw back his head and gave a loud guffaw.

"Formal? Is it Flora? Easily seen you don't know her. My dear Henrietta – don't you think for a moment that she's the kind of person who'd sit down to one of our vulgar spreads. Why, I don't believe Flora knows such orgies exist. After all, they *are* purely middle-class functions. As a matter of fact when I was telling her about this evening's party I must confess that I more or less conveyed that we ourselves didn't ordinarily go in for this kind of gathering. I'm afraid I told a white lie – I rather gave the impression that we were going through with it mainly to please the Crokers, who were a bit old-fashioned. I sort of suggested that for us it was going to be quite an ordeal. So I'd be glad, Henrietta" – this time it was he who reached for her hand – "if you'd help me out a bit and play up that suggestion?"

"Well –" Henrietta said slowly, "if you insist on bringing her, I suppose I can't show you up for a liar. But it will be very hard to do it convincingly."

"I know that," said Theobald dryly.

Henrietta wasn't sure what he meant, and she didn't at all like his tone, but she felt she more or less had him at a disadvantage.

"We must warn the others, Theobald," she said.

"On no account must that be done, Henrietta," Theobald cried. His voice rose urgently and he glanced over Henrietta's head towards the windows of the house in case the wind might have carried their words in that direction. "I don't want anyone to know about it, only you and me and Flora. I want to take everyone by surprise. Indeed those were the only conditions under which I could make Flora consent to come. She wouldn't come under any other."

"But, Theobald!" Henrietta protested once more. She felt her responsibility in the matter come down on her with an insuperable weight. "I'll have to tell James. And I'll have to tell Charlotte. We might get away with keeping it from the others, but we'll have to tell them. You can't possibly expect to land an extra person down on them without notice – and for that matter – you can't let Flora arrive and find no place set for her! There mightn't even be enough chairs!" Henrietta was as embarrassed as if she were the hostess and Theobald's bombshell was about to fall on *her* dinner table.

Theobald only laughed. "Don't worry about that, Henrietta," he said. "We're only going to look in on you for a minute or two towards the end of the meal. We're not going to stay. We're not to be counted as far as place setting and that are concerned." He looked sternly at her. "I thought I made it plain to you that Flora wouldn't understand sitting down to the big gorges that James and Charlotte provide." He gave another laugh, a different sort: a pleased laugh. "Flora doesn't eat as much as a bird."

A bird? All the time they'd been talking, Henrietta had been trying unsuccessfully to visualize the appearance of this person, Flora. Now, all at once, with Theobald's mention of her birdly appetite, Henrietta's imagination rose with a beat of wings, and before her mind's eye flew gaudy images of brightly plumed creatures of the air. They made her quite dizzy, those images, until they merged at last into one final image of a little creature, volatile as a lark, a summer warbler, a creature so light and airy that it hardly rested on the ground at all. Perhaps not a lark – a chaffinch, maybe? A minute little creature with yellowy golden hair.

"Oh, is it wise, Theobald?" she cried again. "Is it wise under the circumstances?"

"What circumstances?" Theobald asked obtusely, but then as he saw Henrietta redden he understood. "Oh, you needn't worry on that score either. Flora's life is too rich, too filled with variety, to notice that at all. I assure you she isn't the kind of person to take in little details."

"Little details!" Henrietta reddened, this time with annoyance. There was only one detail and she wouldn't call it little. You wouldn't have to stare very hard to be aware of it. One of the circumstances to which she had alluded was the fact that she was pregnant again, and beginning to be more than a little remarkable. The other circumstances were the pregnancies of her two sisters-in-law, both of whom were in the same condition, only more advanced. A nice time, she thought, to bring to the house a giddy little bird like this Flora. Because now Henrietta's conception of Flora's appearance had hardened like cement.

"You don't understand, Theobald," she said stiffly. "It could be embarrassing for an unmarried young woman."

"Nonsense!" Theobald said. "But if so, what about embarrassing Honoria?"

"Oh, it's different for Honoria," Henrietta replied, although immediately after she'd spoken, it occurred to her that she hadn't been very kind to Samuel's intended. Honoria's plump, well-fed figure was furred and beribboned as much as any matron in token of her independent means, and there wouldn't be anything like the same embarrassment for her that there could be for a birdy bride-like creature with a name like Flora. Why Honoria might as well have been a matron already.

"Oh, it's altogether different for Honoria," she said, trying to make emphasis do for explanation. It was not a matter one could explain to a man: least of all a man like Theobald who was so lacking in understanding.

Lacking in understanding Theobald certainly appeared to be that day.

"I think you're absurd, Henrietta," he said. "I can only attribute it to your condition. I'm sorry I mentioned the matter. Please forget it." Raising his hat, her brother was about to move away.

Henrietta was speechless. This made things worse. She did not know whether he was going to carry out his intention or not? It was impossible to remain in such uncertainty.

"Theobald!" she called.

Theobald, upon being called, turned with forced politeness.

"Does that mean you are not going to bring her?" Henrietta asked.

"It does not!" Theobald stopped. "I'm not going to miss an

opportunity like this for killing two stones with the one – I mean two birds with the one *stone*. Good morning, Henrietta." This time he quite definitely walked away.

Henrietta stared after him, more upset than ever. Her brother usually affected such a slow and deliberate manner of speech there was seldom danger of a verbal mishap such as he had just suffered. Henrietta shook her head. He must be out of his mind about this Flora, she thought, and she shivered. To think of having to meet and entertain a person capable of turning the head of a man like Theobald!

All during that morning as Henrietta tried to do Charlotte's messages for her, she continued to experience unpleasant shivers of apprehension, and several times when Theobald's slip of the tongue came to her mind, she had a sensation of the ground going from under her. But at bottom Henrietta was a sound and sensible woman. By the time she'd done the messages and got back to James's house she had made up her mind – Theobald's injunctions apart. She'd say nothing at all about the impending surprise. For, unlikely as it seemed that Theobald would play a joke, the thought had occurred to her that he might be having her on. And if that were the case, what a fool she'd make of herself in the eyes of the others. Henrietta deposited with Charlotte the flowers, the frills for the cutlets, and an extra carton of fresh cream, and departed with Robert, taking with her the secret about Flora.

It was really only later that evening when she took her place at Charlotte's beautifully appointed table where she'd been seated between Honoria's father and Ernest that the burden of her guilty knowledge began to tell.

"Are you feeling all right, Henrietta?" Charlotte asked on at least two occasions, once during the soup, and once during the fish, when Henrietta, thinking she'd heard a footfall on the stairs, began to perspire across her forehead.

Oh, why hadn't she told someone – if only Robert? She looked across the table at him in desperation. Could she, even now, convey her fears to him? But Robert was not attending to Julia on his left, much less to Henrietta across the board, because Robert was nervous of swallowing small fish bones. He made it a rule never to talk when eating fish.

The fish, however, had gone the way of the soup and there was no sign of Theobald, and soon the dinner was mid-way through its courses at least with regard to the number of dishes consumed,

although considering the rich nature of these first dishes it might
perhaps be said to be nearing an end. The guests having, as it were,
successfully crossed the biggest of the fences, were coming into the
straight, and would no doubt gather speed now for the gallop home.
In other words, having consumed the turtle soup, the curled whiting,
the crown of roast young pork (accompanied by mounds of mashed
potatoes, little heaps of brussels sprouts and a ladle or two of apple
sauce), might be expected to make quicker progress through the green
salad, the peach melba, the anchovy on toast, the coffee, and the crème
de menthe. Still no sign of Theobald! He must arrive soon if he
expected them to be still at the table as Henrietta understood him to
have intended.

In spite of her irritation with him, Henrietta found herself trying to
go slow with her peach melba, until feeling Charlotte's eye upon her,
and fearing her sister-in-law might think there was something wrong
with the dessert, she had to act like everybody else and gobble it up.

In a trice the anchovies were being passed. In a trice their remains
were being removed, and the cheese and crackers were being carried
on stage.

It was then, just as the crunch of crackers made hearing difficult
that Henrietta once more fancied she heard sounds indicative of
Theobald's arrival. A cab had stopped in the street below, right outside
James's door. It must be Theobald. Henrietta told herself that she
might have known that a person like Flora would have insisted on
arriving by cab. She put down her cracker and listened. Yes, there
were voices in the hall. There was laughing. She looked around the
table. Did no one else hear? Apparently not. Henrietta's heart stood
still. Then, all at once, with a belated access of loyalty she came to a
decision: she'd have to let the others know what was about to befall
them: she must prepare them for the shock.

"Excuse me. Forgive me for interrupting," she cried, breaking in
upon what, unfortunately, was the first time the whole evening that
Honoria had essayed to display the confidence to which her position
entitled her by telling a story. Realizing how unfortunate her interruption was, Henrietta felt she had no option but to continue. "I must tell
you all something," she went on desperately. "I knew it since morning,
but he wanted it to be a surprise."

Normally, having a rather squeaky voice, Henrietta might not have
made herself heard if she tried to address the whole table, but as

everyone was giving punctilious attention to the story Honoria was trying to tell, ever single word of what Henrietta had to say fell on upright ears.

"What's that?" several of the Beckers cried, speaking all together, and looking first at Henrietta and then at each other.

James alone kept his head.

"Who wanted what to be a surprise?" he asked, almost shouting at Henrietta.

"Theobald, of course," Henrietta said impatiently, because surely the others had ears as well as herself and ought to be able to recognize Theobald's laugh, rare as it was, and he had just given a hearty laugh on the stairs. "Theobald, of course, who else?" she said, permitting herself this tick-off, before she fastened her own eyes on the dining-room door.

"Theobald?" James seemed to affect some diminution of interest at the sound of his brother's name. Indeed a curious frigidity had fallen on the company in general, because if Theobald had not come this would have been the first occasion that a member of the Becker family had voluntarily absented himself from a family celebration. And although on this occasion Theobald had been formally excused, there was an underground feeling of dissatisfaction with him.

"Theobald?" Honoria's deaf aunt asked loudly, addressing herself to no one in particular.

"Oh, he's another brother," Honoria replied impatiently.

"Is it the one you dislike so much?" Honoria's father asked, and as the Beckers all seemed to be at hounds and hares, he didn't feel it necessary to lower his voice all that much. Charlotte, in fact, was the only one to hear and as hostess felt obliged to cover up for her brother, Theobald.

"It's nice that he's been able to join us after all," she said. Truth will out, however, and she added an unfortunate rider. "I can't believe that whatever appointment he said he had would have kept him busy all day *and* all evening. I'm glad he has decided to look in on us even for a few minutes!"

"But that –" Henrietta cried, addressing herself to Charlotte first and foremost, and then the whole family – "that is just what I wanted to tell you. He is coming! It was to be a surprise!" In her excitement she rose in her chair. "And now he's here with her!"

"With *her*? With *whom*?" they all cried.

"Flora!" Henrietta almost screamed the name. "Flora was to be the surprise."

"Flora?" James gave a startled look at Henrietta. "Are you out of your mind, Henrietta?" he cried, because at the sound of the name a vague memory stirred in him and gaudy and tinsel images pirouetted before his mind's eye. Hadn't there been an operetta in his youth called *The Flora Doras?* What on earth was coming over Henrietta, he wondered? Flora? Flora? "What are you talking about?" he demanded.

It was all Henrietta could do to refrain from saying that Flora was a bird. But suddenly she recalled Theobald's slip of the tongue about killing two stones with the one bird, and whatever about his fiancée, it seemed to her that when, at that moment the dining-room door was flung open by Theobald, all the seated Beckers, and all their seated guests, seemed to have been turned into stone.

And the bird?

Henrietta stared. Perched on Theobald's arm, or rather hanging from it by one small hand, was the little chaffinch-type of thing she had expected to see.

Flora was small. She was exceedingly small. She was fine-boned as well, so that, as with a bird, you felt if you pressed her too hard she would be crushed. But in spite of her smallness, like a bird she was exquisitely proportioned, and her clothes, that were an assortment of light colours, seemed to cling to her like feathers, a part of her being, a part moreover of which she herself was entirely unconscious. She accepted her clothes as the birds their feathers: an inevitable raiment.

Indeed Flora appeared to be entirely unconscious of her person. She was hardly into the room before her bright eyes darted from one face to another, her own small pointed face eager with interest in them. It was a birdlike face, thin and sharp, and since her chin was slightly undershot, she gave the impression that like a bird her head was tilted at right angles to her little body. She was evidently very curious about them all, but unlike the curiosity of the Beckers that strove to conceal itself, her curiosity had taken open possession of her. It almost seemed that the excited beating of her heart was causing her frail frame to vibrate and tremble, and that she would simply have to find some outlet: beat her wings, flutter her feathers, or clutch at her perch and burst into song, song so rapturous the perch too would sway up and down.

Theobald, however, was not that kind of perch, and no tremor of

Flora's excitement shook the arm to which she clung. Theobald was intent on making his entry.

"Well, everybody?" he said, and with his free hand he possessively clamped to his arm Flora's little hand with its long varnished finger-nails. "Hello, Samuel. Hello, Honoria. I want you all to meet another future Becker bride."

Had the Beckers been totally unprepared for this shock there is no knowing how the seated table would have reacted, but Henrietta had, as it were, broken the fall for them. And so when Theobald looked around for evidence of surprise, all he saw was stupefaction. The faces that stared at Flora and himself seemed to stare at them out of a coma.

"Well?" he repeated, a little half-heartedly. "Aren't you going to welcome us?"

At this, James, who had been the most stunned of all, upon being given a dig in the ribs by Julia, got awkwardly to his feet.

"We are unfortunately nearly finished dinner," he said, looking around the table, "but we are just going to have coffee." He ventured his first real look at Flora – "Perhaps you'd care for a cup?"

Ah! That was better. Good old James! The Beckers relaxed and began to breathe again.

"Where will they sit?" Julia asked, and she went to move her chair to one side. Not that there was much room for movement round the massive mahogany table because it was already so crowded. It was doubtful if a single extra chair, much less two, could be squeezed in at any point. And since, to add to the difficulty, everyone at the table was following Julia's example and trying to make room for the newcomers, there was soon complete confusion. As Julia moved her chair to the right, Henrietta at the same moment was trying to move hers to the left, and on Henrietta's other side Ernest, moving right, was clashing with Charlotte, moving left.

"They look as if they are playing some game," Flora said to Theobald in a whisper, but a whisper which Charlotte to her intense mortification overheard while she was leaning forward to try and catch the attention of that stupid, stupid James, as she crossly apostrophized him in her mind. Giving up discretion, Charlotte shouted at him.

"Why don't we have coffee in the other room?"

"Just a minute!"

To everyone's surprise the voice that sang out was as sweet and melodious as a bar of music. It was Flora's.

"Please don't move, any of you!" she cried. "Please, please stay as you are. We've had dinner. Just ignore us."

There was such poised authority in Flora's voice that one or two of the Beckers who had stood up, sat down again immediately. In fact only James remained standing, and he did so from uncertainty about his duties as host. But Charlotte gratefully seized on Flora's words.

"Don't tease them, James," she said, and she turned to Theobald. "If you're sure you've had your dinner, why don't you both go into the drawing-room while we finish our coffee. You can show Flora the albums while you're waiting."

But as she made the suggestion, Charlotte knew it was not a very good one. Yet what was the alternative? They couldn't be let stand there. Really this was an outrageous thing for Theobald to have done. To bring a strange girl in on top of them like this, and take them at such a disadvantage, particularly when – as Charlotte couldn't fail to see – there was something so distinctive about the girl, something unusual, something indeed downright remarkable.

All at once, irrelevant though it might seem, Charlotte was shot through with bitter regret that she had not had the dining-room redecorated last month as she had intended. But enough of that! What was to be done with the pair now – they didn't seem to be moving off into the drawing-room?

During her brief reverie, however, Charlotte had missed something. Flora had smiled, and Flora's smile was not something to be missed. It was what the Beckers were always to remember about her – her sudden, luminous smile. And on that first occasion that it shone out, it transformed their awkwardness into gaiety. Flora had saved the situation.

"You simply mustn't move!" she cried. "Such a charming group as you make." Then, from the purely exclamatory, her voice changed to the intimately conversational as she turned to Theobald. "Isn't it a wonder photographers never seem to think of posing people around a table this way?" With a charming gesture she indicated the group before her, and smiled again. This time Charlotte didn't miss the smile, and she too, like the rest of the Beckers, felt warmed by it, as by yellow sunlight. "Oh," Flora cried, "oh how I wish *I* was a photographer." Then suddenly she did the funniest thing. "Let's pretend that I *am* one," she cried, and bending down her head in the drollest way, just as if she had a tripod in front of her, and letting her yellow hair fall down over her face like a shutter curtain, she made a circle with her fingers and held them up to her eyes to act as a lens for her make-believe camera. "I think I can get you all in," she said, turning her head from side to side to get them in better focus. "Keep still, everyone. Look at the dickie-bird. And smile! Smile!" Then, when she had them all smiling, she reached down her hand and squeezed the imaginary rubber bulb that controlled the shutter.

It was the most unexpected thing that could possibly have happened. It was exactly as if she was a real photographer. The Beckers had unconsciously stiffened into the unnatural and rigid postures of people being taken by the camera. Then, when the girl straightened up and pushed back her hair, the group came to life again. Realizing how ridiculous they must have looked, Julia laughed. Then they all laughed, even the parlour-maid, even Honoria, who looked as if she didn't often do so. Above all, Theobald laughed. He was delighted with himself. He looked proudly at his fiancée. She'd be able for any situation.

"Isn't she wonderful?" he said to Charlotte.

But they must be introduced to her.

"Come, Flora," he said, starting to lead her round the table, begin-ning, of course, with the head of the house. "This is James," he said, and in no way constrained now, he laid his hand on his older brother's shoulder.

In the hilarious mood that had developed, no one really expected Flora to put out her hand and utter conventional commonplaces. They watched her eagerly.

"James?" Flora said, and there was a pert little note in her voice that made some of the family titter. Then, to the accompaniment of general laughter, she circled her eyes with her fingers again and bent once more over her make-believe camera and took a head-and-shoulders portrait of James.

It was quite a few minutes before anyone could speak, they were laughing so much, and James himself, although he was startled for a second, soon saw what the funny girl was up to, and he too gave way to the merriment.

"I hope I didn't break the camera, my dear?" he said.

Theobald's pride in Flora was infectious. It even infected stuffy old James. He was charmed by her.

Flora herself didn't smile. She was doing something to her camera.

And her serious expression convulsed the group. She straightened again.

"I must take one of each of you," she said, and she turned to her next subject. "Who are you? You're Julia, aren't you?" she asked, while she was adjusting the lens. "Just a minute please. Try not to move." From the intent way she was looking at her it seemed Julia was a difficult subject, which fortunately Julia found flattering. "Smile!" Flora ordered suddenly. But when Julia laughed as the bulb was being squeezed, the photographer was quite annoyed. "You moved," she said severely. "Your picture will be blurred." She turned around. "Who's next?"

It was Samuel, and she had to speak sternly to him too. "I can't take you, you know, while you're grinning like that! Please try to keep still. Look at the dickie-bird!" When she'd taken him she didn't seem altogether satisfied, and she took another shot. "You're Samuel, aren't you?" she said. "You're a bad subject I'm afraid, but with a bit of luck it may come out quite well." She moved her apparatus further along. Her sobriety was the best part of the fun.

"Who have I now?" she asked. It was Henrietta. "You're very photogenic," she said to the delighted Henrietta. "Your face is so angular. Turn your head a little to one side, if you please. Yes – I think a profile would be best in your case."

It was side-splitting. Never in their lives had the Beckers met anyone remotely like this.

"Well, what do you think of her?" Theobald asked James in an undertone. "This performance is nothing! She's a sort of genius really. You've no idea how people stare at her everywhere we go. Of course, she's well-known anyway; she comes from a very old family, but that doesn't account for all the attention she attracts. It's because she's so amazing. There is nothing she cannot do." He laughed. "And nothing she won't attempt too, if she takes it into her head. She's very accomplished. You should hear her play the piano. And she paints. You should see her water colours. She's going to hold an exhibition one of these days. And I believe she has tried her hand at poetry too, if you don't mind! Some publisher has approached her with a view to bringing out a little volume. Oh, there's no end to her gifts. But I always tell her that her real talent is for acting. You've just seen for yourself! And she's a wonderful mimic. You should see her impersonations!"

"Well, if that was any indication!" Samuel said admiringly, coming up to the other two just then, because the party had loosened up and one or two people were going around with Flora pretending to be her assistants, helping to move her equipment and pose those yet to be taken.

They were just about to photograph Honoria's father, and at the expression on the father's face even Honoria burst out laughing, although up to now her laughter had only been following suit.

"Look at my father's face. Please, please," she begged, and she was laughing so much she had to hold her sides to keep from shaking the whole table.

"That girl is a born actress," Samuel said, happy to be able to give free rein to his admiration because up to then he'd had some misgivings about offending Honoria, having noticed that her merriment had been somewhat more subdued than that of his family. Now he could let himself go and enjoy this extraordinarily exciting young woman who unbelievably – thanks to that dry stick Theobald – was about to become one of them.

Samuel ventured a good look at Flora. This he had avoided doing previously, as it didn't seem generous to do so with Honoria present. And he was surprised at a boyish quality about her, because unconsciously, and perhaps because of her name, his first impression had been of quite extravagant girlishness. In fact before he'd met her at all, from the first instant he'd heard the name Flora, it had brought a vision to his mind of a nymph in a misty white dress, with bare feet and cloudy yellow hair, who in a flowering meadow skipped about, gathering flower heads and entwining them in a garland. It was a bit of a shock to see she was wearing a trim black suit and that her small black shoes had buckles, not bows. There was just one thing about her that was flowery though: her perfume. Honoria never wore perfume. Samuel wished she would. It was captivating.

Captivating was the word; all the Beckers were captivated. Flora was not in their midst more than a few minutes before they had all succumbed to her charm. As Ernest expressed it afterwards when he and Julia were going home, there was only one thing that bothered him and that was to think that such a fascinating person should be tying herself up to a bore like Theobald.

"He is a bore, Julia, you know, with all his theories and principles."

"He has put them into practice, though," Julia said, "you must admit that. I'll confess something now, Ernest: it was always my belief he'd make a fool of himself in the long run. People who are too particular always do. I felt certain he'd make a disastrous marriage. I really did."

Ernest would have liked to confess that he too had often thought the same, but at that moment he felt so well disposed towards his young brother that he hedged.

"Theobald hasn't made many mistakes in his day," he said.

"That's what I mean!" Julia cried. "It's that kind of person who makes the worst mistake of all in the end."

But Ernest wasn't listening. He was thinking about his brother. So there had been something behind his nonsense. He wasn't such a blower after all. Ernest felt subdued. He wondered if Flora had money? The jewellery she was wearing must have cost something. He tried to recall it in greater detail, but as he did he got confused. Had she jewellery on at all? He was puzzled. It didn't seem possible that someone as observant as he prided himself on being could be uncertain about such a significant detail. Ernest was so perplexed his wife had to repeat herself twice before she got his attention.

"What is the matter with you, Ernest? Are you deaf? I said her fake photography was the cleverest thing I've seen in years."

"Oh yes, yes. She certainly is a bit of an actress."

"More than a bit I'd say!" Julia replied, but there was something in the tone of her voice that made Ernest look at her out of the corner of his eye.

"What do you mean by that?"

"Oh nothing," Julia said lightly. "Only I thought once or twice that she carried it just a bit too far. I'd say she doesn't believe in hiding her light under a bushel. And quite honestly, I though she went into the realms of absurdity altogether when we were saying good-bye on the steps."

"Why? I didn't notice."

"Oh, you must have heard what she said to James? He was shaking hands with her, when with a deadly straight face, she said she'd let him have the proofs of the photographs as soon as ever she had them developed."

But in spite of the small trace of censoriousness with which she had started to relate the incident, Julia couldn't help laughing herself at the recollection. "James's face was a scream," she said, "and that wasn't all! When James got her meaning at last and started to laugh, she really carried the thing to extremes. She put on an injured air, as if her dignity had been offended, and took Theobald's arm and went off down the steps without another word. Oh, it was really funny. I don't believe one person in ten thousand would have been able to go away like that without dropping the pretence at *some* point."

"There is no doubt about it," Ernest said, "Theobold is right. There is a touch of genius about her. Now that you mention it, I think I did notice that she was carrying the thing a bit far at the end of the evening. I saw her pretending to pack up her photographic equipment, and when Theobald gave her his arm, she made as if she was changing it to her other hand. As a matter of fact Theobald didn't twig it at all: he's a bit slow sometimes in spite of his high opinion of himself. I saw the joke immediately. And I let her see I did. 'Why don't you let Theobald carry it for you?' I said, and went as if to assist her myself. 'That's all right,' she said. 'I can manage.' And she smiled. Good lord, that smile!"

"Oh, she's something new in our lives and no mistake," Julia said, but seeing that they had reached their own street and were approaching their own door, she waited until Ernest had turned the key and admitted them before she gave him a little jab.

"I still can't help thinking it's a pity Theobald has had the satisfaction of knowing he's done so much better for himself than the rest of you."

This just about expressed the reaction of all the Beckers. Not one of them but could see the distinction and talents possessed by his intended, yet not one but felt that in the long run these would only add to his conceit.

Never mind though. Their wedding would be the next thing. They had that to look forward to anyway. When would it be?

The wedding would take place quite soon. Flora didn't believe in long engagements, it seemed, a fact which might have elicited some cynical remarks were it not that the family all agreed. Theobald wasn't half good enough for her, and the quicker he made sure of her the better.

James kept his head, though, and pointed out that family protocol demanded that Samuel's wedding be first. He glanced at Flora's hand; Theobald had not got the engagement ring yet.

But, it appeared, that was another thing Flora didn't believe in –

engagement rings. And this the Becker women found completely baffling.

"She says the feel of a ring on her finger makes her fidgety," Charlotte reported.

"She'll have to wear a wedding ring, won't she?" Julia said.

"I wouldn't be too sure of that either," Charlotte said. "I heard her saying they look dowdy."

Charlotte and Julia looked down at their own thick bands of gold, guarded by big solitaires set in massive claws. They used to be so proud of them, but now at every minute they found their notions of things suffering a jolt. And soon the jolting was as good as continuous.

First of all Theobald broke it to them that he was not going to buy a house. He and Flora were going to live in apartments. It now appeared Flora could not saddle herself with a house. She was at that particular time engaged in bringing out her book of poems, and she had a responsibility to her publisher. Afterwards they might consider the possibility of a house; but not until afterwards.

"That may be all very well now," James said, "but it could be awkward later on."

The others nodded. They knew what he meant.

"Although, mind you, I wouldn't be surprised –" Henrietta said, beginning to say something, but stopping. She had recollected the presence among them of Honoria, who although only one month married might take offence. Afterwards she had a private word with Charlotte.

"Of course," she said to Charlotte, "it would not matter so much in Flora's case, she is so gifted in other directions. And I don't believe Theobald would mind as much as another man – he'd have such a lot of compensations."

Flora's gifts were indeed many. A few weeks before the wedding her book of poems came out, and although frankly the Beckers were unable to understand two words of it, their pride in her was even greater than Theobald's. Samuel was particularly pleased. He made it his business to go down to the club every day to see if there were any reviews of the book.

"She should have had it illustrated," he maintained every time the book was mentioned. "She should bring out an illustrated edition."

Samuel in fact went one further than them all at times in his admiration for her, and actually took a censorious attitude towards poor

Theobald. "That fellow doesn't realize a man has responsibilities towards a woman like Flora," he muttered. "He should take her around more. There was an exhibition of modern paintings last week in Charleville House. I read about it in the paper. But I bet Theobald knew nothing about it. I hope she didn't have to go without an escort, because I'm sure it's the kind of thing she wouldn't want to miss."

And there and then he promised himself that when she was his sister-in-law, he'd make a point of remedying Theobald's deficiencies in such matters. He was beginning to suspect that Theobald, for all his talk, did not really have a very deep feeling for the Arts. He, Samuel, might not understand a great deal about art, and with one thing and another he hadn't had much time for it, but he intended to do something about it. And now, with the added security of Honoria's dowry he might even venture to buy a few pictures; start a small private collection perhaps. If bought wisely, pictures could be a profitable investment he'd heard. And in this sphere Flora's advice would probably be invaluable. He'd make a start at once; go to a few galleries, make a few enquiries. If Flora were with him he'd feel safe. Yes, they'd make a few tentative expeditions.

The prospect of entering the realm of art in the company of Flora was a particularly pleasant one for Samuel just then, because he would soon be temporarily deprived of Honoria's company. A few weeks after Henrietta's tactful regard for her feelings on a certain subject, Honoria had given evidence that such tact was superfluous. But he must not let his enthusiasm run away with him. The proprieties had to be considered. Oh well! The wedding was just around the corner.

Meanwhile there was the question of the wedding presents.

Presents were a main concern with the Beckers. Every occasion for making an exchange of gifts was eagerly seized on by them, weddings of course being the best occasions of all. The giving and receiving of presents had always been a way of expressing emotions which nervous reticence made it impossible to express in any other way. Presents were a silent symbol of their family solidarity. They spoke loud to the Beckers, and in a language they understood. Thus, when the James Beckers went to visit the Ernest Beckers it always gave them a feeling of family unity to drink coffee after dinner from the Crown Derby service they themselves had given the couple on their wedding day. The Ernest Beckers in turn felt something identical when having

spent an evening with James and Charlotte, they were obliged to
acquaint themselves with the time by consulting the big ormolu
clock of which they were the donors on a recent anniversary of the
marriage of their host and hostess. And both the James Beckers and
the Ernest Beckers found it pleasurable, when visiting Henrietta and
Robert, to be given tea from an old Georgian silver service, the tray
of which had been the gift of one and the service itself of the other,
both bought separately, as it happened, but matching exactly due to
the tact and intelligence of the very reliable antique dealer from whom
the Beckers had bought all their furniture, porcelain and silver since
time began.

The Becker men, and Henrietta, of course, had grown up in an
aura of good sound taste, and it hadn't taken the Becker wives long to
learn from them. It hadn't taken them long to profit by good example
and to realize the stigma that attached itself to the brand-new furniture
that in their single state they used to admire in the shop windows of
Grafton Street. Just exactly what the stigma was they were not certain,
but nevertheless they weren't long in resolving at all costs to avoid
having it attach itself to anything belonging to them. They rapidly
reduced their disturbing new knowledge to the working formula
that nothing was worth buying that was less than a hundred years
old.

It was therefore the biggest jolt of all for the Becker wives to learn
that Flora had other ideas about furniture and decoration. Flora, or so
she declared, would not tolerate anything in her home that wasn't
as fresh as paint. They were not only startled; they were dumbfounded.
This was clearly not another case of their own former ignorance,
when they had been unable to distinguish between the merely old and
and the antique and had contemptuously classed both as second-hand.
Not that they often dwelt on those days. Sometimes, however, they
had to entertain friends from those early days, friends who had made
less fortunate marriages – and who were inclined to voice surprise
that they, the Becker wives, having married money, did not have
newer furniture, and then, smugly, Julia and Charlotte would put
these people right. And if they failed to convince their friends they
contented themselves by thinking to what zenith their own taste had
soared.

Yet here was Flora making positively heretical statements, not only
about tables and chairs, but about glass and table-ware and even

jewellery. And with her it was clear they were up against something different from their own early lack of knowledge. There was more behind her prejudice than there had been behind their former ignorance, no matter what the surface similarities. It was most bewildering, and a disturbing thought entered their minds – was there perhaps another world more esoteric even than the world of antiques? A world of which they yet knew nothing? Oh, but how willing and eager they were to learn!

Flora had a phrase and they grasped at it. *The antiques of tomorrow*. That was what the new bride intended to have in her apartment, and for weeks prior to the wedding her conversation abounded in the names of joiners and cabinet-makers, designers, brass-workers and handlers of gold leaf, craftsmen of whom neither James nor Ernest had ever heard, living in streets not even Robert knew existed, peculiar lanes, dead ends, and back alleys. It was odd. It was distinctly odd. And although the James Beckers and Henrietta and Robert too made valiant efforts to catch and memorize the names of some of these obscure craftsmen, and track them down to their haunts, they found it exceedingly hard to believe that any value could be set upon the shapeless and colourless articles they were seriously offering for sale.

Samuel was the only one with an ounce of real courage, and one day he instructed Honoria not to hesitate any longer, but go out and buy, as their present for Flora, a large canvas on which there was inscribed a name he had definitely heard Flora mention, although, apart from the signature, there was nothing else intelligible to him on the canvas.

After Samuel had purchased the painting and Flora had been quite pleased with it, some of the others took courage. Ernest and Julia bought an etching, and Henrietta a most uncomfortable modern chair. But they never got the same feeling of pride in these presents that they formerly used to get buying things for each other. They could not feel either that they would get the same pleasure when dining with the Theobalds that they got when dining with each other, that is to say the feeling of pride in their own selective judgment. There would be little or nothing of themselves in their gifts, and they had had no fun in buying them. Of course they had to allow that they might not see very much of these presents after they left their hands, because they might not be very prominently displayed by the Theobalds, or even displayed at all. Not that they would resent this, recognizing that the fault could be in themselves: they might not have really mastered all the nuances of the new brand of good taste.

In consequence Flora became vested with still greater charm. Only Samuel claimed to come anywhere near understanding her. He had in fact confided to Henrietta that in some ways he had a greater affinity with her than Theobald. And when he was requested to be the best man at their wedding, he felt it was a tribute to this affinity and that Flora was behind the request.

"My height is about right, I dare say," he said deprecatingly when talking to James. "I expect they have to look into that kind of thing at a large fashionable wedding where there will be newsmen galore and photographers."

"Will there be a lot of photographers?" James asked. He really was stupid at times, Samuel thought, in spite of his business capabilities.

"Don't you know there will!" Samuel said curtly, "with a bride like that!"

"I suppose you're right," James said, and he began to feel nervous at the prospect of such publicity. But his nervousness was quickly superseded by a feeling of family pride. Theobald's acquisition of Flora was the best thing that had happened to the Beckers for a long time.

Everywhere she went Flora attracted attention. Shades of the days when Theobald had sighed over the nonentity of his family! Now, wherever they went – that is to say if Flora was with them – they were followed at every step by glances of admiration or curiosity. And if they happened to take a meal out in a public restaurant, which they did not do so often nowadays, far from worrying Theobald by staring around the room, it was almost absurd the way the Beckers fastened their eyes on Flora and kept them on her. They certainly had a common focus now, as indeed did everyone in the room. The funny part of it was that it began to look as if in this regard Theobald could have had too much of a good thing. To the amusement of his brothers and sister it seemed at times that he rather wished he could hide Flora's light under a bushel.

"I think he's jealous," Flora herself said jokingly in his hearing to Samuel the day she and Theobald came home from their honeymoon, when he and some of the others called at the apartment to pay their respects to the happy pair.

"That is absurd," Theobald replied, disclaiming such unworthy motives. He'd only been trying to put some small curb on a wife who didn't really seem to know when to stop. It wasn't everyone who could appreciate her high-flying acts and antics. At the hotel where they'd been staying when they were away she had been unique. To the other guests her energy, her fire, her undiminishable vitality had made her seem like someone from another planet. Her wit, her sallies, her vivid word-pictures had left them breathless. As for her impersonations, these had left everyone, including himself, exhausted.

"You have no idea, Flora, the effect you had upon those people," he said, trying to speak a little crossly to her because it really had been embarrassing. He turned to the others. "She was like a flame playing over them incessantly, withering the life out of them."

"A flame?" Flora had heard him. "Oh, how lovely!" she cried. She ran over and gave him a kiss. "That's the nicest thing you've ever said to me, Theobald." She closed her eyes and a frail smile played over her face, a reflection perhaps of some inward thought that caused her also to sway slightly from side to side and then, after a minute, to tremble.

Watching her Samuel saw that she had begun to glow, to grow more vivid and more vital. Under the influence of the compliment she seemed to vibrate as if a strange new force ran through her. The flesh and blood Flora had vanished, and where her feet had rested a flame struggled in the air.

But that was absurd, he thought. He was getting over-imaginative and he would have been a bit worried about himself only Theobald just then got very cross with her.

"I know what you're up to, Flora. Stop it," Theobald said. "See! She's at it again," he said, turning to Samuel. "Trying to imagine what it's like to be a flame!"

Samuel sighed with relief. It had not been his imagination then. He was greatly reassured and pleased, too. It just showed how alive he was to Flora's moods. No longer alarmed, he looked at her appraisingly. It was hard to see why Theobald was so put out. What a dull dog he was!

"It was this way all the time at the hotel," Theobald said. "You'd only to mention something and Flora would start to personify it." He took her arm and shook it, rather violently. "Stop it, Flora."

As if drenched with cold water, the flame that was Flora died down. Theobald looked ridiculously relieved. He laughed uncomfortably.

"I wish you wouldn't encourage her, Samuel," he said, because Samuel was complimenting her.

"You have a great gift, my dear," his brother was saying as he pressed her hand.

"Now, Theobald! Do you hear that?" Flora cried. She turned confidingly to Samuel. "I wish Theobald had your appreciation of things. Why! he was even annoyed with my little green dragon."

In spite of himself Theobald had to laugh at her this time. He didn't approve greatly, but there was something irresistible about the casual, intimate way Flora spoke of these imaginative creations of hers.

"What green dragon? Is this something new?" Samuel asked.

"A green dragon?" At the other end of the room Henrietta had overheard and given a little fictitious scream as she hurried over to them. "What are you talking about?" she cried, and in a minute everyone was clamouring for an explanation.

The green dragon was evidently one of Flora's most successful performances, and the one she had put on most frequently at the hotel. The affair of the photography on the first day they met her had been impromptu, but the green dragon was apparently part of a steady repertoire.

"Oh, do it for us. Do it! Please, Flora," several of her new relatives cried, speaking all together.

"I don't *do* it," Flora said. "I *see* it."

They did not understand.

"It's really very clever." Theobald was softening. "I have to admit that. It's absurd of her to say I was annoyed about it. It was only that I thought she put on the act too often. And that strangers wouldn't understand anyway. They were a dull lot on the whole in that hotel!"

Samuel appealed to his new sister-in-law.

"I beg you, Flora, please remove the imputed stigma that we are no better than that dull lot. May we please see the green dragon?"

Theobald nodded his consent. He even tried to make it easier for his family to enter into the spirit of the thing.

"It's quite a simple trick, basically," he explained. "Flora just stands up and looks in front of her and claims she sees it – sitting on the table or on a chair – anywhere in fact. That's all there is to it, but the way she stares at it you'd swear it was there. Her way of looking at it is so convincing. And she puts on such a comical expression."

"Oh, it sounds most amusing," Henrietta said. "Please, Flora, please."

"Please what?" Flora asked, and truly her expression was masterly at that moment. No one could have been more serious. That was the core of her genius: that she could keep her face straight when everyone else was doubled up with laughter. They were all sure that she was going to oblige with the entertainment. There was a look of expectancy on every face.

But Theobald, who was able to read Flora's face a little better now than before they were married, saw an obstinacy in it that the others didn't see. For a moment he had the feeling that he used to have years earlier, when Henrietta was a girl – a big awkward girl – who when asked to perform on the piano used to wear away the whole evening with wearisome refusals that were part vanity, part hysteria. There wasn't going to be that kind of stupid scene now, was there? He looked uneasily at his wife. But he'd misjudged her. Turning suddenly she looked around at one of the small gilt chairs that were so fragile the Beckers were afraid to sit on them, and then at the curious marble table that they found so hard to consider suitable for a meal, and when finally she looked at Henrietta it was with the faintest trace of contempt.

"I'm sorry I can't show it to you," she said. "I don't see it anywhere. It must have gone into the garden."

Such roguishness, but at the same time such a graceful way to refuse. It was almost as good as putting on the act. Everyone was looking around the room, and Samuel stepped over to the window and looked out. The green dragon's absence was almost as positive as his presence would have been. Theobald saw that his family could almost visualize the little creature. All his own pride in Flora came back. He didn't mind how she showed off in the bosom of the family. And this wasn't just showing off. She had handled the situation very neatly. She hadn't felt like performing and she'd got out of it with tact. That of course was the reason her little charades were always so successful: she did not attempt them unless she felt the compulsion, or the inspiration, or whatever you fancied calling it.

Then, as if to corroborate her husband and just as the others were taking their leave and were about to go, the wives secure in their warm wraps and James and Ernest with their mufflers already round their necks, Flora, who had come to the door with Theobald to see them off, peered suddenly out of the open doorway into the dark street.

"Ah, there he is!" she cried. "I'm glad he came back before you left. See him?"

"See who?" some of the slower ones asked, staring out.

"The green dragon, of course – who else?" Flora said, affecting impatience as she bent down and held out her arms. "Come here, my pet," she said, and she made a feint of catching something that had, as it were, leapt through the air at her bidding and was now cuddled against her.

"Well, isn't that the most amazing thing you could see in a month of Sundays," James said. "You'd swear she had something in her arms."

"Isn't he a darling?" Flora said. "Look! He likes me to tickle him behind his ear."

"Oh please, please, Flora." The Becker ladies begged for mercy. They had already laughed so much they couldn't bear to watch any more. But Flora went on. It was exactly – oh but exactly – as if she had a little animal in her arms, cuddling it and talking to it and tickling it, in much the same way that they themselves – some of them anyway – Robert perhaps? – might play with a kitten or puppy; except – and this was important – except that Flora's fingers moved delicately, guardedly, as if her pet had some prohibitive quality, such as a scaly skin.

"Genius. Sheer genius," Samuel said.

Even James rose to the occasion with another rare flash of wit.

"Take him inside, my dear," he said. "Good night, good night. We'll find our way ourselves. Don't stand out here in the night air. *The little fellow might catch cold.*"

The little fellow! He meant the little dragon. James had never been known to make such a good joke. It showed how he responded to his new sister-in-law.

There was a further peal of laughter, and shaking with merriment the women had difficulty finding their feet on the steps. Theobald stared after them. Had the Beckers ever before laughed out loud like that in the street? A change had certainly come over them. And this was only the beginning. With Flora around, new and surprising things would be happening every hour.

Some days, with no more than a few hours' warning, the Theobald Beckers would invite the whole family to join them at the theatre, and all because Flora, when she went out to buy fish, had booked a whole row of seats for the theatre, and it would take every available Becker to fill them if Theobald's money was not to be thrown upon the waters.

Another time it would be a picnic in the country. Theobald would have to make a hurried round of calls to gather the James Beckers or the Ernests or the Samuels or Henrietta and Robert to fill the seats on a side-car that Flora had seen outside the Shelbourne Hotel and couldn't resist hiring. And if any of them felt it made them too remarkable to be seen sitting up on an old-fashioned vehicle, no matter, the next week it could be a char-à-banc. Forward in time or back in time, it made no difference to Flora as long as she could escape from the tedium and boredom of the present, just as it didn't matter to her whether it was Henrietta or Honoria she was impersonating as long as she stepped out of her own personality and became another being. When this desire for change came over her nothing was allowed to come between her and making the change. Often in the middle of a conversation, a sentence, a word, she had been known to spring to her feet and turn a picture face to the wall.

"I couldn't stand it a single minute longer," she'd explain. In her own apartment this didn't matter so much, of course, but Julia felt it was going a bit far when she did it in Charlotte's to a water colour which, as a matter of fact, Julia herself had given to James and Charlotte. Another day it was a vase to which she took exception and put out of sight.

"It may be only a little affectation," Charlotte said, when she and Julia were discussing the matter later.

"That's no excuse," Julia said. She was still the only one of the Beckers who had not completely capitulated to Flora's charm.

"Julia is jealous if you ask me," Honoria said to Charlotte when Charlotte told her about Julia's attitude. "She's just plain jealous because Flora has got such good taste. I think Flora was quite right about the vase. It was hideous," she added, feeling no disrespect in speaking her mind about the vase because it was she who had given it to Charlotte. "As a matter of fact," she went on, looking around her own lavishly furnished drawing-room, "I'm always nervous when her eye falls on those china dogs my aunt gave me." She stood up, moved heavily over to the mantelpiece and took down the dogs. Holding them out from her, as if they had the mange, she rang the bell for the servant.

M

"Throw these out, please," she said to the astonished maid, "and this too," she added as an afterthought, reaching up and taking down a water colour that was over the mantelpiece. "And if I were you, Charlotte," she said, "I'd take your condition into consideration and get rid of that Buddha James gave you last year. It can't be good for you at present to have to stare it in the face – well, to have to stare at it anyway – every time you sit down in your own drawing-room."

"But what could I do with it?" Charlotte asked, although after seeing Honoria's treatment of the china dogs she could guess what her sister-in-law would say. Honoria did not go in for short measures.

Honoria's vandalism was of course a lot easier to take than Julia's and Charlotte's, neither of whom had brought a penny of dowry into the family, and when they too began to throw things out their husbands were more critical. The only good that could be said for taking such drastic steps was that they were influenced by Flora. That and the fact that their rooms looked unquestionably better without the old junk. Into all their homes, as into their lives, more air had come, more colour, more light. Even Henrietta made changes, and Charlotte finally did throw out the Buddha, or rather she gave it to the washerwoman.

Charlotte's washerwoman was what was called a "character". She was one of the people that Flora could imitate to the life. If there was a dull moment in a conversation, or even a lull, Flora was liable to say something in a voice utterly unlike her own.

"Charlotte's washerwoman!" four or five people would shout out at once, as if it was a guessing game. There was never any need to tell them who was being impersonated, yet Flora's appearance hadn't altered in any way. Of course there were times when she took more trouble, pulled her hair over her face and dragged her clothes half off to make herself look disorderly. When she did that you'd swear it *was* the washerwoman: she even looked like her.

Flora really enjoyed impersonating people but she liked them to recognize at once who it was she was representing. And it was surprising how irritable she could become if anyone guessed wrongly.

"No! How could you be so stupid!" she said crossly to poor James one evening when he took her to be doing Henrietta. "I'm Charlotte," she said. "Are you blind? Didn't you see me bending when I came in the door?" For Charlotte being unusually tall had a nervous tendency to dip her head when she came through the doorway although there was no danger of hitting her head in her own home where the rooms were spacious and high-ceilinged.

"But you weren't Charlotte when you were coming into the room!" James said a bit argumentatively, Samuel thought, because looking at Flora now anyone could see she was holding herself exactly like Charlotte.

Flora herself gave James a deadly look.

"Charlotte I was born," she said, "and Charlotte I will remain!"

There was a peal of laughter at this which James did not quite understand, not having been of the company on the previous evening when, in answer to a suggestion from Flora that she should call herself Lottie, Charlotte had taken umbrage, and uttered almost the same words in identically that tone.

"Charlotte I was born and Charlotte I will remain until I die!" Flora was Charlotte to the life.

There were, however, times when Flora's impersonations were a bit too subtle for anyone to guess. These were times when avoiding the obvious landmarks of voice and gesture, she ventured into the interpretation of some inner characteristic, some quality normally hidden in the other person. There were even times when regardless of an audience, almost it seemed indifferent to one, undesirous of one, for some purely creative satisfaction she could be observed trying to project herself into another person. That, Samuel thought, was the mark of the real artist. He had caught her at this on a number of occasions. He'd see her stare at someone, and then after a minute her lovely agate eyes would alter and fill with curiosity, a curiosity which would grow stronger, would make her eyes deeper and their light more inward. It was really awe-inspiring then to see how her whole face would change, and her eyes would lose their lustre, their vivacity, their depth, but above all, their luminous glow and take on instead an actual physical resemblance to the eyes of the person at whom Flora had been staring. He had seen her lovely eyes grow narrow, and the lids come down obliquely as into them crept the chilly, supercilious expression that was habitual to Julia. He had seen them empty of all depth and stare outward with the naive and childish expression of Honoria. He had seen them become so cold and shallow they seemed to have changed colour like the sea over sand, and he knew Flora was being Theobald.

It was becoming Samuel's biggest pleasure to watch his new sister-in-law in the act of departing from her own body and entering that of someone else. But he was careful to guard her secret for her, and even when he saw the transformation coming, he'd bend one part of himself to the task of diverting the attention of the family, while the other part of him he'd give over to furtively watching her and sharing in her adventure. Only when he was in doubt as to who she was taking off, would he venture to intrude his curiosity upon her. He'd go up to her then, quietly, and bending down understandingly, he'd whisper a name in her ear.

"Charlotte?"

If he was right Flora would look up and smile. If he was wrong – but this rarely happened – although she was not able to conceal her annoyance, she never failed to make a witty answer, correcting his error in some original or comical way.

"What's the matter with you?" she would ask. "Are you blind? That's Charlotte over there!"

Samuel, however, was seldom wrong. Even when one evening in the very act of raising a glass of claret to her lips at a small party given in a restaurant by the Ernest Beckers, he saw Flora pause and look into her glass for a second before she drank, in that instant, although there had been neither word nor gesture to fasten upon, he knew Flora had become Theobald – Theobald arresting the flow of his consciousness, becoming aware of himself, trying to catch himself as it were, in the act of living. That evening Samuel could not forbear leaning across the table to her.

"Theobald?" he whispered.

For a moment Flora seemed startled. Then she nodded, but curtly, and at once for some reason – possibly to cover embarrassement – she answered out loud, and her voice was impatient. "What do you want?" she said.

Samuel was always very understanding. He made allowances. She was probably afraid the others would discover her secret game. He resolved not to intrude on her in that way again. And when a few days later he did, it was only under the compulsion of unbearable curiosity, because not for the world would he want to forfeit her friendship. He was becoming more and more dependent on it, particularly of late, because Honoria, although in no way noticeable yet, had already taken to staying home in the evenings and having Charlotte or Henrietta come over to sit with her. Very considerately she refused to keep Samuel tied to the house. One or two nights a week at least she insisted he go out, and if it weren't for having Theobald and Flora, where would he spend those evenings? Certainly not with James or Ernest. And to put oneself voluntarily into Robert's company would, of course, have been ludicrous. So to Flora's he went, every evening Honoria could spare him.

Then came one particular evening. Samuel had had dinner at home, but after dinner he walked over to the Theobald Beckers to spend a short while with them before retiring. It was a summer evening and the lamps were not lit when the servant admitted him. The master, she said, was dining at the club that evening, but the mistress was in the drawing-room. Would she announce him, or would he go in to her?

Samuel went across the hall and opened the dining-room door. For a moment he thought there was no one at all in the room. It was only faintly lit by the paling daylight and the furniture had begun to confound itself with its own long shadows on the wall. Beyond the window the trees in the garden were still visible. Samuel was staring at the black branches when he saw Flora.

She was standing by the side of the window, leaning back against the white woodwork to which her back was closely pressed, her shoulder blades drawn downward, and her face tilted upward more than usual. She seemed to be staring through the upper panes of the glass, and when he moved nearer, Samuel saw the thin spikes of the first stars. She was like the bowsprit of an ancient ship, he thought, and as sightless – at any rate sightless so far as he was concerned. She was unaware of him until he came close – or so it seemed, although he did not think it possible she had not heard him when he first entered. But then, when he'd come close and seen the rigidity of her body and the intensity of her expression, he was paralysed with embarrassment. He did not dare to break in upon her, but stood silent too, afraid to breathe. He felt as if he was in the presence of someone he had never known, and he began to tremble and his face to twitch in a way it had not done for a long time.

This was not Theobald's wife. This was someone else. But who? It was someone Samuel had never seen before. He pulled himself together. It was, of course, quite possible that it was some former acquaintance of hers. Or it could even be some person who did not exist at all except in her imagination, someone who borrowed life from her as characters in a book borrow life from their creator. If novelists and dramatists could invent people, well then, why not Flora? She must write, he thought. A play perhaps? She must! She must! She must! Breathing more than speaking it, he whispered the question that tormented him.

"Who is it?" he whispered. "Who are you now?"

First Theobald's wife shuddered. Then she turned, and her eyes were sad and wearied. Samuel felt a catch at his heart. Was there something wrong? But her voice was normal enough when she spoke.

"Why Samuel! What a strange thing to ask! I'm Flora, of course, who else?"

Who else indeed? Who else would have made such an answer?

Yes, it was Flora: but if ever a person was caught in the act of self-impersonation, that person was Theobald's wife, for in that tense, motionless figure which a moment before had been unaware of his presence, he realized that Flora had concentrated her whole personality. And the essence of that personality was so salt-bitter that a salt-sadness came into his heart too.

"I understand," he said quickly. "I won't intrude." Turning away swiftly he went out of the house.

Yet, the next evening Flora was as gay as ever. If possible she was more hilarious, in higher spirits, and more irrepressible than they'd ever seen her. Except for Julia, the Beckers were all enthralled.

"Irresponsible is what I'd call her, not just irrepressible," Julia said when during the course of the evening Flora had twice mimicked Theobald when he was out of the room. "If he ever finds out he'll never forgive her."

"Oh, he won't find out," Charlotte said. She'd hate to have missed that particular take-off: it was the one she enjoyed the best of the lot. "It was so amusing," she said, laughing again at the thought of it. "She only stood with her back to us but there was something about her that would make you swear she was Theobald."

"All the same," Julia carped, "I think it is disloyal of her, and what is more, I think some of her other impersonations are coarse."

"Coarse? Julia!" Charlotte was astonished at the viciousness of the accusation.

"Well," Julia said, determined to be even more explicit, "I suppose I oughtn't to mind as long as Honoria herself doesn't seem to care."

"Oh that!" Charlotte was relieved and she laughed again. It was, perhaps, a bit coarse, but at the same time it was comical to watch a

little scrap of a thing like Flora imitating – and with such success – a
big lump like Honoria, particularly in view of Honoria's increased
size. "Anyway, Honoria enjoys it as much as any of us," she said,
defending Flora further. Charlotte, being the most insipid of the
Beckers except for her height, had up to then been relatively safe from
Flora's mimicry, and so, next after Samuel, she had the keenest
appreciation of it. But it was true that Honoria took the imitations in
surprisingly good part, considering how often she was the victim.

In fact, where, at the beginning of her relationship with the Beckers,
Flora had been continually calling upon them to witness that she was
now Henrietta, now Charlotte, now James, now Julia, now Ernest,
and now perhaps one of the servants, or a tradesman with whom they
were all familiar, of late she had confined herself to making Honoria
the butt of her humour. She had merely to smile in a certain way, or
go up to Samuel and pick a bit of fluff off his sleeve, or do no more than
take out her handkerchief and blow her nose, and everybody screamed.

"Look at Honoria!" they'd cry.

Once or twice Flora carried things so far as to answer for the real
Honoria when Samuel came into the room and called his wife.

"I'm here, Samuel," she said. "What do you want?" And once when
Honoria answered at the same time, Flora was so funny, so amusing.
She turned on the real Honoria and gave her a chilling look, calling
her Flora.

"Please, Flora," she said. "Please give up these childish impersonations." As if it was Honoria who had been pretending!

It was side-splitting.

And in spite of Julia's misgivings, when summer came and at
Flora's instigation the Beckers made a big family party and rented a
villa on the coast, it was enlivening for them all in the monotony of
their rural surroundings, to have her with them, up to her pranks and
antics.

"I realize all that," Julia said, when this was pointed out to her,
"but I still say she shouldn't pick on Honoria. If I were you, Samuel,
I'd put an end to it quick, now that Honoria is so near to her time."

"Oh but surely," Charlotte interrupted, and she was about to say
that Flora would have too great a delicacy to continue making fun of
Honoria much longer, until at that very moment she saw Theobald's
wife going over to Samuel, and she was walking with a most peculiar
gait. Julia saw her too.

"Look at her now!" Julia cried. "What did I tell you! It's disgusting. It's shameless. Poor Honoria: it's so unfair! Her first baby, too!"

It being the third time that her own figure had become somewhat grotesque – and the fourth time for Charlotte – she felt they could be supposed less sensitive than Honoria who was pregnant for the first time. "I'm going to put a stop to it at once," she said, and she went straight over to Flora. "Look here, Flora, what do you think you're doing?" she asked in a harsh tone.

But Flora answered so sweetly Julia was momentarily disarmed.

"Please don't call me by the wrong name, Julia," Flora said sweetly. "Can't you see I'm not Flora: I'm Honoria. How can you mix us up, particularly now?"

In spite of himself Samuel chuckled. Julia turned on him. "What is wrong with you?" she cried. "Why do you think it so funny?" Then she shrugged her shoulders. "If that's the attitude you intend to take, I may as well mind my own business."

It was on the tip of Samuel's tongue to say "Please do," but instead he smiled falsely and turned to the rest of the company.

"How about some music, ladies?" he asked, and only after he'd spoken did he realize how rarely it was they played the piano since Flora had come among them with her diverting ways. "Well, how about some music?" he repeated, although he was surprised at his duplicity because Julia was the musician of the family, and his suggestion might appease her. But before Julia had time to lift the piano-lid, Flora had snatched at the suggestion and converted it to her own use.

"I'll play," she said, still speaking with the voice of Honoria. "I'll play the tune Samuel likes best!" she cried, and the next minute she was seated on the piano stool playing the only tune that Honoria's memory had managed to retain from all the long and expensive music lessons that had formed the largest part of her education.

Flora played Honoria's tune. She played it and replayed it. And she might as well have been Honoria, so faithfully did she reproduce all the little twists of the wrist, turns of the waist and nods of the head by which Honoria had learned to make up for the deficiencies of her musical talent.

"Well?" Charlotte whispered to Henrietta. "That seems harmless enough."

"Do you think so?" Julia hissed, cutting in on them. "Well, if you think that, please look at the way she is sitting on the piano stool."

True enough, Flora was sitting peculiarly. Charlotte and Henrietta both had to admit there was something awkward about it. She was sitting at least a foot further away from the keyboard than was either necessary or normal.

"It's disgusting! I've said so before," Julia said, "I'll say it again." She glanced around her to make sure the women were alone. "I hope the men don't notice," she said. "It's making a mockery of motherhood." And having glanced pertinently at the waist-line of the other two, she indicated her own loosely slung garments. "It's all due to jealousy, I hope you realize that. Flora is jealous of all of us, but particularly of Honoria because they were married so nearly the same time."

Whatever malice underlay these words however miscarried of its effect because both Charlotte and Henrietta suffered a sudden suffusion of pity for Theobald's poor little bride.

"Oh, poor, poor Flora," they cried, and then both together they looked in her direction. "Perhaps –?" they began eagerly, but Flora's waist was as slim as ever, and her figure gave a complete denial to their kindly hopes for her. Julia hadn't bothered to look at Flora at all.

"Quite the contrary," she said, then she lowered her voice. "And if I'm any judge of these things, *that* will be the fly in Theobald's ointment."

"Oh!" Charlotte exclaimed. "You don't think so, really, do you? It would be such a pity." Her thoughts raced to the nursery upstairs where her big pale baby lay sucking its thumb. "Why, I've heard of dozens of cases where there was no sign of anything for much, much longer than this, and yet there was success before the end!"

But two days later, it was Charlotte herself who had to bring up the subject again.

"Are you sure, Julia?" she asked. "Are you sure there couldn't be some possibility of mistake in what you said yesterday?"

"Why?" Julia said coldly.

"Because," Charlotte said, "I couldn't help noticing how she acted at supper last night." No need now to name names. "She used to love pickled onions, you know that? Well, last night she didn't have any. Wouldn't touch them in fact! And it was the same with the apple sauce. She used to love that too. I couldn't help thinking it odd after what you were saying because I myself couldn't bear anything with the slightest flavour of onion in it when I was expecting, and I couldn't touch apple sauce. It used to give me the most appalling heartburn. But that wasn't all. During supper – the whole time in fact – she sat – well she sat a foot out from the table just like when she was playing the piano. It may be that the thing has got on my nerves, but as well as everything else, I thought she was *walking* queerly after supper when she and I went for a short stroll in the garden. The stroll was at *her* suggestion, mind you, which I thought odd – and here's another thing! – I hope you won't think me coarse to mention it, but I couldn't help noticing that she never buttons her coat, not properly anyway: she lets it hang out loosely from her. Now why on earth is that, do you think?"

"Why do you think?" Julia asked. But she was only leading Charlotte on for a fall.

"Well," Charlotte said, "I was wondering if there was any possibility that you could be wrong, and that she might be going to have a baby after all?"

This was what Julia had anticipated, and she was ready for it.

"In that case," she said acidly, "isn't it odd that it's thinner Flora is getting, not stouter?"

For a moment Charlotte was defeated. Then she came to the fore again. "Some women do get thin in the early stages."

"Is that so?" Julia was more than doubtful. "Then tell me, in a case like that does the woman have to sit a full foot out from the table? Does she have to wear her coat unbuttoned? And above all, does she have to walk like Flora walks?" For Flora had certainly taken to a most peculiar gait. "No," said Julia, answering her own questions so emphatically that Charlotte was silenced. "I tell you, I'm tired of your talk of impersonations. It's not impersonation. It's mockery. Flora is making a mockery out of poor defenceless Honoria."

"Oh for goodness' sake, Julia," Charlotte cried. "Are you losing your sense of humour? Anyway, if what you say is true, why would Flora be doing it when she's alone?"

"What on earth do you mean, Charlotte?"

Julia's startled look made Charlotte falter.

"Well, I wasn't going to mention it," she said, "but the evening before we came down here, I called in to Theobald's with a message from James, and I was shown into the drawing-room, and for an instant I thought I was alone there until suddenly I saw there was someone else there after all. Oh, Julia, I know it sounds a bit daft – the lamps weren't lit – but for a minute I was positive it was Honoria. I nearly said the name. But it was Flora. She was walking up and down her own drawing-room floor, and if you only saw the way her hips were swaying. Why, even Samuel would have been forgiven if he mistook her for his wife. And when the maid had carried in the lamps and after I knew it was Flora, I still couldn't take my eyes off her, because I could still have sworn she was twice the size she'd appeared when I first came in the door. I've often heard of optical illusions, but I never thought I'd experience one!"

Julia said nothing for a minute.

"It seems to me," she said then slowly, "that we are all experiencing them these days. Ernest was saying only this morning that James had commented on the resemblance between Flora and Honoria. Resemblance! Did you ever hear anything more absurd?"

"It does seem a bit absurd, doesn't it?" Charlotte said. "On the other hand, I must say I did think once or twice that Flora was beginning to have a look of Honoria. I'm interested to hear James noticed it. I wonder if any of the others did?"

When discreet enquiries were made in the course of that same afternoon, Henrietta too thought she had noticed a slight resemblance.

"I thought it was only my imagination," she declared, "and I didn't like to mention it to anyone in case it might be put down to my condition. I'd hate anyone to think I was getting nervy or hysterical, or beginning to get fancies."

That, however, was just exactly what was happening to all the Beckers, and especially to the Becker wives.

"It's all Flora's fault," Julia said.

"Isn't it strange, though, that Honoria doesn't appear to notice?" Charlotte said.

"Oh, that's part of her nature," Henrietta said, "but all the same it's my belief she's more upset than we think. I came across her by surprise the other day and I could have sworn she had been crying."

"Crying?" The other two women started up in matronly concern.

"A fit of crying would be the worst thing in the world for her at the present time. It could be the cause of anything!" With this far from lucid statement Julia stood up. "I'm going to speak to Samuel again," she said.

Charlotte felt her knees tremble. Samuel was Flora's stoutest champion. She'd have thought it would be more difficult to approach him than Theobald, and to approach Theobald of course was unthinkable.

Samuel, however, was no match for Julia. When he tried to pooh-pooh her complaints, she went for him with fire in her eyes.

"Samuel Becker," she cried. "Are you going to put Flora before Honoria? I'm telling you that for some reason or other, Theobald's wife is deliberately trying to make your wife look ridiculous, and what is more, Honoria is beginning to notice."

Samuel's face was white and drawn. He made one last effort to evade the issue.

"It's not deliberate," he said speaking lowly. "If Flora is giving offence I am certain she is unconscious of it."

So he was willing to admit offence was given. Julia relaxed somewhat.

"Consciously or unconsciously," she said, "it has got to stop, and stop immediately. Today! Did you know that Honoria has been having fits of crying lately? And what do you think is the cause of that? Above all, may I ask what effect you suppose this state of mind will have on your unborn child?"

Samuel's face went whiter.

"Where is Flora now?" he asked. "I'll speak to her."

Flora was not far away. She was in the breakfast room sitting by the window, sewing. As a matter of fact Charlotte and Julia thought Samuel could hardly have gone farther than the end of the passage when he was back again, but they knew at once by his face that something had happened.

"What's the matter?" Charlotte cried. Then a sudden inexplicable fear came over her and she shouted for James.

"James, James!" she called, relieved to remember that he was sitting on a garden seat just under the open window, reading in the sunshine.

"What in heaven's name do you want, Charlotte?" James said, starting up and leaning in across the window-sill, but instantly he too felt there was something wrong. "Ernest! Robert!" he cried, seeing the two men walking along a gravel path to one side of the villa. Then, without waiting to go around to the door, stiff as he was, he put his leg over the window ledge and joined the women at once. "Oh, you're here too, Samuel," he said with relief.

But whatever had upset Samuel he was now fuming at the fuss that was being made. "What is the matter with you people?" He turned to Julia. "I only wanted to speak to you, Julia," he said. "I don't understand – what is the meaning of this commotion?" Yet when Ernest and Robert hurried in he couldn't help deriving some comfort from the proximity of so many Beckers. "There's nothing wrong," he said. "I only wanted to have a word with Julia – or Charlotte – or Henrietta." He hesitated. "I wanted one of them to step to the door of the other room with me." He hesitated again. "It's Flora."

Charlotte put her hand to her heart. "Is there something the matter with her?" she cried.

"Oh no – at least I don't think so," Samuel said, "but I was a bit worried because she didn't answer when I spoke to her. She was sewing, and when I called her she just went on drawing the needle in and out and didn't even turn her head."

"She didn't hear you: that's all," James said, with an elderly frown. He'd given his knee a knock on the window ledge. It was vexatious. "Was it to tell us she was deaf you brought us in from the sunshine? I thought the place was on fire." He was turning to go out again when Samuel put out his hand and laid it on his older brother's arm.

"Wait a minute, James. The odd thing is that I know she heard me." He turned back to the women: they were more understanding. "I know she did. I called her by name, not once, but twice or three times, and yet she went on sewing. And the last time I called she was putting the thread between her teeth to break it, and I could see by the way she paused that she was listening. Then, ignoring me, she bit the thread and broke it and bent her head again."

It wasn't much – but it was decidedly odd.

"What is she sewing anyway?" James asked suddenly. "She's at it all the time."

"Oh, for goodness' sake, James," Charlotte said, "what does it matter what she's sewing!" It was so like James to fasten on something trivial. She turned back to Samuel. "Why didn't you go over to her?"

It was only after Samuel answered that they all began to feel anxious.

"I thought one of you women should do that," he said. "That's why I came back for one of you," He looked at Julia. "I thought you might be best, Julia."

"Me?" In spite of being the most aggressive earlier on in her assertions that something ought to be done, Julia was most reluctant to put herself forward now. "Will you come with me, Charlotte?"

"I will of course," Charlotte said readily enough, but she made a sign to the men. "Please stay near at hand," she said. Then she addressed herself to Samuel in particular, and her voice was very kind. "We'll leave the door open," she said, "and you can stand outside and listen."

"But be quiet," Julia warned, because James was still inclined to protest that they were making a fuss about nothing. "Where is Theobald?" they could hear him ask. "Why isn't he here? Why didn't someone fetch him along? If there's anything wrong it's his business more than it's ours."

Afterwards everyone remembered what James had said, but they all felt it was fortunate that Theobald was not there. For Flora gave Julia and Charlotte a very different reception from the one she had given Samuel. Being prepared for similar treatment, they were paralysed with fright when she sprang to her feet the instant they called her name. They'd only called once, and as casually as possible.

"Flora?" they'd said timidly. "Flora?"

But the name had hardly left their lips when Flora sprang up. Lithe as a cat, she swung herself around, and gripped the back of the chair in which she had been sitting. Her sewing had fallen to the floor. Her eyes were blazing.

"What is the matter with you all?" she demanded. "Have you gone mad? Why are you coming in here and calling me names?" And then, as if she saw – or in some way divined – that the rest of the family was there too, huddled together outside the door, she shook her fist in their direction. Julia and Charlotte drew together, and didn't advance any further. "Tell me this, Julia Becker, or you, Charlotte Becker!" Flora cried. "Is it a joke? Because, if it is, you'd better stop it at once. You must know by now that one thing I detest is being called names."

"But I never called you names, Flora," Julia cried.

"None of us did, Flora," Charlotte said.

They seemed to have only made things worse, however. Flora's face became convulsed.

"There you go again," she cried, and she nodded towards the hallway where the others were rooted to the ground. With her long thin finger she pointed out through the window that looked on the garden. "As for that one," she said, "that wretched creature out there: if someone doesn't stop her from driving me mad, I won't answer for what will become of her."

They looked.

Out in the sun, on a stone bench, not too far from the house but just beyond earshot of what had gone on within it, Julia saw that Honoria was taking her mid-day rest with her eyes shut and a newspaper over her face to keep her skin from getting too red.

Sensing that behind her the others had come close, Julia called out to them.

"You'd better come in altogether," she said.

Flora swung around. "Yes, come in. All of you," she cried. "Let's have this out. And make her come in too," she added, nodding back over her shoulder to indicate the figure at the end of the garden.

James was the first to enter the room.

"Now, now," he said placatingly, "there's no need to disturb Honoria. If we have had some little disturbance among ourselves, there is no need to drag poor Honoria into it. It's best for her to be kept as quiet as possible under the circumstances."

Something in James's words seemed to sting Flora into another ungovernable fury. There was moisture gathering on her forehead and more alarmingly at the corners of her mouth –

"Honoria?" she echoed. "Under the circumstances? So you are all playing the same game." She caught at the neck of her dress and tore it open. "Very well. I warned you. I won't stand it. It was bad enough when it was only her that was tormenting me" – she pointed again at the unsuspecting Honoria. "I pretended not to take any notice. But if you're all at it, I can't stand it. I can't and I won't!" She clapped her hands over her ears, and tears sprang into her eyes.

"But what are we doing?" Charlotte cried. "We don't know what you're talking about, Flora!"

"Flora! Flora! Flora!" The girl was almost beside herself. "You *do* want to drive me mad. You do! You do!" Her eyes ran over the faces one by one, and then she scanned them all as a group in a wild sweeping glance. "It's a shame for you!" she said. "You ought at least to consider my condition."

From where he stood at the back of the group, looking down at the carpet, Samuel started violently and looked up.

"Yes – a shame," Flora repeated. "If people only knew how I'm treated," She wrung her hands. "Oh, how terrible – I have no one to help me." Suddenly she placed her hands on her small flat abdomen. "It's not myself I'm thinking about – it's the child!"

At that the Beckers, all except Charlotte, went rigid. Charlotte laughed hysterically.

"Oh, it's only an impersonation," she shrilled, but even as she spoke her blood ran cold. Flora's tears had dried as quickly as they'd rushed forth.

"If it's only an impersonation," she cried, "then it's time an end was put to it!" She ran over to the window. "Look at her now. Look at the brazen creature. At this very moment she's out there making a mockery of me. Oh, how can she do it? How can she be so coarse? How can you all see her at it day after day and not be revolted? Don't you notice the way she sits at the table? Don't you notice the way she wears her clothes, not fastening the buttons?" Suddenly she stooped and picked up the piece of material she had been sewing. "She even went to my work-basket and took out this and pretended it was hers."

The frightened gaze of the Becker women fell on a small white flannel chemise that was only half-finished. But as she held it up the sight of it made Flora wail. "I wouldn't mind if she were a normal woman," she cried, "a woman that might have a child of her own some day, but look at her, with her hips like a scissors, and her chest like a cardboard doll! *She'll* never have a child. It's just that she's jealous; jealous of me. That's what it is!"

For one moment Flora's face became radiant, glorified, and then the light died out and it was once more haggard and harassed and aged-looking. "Oh, I can't stand it," she said in a voice that was now small and whimpering. She put her hand up to her head as if it ached. "She's got me so confused." Then, as if she was taking them into her confidence, she tried to steady her voice. "I'm fighting against it," she told them. "See!" Fumbling among the laces on the front of her dress she pulled out a crumpled piece of paper. "When she says something to put me astray I look at this paper. It has my name written on it. Oh, I won't let her get the better of me. She won't drive *me* mad!"

Urgently, frantically, she pushed the paper into James's hand, then before he had time to uncrumple it, she pulled it back and shoved it into another hand and then into another and another. But all any of them could see was a blur of wretchedly bad handwriting. Snatching it back she stuffed it back into her bodice. And now the look on her face was crafty.

"You see, I'm able for her," she said. "I'm able for all of you." She spread out her fingers and again placed them over her boyish body.

"I have to think of my child," she said. And it was the change in her voice that was hardest to bear: it had become wondrously gentle again.

"Oh my God!" Charlotte said, muffling her cry with her handkerchief. Next minute she was sobbing convulsively and James had to call on Samuel and Ernest.

"Get her out of here quick," he ordered.

Flora, however, had not understood it was Charlotte he meant.

"Get who out of here?" she screamed, starting up like a hare. "No one is going to lay a hand on me."

"Hush, hush, he wasn't talking about you, my dear," Samuel said, and he endeavoured to take her hand.

"Are you sure?" Flora's eyes filled first with suspicion and then with fear, and finally with something else, indefinable to the Beckers. They stared at their brother Samuel, who had pushed James aside and seemed to have taken over command of the situation. Flora too recognized that Samuel had put himself in authority. She caught at his lapels. "That's what she wants, you know – to have me sent away." She let go the front of his jacket and seizing his hands she clutched them so that the skin went thin on her knuckles and the bone showed through. "You'll help me, won't you?" she pleaded. "You're the only one I trust. You won't let her drive me mad, will you, like she's been driven mad herself. That's it, you see. No one knows but me and I didn't tell anyone before now. But I knew it all the time. She's mad. Mad! She was really always mad. Her family was mad – all of them. Her father died in a madhouse. She didn't tell that to Theobald, I bet? She didn't tell it to any of you. But I found out and that's why she had this set against me. She wants to make me mad too. But she won't. None of you will. You can keep on calling me Flora all you like. Flora! Go on! Call it to me, Flora! Flora! Flora! I won't listen. I'll stick my fingers in my ears so I won't hear." With a wild distracted gesture Theobald's wife pulled her hands away from Samuel's again and went to stick her fingers in her ears, but halfway through the gesture her hands dropped to her sides. "Where is my piece of paper?" she cried and again she fumbled and found it once more. "As long as I have my name written down on this bit of paper no one will succeed in getting me mixed up," she said. Then, having stared at the piece of paper and soundlessly moved her lips two or three times as if memorizing something, she stowed it away again, and rammed her fingers into her ears as far as they'd go.

N

"She'll pierce her ear-drums," James said. And as if Flora had gone out of the room the Beckers' tongues were loosened.

"What happened to her?" that was what they all wanted to know.

But Samuel raised his hand and it looked as if he'd scourge them. "Oh, you fools!" he yelled. "Get out of here, all of you. Leave this to me." There was such a look on his face that Robert was already backing out of the room.

"Are you sure it's all right for you to stay alone with her?" James asked from the doorway.

"Oh, James, what do you mean?" Charlotte cried. "You don't mean –?" But she didn't dare finish the sentence.

James's meaning was made clear, however, before the door shut. They saw Samuel put his arm around Flora's thin shoulders, and his words sent a chill through their hearts.

"Hush, Honoria. Hush, hush," Samuel was saying. To Flora!

"Please, Honoria – please hush!"

Then the door shut them out.

"Oh God in heaven," Charlotte said, and burst into tears again.

"What on earth will we do with her?" Julia asked.

"How was it we didn't find this out before now?" That was what puzzled Henrietta.

"I kept telling you all that something was wrong," Julia said, "but none of you wanted to believe me."

"What good would it have done if we had listened to you?" Henrietta said tartly. "Sooner or later – what difference does it make – the disgrace is the same."

"Disgrace? Oh, how can you speak about it like that?" Charlotte stopped crying out loud but tears ran silently down her face. "How can you use such a word! It's all so terribly sad."

"And there's Theobald to think about!" James said suddenly. "What about him? Where is he? When will he be back? And who is going to break this to him?" But knowing it would probably be up to him to do it, he sank down on a chair in the hall and began to mop his forehead with the handkerchief out of his breast pocket that was normally only for show. "This is only the beginning," he said.

But inside in the room with Flora this was not what Samuel was thinking as he held her hands tightly in his, and tried to keep her calm by lending himself to her delusion, calling her Honoria over and over again. It was all over. That's what Samuel was thinking.

"Hush, Honoria. Hush, hush," he said. They would have to send for Theobald. They would have to get a doctor and make arrangements to have her taken away somewhere – for a time at least – to try and restore the balance of her poor jangled mind. It might not be for ever, or even for very long, but all the same Samuel knew that the terrible, terrible sadness that had settled on his heart would lie upon it for ever.

It was all over; the fun and the gaiety. Their brief journey into another world had been rudely cut short. They had merely glimpsed from afar a strange and exciting vista, but they had established no foothold in that far place. And the bright enchanting creature that had opened that vista to them had been but a flitting spirit never meant to mix with the likes of them.

Across Flora's shoulder he looked out the window into the garden. The children of Charlotte and Julia and Henrietta had come back from a walk with their nanny and were playing under a tree: a heavy-set little girl, and two stodgy boys. And on the grass Charlotte's fat baby sat sucking its thumb. Beckers to the bone, all of them And the child that his wife Honoria was carrying would be like them, as like as peas in a pea-pod.

His eyes came back to rest on Flora. The tempest of her passion had died down.

"You'll be all right in a little while, my dear. Try to rest. Try to forget everything. Rest on me –" he paused. "– rest on me, Honoria."

But when Flora's sobbing finally ceased and, exhausted, she rested against him, her weight was so slight he started. It was as if she had begun to dissolve once more into the wraith-like creature of light that had first flashed on them all in its airy brilliance on the night of his own betrothal party; a spirit which they in their presumption had come to regard – so erroneously – as one of themselves, just another of the Becker wives, like Julia or Charlotte, or the real Honoria.

A Likely Story

Once upon a time there was a widow who had one son. He was her only son: her only joy. His name was Packy. Packy and the widow lived in a cottage in the shadow of the old abbey of Bective. The village of Bective was opposite, on the other side of the river Boyne.

Do you know Bective? Like a bird in the nest, it presses close to the soft green mound of the river bank, its handful of houses no more significant by day than the sheep that dot the far fields. But at night, when all its little lamps are lit, house by house, it is marked out on the hillside as clearly as the Great Bear is marked out in the sky. And on a still night it throws its shape in glitter on the water.

Many a time, when the widow lit her own lamp, Packy would go to the door, and stand on the threshold looking across the river at the lights on the other side, and at their reflection floating on the water, and it made him sigh to think that not a single spangle of that golden pattern was cast by their window panes. Too many thistles, and too many nettles, and too much rank untrodden grasses rose up in front of their cottage for its light ever to reach the water.

But the widow gave his sighs no hearing.

"It's bad enough to have one eye-sore," she said, "without you wanting it doubled in the river!"

She was sorely ashamed of the cottage. When she was a bride, its walls were as white as the plumage of the swans that sailed below it on the Boyne, and its thatch struck a golden note in the green scene. But now its walls were a sorry colour; its thatch so rotten it had to be covered with sheets of iron, soon rusty as the docks that seeded up to the doorstep.

'If your father was alive he wouldn't have let the place get into this state,' she told Packy every other day of his life. And this too made him sigh. It was a sad thing for a woman when there was no man about a house to keep it from falling down.

So, when the rain dinned on the tin roof, and the wind came through the broken panes, and when the smoke lost its foothold in the chimney and fell down again into the kitchen, like a sack of potatoes, he used to wish that he was a man. One day he threw his arms around his mother's middle.

"Don't you wish I was a man, Mother," he cried, "so I could fix up the cottage for you?"

But the widow gave him a curious look.

"I think I'd liefer have you the way you are, son," she said. She was so proud of him, every minute of the day, she couldn't imagine him being any better the next minute. He was a fine stump of a lad. He was as strong as a bush, and his eyes were as bright as the track of a snail. As for his cheeks, they were ruddy as the haws. And his hair had the same gloss as the gloss on the wing of a blackbird.

"Yes, I'd liefer have you the way you are, son," she said again, but she was pleased with him. She looked around at the smoky walls, and the broken panes stopped with old newspapers, "What would you do to it, I wonder – if you *were* a man?"

Her question put Packy at a bit of a loss. Time and again he'd heard her say that all the money in the world wouldn't put the place to rights.

"Perhaps I'd build a new cottage!" he said cockily.

"What's that?" cried the widow. But she'd heard him all right, and she clapped her hands like a girl, and a glow came into her cheeks that you'd only expect to see in the cheeks of a girl. "I believe you would!" she cried, and she ran to the door and looked out. "Where would you build it, son? Up here on the hill, or down in the village? Would you have it thatched, or would you have it slated?"

"Slated, of course," said Packy decisively, "unless you'd prefer tiles?"

The widow looked at him in astonishment. Only the Council cottages had tiles.

"Would there be much of a differ in the price?" she asked timidly.

"Tiles would cost a bit more I think," Packy hazarded. "And they mightn't be worth the differ.'

A shadow fell on the widow's joy.

"Ah well," she said. "No matter! If we couldn't do everything well I'd just as soon not build it at all! I wouldn't want to give it to say that it was a shoddy job."

There would be nothing shoddy about it though.

"I was only thinking," said Packy, "that it might be better to put the money into comfort than into show. We might get a range in the kitchen for what we'd save on the tiles!"

"A range?" cried the widow. Never, never, would she have presumed to think that she, who had stooped over a hob for forty years, would ever have a big black range to stand in front of and poke with a poker. But all the same she felt that it might be as well not to let Packy see she was surprised. Better to let him think she took a range for granted. So instead of showing surprise she looked at him slyly out of the corner of her eye. "What about a pump?" she said. "A pump in the yard?" But she saw at once by the way his face fell that she'd gone a bit too far. The Council houses hadn't as much as a mention of a pump.

"I thought maybe it would be good enough if we built near the pump in the village," Packy said uneasily.

'Sure of course it would be good enough, son," she conceded quickly. After all, a pump in the yard was only a dream within a dream. But she would have given a lot to stand at the window and see her neighbours passing on their way to the pump in the village, and better still to see them passing back again, their arms dragging out of them with the weight of the bucket, while all she'd have to do would be to walk out into her own yard for a little tinful any time she wanted. It would make up for all the hardship she'd ever suffered. Oh, she'd give a lot to have a pump in her own yard!

And looking at her face, Packy would have given a lot to gratify her with a pump.

"I wonder would it cost a lot of money?" he asked.

'Ah, I'm afraid it would, son," said the widow, dolefully. Then all at once she clapped her hands. "What about the money we'll get for this place when the new cottage is built? Couldn't we use that money to put down a pump?"

Packy stared blankly at her. Up to that moment he had altogether forgotten that building a new cottage would mean leaving the old one. To him, the little cottage never seemed as bad as it did to the widow. He had listened, it is true, to her daily litany of its defects, but out of politeness only. Never had he seen it with her eyes, but always with his own. According to her, its tin roof was an eyesore, but he liked to hear the raindrops falling on it clear and sweet. According to her the windows were too low, and they didn't let in enough light by day, but in bed at night he could stare straight up at the stars without raising his head from the pillow. And that was a great thing surely! According to her, the cow shed was too close to the house, but if he woke in the middle of the night, he liked to hear Bessie, the old cow, pulling at her tyings, and on cold winter nights it comforted him to find that the fierce night air was not strong enough to kill the warm smell that came from her byre.

There was one wintry night and he thought he'd die before morning, like the poor thrushes that at times fell down out of the air, too stiff to fly, but when he thought of Bessie and the way the old cow's breath kept the byre warm, he cupped his own two hands around his mouth and breathed into them, and soon he too began to feel warm and comfortable. To him, that night it seemed that together, he and the old cow, with their living breath were stronger than their enemies, the elements. Oh, say what you liked, a cow was great company. And as far as he was concerned, the nearer she was to the house the better. So too with many other things that the widow thought were faults in the little house; as often as not to Packy they were things in its favour. Indeed, it would want to be a wonderful place that would seem nicer and homelier to him than the cottage where he was born. After all, his Mother came to it only by chance, but he came to it as a snail comes to its shell.

"Oh, Mother!" he cried, "maybe we oughtn't to part with the old cottage till we see first if we're going to like the new one!"

To hear the sad note in his voice you'd think the day of the flitting was upon them. The widow had to laugh.

"Is that the way with you, son? You're getting sorry you made such big promises! Ah, never mind. It'll be a long time yet before you're fit to build a house for any woman, and when that time does come, I don't suppose it will be for your old mother you'll be building it."

But her meaning was so lost on him.

"And for who else?" he cried.

But the widow turned away and as she did she caught sight of the clock.

"Look at the time! You're going to be late for school. And I have to cut your lunch yet," she said crossly. Bustling up from the bench she seized the big cake of soda bread that she had baked and set to cool on the kitchen window-sill before he was out of bed that morning. "Will this be enough for you?" she cried, cleaving the knife down through the bread and mortaring together two big slices with a slab of yellow butter. Then, as he stuffed the bread into his satchel and ran out of the door, she ran after him. "Hurry home, son," she called out, leaning far over the gate to watch him go up the road.

Hardly ever did he go out of the house that she didn't watch him out of sight, and hardly ever did he come home that she wasn't there again, waiting to get the first glimpse of him. And all the time between his going and his coming, her heart was in her mouth wondering if he was safe and sound. For this reason she was often a bit edgy with him when he did come home, especially if he was a few minutes late as he was sometimes when he fell in with his friends the Tubridys.

The widow was death on the Tubridys, although nobody, least of all herself, could say why this should be so. Perhaps it was that, although she often said the whole three Tubridys – Christy and Donny and poor little Marty – all sewn up together wouldn't put a patch on her Packy, still – maybe – it annoyed her to see them trotting along behind Rose Tubridy on the way to Mass of a Sunday while she had only the one set of feet running to keep up with her.

"Well! What nonsense did the Tubridys put into your head today?" she'd call out as soon as he came within earshot.

"Oh, wait till you hear, Mother!" he'd cry, and before he got to the gate at all, he'd begin to tell all he heard that day.

One day he was very excited.

"What do you know, Mother! There is a big pot of gold buried beyond in the old abbey! Christy Tubridy is after telling me about it. He didn't know anything about it either until last night when his father told him while they were all sitting around the fire! He said he'd have got it himself long ago, only every time he put the spade into the ground, a big white cock appeared on the top of the old abbey and flapped its wings at him, and crowed three times! He had to let go the spade and run for his life! What do you think of that, Mother?"

But the widow didn't give him much hearing.

"A likely story!" she said. "What harm would an innocent old cock have done him? Him of all people: that ought to be well used to the sound of cocks and hens, with the dungheap right under the window of the house. It's a wonder he wasn't deafened long ago with cocks crowing right into his ear! Oh, it would take more than an old cock to scare that man! And furthermore, let me tell you that if there was something to be got for nothing in this world, the devil himself wouldn't knock a feather out of him till he got it. You mark my words, son, if there was as much as a farthing buried in the old abbey, by now old Tubridy would have scratched up the whole place looking for it. He wouldn't have left one stone standing on another. He'd have done a better job on it than Cromwell! A pot of gold, indeed! A likely story!"

"I suppose you're right," said Packy, and he left down the spade that he had grabbed up to go digging for the gold.

"Don't be so ready to believe everything you hear!" said his mother.

But barely a day later he came running home again to tell something else he had heard.

"Mother! Mother! Do you know the heap of old stones at the bottom of the hill in Claddy graveyard, where there was an old church one time? Well, last night Christy Tubridy's father told him that when they were building that church long ago they never meant to build it there at all, but at the top of the hill, only the morning after they brought up the first load of stones and gravel, where did they find it all but down at the bottom of the hill! Nobody knew how it got there, but they had to spend the day bringing it all up again. And what do you suppose? The morning after when they came to work, there were all the stones and the gravel down at the bottom once more. And the same thing happened the day after that again and on every day after for seven days! But on the seventh day they knew that it must be the work of the Shee. The Shee didn't want a church built on that hill at all. There was no use going against them, so they built it down in the hollow."

But the widow didn't give him any hearing this time either.

"A likely story!" she said. "It's my opinion that the workmen that carried those stones up the hill by day, were the same that carried them down-hill at night. I don't suppose the men that were going in those days liked work any better than the men that are going nowadays, and it's likely they decided it would pay them better to put in a few hours overtime taking down the stones, than be lugging them up there for an eternity – as they would be in those days with not many implements. The Shee indeed! How well no one thought of sitting up one night to see who was doing the good work? Oh no. Well they knew it wasn't the Shee! But it suited them to let on to it. The Shee indeed! If that hill belongs to the Shee – which I very much doubt –

what harm would it do them to have a church built on it? Isn't it *inside* the hills the Shee live? What do they care what happens outside on the hillside? A likely story! I wonder when are you going to stop heeding those Tubridys and their nonsense?"

Never, it seemed, for the very next day he came running down the road as if he'd never get inside the gate quick enough to tell another story.

"Oh Mother!" he cried, jumping across the puddles at the door. "Are you sure I'm yours? I mean, are you sure I belong to you – that I'm not a changeling? Because Christy Tubridy told me that their Marty is one! I always thought he was their real brother, didn't you? Well, he's not! One day, when he was a baby, their mother was hanging out the clothes to dry on the bushes, and she had him in a basket on the ground beside her, but when she was finished hanging up the clothes she looked into the basket, and it wasn't her own baby at all that was in it but another one altogether that she'd never seen before, all wizened up, with a cute little face on him like a little old man. It was the Shee that came and stole her baby, and put the other crabby fellow in place of him. The Tubridys were terrible annoyed, but they couldn't do anything about it, and they had to rear up Marty like he was their own."

But this time the widow gave him no hearing at all.

"A likely story!" she cried. "A likely story indeed! Oh, isn't it remarkable the lengths people will go to make excuses for themselves. That poor child, Marty Tubridy, was never anything but a crabby thing. He's a Tubridy, all right. Isn't he the dead spit of his old grandfather that's only dead this ten years? I remember him well. So they want to let on he's a changeling? God give them wit. The Shee indeed! The Shee are no more ready than any other kind of people to do themselves a bad turn, and if they make it a habit to steal human children – which I very much doubt – I'd say they'd be on the watch for some child a bit better favoured than one of those poor Tubridys. Now, if it was *you* they put their eye on, son, that would be a different matter, because – even if it's me that says it – you were the sonsiest baby anyone ever saw. Not indeed that I ever left you lying about in a basket under the bushes! It would want to be someone smart that would have stolen you! I never once took my eyes off you from the first minute I clapped them on to you, till you were big enough to look after yourself – which I suppose you are now? Or are you? Sometimes

I doubt it when you come home to me stuffed with nonsense! Changeling indeed! A likely story."

But as a matter of fact it would have been hard to find a story that would not be a likely story to the widow. The gusts of her wisdom blew so fiercely about the cottage that after a while Packy began to feel that it wasn't worth while opening his own mouth at all so quickly did his mother rend his words into rags. And when, one spring, he began to fancy every time he went out of doors that there was someone beckoning to him, and calling him by name, he said nothing at all about it to his mother. For of course he could be mistaken. It was mostly in the evenings that the fancies came to him, and the mist that rose up from the river and wandered over the fields often took odd shapes. There were even days when it never wholly lifted, and like bits of white wool torn from the backs of the sheep as they scrambled through briars and bushes, or rubbed up against barbed wire, the mist lay about the ground in unexpected hollows. It lay in the hollows that are to be found in old pasture that once was broken by the plough, and on the shallow ridges where the fallow meets the ley. Ah yes! It was easy enough then to mistake it for a white hand lifted, or a face turned for an instant towards you, and then turned swiftly aside.

It is said however that a person will get used to anything, and after a while Packy got used to his fancies. He got used to them, but he was less eager than usual to go out and wander in the fields and woods, above all after the sun went below the tops of the trees. And the widow soon noticed this. It wasn't like him to hang about the cottage after school.

What was the matter, she wondered? Did something ail him?

"Where are the Tubridys these days, son?" she asked at last. "God knows they're here often enough when they're not wanted. It's a wonder you wouldn't like to go off with them for a ramble in the woods."

She went to the door and looked out. It was the month of May, the very first day of it. But Packy didn't stir from the fire. Nor the next day either. Nor the next. Nor the next.

"That fire won't burn any brighter for you to be hatching it," said the widow at last.

That was true, thought Packy, for it was a poor fire surely. He looked at it with remorse. It was nearly out. There was nothing on the hearth but a handful of twigs that were more like the makings of a jackdaw's nest than the makings of a fire. It was like a tinker's fire, no sooner kindled than crackled away in a shower of sparks. He looked at his mother. He knew what was wrong. She had no one to depend on for firing now that he never went out for he never came back without a big armful of branches from the neighbouring demesne. He looked at her hands. They were all scratched and scored from plucking the bushes.

"Oh, Mother," he cried in true contrition, "tomorrow on my way home from school I'll go into the woods, no matter what, and get you an armload of branches!"

But the next day – and in broad sunlight too – his fancies were worse than ever.

Just as the bell rang to call in the scholars from play, what did Packy see, around the corner of the schoolhouse, but a finger beckoning: beckoning to him! It turned out to be only the flickering of a shadow cast on the wall by an old hawthorn tree beyond the gable, but all the same it unsettled him. And when school was over he made sure to keep in the middle of the little drove of scholars that went his way home.

For there is no loneliness like the loneliness of the roads of Meath, with the big, high hedges rising up to either side of you, so that you can't even see the cattle in the fields, but only hear them inside wading in the deep grass and pulling at the brittle young briars in the hedge. Closed in between those high hedges, the road often seems endless to those who trudge along it, up hill and down, for although to the men who make ordinance maps the undulations of the land may seem no greater than the gentle undulations of the birds rising and dipping in the air above it, yet to those who go always on foot – the herd after his flock, the scholar with his satchel on his back – it has as many ripples as a sheet in the wind, and not only that, but it often seems to ripple in such a way that the rises are always in front, and the dips always behind.

It was that way with Packy anyway.

Oh, how good it would be at home: first to catch a glimpse of the little rusty roof, and then to run in at the gate and feel the splatters of the mud on his knees as he'd dash through the puddles in front of the door.

It was not till he got to Connells Cross that he remembered his promise about the fire-wood. Oh sorely, sorely was he tempted to break that promise, but after one last look at the far tin roof that had

just come into view above the hedge he let the little flock of scholars
go forward without him. Then, with a sad look after them he climbed
up on the wall of the demesne and jumped down on the other side.
Immediately, under his feet twigs and branches cracked like glass, and
for a minute he was tempted to gather an armful although he knew
well they were only larch and pine. But he put the base temptation from
him. Try to light a fire with larch? Wasn't it larch carpenters put in the
stairs of a house so the people could get down it safely if the house took
fire! And pine? Wasn't it a dangerous timber always spitting out sparks
that would burn holes the size of buttons in the leg of your trousers!
Oh no; he'd have to do better than that; he'd have to get beech or ash
or sycamore or oak. And to get them he'd have to go deep into the
woods to where the trees were as old as the Christian world. He'd
have to go as far as the little cemetery of Claddy. There, among the
tottering tombstones and the fallen masonry of the ancient church,
there was always a litter of dead branches, and what was more, every
branch was crotched over with grey lichen to make easier to see against
the dark mould of the earth.

Like all cemeteries, the cemetery of Claddy was a lonely place, and
to get to it he would have to cross the hill that Christy Turbridy said
belonged to Shee, but he remembered that his mother had heaped
scorn on that kind of talk. All the same, when he came to the small
pathway that led up to the hill, he faltered, because it was so overgrown
with laurel it was more like a tunnel than a path. Away at the far end
of the tunnel, though, there was a glade and there the light lay white
and beautiful on the bark of the trees. Shutting his eyes, Packy dashed
into the leafy tunnel and didn't open them until he was out of it. But
when he did open them he had to blink, because, just as the sky would
soon sparkle with stars, so, everywhere, under his feet the dark earth
sparkled with white wind-flowers. Who could be afraid in such a
place?

As for branches: the ground was strewn with them. Ah! there was a
good one! There was a fine dry one! And there was one would burn
for an hour!

But it didn't pay to be too hasty. That last was a branch of blackthorn and it gave him a nasty prick – "Ouch," it hurt. Letting fall his
bundle, Packy stuck his finger into his mouth, but the thorn had gone
deep and he couldn't suck it out. He'd have to stoup his finger in hot
water, or get his mother to put a poultice of bread and water on it. He'd

better not forget either, he told himself, because there was poison in thorns. Christy Tubridy knew a man who . . . At the thought of the Tubridys though Packy grew uneasy. All the stories they had ever told him again crowded back into his mind. Supposing those stories were true? Supposing the Shee really did still wander about the world? Supposing they did steal away human children?

Suddenly his heart began to beat so fast it felt like it was only inside his shirt it was instead of inside his skin. And the next minute, leaving his bundle of twigs where it lay, he made for the green pathway up which he had come, meaning to fling himself down it as if it were a hole in the ground.

And that is what he would have done only that – right beside him – sitting on the stump of a tree, he caught sight of a gentleman! A stranger it is true, but a gentleman. At least, Packy took him to be that – a gentleman from the Big House, perhaps? Now although Packy was glad he was not alone, he was afraid the gentleman might be cross with him for trespassing. But not at all. The gentleman was very affable.

"There's a fine dry limb of a tree!" he said, pointing to a bough of ash that Packy had overlooked.

He spoke so civilly that Packy ventured a closer look at him.

Was he a man at all, he wondered? The clothes on him were as fine as silk, and a most surprising colour: green. As for his shoes, they were so fine his muscles rippled under the leather like the muscles of a finely bred horse ripple under his skin. There was something a bit odd about him.

"Thank you, sir," said Packy, cautiously and he bent and picked up the branch.

"Don't mention it: I assure you it's a pleasure to assist you, Packy." In surprise Packy stared. The gentleman knew his name!

"Yes, Packy, I know your name – and all about you," said the little gentleman smiling. "In fact I have been endeavouring all the week to have a word with you – alone, that is to say – but I found it impossible to attract your attention – until now!"

Packy started. So he wasn't mistaken after all when he fancied that someone was beckoning to him, and raising a hand.

"Was it you, sir?" he cried in amazement. "I thought it was only the mist. Tell me, sir – were you at it again today?" he cried. The little gentleman nodded. "Well doesn't that beat all!" said Packy. "I thought it was a branch of hawthorn swaying in the wind."

The gentleman bowed.

"I'm complimented. A beautiful tree; always a favourite of mine, especially a lone bush of it in the middle of a green field. But to come to practical matters. I suppose you're wondering what I wanted to see you about. Well, let me tell you straight away – I understand that you are dissatisfied with the condition of your cottage – is that so?"

He was a County Councillor! That was it! – thought Packy. He'd come to make a report on the condition of the cottage. And to think that he had nearly run away from him!

"It's in a very bad state, sir," he said. "My mother is very anxious to get out of it."

To a County Councillor that ought to be broad enough! Better however leave nothing to chance. "Perhaps there is something you could do for us, sir." he said. Throwing down his bundle of kindling, he went nearer. What were a few bits of rotten branch to compare with the news he'd be bringing home if the gentleman promised him a Council cottage?

"Well, Packy, perhaps there may be something I can do for you!" said the gentleman. "Sit down here beside me, and we'll discuss the matter, or better still, let us walk up and down; it gets so chilly out on the hillside at this hour of evening."

And indeed it was more than chilly. The mist had started to rise. Already it roped the boles of the trees, and if it weren't for the little gentleman's company Packy would have been scared. As it was, he set about matching his pace to the pace of his friend, and stepped out boldly.

"I suppose you're a County Councillor, sir?" he asked, as they paced along.

"Eh? A County Councillor? What's that?" said the little man, and he stopped short in his stride, but the next minute he started off again. "Don't let us delay," he said. "It's mortally cold out here."

So he wasn't a County Councillor? He didn't even know what a Councillor was! Packy's heart sank. Where did he come from at all? And was it all for nothing he'd lost his time and his firewood. It was very tiring too, striding up and down on the top of the hill, because at every minute the little gentleman stepped out faster and faster, and where at first, when they passed them, the windflowers had shone out, each single as a star, now they streamed past like ribbons of mist. Even the little man was out of breath. He was panting like the pinkeens that Packy and the Tubridys caught in the Boyne and put into jam-jars where they swam to the sides of the glass, their mouths gaping. Chancing to glance at him it seemed to Packy that the little man had got a lot older looking. His eyes looked very old!

"What's the matter, Packy?" asked the little man, just then, seeing him stare.

"Nothing, sir," said Packy – "I was just wondering if it is a thing that you are a foreigner?"

"Is it me?" cried the gentleman, "a foreigner!" He stopped short in astonishment. "I've been in this country a lot longer than you, Packy!" He paused, " – about five thousand years longer, I should say."

Packy too stopped short.

Was the little man cracked, he wondered? This, however, was a point he could not very well ask the gentleman to settle. He would have to decide it for himself. So he said nothing. But he wasn't going to pace up and down the hill any more.

"I think I'd better be going home, sir," he said politely, but decisively.

"Oh, but you can't go back to that wretched cottage," cried the gentleman. "Not till I see if I can do something for you!" he cried. "Have you forgotten?"

Of course he hadn't forgotten. But if the gentleman was cracked, what use was there placing any hope in him?

"I've been thinking of your problem for some time past, Packy, as it happens," he said, "and it seems to me that there is very little use in trying to do anything to that old place of yours – "

That was sane enough, thought Packy.

" – and so," he went on, "what I have in mind is that you come and live with *me*!"

So he *was* cracked after all! Packy drew back. But the little man went on eagerly. "I live right near here – yes – just down there – only a few paces," he cried, pointing down the side of the hill towards the water's edge.

Now Packy wouldn't swear that he knew every single step of the ground at this point, because a great deal of it was covered with briar and scrub, but he'd be prepared to swear that there wasn't a house the size of a sixpence on the side of that hill!

"I see you don't believe me!" said the little man. "Well – come and I'll show you!"

Now, the little man was so insistent, and Packy himself was so curious, that when the former set off down the slope, Packy set off after him, although it was by no means easy to follow him, for the undergrowth was dense, and the branches of the trees, that had never been cut back, or broken by cattle, hung down so low that in some places they touched the ground. To pass under them Packy had almost to go down on his knees. But the little fellow knew his way like a rabbit. He looped under the heavy boughs as easily as a bird, while Packy stumbled after, as often as not forgetting to lower his head, and getting a crack on the pate. "Ouch!" he cried on one of these occasions.

"What's up?" asked the little man, looking irritably over his shoulder.

"I hit my head against a branch; that's all," said Packy.

The little man looked crossly at him.

"That wasn't a branch you hit against," he said sharply, "it was a root!"

And indeed he was right. At that point, the hill sloped so steeply that the rain had washed the clay from the roots of the trees till you could walk under them in the same way as you'd walk through the eye of a bridge. It was just as he was about to duck under another of these big branching roots after the little man, that Packy noticed how dark it was on the other side, as if something had come up between them and the sky. He came to an abrupt stand. The little man, on the other hand, darted into the dimness.

"Mind your step there," he cried, looking back over his shoulder. "It's a bit dark, but you'll get used to it." He fully expected Packy to follow him.

But Packy stuck his feet in the ground.

"Hold on a minute, sir," he said. "If it's a cave you live in, I'm not going a step further."

He hadn't forgotten how, once, an uncle of his had come home from America, and hired a car and took him and his mother to New Grange to see the prehistoric caves. His mother couldn't be got to go into them, but he and his uncle crawled down a stone passage that was slimy and wet, and when they got to the caves they hardly had room to stand up. They could barely breathe either the air was so damp. And it had a smell like the smell that rises from a newly-made grave. All the time Packy kept thinking the earth would press down on the cave and crack it like an egg – and them along with it. No thank you! He had seen enough caves!

"You're not going to get me into any cave," he said stoutly. The little man ran out into the light again.

"It's not a cave!" he cried. "Do you think we had to scratch holes for ourselves like badgers or foxes? We may live inside the hill but we move around under the earth the same way that you move around over it! You've a lot to learn yet, Packy, you and your generation."

"Is that so?" said Packy. "Well, we can move about in the air! And under the sea!"

"Bah!" said the little man. "Not the way I meant! Not like the birds! Not like the fishes!"

"I suppose you're right there," said Packy, but half-heartedly.

"What do you mean by supposing everything?" said the old man crossly. "Don't you ever say yes or no? I hope you haven't a suspicious streak in you? Perhaps I should have known that when you kept running home all the week every time I tried to get your attention!"

"Oh, but that was different, sir," said Packy. "I thought then that you were one of the Shee!"

At this, however, the little man began to laugh.

"And who in the name of the Sod do you think I am *now*?" he said.

"I don't know, sir," said Packy, "but I'm not afraid of you anyway – a nice kind gentleman like you – why should I?"

"And if I were to tell you that I *am* one of the Shee," said the little man, "what would happen then?"

Packy pondered this.

"Perhaps you'd be only joking?" he said, but a doubtful look had come on his face.

"And if I wasn't joking," said the little man, "what then?"

"Well, sir," said Packy, "I suppose I'd be twice as glad then that I didn't go into the cave with you!"

"I tell you it's *not* a cave!" screamed the little man. "And by the same token, will you stop calling us the Shee! What do they teach you in school at all, at all? Did you never hear tell of the Tuatha de Danaan? the noblest race that ever set foot in this isle? In five thousand years no race has equalled us in skill or knowledge."

Five thousand years! Packy started. Had he heard aright?

"Excuse me, sir," he said then. "Are you alive or dead?"

It seemed quite a natural question to ask, but it angered the little man.

"Do I look as if I was dead?" he cried. "Wouldn't I be dust and ashes long ago if so?"

"Oh, I don't know about that," said Packy. "When my uncle hired the car that time – the time we went to New Grange – we passed through Drogheda, and we went into the Cathedral to see Blessed Oliver Plunkett's head. It's in a box on the altar. He's dead hundreds of years: and he's not dust and ashes!"

But truth to tell, there was a big difference between the little gentleman's head, and the head of the saint, because the venerable bishop's head looked like an old football, nothing more, while the little gentleman looked very much alive, especially at that moment, because he was lepping with anger.

"Are you taught nothing at all nowadays?" he cried in disgust. "Do you not know anything about the history of your country? Were you not taught that when we went into the hills we took with us the secret that mankind has been seeking ever since – the secret of eternal youth? But come! that's not the point. The point is – are you coming any further, or are you not?"

Now there was no doubt about it, the situation had changed. Packy stared past the little man, and although he could see nothing, his curiosity undecided him. What a story he'd have for the Tubridys if he'd once been inside that hill!

"Will you bring me back again, sir?" he asked, having in mind the story about the changelings.

The little man looked at him.

"Well, Packy, I may as well be straight with you. An odd time – now and again only – we take a notion for a human child and try to lure him away to live with us forever under the hills, but we always look for one who is dissatisfied with his lot in the world."

"Oh, but I'm not dissatisfied with my lot," cried Packy apprehensively.

"Oh come now!" said the little man, "didn't I often overhear you and your mother complaining about that wretched cottage of yours?"

"Oh, you might have heard us talking, sir, but it was my mother that was discontented: not me. I was only agreeing to keep her in good humour.'

"What's that?" said the little man sharply. "Don't tell me I've got the wrong end of the stick! Are you sure of what you're saying, Packy? Because if that's the case I may as well stop wasting my time." He scowled very fiercely. After a minute though he seemed to remember his manners. "It's too bad" he said, "because you're the sort of lad I like."

"Thank you, sir," said Packy. "My mother will be pleased to hear that." Then as he made a move to go, upon an impulse he stopped. "I wonder, sir, if you'd mind my asking you a question before I go?"

"Why certainly not," said the little man. "But be quick, boy; it's very cold out here on the hillside."

"Well, sir," said Packy, "I'd like to know if it's true about Marty Tubridy – I mean – is he a changeling, sir?"

"Is it Marty Tubridy! Of course not!" said the old man. "Your mother was right there," he conceded. "We have no use for weedy little creatures like the Tubridys: it isn't everyone we fancy, I can tell you."

That was very gratifying to hear. His mother would be pleased at that too, thought Packy. Then he remembered that she would probably say it was all a likely story. He sighed.

The little man looked keenly at him.

"Are you changing your mind?"

Packy said nothing for a minute. Then he looked up.

"You didn't tell me whether I'd be able to get out again?" he asked.

"Really, Packy, you are an obstinate boy! I have no choice but to tell you the truth, which is that at the start I had no notion of letting you out again if I once got you inside, but as it's getting late, and I'm getting sick and tired arguing, I'm willing to make a bargain with you. I won't stop you from going home – if you want to go yourself, but don't blame me if you don't want to go!"

Well, that seemed fair enough.

"Oh, there's no fear of me wanting to stay!" he said confidently. "Thank you kindly for asking me, sir. I'll go on for a short while. But wait a second while I take off my boots so I won't dirty the place: my feet are shocking muddy after slithering down that slope."

For a minute the little gentleman looked oddly at him.

"Leave on your boots, Packy," he said; then slowly and solemnly: "Don't leave anything belonging to you outside. That's the very thing I'd have made you do, if I was not going to let you out again. I'd have had you leave some part of your clothing – your cap, or your scarf, or something, here on the outside of the hill – like a man would leave his clothes on the bank of the river if he was going to drown himself – so that people would find them and give up hopes of you. Because as long as there's anyone outside in the world still hoping a child will come back to them, it's nearly as hard for us to keep him inside as if he himself was still hoping to go back. Keep your boots on your feet, boy. You can't say I'm not being honest with you, can you?"

"I cannot, sir," said Packy, "but tell me, sir, those children you were telling me about – the ones that didn't want to go back to the world, did they always leave their shoes outside?"

"They did," said the little man.

"Did they now?" said Packy reflectively. "Wasn't that very foolish of them? How did they know they wouldn't be sorry when they got inside?"

The little man shrugged his shoulders.

"Ah sure don't we all have to take a chance some time or another in our lives?" he said. "Look at us! Before we came to Erin we were endlessly sailing the seas looking for a land to our liking. And many a one we found. But it never satisfied us for long. No matter how often we beached our boats, we soon set sail again, till one day we saw *this* island rise up out of the seas and we put all our trust in the promise of her emerald shores. Before we went a foot inland do you know what we did? We set fire to our boats, down on the grey sands! That was taking a chance, wasn't it? So you can't expect me to have much sympathy with people that won't take a chance with their boots! Have you made up your mind about yours, by the way? You won't leave them? Very well then, lace them up again on you, and don't mind them being muddy. I'll get one of the women inside to give them a rub of a blacking-brush. They're very muddy all right. Never mind that now though – follow me!" Then he turned around and ducking under the root of the tree again, he walked into what seemed to Packy to be a solid wall of earth.

But just as fog shrinks from light, or frost from fire, so, as they went inward, the earth seemed to give way before them. Nor was it the cold wet rock of New Grange either, but a warm dry clay in which, Packy noticed with interest as they went along, there were different layers of clay and sand and gravel and stone, just like he had seen in Swainstown Quarry when he went there once on a tipper-lorry. In fact he was so interested in the walls of clay that he hardly realized how deep into the hill they were going until the little man came to a stop.

"Well! Here we are!" he said, and Packy saw that they had arrived at what at first seemed to be a large room, but which he soon saw was merely a large space made by several people all gathered together.

But apparently these people rarely moved very far from where they were, for around them they had collected a variety of articles that suggested permanent habitation, in the way that furniture suggests habitation in a house. Not that the articles in the cave were furniture in any real sense of the word. Tables and chairs there were none. But in a corner a big harp gleamed, and randomly around about were strewn a number of vessels, basins and ewers and yes, a row of gleaming milking pails! With astonishment, Packy noticed that all these vessels, and the harp too, were as bright as if they were made of gold! He was staring at them when the little man shook him by the arm.

"Well, how do you like it down here?" he cried, and he was so feverishly excited he was dancing about on the tips of his toes.

Now, Packy didn't want to be rude, but the fact of the matter was that only for the gold basins and the gold pails, and the big gold harp, he didn't see anything very wonderful about the place. But of course, they would be something to tell the Tubridys about.

"They're not real gold, sure they're not?" he asked.

"Of course they are gold," said the little man. And then, seeing that Packy seemed to doubt him, he frowned. "In our day Ireland was the Eldorado of the world. I thought everyone knew that! Everything was made of gold. Even our buttons! Even the latchets of our shoes!" And he held out his foot to show that, sure enough, although Packy hadn't noticed it before, the latchets were solid gold. "It was a good job for us that gold was plentiful," he said irritably. "I don't know what we'd do if we had to put up with some of the utensils you have today."

"Oh, they're not too bad," said Packy. "There are grand enamel pails and basins in Leonards of Trim!"

"Is that so?" said the little man coldly. "Perhaps it's a matter of taste. To be candid with you though, Packy, I wouldn't like to have to spend five thousand years looking at some of the delph on your kitchen-dresser!"

Packy laughed. "There'd be no fear you'd have to look that long at them," he said. "They don't last any time. They's always getting broken."

"Ah, that's not the way in here," said the little man. "Nothing ever gets cracked down here; nothing ever gets broken."

Packy stared. "You don't tell me!" he said. "Do you never knock the handle off a cup, or a jug?" That was a thing he was always doing.

The little man shook his head.

"Oh, but I forgot," said Packy, "gold wouldn't break so easily." Not that he thought it was such a good idea to have cups made of gold. When you'd pour your tea into them, wouldn't it get so hot it would scald the lip off you?

One day in the summer that was gone past, he and the Tubridys went fishing on the Boyne up beyond Rathnally, and they took a few grains of tea with them in case they got dry. They forgot to bring cups though, and they had to empty out their tin-cans of worms and use them for cups. But the metal rim of the can got red hot the minute the tea went into it, and they couldn't drink a drop. Gold would be just the same?

But in fact, there were no cups at all it appeared.

"One no longer has any need for food, Packy," said the little man, "once one has learned the secret of eternal youth!"

"Do you mean you don't eat anything?" cried Packy, "anything at all? Don't you ever feel hungry?"

"No child," said the little man sedately. "Desire withers when perfection flowers. And if you stay here with us for long, you'll lose all desire too."

"You're joking, sir!" said Packy, doubtful. At that very minute he had a powerful longing for a cut of bread and a swig of milk. Indeed he glanced involuntarily at the gold milking pails. The Tubridys said the Shee often stole into byres and stripped the cows' udders.

The little man had seen his glance and must have read his thoughts.

"A little harmless fun now and then," he said, shamefacedly.

Had they been stripping cows lately? Packy wondered. Perhaps there might be a dreg in the bottom of one of the buckets? He craned his neck to see into them. They were all empty!

"I'm very dry, sir," he said.

"That's only your imagination," said the little man crossly. "Stand there for a minute, like a good boy," he said then, and he darted over to one of the women. "There's something wrong somewhere," he said to a woman that was sitting by the harp. And then he snapped his fingers. "It's the boots," he cried.

The young woman stood up. "Give me your boots, son," she said, "and I'll get the mud off them."

Now Packy was always shy of strange women, but this one spoke so like Mrs. Tubridy that he felt at home with her at once. And indeed, just as Mrs. Tubridy would have done, she caught the sleeve of his coat in her two fists and began to rub off the mud that was caked on it. It didn't brush off so easily though.

"I'll have to take a brush to it," she said. "Take your coat off, son, and I'll give it a rub too when I'm doing your boots."

"That's very kind of you, ma'am," said Packy, and he took off his coat. It was the coat of his good suit. His mother made him wear it that day so she'd get a chance to put a patch on the elbow of his old one. His vest was the vest belonging to the old suit.

"Is there mud on your vest as well?" asked the young woman.

"Oh no, ma'am," said Packy. "That's only splatters of pig-food and chicken-mash."

"What matter! Give it to me," she said. "I may as well make the one job of it."

But when he took off his vest his shirt was a show.

"That's only sweat-marks," he protested, knowing she'd proffer to do the shirt as well. But there was no holding back from her any more than from his mother.

"Here, sonny," she cried. "Go behind that harp over there and take every stitch off you and we'll get them all cleaned and pressed for you. You can put this on while you're waiting," she said, and she whipped a green dust-sheet off another harp.

It seemed to Packy that such courtesy was hardly necessary, but he went obediently behind the harp and stripped to the skin. Just as he reached out his hand, however, for the dust sheet, the young woman came back with a big gold basin of water.

"What's that for?" cried Packy, drawing away from her.

She shoved a towel into his hands.

"Wrap that towel around you," she said, "while I try to get some of the dirt off you before you get back into your clean clothes."

"Mud isn't dirt!" cried Packy indignantly. "My mother washes me every Saturday night," he cried, "and this is only Tuesday."

At this point the little man hurried over to them.

"It's not a question of cleanliness, Packy," he said. "It's a question of hospitality. Surely the ancient customs of the Gael have not fallen into such disuse in Ireland today? Does your mother not offer ablutions to those who cross your threshold?"

"What's that, sir?" said Packy, but he recollected that one day when his teacher called at the cottage, he slipped on the spud-stone at the gate and fell into a puddle, and that day his mother ran into the house and got out a big enamel basin and filled it with water for him to wash his hands. Then she got a towel and wiped the mud off the tail of his coat. She offered him an old pair of his father's pants too, but he wouldn't put them on. Oh, his mother wasn't far behind anyone, he thought, when it came to hospitality. And so, to show that he was very familiar with all such rites, he made an opening in the towel, and unbared first one hand, and then the other.

"That's a good boy," she said. "Now your foot. Now the other one!"

She didn't stop at his feet though, and before he knew where he was, there wasn't a cranny of him she hadn't scrubbed.

Never in his life had he been washed like that. It reminded him of the way Mrs. Tubridy scoured old grandpa Tubridy's corpse the night he was waked.

He was especially struck with the way the black rims of his nails stood out against his bone-white hands. And he greatly regretted it when the young woman prised out the dirt with a little gold pin. And when she was done with his finger-nails, she began to prod at his toe-nails!

They must be terrible clean people altogether, he thought. His own mother was supposed to be the cleanest woman in the parish, yet she'd never dream of going that far. When his father died, and she was describing the kind of mortuary card she wanted to get for him, she held up her hand to the shopkeeper and showed him the rim of dirt under her nail.

"I want the border of the card as deep as that!" she said. Indeed, she'd speak of the black of her nail as readily as another person would speak of the white of his eye!

These people must be terrible particular people, he thought. All those gold basins and gold ewers were for washing themselves, he supposed. And just then the young woman took out a comb and began to rake his hair so hard he felt like as if he'd been sculled. But the comb was solid gold too.

"Oh wait till the Tubridys hear about this," he said ecstatically.

The young woman looked at him in a very peculiar way, and then she looked at the little man.

"There's something wrong still," said the little man.

"Are you sure you washed every nook of him?" he asked. He'd got very cross again.

"I did," said the young woman, and she was cross too.

I hope they're not going to start fighting, while I'm standing here in my skin, thought Packy, and he shivered. He ventured to pluck the little man by the sleeve.

"Excuse me, sir," he said as politely as possible. "Are my own clothes near ready do you think?"

But these innocent words seemed to infuriate the little man, and he turned on the young woman again.

"You missed some part of him!" he shouted. "What about his ears? Did you take the wax out of them?"

"Oh, I forgot," cried the young woman, and whipping the gold pin out of her bodice again she began to root in his ears.

There was such a lot of wax in his ears, Packy was shamed and he thought he'd better pass it off with a joke.

"I'll have no excuse now but to get up when my mother calls me in the morning," he said.

But the little man seemed ready to dance with rage at that. "What about his teeth?" he cried, ignoring him and calling to the young woman. "Maybe there's a bit of food stuck between them?"

"That's it surely!" cried the young woman. "Open your mouth, Packy," she said, and she began to poke between his teeth with the needle, but to no avail. There was not a thing between his bright white teeth.

He had to laugh. "That's the way the vet opens Bessie's mouth," he said. "Bessie is our cow."

"Bother your cow Bessie," said the little man, and he caught the young woman by the arm and shook her. "Could there be a bit of grit in his eye?"

"I don't think so," said the young woman, "but we can try!" and she reached out and pushed up his eyelid. "Nothing there," she said. Then she looked into his other eye. "Nothing there either."

What was all this about? Packy wondered. What were they looking to find? And what about the milk? He thought they were going to try to get him a cup of milk after they'd washed him. He was still thirsty. But it was hardly worth while troubling them to get it for him, because he'd have to be going home. It would be getting very dark in the woods outside, he thought, and he looked around.

"Have you no windows?" he cried.

"What would we want with windows!" the little man exclaimed. "If some people like to wake up and find the quilt all wet with rain, there are other people who don't" he said venomously.

"Oh, but it isn't always raining!" cried Packy, knowing it was his own little window at home to which the little man was referring. And thinking of that small square window on a sunny morning his face lit up. There was something to be said for a broken pane at times. "Once a swallow flew in my window – through the hole in the glass," he said, and he gave a laugh of delight at the memory of it.

But the young woman made a face.

"Don't talk about birds!" she said. "Dirty little things, always letting their droppings fall on everything."

"It's great manure, though," cried Packy. "If you could get enough of it, you could make your fortune selling it to the people in the towns."

At this however the little man shuddered violently.

"We may at times have vague regrets for the world outside, Packy," he said in an admonitory tone, "regrets for the stars, and the flowers, and the soft summer breezes, but we are certainly not sorry to have said farewell to the grosser side of life to which you have just now – somewhat indelicately – alluded."

Packy stared, and there was a puzzled look on his face but suddenly it cleared and he nodded his head sagaciously. "I suppose you were born in the town, sir?" he said. "My mother says when people from the towns come out for a day in the country, they never stop talking about the smell of the flowers and the smell of the hay, but give them one smell of a cow-shed and they're ready to run back to the town. But it's not a bad smell at all when you're used to it. I suppose it makes a difference too when you have a cow of your own; like us. I love the smell of the dung in Bessie's byre!"

"Indeed?" said the little man. "You don't tell me!" He must have been sarcastic though, because he turned to the young woman. "That's the limit!" he said. "I think we may give him up as a bad job." He turned back to Packy. "Do you still feel the need of a cup of milk?"

"If it's not too much trouble, sir, please," said Packy.

"I didn't say you were going to get it," said the little man testily. "I asked if you felt the need of it."

"I do, sir," said Packy," but perhaps it's not worth while bothering you. I ought to be thinking of getting home."

"Did you hear that?" the little man cried, fairly screeching, as he turned to the young woman. "Oh, there is no doubt about it, there is something wrong somewhere. We'd better let him go home."

The young woman looked very sour. "The sooner the better, if you ask me," she said. "What kind of a child is he at all? Why didn't you pick an ordinary one?"

"But he *is* an ordinary child," screamed the little man. "It's not my fault, and it's certainly not his!" He turned to Packy. "Don't mind her, Packy. Women are all the same, under the hills, or over the hills. You may as well go home. And you'd be advised to start off soon, because it will be dark out on the hillside. Wait a minute till I get your clothes!"

When they got the clothes, Packy couldn't help noticing that the mud was still on them. And his boots were still in a shocking state.

"Tch, tch, tch!" said the little man. "Women again! Try to overlook it, Packy, as a favour to me. – Well? Are you ready? Better take my hand: it's always easier to get in here than it is to get out!"

Yet a second later Packy saw a chink of light ahead, and it widened and widened until suddenly he was at the opening of the hill again, and above him was a great expanse of moonlit sky.

"I'm afraid there was a shower while we were inside," said the little man. "I hope your twigs didn't get wet!"

"Oh, I may leave them till morning anyway," said Packy. He had been wondering how he'd carry them the way his finger had begun to throb with the pain of the thorn in it.

"And why would you do that?" said the little man. "Won't your mother want them first thing in the morning?"

"She will," said Packy, " – but my finger is beginning to beal, I'm afraid," and he stuck it into his mouth again.

"What is the matter with it?" cried the little man. "Show me!"

"Oh, it's nothing, sir," said Packy. "Only an old thorn I got when I snatched up a bit of blackthorn."

But the little man was beside himself.

"Show me! Show me!" he screeched. "A thorn!" and he caught Packy's hand and tried to peer at it, but the moon had gone behind a cloud. He stamped his foot angrily. "You don't mean to tell me it was there all the time! Oh, weren't we blind! It was *that* thorn kept pulling your mind back to the world. Oh, how was it we didn't see it?"

"How could you see it, sir?" said Packy. "It's gone in deep. It'll have to have a poultice put on it."

At that moment the moon sailed into a clearing in the clouds and shone down bright. The little man caught him by the sleeve.

"Will you come back for a minute and we'll take it out for you?" he cried. "There's nothing safer than a gold pin when probing for a thorn."

Packy held back. The little man meant well, he supposed, but God help him if he was depending on that same young woman who was supposed to have polished his boots and brushed his suit.

"I'd better go home and get my mother to do it," he said.

The little man let go of his sleeve.

"All right, Packy," he said. "Go home to your mother. I can't blame you. I suppose you see through the whole thing anyway! As long as there was any particle of the earth still on you, you'd never lose your hankering for home. But I hope those women didn't handle you too roughly."

"Oh not at all, sir," said Packy politely.

His mother wouldn't have to wash him again for a year of Saturdays.

"Well I'm glad to think you bear no ill will," said the little man. "I wouldn't like you to have any hard feelings towards us." Then he shook his head sadly. "You must admit it was a bit unfortunate for me to be bested by a bit of a thorn. Ah well, it can't be helped now."

He looked so sad Packy felt sad too.

"I suppose I'll see you around the woods some time, sir," he said.

But the little man shook his head from side to side.

"I don't think you will," he said.

There seemed no more to say.

"Well, I suppose I'd better be going," said Packy. "I hope I'll find my way."

"Oh, you'll find your way all right," said the little man. "The moon is a fine big May moon. I'm sorry about your boots," he added, calling after him, but he couldn't resist a last sly dig. "Anyway you'd only destroy them again going in through the puddles around your door!"

"Oh, I don't mind the puddles," said Packy. "Only for the puddles we couldn't keep ducks; they'd be always straying down to the Boyne, and in the end they'd swim away from us altogether. Puddles have their uses."

At that the little man laughed.

"I never met the like of you, 'Packy!' he said. "Good-bye!"

"Good-bye, sir," said Packy.

And then he was alone.

Slowly he started up the hill until he came to the top where the windflowers were all closed up for the night. But on their shiny leaves the moon lay white. And there, a dark patch in the middle of the glade, was his bundle of twigs.

He gathered them up. His finger was still throbbing but he paid no heed to the pain. Only for that thorn he might never have got out of the cave. Because it wasn't much better than a cave, no matter what the little man said about it. He began to whistle. And when he came to the pathway leading to the gap in the demesne wall he ran down it full-tilt. In a minute he was out on the road again.

There had been a shower all right. All along the road there were puddles. But in every puddle there was a star. And when he got to the cottage the puddles around the door were as big as ever, but in them shone the whole glory of the heavens.

"Is that you, Packy?" cried the widow, running out to the door in a terrible state. "What kept you so late, son?"

"Oh, wait till I tell you," cried Packy, although he knew right well what she'd say:

A likely story!